# MEANT FOR ME

# ALSO BY TAY MARLEY

*The QB Bad Boy and Me*

*The Summer of '98*

# MEANT FOR ME

## TAY MARLEY

wattpad books — FRAYED PAGES

**FRAYED PAGES**

Content warning: scenes including sexual assault and death.
Please read with caution.

Published in Canada by Wattpad WEBTOON Book Group, a division of
Wattpad WEBTOON Studios, Inc.

36 Wellington Street E., Toronto, ON M5E 1C7

*www.wattpad.com*

First Frayed Pages x Wattpad Books edition: February 2024

*www.frayedpagesmedia.com*

ISBN 978-1-99885-439-4 (Trade Paperback)
ISBN 978-1-99885-441-7 (eBook)

Names, characters, places, and incidents featured in this publication are
either the product of the author's imagination or are used fictitiously. Any
resemblance to actual persons (living or dead), events, institutions, or
locales, without satiric intent, is coincidental.

Library and Archives Canada Cataloguing in Publication and U.S. Library
of Congress Cataloging in Publication information is available upon
request.

Printed and bound in Canada

1 3 5 7 9 10 8 6 4 2

Cover design by Lesley Worrell
Cover image © Diana Taliun, © Luimi via Shutterstock
Author Photo © Tay Marley
Typesetting by Delaney Anderson

To the readers and dreamers

# CHAPTER ONE

## August

When my big sister, Margo, was fourteen, she caught our father having an affair with my mother. She told me how shocking it was: even if our father was a good-looking Italian man who had women walking through his restaurant doors in droves, the question of his faithfulness would never have been called into question.

That was until Margo, who had never even held hands with a boy, walked into the storeroom to collect a can of pizza sauce and saw her father's pants around his ankles and a woman's legs around his waist.

My father brought great shame on the Bianchi name and, as I was told, was given an earful from my Nonna, who was appalled at his actions. She never accepted my mother, who, while of Italian descent, had been born and raised in America. My mother didn't like to cook; she was career-focused; she didn't want a lot of children. That didn't sit right with Nonna; as if the fact that she was a mistress wasn't bad enough, she didn't equate to a good Italian housewife either. But she was beautiful, elegant, dazzling in diamonds and wealth. And she had a good heart; she was kind and welcoming.

Dad left Sicily with my mom, both heading back to her home in California. Six months later, Margo was sent to live with them as her own mother had fallen deep into drugs and alcohol. A year and a half later, I was born. As I grew older, I asked Margo how she wasn't angry with my mother for tearing her family apart. All she ever said was that her father was happier in America, with my mom, than he had ever been before, and that there were probably things that went on that she didn't understand because of her age. The universe brought people together in mysterious ways, who was Margo to argue?

Margo was like that. She tended not to dwell on circumstantial matters. She couldn't change the relationship that her dad had with my mom. So she embraced it—and she embraced me.

As I watched the expansive land from the bus window, the Colorado river winding through miles of pasture and hills, I tried to hear what Margo would tell me about *this* situation. What advice would she have for me now? She was practical, so the first thing she would tell me was that traveling on a bus from Beverly Hills, California, to Austin, Texas, was impulsive and stupid, and I needed to go home and deal with reality regardless of what I felt.

There was no chance I could go home. It didn't matter what I'd left behind; our event planning business, May We?, didn't matter, nor did the clothes and shoes, the condo, the friends and clients. None of it mattered. I couldn't be sure what had pushed me into choosing Austin as the final stop. I'm not sure I chose it at all. But I started going east, and I just kept going in the hopes that the oozing heart-sized hole in my chest would heal the further I got from home.

Of course, I couldn't see that happening.

My head fell onto the warm windowpane, and I watched the road whirring past, fast. So fast that the lines separating the lanes were a blur. The road signs were a blur. My fingertips touched the bottom of my eyes just to be sure that I wasn't sobbing in public again and that the blur wasn't gathered tears refusing to spill. Nope, not a tear so far. I'd thought keeping it together would have been a lot harder, but I had a feeling the hollow pit in my chest was a black hole, draining the emotion and pain before I knew what to do with it.

• • •

Stepping off the bus, I was reminded that August in Austin is peak heat. I could feel the relentless sun piercing my skin the moment I hit the pavement, where dozens of bodies shuffling past made it even hotter. For a moment, all I could do was stand still and watch the world move around me.

The colors, the beautiful sundresses and wide-brimmed hats. Flip-flops and sandals. Smiles that said all was well in the world. It never ceased to amaze me how one tragic event, one event that felt so enormous that it should have had the entire population reeling and falling to its knees, was in fact not earth-shattering at all. It existed only to me and a handful of people back in California.

It made me wonder how much darker life would be if grief was physical. If we could walk past someone and see exactly what it was they felt. If we could see their heart tearing right down the middle, if we could see the never-ending slow bleed of their mind turning into a dismal mess. I suppose there was a good reason it wasn't like that. It would be too much. Humans are empathetic. Having to experience everyone else's grief would be a quick descent into madness.

I hoisted my backpack on over my black T-shirt dress, and I began walking. Black was the right color. Not just because it represented how I felt but because the sweat would be less obvious. And I did sweat as I started walking with no destination in mind. I'd always loved to walk, to watch the world around me shift as I sorted through thoughts and feelings. I'd walk on the beach, sand between my toes, though today I headed out in my worn sneakers down unfamiliar streets.

The Colorado River running right through the heart of Austin was beautiful on a day like today. The sun hit the rippling surface, appearing as if it were glittering with diamonds. I stood on the Pennybacker Bridge and looked across the river, its expanse stretching hundreds of feet. Rolling hills flanked either side, with trees and grass and water for miles. For a moment, I inhaled the clean air, searching for peace or a flicker of appreciation for the scene. The fact that I felt hollow—less than hollow; I felt nothing—scared me. I knew the view was beautiful, and yet any emotion refused to stir.

Night began to fall after some hours of aimless wandering. The sky turned dusted orange, the sliver of blue became an almost purple shade, and the clouds looked like cotton candy. There was an obvious ache in the sole of my feet, and it traveled right up into the core of my thighs. I hadn't eaten, and I hadn't had anything to drink. I hadn't healed one fucking bit, and that was the point. To move and think until the pain subsided. Just a little bit. That was all I asked.

When it was dark and there were crickets chirping, stars overhead, and headlights illuminating the road in front of me, I wondered if I should have booked a room for the night. Especially because as I peered around, I realized how far from town I now was. There were no storefronts, no people, no homes. Just the occasional gravel driveway that was so long I couldn't see the end of it, trees, and fields.

The night didn't bring much in the way of relief from the heat. It was still humid, and I felt drenched. I came to a standstill. What should I do? What would Margo do? Well, she'd never have spent an entire day walking across Austin in the first place. She'd have caught a cab, rented a room, carefully allocated her hours into set activities so that she could make the most of her adventure.

I knew her so well. I knew what she would do, and still, I couldn't bring myself to do it. I'd never have done it as well as her. There was no point in attempting to be half of who she was.

*Bullshit, Addie. You're an event planner. Organization is what you do!*

"Excuse me, ma'am?"

I startled and turned around to the harsh glare of the bright lights behind me. A shadow stood there, a woman, her figure thin. My breath caught.

"Margo?"

"Uh . . . ma'am, are you all right? It's not too safe walking around these parts alone. A lot of traffic passes through, and I—"

Her words became static, and the world started to topple as I lost my balance. The woman rushed for me as I went down, cold, hard asphalt hitting my aching legs and arms.

"It'll be okay," she said. I knew it was a promise as her hand cradled my head and darkness seeped in.

# CHAPTER TWO

*Two years ago*

The last thing I wanted to be doing on a Saturday evening was making a brief appearance at some swanky event on Rodeo Drive where there'd be more celebrities than the Met Gala. That might have sounded a bit backward. Don't all women in their early twenties want to be rubbing shoulders with the rich and famous at designer store openings?

Well, no, not all women. I was required to be here, though. Even if just for a few minutes. I had put the whole thing together, after all. It was customary to go and make sure things were in order. The smell of rich fabrics and wine lingered in the air. Music rattled the clothes hangers on their steel racks, and I winced at stilettos piercing the brand-new wooden floor.

"Addison!"

I'd been hoping to slip out before the client caught me. However, at the sound of her harsh, nicotine-damaged voice calling me, I turned and found Klarise Klauden approaching. She glittered with diamonds and stunk of four-hundred-dollar champagne. Still, I let her give me one of her awkward half hugs that made it quite clear she also preferred her personal space.

"This is perfect." Her frosted fingertips wiggled as she waved around the room. "You've made an impression too. There have been whispers circulating. You could make a lot of connections here. People want to hire *the* Addison and Margo May. This'll do wonders for the business, sweetheart."

"It's just Addie." I gave her a polite nod and watched her touch the piercing on her thin nose. "You have our card, Klarise. So, whoever's interested, just pass the information along."

Her brows pinched, like she'd heard a bad joke and was contemplating how to react. "Yes, well, I think that's your job, sweetheart. You have all of this potential. Don't leave it to someone else to give you a break."

She wasn't wrong. But she also wasn't desperate to get home, wrap up in a dressing gown, and finish the most delectable romance I'd read to date. I'd just reached the pivotal moment when the hero does something stupid and has to get on his knees and grovel. It didn't matter that it was July in Beverly Hills. I wanted bed. I wanted books.

Our business, May We?, was well known in California. Margo and I had inherited the company from our parents and rebranded it—and ourselves—in order to make it our own. Our workload had tripled since we'd taken over. We weren't lacking in clients, but the more that we had, the better, and Margo would be furious if I didn't at least attempt to expand our client base. She usually came to the events. I preferred the office work. But I'd granted her the night off so she could go on a date. It better have been worth it.

I turned on the best "fake it until you make it" smile and proceeded to take a few laps around the store. In the dark, the walls were glowing from neon lights that were fixed behind the boards. It was cute and enchanting. Posters of models wearing the brand's items were hung, and mannequins were dressed in their new outfits.

And then, as I was about to make a graceful exit, I saw him. My sister's lowlife ex-husband, a coward, a pathetic excuse for a person.

I considered slipping out, but somehow I found myself standing in front of him with a glass of champagne and a brutal bitch glare in place. Ignoring the couple he was having a conversation with, I cleared my throat and smiled at him. The smile was laced with disgust. Which I think he received when he finally looked at me.

"Addie." His brows shot up in surprise, but his nerves weren't slow to seep in, and I watched that familiar red rash crawl across his throat. He might have been a heartless bastard, but he didn't have an ounce of confidence either. Not the sort that was needed to survive in this world. It was no wonder he lived behind a desk.

He swallowed, and his nervous laugh showered saliva. I recoiled with a scowl as he waved his hand at the man and woman behind me. "Addie, this is Cecilia and her brother, Charles. Cecilia is . . . well, we're engaged."

Oh.

When I'd first approached, I hadn't paid any mind to the couple. But now I turned and looked at the woman. Her elegance was striking. Her beauty wasn't blatant. It was subtle, and it took a moment of staring to appreciate her regal features. A strong nose, prominent cheekbones, and a soft gaze that all seemed to work rather well together. Though the part of her I was most interested in was her protruding stomach.

He'd left Margo and filed for divorce less than two years ago, and here he was with a new fiancé and a child on the way. It wasn't that surprising when I thought about it. Pete had never been one to deliberate on his choices. He'd proposed to Margo within six months of meeting her. I'd argued it was too fast, but Margo, the romantic she was, didn't see it that way.

I supposed when he'd met this Cecilia woman, he was quick to deduce where their futures sat and started immediately on building his family.

"You don't waste time," I said, already thinking about Margo and how heartbroken she'd been when her marriage fell apart. Anger bubbled, causing me to clench the stem of my glass so hard I thought it might shatter.

Pete's nervous laugh was grating as he looked at his soon-to-be wife and then back at me. "Uh, what? What do you mean?"

"Use those analytical powers of deduction and figure it out, Pete."

"Look, Margo and I . . . that's over. What am I meant to do? Never move on?"

"You should move on all you like," I said, watching him become flustered over the fact that we weren't alone. I didn't care. In fact, I looked at his fiancé and attempted to smile because none of this was her fault, but why shouldn't she know what he'd done to the last woman he'd claimed to love? "It's just the fact that you left my sister because she couldn't carry a pregnancy. As if that wasn't hard enough."

He ran his hand across his thick beard. Admittedly, Pete wasn't unattractive; what he had done made him hideous to me, but superficially, he was good-looking. Not a lot taller than me or Margo, but that was fine because we were both small. He had a nice build and big eyes and a thick head of hair. But he was still a piece of shit, and that was all that I could ever see after what he had done.

"I just knew it wasn't going to work. It had nothing to do with the miscarriages. It wasn't a malicious breakup . . . it was just doing what was best for me."

I had the strongest urge to stab him with my heel. "Really? Nothing to do with the miscarriages? How convenient you left after she suggested spending money on a surrogate, then."

He lowered his gaze, and I let out a harsh laugh, casting a glance to poor Cecilia, who was cradling her bump and staring at the floor. I wasn't sure what she knew of Pete's failed marriage, but with the look her brother was giving Pete, I had to assume it wasn't the whole truth.

"Coward," I spat and threw the champagne at his face, grinning when he gasped, blinking the alcohol from his lashes.

He could justify himself until he was blue in the face, and I still wouldn't forgive him for hurting the one person I loved more than anything in this world. She deserved better, and I hated that he was getting what he wanted while she was still going on dates with losers in the hopes that she would find her Mr. Right.

• • •

The condo I shared with Margo was on the second floor. We had a cute awning covered in lustrous green vines over the front gate, a digital code for access, and gorgeous potted flowers along the short footpath that led to the front door of the building. As soon as I walked inside the condo, the sound of Whitney Houston blasted through the small two-bedroom home, and I rounded the foyer wall to find Margo standing in the middle of the living room, belting the chorus out at the top of her lungs.

"And I-i-i-i-e-i-i-i will always loooooooooove you uuuuu-ooooo—"

"What is happening in here?"

She paused her solo and fixed me with a grin I knew well. Pride. I'd seen it a lot over the course of my life, considering she had been raising me from the time I was thirteen and she was twenty-nine. The privilege of telling me how proud she was at the achievement of my milestones had fallen to her. She'd never let me down. I couldn't have asked for a better caregiver. While I was now twenty-two, she was still the parent I needed.

My high-heeled shoes fell to the hardwood floor with a thud as she skipped forward, held up her phone, and pressed Start on a video. The music faded as the video began, and the surround sound was soon filled with the chattering and laughter of the party I had just been at. To my shock, there I was on the screen, flinging a glass of champagne at Pete's face.

"How—"

"It's not viral. Irie was there," Margo explained, locking her phone and tossing it onto the sofa. I did remember seeing her supermodel best friend, but I had done a good job of avoiding talking to her. Irie was fine and all, just a bit overwhelming at times. "She told me she saw you storming over to Pete and hoped something would go down. She had her phone ready just in case."

"I shouldn't have done that."

"No, probably not. But what's done is done." She pursed her lips, but her eyes were full of mischief. Much like mine must have been when I tried and failed to hide a giggle of amusement.

Margo and I were a lot alike in the sense that we both had golden, tanned Italian skin, long, dark hair, and almost black eyes. But Margo had angular, more chiseled features, a sharp jaw and cheekbones, thin but beautifully shaped lips, crow's feet around her eyes, and laugh lines around her mouth. I had the advantage of being sixteen years younger than her, but regardless of age, she was gorgeous. Where she had definition, I did not. I had never grown out of my baby face, round and soft with a curvier waist and legs.

Margo and I constantly bickered and wished we could trade bodies. Of course, neither of us had the height we envied in other women.

She wandered over to the sofa and fell into it with an exasperated sigh. She no longer cried over her ex-husband, but I knew the wasted six years of marriage hurt her a lot. After watching what she'd gone through, after watching a "perfect" marriage crumble right in front of me, I'd become skeptical about the notion of investing in a relationship that could implode no matter how well I believed it to be going. She knew how I felt, and I think that's why she was so cautious about showing her pain in front of me.

"You met Cecilia."

I sat beside her and pulled my legs up underneath me. "You knew?"

She nodded. "I ran into them last week, and he introduced me to her, told me all about their soon-to-be newborn."

"You didn't tell me."

She rolled her head toward me and fixed me with a narrow stare. "I was afraid you would be out for blood. If I'd known all I had to be concerned about was a face full of champagne, I'd have mentioned it sooner."

"He deserved more than a face full of champagne. A face full of fist. Or hot coal."

She waved a dismissive hand. "He's not worth it. I want to forget he was ever part of my life. He's just another human being as far as I'm concerned. Tell me how the event went."

"Fine." I shrugged. I reached to run a hand down the large leaf of my peace lily plant. We had a lot of houseplants scattered throughout the condo. A little slice of nature in our suburban jungle life. "Tell me about the date."

"Same old, same old."

I pouted at the fact Margo had endured another dead-end date. If it had gone well, she'd have never waited this long to talk about it.

"Addie, I just want to be a mom." She stared at her thin fingers in her lap. "I'm going to be thirty-nine in a few weeks. I never, ever thought I would have waited so long to have a child."

My heart squeezed for her. Margo had been a mom from the moment our parents died, but I knew she wanted her own baby, and if it was possible, she'd wanted it even more after she found out her chances of ever carrying a baby to term were slim to none. After seven miscarriages, she'd decided surrogacy would be her best route. She'd considered adoption—once. It didn't work out, and since she'd frozen her eggs a few years ago, she wanted to use them and have a child of her own.

I subconsciously pinched the skin on my wrist and mumbled, "I wish—if I'd—"

"Don't." She cut me off. "Don't think it. Don't speak it."

I was getting a headache. That was no surprise, though; it was almost guaranteed to happen when we discussed my sister's shortcomings. She deserved so much more than she'd been given.

"I've been thinking about a donor." She swallowed and pinched her lip, a nervous habit that made the skin dry and chapped. "Forget about a man, right? What if I just do it alone? Have a surrogate and a donor instead of waiting to find the right man to be the father of my child?"

My sister was one of the most selfless people I knew. She'd put aside her entire life and stepped up to raise a teenager when she was in the middle of living her own life and running her own business and meeting men who might have been her future, but she'd settled for Pete because she didn't have time to date around.

If there was anything I could do to thank her for her sacrifice, I would do it.

"I'll be your surrogate."

Her mouth fell open. "What?"

"I'll be the surrogate. I'll carry the baby for you."

# CHAPTER THREE

I've never been much of a drinker. I've been drunk before, but it didn't hold a lot of appeal after one time when I woke up with a hangover from hell. I couldn't see how it was worth the nausea, the headache, the overall feeling of death that crawled beneath the skin. It wasn't something I wanted to experience ever again.

Yet there I was, feeling much the same even though I had no recollection of touching alcohol the night before.

I rolled over, eyes still closed, and my hand thudded against cold steel. The smell of hand sanitizer stung my nose, and plastic tubing tugged on the inside of my elbow. When I did manage to peer through one half-lidded eye, I saw an IV bag hanging above me, taupe walls, and a worn leather armchair beside the bed. Hospital. How on earth had I ended up in the hospital?

There was no one else in the room, so I sat up, careful not to lean on the tube that stemmed from a vein in my arm. A small remote dangled over the bed rail, so I picked it up and pressed the button that I assumed called the nurse based on the little stick figure and exclamation mark on it. The other button read "emergency," and I didn't think it would be wise to cause that sort of panic.

A few moments later, the door opened, and two women appeared, one wearing pale-blue scrubs and the other in a police uniform.

"Honey," the nurse said, resting her hand on my shoulder. "Are you feeling all right?"

"What happened?"

"Oh, Officer Ryan brought you in last night dear. She said you were wandering alone and collapsed right in front of her. You were very dehydrated, but there were no injuries apart from some surface abrasions on your arms and legs."

"You're Officer Ryan, I assume?"

The policewoman stood at the foot of the bed with a kind smile. She was lean and tall with light-brown skin and tight ringlets pulled into a bun at the nape of her neck. "I am. You can call me Raine, though." She looped her thumbs through her belt loops and rocked back on her heels. "You had me worried, honey. Can I ask what you were doing walking alone at night?"

I swallowed and tried to recall what it was I'd been doing or planning on doing. As far as I could remember, it wasn't much. "Just walking," I said. "My bus arrived at nine in the morning, and I didn't really have anywhere to go, so I was just . . . walking."

"Where did that bus arrive?"

Peering up from the stiff white bedding, I met her expectant stare. She wasn't demanding answers, not in the same tone a cop might question someone suspected of a crime. It was more like she wanted to find out what had happened that had put me in such a vulnerable position.

"Uh, in Austin somewhere." I grasped for the street name, but it evaded me. "I can't remember where the bus terminal was."

"You walked from Austin? Walked?"

I nodded, brow furrowed at her disbelief.

"You were on the outskirts of Georgetown, miss. That's almost twenty-eight miles on foot."

"Like I said, I was just walking. I like to walk."

The nurse stepped in at that point. Her aged white hands were covered in bright-blue veins, and she held up the chart, reading it over. "The doctor has cleared you to be discharged. So, is there someone we can call, sugar?"

Sugar? Honey? These people were fond of their sweet nicknames. Inhaling a deep breath, I shook my head. "No. I'm here alone."

"Where are you from?" Raine asked, hands resting on her belt.

"Beverly Hills. In California."

The nurse pushed her glasses up her nose. Her name tag read Helen. She didn't look like a Helen. She looked like a Jan. "Are you here on vacation?"

"I don't know."

Raine and Helen shared a brief look of concern. It was all I could do not to scoff. I'd seen that pitiful look of concern about several thousand times over the past week. Wren, Sam, and Lo—coworkers who helped Margo and me run the business—had all looked at me like that while they asked me over and over again if I would be all right.

The answer was no. I fucking wouldn't be all right. But I'd accepted that.

"Can I just . . . go?" I kept a gentle tone. I didn't want to seem ungrateful or demanding. Raine had done me a huge favor not leaving me on the side of the road in the middle of the night. "I'm not a minor, I don't need to be let go to a parent or whatever, right?"

"Oh, of course not, sugar." Helen laughed and gave me a pat on the hand. "We just thought that you might need a ride or something of the sort. I'll get those discharge papers sorted. It should only be another few minutes. I'll be right back."

After she'd removed the IV line, she left me alone with Raine, who was still smiling. "I can give you a ride somewhere," she offered. "I work nights, and I came back after my shift ended to make sure you were okay. So, I'm not working right now, and I can give you a ride. Somewhere. Wherever."

As much as I wanted to answer her, I couldn't. Every time I

opened my mouth, I realized I had no place to be. Nowhere to go. No plan.

"Um." Her brows pulled, and she held the rail as she rounded the bed to stand beside me. "Look, it's kind of a Sunday tradition to have brunch at my dad's farm. I don't work Sunday nights, so I don't have to get straight to sleep. You should come and have something to eat, and you can figure out what the next step is?"

"You—you don't even know me."

She widened her gaze with exaggerated fear. "Were you out and about to commit murder last night?"

"No."

"I know." She laughed. "I had a peep through your backpack. Nothing but beautiful clothes and shoes."

"You went through my backpack?"

"Had to. I was looking for some ID."

"You wouldn't have found that," I mumbled and threw the sheets back. I was still in the T-shirt dress I'd been wearing last night. The sweat had dried, but it stunk. "I left my clutch at home. All I have is my phone."

"Yes," she said, nodding. "I did see that in the backpack."

She seemed nice. Nice enough to extend an invitation to brunch when I was a complete stranger. No one had ever shown that sort of hospitality to me before, but perhaps that was just how things were done around here. Or at least that was how she did things.

"Yeah, I'll come for brunch. Thanks. I don't have much else to do. Can I shower and change first?"

Her eyes darted around the room and then landed on the bathroom door. "Go ahead. I'll wait."

The hospital shower wasn't half bad. The pressure was decent, and the temperature was warm. After I felt cleaner, I slipped into a dark-green sundress. The straps were thin, and the bodice was fitted tight. After experiencing the heat yesterday, I was going to wear as little as possible. That included bras. The main reason for not wearing one was actually because I'd forgotten to pack spares. It was times like this I was glad to be a small B cup. All of my curve began at the waist down.

My trainers were almost ruined to the point of no return, so I slipped into a pair of Havaianas flip-flops, tied my hair into a loose knot, and slipped out of the bathroom to meet Raine, who was in the armchair on her phone with what looked like my discharge papers and insurance forms in her lap.

"Ready?"

• • •

In the front seat of Raine's cruiser, I watched the old Victorian-inspired buildings of Georgetown pass in a rushed blur. There was a lot of peaked roofing, old red brick, and quaint charm that surrounded the historical Georgetown central district.

"There won't be a lot of people there," Raine said abruptly. Perhaps she'd taken my silence as nerves or concern over brunch with strangers. Crowds and strangers weren't my favorite thing, but I was numb to concern and fear at the moment.

Raine continued. "It'll just be my dad, my fiancé and his daughter, and maybe some of the farmhands. Oh, an—"

"You don't have to explain," I told her. "I'm not worried or whatever."

"Can I ask you something?"

"I guess."

"What are you doing so far from home? Why were you walking for miles and miles?"

It wasn't an unreasonable question; even if she hadn't been a cop, she'd still have been curious. I was just as curious as she was. Why had I decided to walk for close to twelve hours in a state I'd never been to before? I loved to walk, but that was a long time, even for me. The truth wasn't a secret that I wanted to keep a lid on, but finding the words was a challenge in itself. I hadn't said it out loud, and I wasn't sure if I could.

"My sister died, and I—I just needed a break." I exhaled, a harsh band of tension forming around my head. I could see Raine looking from the road to me and back again. No doubt she would tell me she was sorry or something, but I didn't want to dwell on the subject.

"You have a fiancé?" I asked. "And a soon-to-be stepdaughter? That must be nice."

"Oh." Her voice was tight for a moment, and I saw her nod. "It is. Willa is the sweetest little thing. She was part of the proposal. Milo proposed on the fourth of July. We were all out on the farm, and there were fireworks, and Willa and I were passing a ball back and forth, and it was dark, but when I caught one of her throws, it wasn't a ball, it was a ring box, and then Milo appeared, and I cried and *ugh*—it was beautiful."

"Congratulations," I said, admiring the ring on her finger. It was a simple white gold band with a teardrop-shaped diamond that glittered in the morning sun. "How old is Willa?"

"She's ten. Her mom died when she was two, so it was just her and Milo up until about three years ago. He transferred here from a station in Austin. Milo is a police officer too."

I smiled and watched the outskirts of Georgetown. There were a lot of large acreages that held beautiful farmhouses and ranches. Trees were scattered in fields and lined long, winding driveways.

"It's so green here," I murmured. Then a thought occurred to me, and I panicked, reaching down into my backpack between my feet.

"What's the matter?" Raine questioned as I swiped past the dozens of missed calls from staff and friends at home. Instead, I dialed Pete's number and waited with a bouncing leg until he answered.

"Hello? Addie?"

I swallowed and tried not to sound murderous when I spoke. "Pete, I need you to go to the condo and get all of the houseplants. Re-home them. Give them to someone who will water them, all right?"

"Uh . . . sure. Yeah, I can do that, I guess. Is the gate code the same?"

"Yeah. There's a key in the third-to-the-left potted plant on the doorstep."

"Got it," he said, and I could hear his toddler babbling in the background. "Uh . . . how are you doing, Addie? Are you—"

I hung up before he could ask me if I was okay. Margo had moved on with her life. Pete was nothing more than an ex-husband who had found his forever with someone else. But I still hated him. I hated that he'd shown up at her funeral, weeping and sobbing as if he'd lost someone he cared about. I hated that he was living, laughing, in love with some other woman who had given birth to his perfect son. He was living the life Margo deserved, but instead, she was six feet under dirt. I hated Pete.

"Ex?" Raine asked, and I realized my knuckles had turned white while I clutched my phone.

"No," I answered. "Not mine."

• • •

We arrived at one of the long, winding driveways that was shaded with trees on either side, the thick branches full of leaves creating an overhead awning. The gravel crunched beneath the tires, and there was nothing but green for what felt like forever.

We approached an enormous home that looked to be from the Victorian era but had been renovated and was modern and sharp. The weatherboard was a crisp white and the shutters were midnight black. There was a wraparound porch on both floors. The railing was thick steel, and there were wide windows and French doors everywhere.

On the other side of the parking area was a second driveway that led toward the acres of open fields, where I could see sheds and barns and horses. I stepped out of the cruiser and was hit with an array of different smells. Clean air was the first, and the rest I couldn't put a name to. It wasn't bad; it was just so different. The air was different. I had never experienced it before.

"Yep, that's horse shit." Raine stood beside me and inhaled a deep breath; she had a pair of sunglasses on now. "Or it might be Noah, the donkey."

"Noah?"

She shook her head with a small smile. "Willa named him after Noah from *The Notebook*."

"She watched that?"

"Loves it," Raine said. "We fast-forward through the sex scenes, but she's obsessed with those classic romance movies. Milo thinks it's better than her watching some of the trash that's on television now. He's hoping it'll raise her standards and she'll settle for nothing less than being courted by a gentleman."

I nodded. "Not a bad idea."

"Yeah, but I said the best chance she has is seeing her dad's example." Raine grinned. "So, Milo is the Noah to my Allie. Flowers, cute dates, compliments. He's a catch."

"Noah and Allie fought a lot and then had an affair while she was engaged."

Raine's smile slipped, and she was quiet for a moment. "Well, shit."

I laughed, and it was so sudden and abrupt that I almost missed the fact it had come from me. "It's all for true love, right? I mean, Noah and Allie loved each other until death. So, that's the main thing."

She laughed as well, and then we wandered up to the front of the house, but instead of going in through the front door, we went around the porch to the back garden, where the deck extended. Covered in outdoor sofas, a large table, a fireplace, and an egg-shaped swinging chair, it was gorgeous. It overlooked a large stretch of rolling land: there were tall trees with tire swings hanging from the thick branches, flower beds, vegetable gardens, bench seats, and large, tidy doghouses lining the back.

"Wow," I murmured, wanting so much to see it for what it was rather than having a looming dark cloud of despair distorting the view.

"I'm going to go in and find out how far off brunch is. Want to come?"

I looked over at the open French doors, which looked as if they led to a dining area. The kitchen couldn't be far; I could smell hot bread and bacon.

"I'm just going to make another call." I was still holding my phone; the sundress had no pockets. "I'll come in after. Where do I go?"

"Unless we're back out here, we'll be in the kitchen. Straight through those doors and to the left."

"Great."

She headed inside, and I stepped down from the deck, wandering across the neatly trimmed lawn toward the back where the garden beds were. A sprinkler was showering two of the seven beds, but three others were glittering with water droplets. Someone must have been rotating the sprinkler so it covered the entire area.

I crouched and touched a soft, wet purple petal with a white middle that spread outward and morphed into a deep violet. The soil was damp, and I could smell what I'd detected when I'd first hopped out of the car. Damp soil. It was nice, just different from the potted plants I watered at home.

While I was still crouched, stalling calling Lo back at home to find out how the event had gone last night, I heard the creak and spring of a gate being opened behind me. I twisted to see a man wandering through with a bucket in each hand.

He was tall, six foot two at least. He had dark-brown hair and sun-kissed skin that was damp with sweat. He set the buckets beside a garden bed, stripped off his black T-shirt, and cupped his hands to collect some of the sprinkler water, which he then ran over his face. He hadn't even seen me, and I kept still, hoping he'd leave without seeing me hiding in the garden.

His light-wash jeans hung low on his sharply cut hips and were covered in dirt; his chest was defined, with a dusting of dark hair. He had those pillowed pec muscles, soft but strong, and broad shoulders rounded with strength. And then, as I was imagining what they might feel like, my phone started ringing.

"Shit." I tapped Ignore and stood up, feeling exposed and stupid when I saw the man standing a few feet from me with his hands on his hips and a brow raised in question.

"I'm—This is—I'm here with Raine."

His curious stare narrowed, sweeping me slowly as he nodded and picked up his buckets.

I watched him walk off across the lawn, his back just as defined as the front, until he turned the corner around the house and disappeared. That was a bit awkward, but I decided not to dwell on it. He must have been one of the farmhands Raine had told me about earlier.

I exhaled a deep breath. I couldn't call Lo. I sent her a text message instead.

> How did the event go? Out of town for now. Don't call me, just keep business running. You're in charge.

Her response was almost immediate.

> Of course. Take care. X

Lo was good like that. She didn't ask a lot of questions; she didn't pester me to be her friend or put her nose in other people's business. She just got on with her job, and we kept our personal lives private.

"Addie?"

I peered up and saw Raine on the deck with a platter of food that was steaming hot. She set it on the table, and I jogged back up the steps, asking if I could do something to help. Before she could answer me, a little girl came bounding outside. She was dressed in a pair of wide-leg shorts that were cream and blue pinstripe. *Vintage* was the word that came to mind. After what Raine had told me, I guessed this was her stepdaughter, in love with *The Notebook* and likely the fashion in it too.

"Oh, Willa, this is Addie," Raine said, her smile full of affection as she watched the little girl, who, in turn, was watching me. "Addie, this is Willa, Milo's daughter."

She was cute, super cute. She had long black hair in a braid down her back, a little button nose, and one dimple in her right cheek when she smiled. There was something about her that was so familiar. She reminded me of someone. With a pang of anguish throughout my entire body, I realized she reminded me of Margo, and I longed for the chance to see Margo's face one more time.

I shook off the haunted feeling and forced a smile. "Hi."

"Hello," she said. Her gaze was cautious, but she politely extended her hand, and I couldn't help but grin a little harder at her good manners. "I'm Willa."

"I love your shirt." I pointed at the tee, which had the quote "Obstinate, headstrong girl" written across the front of it. *"Pride and Prejudice."*

Her stare went from cautious to somewhat more curious. "Do you like that movie too?"

"I do. But I also love the book."

"I haven't read the book."

"I really recommend it."

She sat down on the bench seat at the table. "I'll get it from the library next time I go."

Raine spun and went back inside, calling over her shoulder that she needed to bring the rest of the food out and gather the team.

The sun touched my back as I sat opposite Willa. She was staring at me again, rather intensely—it was almost a look of distrust. Perhaps that was just how a child stared at someone who was new. I wanted to make conversation with her, but I had no clue what to ask. *How is school?* No one liked school. *Got a man?* No, she was ten.

"Favorite movie?" I asked.

She tilted her head with thought. "*The Notebook*. For now."

I nodded as if Raine hadn't told me that.

"Favorite book?" she asked.

*"A Walk to Remember."*

Her expression lit up. "I like that movie."

I smiled and wanted to tell her the book was incredible and she needed to read it, but I couldn't blame her for favoring movies over novels. For a child, her taste was impressive enough on its own.

"I'll read the book," she added after a moment. "I love reading."

"Me too."

Raine reappeared with another platter of food and a man following behind her with his arms also full of food. It wasn't the one I'd run into in the garden. He was a fair-skinned middle-aged man with a beard and thinning dark hair that fell around his ears. He was handsome, well-built, and seemingly confident in a way that wasn't arrogant.

"This is Addie," Raine said. "Addie, this is Milo."

"How's it going?" He set the plates down and sat next to his daughter. "Raine said you came from Beverly Hills. Quite a change."

"It's different, but this place is . . . lovely."

"It is. I went to California on a trip with the fellas to see some concert in college. It was fun and all but a bit too much going on, if I'm honest. I prefer a slower pace."

I nodded, understanding more than he knew. It was part of the reason I was at home a lot, curled up on the sofa with a book. Raine sat beside me and started handing out plates. She'd made it seem like there would be more people here, so I was surprised when Milo and Willa started piling their plates with food.

"Your dad isn't joining us?" I asked.

Raine scooped fruit salad onto her plate, her dark ringlets now out of the bun and falling around her shoulders. "Yeah, he's not up for it this morning. He's got a migraine. He gets them a lot, so he's in bed resting at the moment. And most of the farmhands are off for the Sunday. Zac shouldn't be far, though."

I'd just finished putting scrambled eggs, bacon, fruit salad, and bread rolls onto my plate when the man from the garden rounded the corner and came striding down the porch. He was dressed in a fresh pair of jeans and a clean white T-shirt. His hair was tousled with a slight wave into a styled mess, and he had a light stubble coating his jaw. He sat down beside Milo and leaned his forearm on the tabletop. He had incredible shoulders, and my mind flashed back to the moment I'd been crouched in the garden, watching him shirtless like an absolute creep. My cheeks warmed with embarrassment.

"This is Zac." Raine covered her full mouth while she spoke. "Zac, this is Addie—"

"We've met." He interrupted her and dragged the bowl of eggs toward him. "Fuck, I've got so much work to do, Raine. Winnie has a broken shoe. I called Kent, and he'll have a new one for her tomorrow, but for now, she's limping and refusing to walk on the gravel. She's in the paddock, but I'm not sure how I'll get her back in the stables without dragging her ass."

Raine smiled, nodding along while he gave her a few other casual updates about farm life. It didn't sound like there were a lot of animals apart from horses, and it seemed like a reasonable assumption that they could be breeders or trainers. It wouldn't have been surprising after seeing the size of the home. Good horse breeders and trainers could bring in a lot of income. Well, that was what I had read.

"Addie here is from California," Raine said, almost sounding as if she'd been holding that in and desperately waiting until Zac was done so she could say it. "Beverly Hills, to be specific."

Zac leaned back in his seat, his thick, dark lashes sweeping over me while his face remained impassive. "What brings you to the outskirts of Georgetown?"

"I don't know," I answered and felt grateful that Raine didn't decide to fill them all in on how I'd passed out on the side of the road after an attempt to walk off the pain of losing my sister last week. The less I had to relive that truth, the better.

Of course, the answer "I don't know" in response to asking what I was doing in another state was enough to raise their brows.

"I'm just getting a breather," I said, swallowing breathtaking grief before it could wind me. "A change of pace."

"Good place to come for that." Milo winked and stabbed a sausage with his fork. It dawned on me that he was also a cop, and he didn't seem the least bit suspicious about my being here with no explanation. Perhaps Raine had filled him in earlier.

"You wanna meet my donkey?" Willa asked. "Zac, can we take her down to the paddock to meet Noah?"

Zac chewed his food, his strong jaw moving as he gave me a slow once-over. It made me feel exposed and nervous until he lowered his head with a quiet scoff. "Might be a bit much dirt for our guest, Will."

How rude. No doubt he'd seen the dress and flip-flops and, more than anything, taken into consideration that I was from Beverly Hills and assumed I was some prissy California princess that thought these parts were full of hicks.

"I would love to meet Noah," I told Willa.

"Zac, take Willa and Addie to meet Noah." Raine gave him a pointed look before she turned to me. "Willa isn't allowed down at the paddock alone. There's not a lot of trouble to get into, but there is the occasional snake, and a few months ago we had a puma attack one of our horses. Super rare, but it's for peace of mind that Willa doesn't wander alone."

"Of course."

"Still want to meet Noah?" Zac asked, elbows on the tabletop.

His judgment was getting a little old, and it'd been less than fifteen minutes since we sat down at the table. "Yeah, I'm sure."

He quirked his brows. "All right then."

"You promise you'll take us?" Willa demanded.

He sighed as if making promises to this little girl was nothing new. She stood up and skipped toward where he sat, and then she held up her pinkie finger.

"Promise."

He gave her a tight smile, silence settling while we waited with anticipation. Finally, he lifted his pinkie finger, wrapped it around hers, and solidified the agreement with a quick bounce of their conjoined fingers.

"Now pinkie promise Addie." Willa pointed at me. "I'm not new to your loopholes. Promise her too."

"Loopholes." He narrowed his amused glare at Raine. "You teach her that?"

She shrugged.

"Promise," Willa sang. Zac turned to me, and I quickly lifted my pinkie, even though we were too far apart to touch. I preferred it like that, though: his stare was doing enough to my nerves without adding contact on top of that.

"I do mine like this," I lied, coming up with something on the spot. I gestured for Zac to raise his finger, and so he did, and then I touched mine to my nose with a swift flick. "You do the same."

He looked as if he were fighting a smile. He held my eyes, his impossibly thick lashes fluttering as he swiped the side of his nose with his little finger and nodded.

"There." He finally tore his piercing gaze from me and looked at Willa. "We're all locked in, all right? Relax. I'll take you down to see Noah for a few minutes. I have a lot of work left to do."

"I know, it's just fun messing with you."

There was a collective laugh at Zac's expense. Mine too, I suppose. I could still feel the ghost of his stare seeping into my skin.

After we'd eaten and I'd helped wash up in a gorgeous, immaculate kitchen that was bigger than the condo's whole living room back at home, I followed Zac through the garden gate with Willa strolling along beside me. She was wearing a pair of blue rubber boots, which she used to kick the gravel as we walked downhill. It wasn't steep, but I could feel the natural lean of my body adjusting to the descent. Zac had his hands in his pockets as he peered at my feet. Flip-flops weren't the best footwear for the situation, but I wasn't going to admit that.

"Managing there, Beverly?"

"It's Addie." I kept my tone even. "And I'm fine."

"That's pretty nail polish," Willa said, staring at the nude pink on my toes. Margo and I had gotten manicures and pedicures almost two weeks ago. She was buried with this shade on her nails. *Immortalizing the perfect shade for our tan skin*—that was what she'd said. She was right. But mine was starting to grow out, putting me further and further from the memory of our last girls' date.

"Thanks."

We must have walked for ten minutes before we came to a series of gates and fences, then a little shed where Noah was standing, eating apples from a rope that hung from the roof.

Zac made a clicking noise with his tongue and leaned his forearms on the fence. "Noah, here, boy."

Noah ignored him.

"Noah," Willa sang, climbing the fence rails until she was sitting perched on the edge with her legs inside the pen. "Noah, come here."

Noah snapped to attention as soon as he heard her voice, and he trotted toward her and nuzzled her outstretched hand. I couldn't help but giggle, as strange as it felt, at Zac, who rolled his eyes and sighed. "Traitor," he mumbled.

"Hi, Noah," I said, petting the animal. His hair was so soft, and his little tuft of black hair was cute. His lids closed and opened slowly with satisfaction while Willa and I rubbed his head.

"He's soft, right?" Willa looked at me but burst into a fit of giggles when Noah started nuzzling her cheek with his nose. "Noah!"

She tumbled backward off the fence and would have landed on the grass below if it weren't for the strong set of arms that caught her just in time. "Willa," Zac exhaled and sounded relieved that he'd been there. "On the ground or stand on the fence rails. He's too rough."

"He's not rough," Willa scolded, but she did as she was told. "He's affectionate. He loves me."

Zac chuckled but stood closer from then on. It was sort of . . . sweet. Even if he didn't talk to me a whole lot and seemed sort of standoffish, I could appreciate that he cared about this little girl. I wondered how much time Willa spent on this farm. She was Raine's stepdaughter, and Raine didn't live here, but she must have frequented the house enough for the farmhand to become a good friend. I guessed I didn't understand much about the dynamics of running a farm, though.

After we'd had a little time with Noah, peeped at some of the horses in the paddock, and wandered back to the house, Raine let me know that she needed to get home for some sleep before she passed out. Milo had a few things to do before he left, so Willa hung behind with him. I said goodbye to Zac as well, receiving a simple nod in return.

In the car, I fastened my seat belt and settled in. "Thanks for brunch."

"Not a problem," Raine answered, yawning. "I think Willa liked having someone to talk classic romance with."

"She's a nice girl." I nodded. "Does Milo help at your dad's a lot?"

"Yeah, just on his weekends. He fixes things around the house or feeds the animals. Whatever needs to be done."

"That's nice of him."

"Oh, and he cooks Sunday brunch, of course."

"That was one of the best meals I've had in a long time." I recalled the fluffy eggs and crisp bacon.

When we got into Georgetown central, Raine asked me where I wanted to go.

"Oh." That had been the point of brunch. I was meant to be thinking about what to do next, but the whole morning had been a distraction—a pleasant one—from the truth that was my life right now. "Just drop me off at the closest motel."

"A motel? You could come and stay with me, if you need somewhere to go."

"No, no. I'm good. This is just for a night or two. Until I move on."

Move on to where? I had no idea. But what I did know was that it wouldn't be home.

# CHAPTER FOUR

*Two years ago*

There was probably a butt mold from where I'd been sitting on the couch for an entire weekend. Margo was taking the lead on our planned events this time, back to normal, and I had been curled up with three books, which I'd finished from beginning to end, getting up only to pee, eat, and drink.

Like a cat.

Sunday afternoon sunshine was pouring in through the living room window and I was closing the fourth book on chapter two when the front door opened and closed. Margo appeared in the living room a moment later, fatigue all over her made-up face. She was wearing tall heels and a slim full-length jumpsuit.

"Who plans weddings on a Sunday?" she groaned, leaning on the doorframe. "Sunday?! I need sleep."

"I'd get married on a Sunday."

"You would not."

I grinned and followed her through to the kitchen, where she started rummaging through the cupboard for Advil. While she searched, I poured her a glass of water and sat on the edge of the counter. My beautiful Boston fern plant sat next to me, and I ran my palm along the underside of its long-leafed stems. I'd loved plants, flowers, and trees for as long as I could remember. I spent hours reading up on how to grow and care for different foliage. I'd told Margo that I wanted to do horticultural studies, but she'd said it would have to wait until we weren't as busy with May We?

I plucked an apple out of the fruit bowl. "Have you thought more about the offer that I made last weekend?"

She let out a deep breath and shook her head as she pulled her hair up into a knot. "It's a no, just like it was then and will remain."

"I'm kind of offended that you don't want me to carry your child."

"Well, don't be offended. I'm saying no *for you*. You're twenty-two. You're at an age where you should be going out and meeting people and having fun. You should not be walking around, pregnant with someone else's child."

"Margo."

"No, no." She waved a finger at me, but her brows were pinched, and I could tell that her headache was worsening at the mere thought of having an argument with me. "Don't come at me with any of your logical arguments. This is not negotiable."

"Honestly, it's weird that you're not all for the idea. I mean, you'd want to trust the person carrying your child, right? Who could you trust more than me? We live together. You'd be right beside me through the entire experience, which would make it all the more meaningful for you."

"I get all of that," Margo said after she'd swallowed her mouthful of water and pain relief. "But I can't do that to you, Addie. And you know the reason I can't. It blows my mind that you'd even ask me."

"It—"

"Moving on." Margo cut me off before I could continue giving her logical arguments and explain further what a great idea it was. "How's next weekend's bridal shower coming along?"

As much as I wanted to keep discussing the potential of me being her surrogate, I paused because I needed to ask her this question before I forgot, and she'd opened the subject for it. "The client wants to know if she should put a tab on at the bar or hire a private room and have her friends BYO."

"What does her budget allow?"

"A private room or a very small tab."

She lowered her head in thought and tapped the countertop. "I'd do the private room and tell her girlfriends to bring their own alcohol. It ends up being the biggest expense, so it'll save her in the long run. Plus, they can order more from the bar if need be, but they can't bring their own alcohol without the private room. So that's what I'd suggest."

"Hopefully it's not too late to get the private room," I said, thinking out loud. "It's next week."

"No, it won't be too late. It's at High Flyer's, right?"

"Mm-hmm."

"There will still be rooms available. Give them a call tomorrow, though. The sooner the better."

"All right."

"The best man kept asking after you today. Harlow." Margo raised her brows suggestively. "You should call him."

I racked my brain to remember who the best man even was, and it must have been obvious that I couldn't put a face to the name.

"He was the cute one with the man bun. Five-five. Tattoos and a lip piercing."

"You sound like an ad for a dating website."

"Call him."

"Eh." I shrugged, now recalling the guy she was referring to. "We had two conversations, and he talked about gaming and weightlifting the entire time."

"I'm sure he has more hobbies than that. More going for him. You'll never know if you don't give it a chance. You have to get out of the house once in a while, Addie. You're never going to meet someone with your face in a novel all the time. Those men are not real. They are not going to pop off the page and sweep you off your feet."

"I know that," I snapped and felt a blush trickle across my cheeks. "It's nice to pretend, though."

"To be fair, I wish that could happen. Fictional men are perfect."

"That's because they're fictional."

"More men should read romance novels," she said. "It's like, the secrets are all right there. Want to win us over? Do some research."

"I feel like they have no problem winning us over, it's the reveal after a few months of dating when the disappointment begins."

She nodded. "You might be right."

"I am right."

She giggled and snatched up her own apple, holding the stem with a knowing grin. "How about the fate is in the apple's stem?"

I rolled my eyes. We'd been doing this for as long as I could remember. A schoolyard game that determined who you were destined to love. At the same time, we held our apple stems and twisted, chanting the alphabet. Margo's was the first to snap.

"K," she said, disappointment furrowing her brow. "K? What name—"

"Keegan?" I offered, having paused my twisting.

She scowled. "No. Douchebag name. Carry on. Let's see who you're going to get."

I carried on and carried on, and I got all the way to Z and it still hadn't snapped. I forcefully pulled it off the apple and huffed with disappointment. "Well, if that's not a damn sign I'm destined to be alone, I don't know what is."

"You got Z." Margo gave me a light slap on the leg. "Don't be so pessimistic."

"Don't be so optimistic. Names that start with Z are so few and far between I might as well accept I'm going to die alone."

She shook her head and pushed off the countertop, skipping toward the corridor. "There's someone out there for all of us, Addie." Her voice echoed from where she'd disappeared.

How she remained so optimistic after what Pete had done to her, I had no idea. The fact she was considering an anonymous donor rather than waiting for Mr. Right was unbelievable on its own. That wasn't like Margo. She was so invested in finding her forever. But after watching what she'd been through, I had to admit that real-life relationships looked somewhat disappointing.

I was more in favor of her achieving her dream of having a baby without the help of a man. I understood why she was reserved when it came to the idea of me being her surrogate. But I wanted to do this for her, and I wasn't giving up that fast.

• • •

"What the fu—"

Night had fallen, and Margo emerged from her afternoon snooze to find me in the office at the end of the corridor.

"Surprise!"

Margo walked into the room, slow and blinking, as if she thought she was still asleep. I'd had a busy afternoon, with an expensive trip to Target and then some redecorating.

I spun around and gestured at the room.

"So?"

Margo took in the change table against the wall, art decals above it, the crib in the corner, a Finding Nemo mobile hanging from the ceiling. There was a new chest of toys, diapers, wipes, a small set of drawers with a tiny outfit laid across the top. A bouncer and a stroller were in the closet, but I'd left the sliding door open so she could see them. The desk, cabinet, and armchair from our office setup were still there, but tucked off to one side. I figured it would work to get my point across, and if needed, we could make permanent rearrangements later.

She looked at me with her mouth hanging open. "Addison?"

"Yes?"

"Wha—"

"You have to let me have the baby now. Or I bought all of this stuff for no reason."

She rubbed her temples, eyes closed and breathing deep.

"Relax, huh? Just . . . let me do this. Please?" I didn't know what else I could do to convince her.

She folded her arms across her chest. "Why is it so important that you're the one who carries the baby?"

"Because." I took her hand and gave her a soft smile, one I liked to use whenever I was in trouble and needed to butter her up. She was a mom already, even if I wasn't her daughter. "You've done so much for me, Margo. I would have been so lost if you hadn't stepped up and taken me in after Mom and Dad died. I was a teenager, and that can't have been easy. I want to give back, so much. This feels like such a small gesture in the grand scheme of things. I want to do this. For you."

Her lip quivered, and she bit down on it.

"Don't," I giggled, wiping at her face when a tear escaped. "You're so emotional."

She slapped me on the arm. "You say stuff like that and expect me not to be?"

I shrugged. "So? Mmm? Doesn't it look great in here? The only thing that's missing is a bubba."

She searched the room with her tearful gaze again. I knew I was winning her over; she was caving, and I felt a little surge of excitement bubble under the surface. It escaped, though, in the form of a clenched-jaw squeal, and I started bouncing on the spot.

"I can't wait to give birth to my niece or nephew."

Margo curled over with an exhausted laugh and held her palms to her face. "No, no. I haven't decided."

"Nonsense. It's the perfect solution."

# CHAPTER FIVE

Hanna, the nice older woman who ran the little bed-and-breakfast in town, was waiting for me outside of my room on Friday morning. The Lemon Inn looked like a regular home for the most part. It had the appearance of an early 1900s villa that had been restored. The weatherboards were a mint green, the trimmings and window frames were white. It was quaint.

There was also a café called the Sweet Lemon Kitchen that served a decent breakfast each morning. It was the sort of place I'd have loved to spend a week with a good book in the middle of winter. But it was too hot to hide in my room, despite my best efforts to do just that. Apart from stepping out to get a few clothes and bras, I'd been sitting in front of a barely functioning AC unit and reminding myself that it was better than being at home. It didn't help that the first few days after I'd arrived, my legs had been crippled with pain from the absurd distance I'd walked.

This morning, though, now that I'd recovered, I wanted to go for a walk. My body was restless, my mind was restless, and even though I would be alone with my thoughts no matter where I went, there was something about being outside that changed how I processed the murky waters in my mind. When I could see the sky, when I could feel the sun, when I could hear the wind, it spoke to me in a much gentler voice than the harsh bite of a small space.

"Hanna." I gave the overeager hostess a tight smile, noting her pleated dress and penny loafers. Her pale-blond hair was almost white and pulled back in a low bun. Stepping around her in the narrow corridor, I kept walking, my flip-flops slapping the hardwood floor. My trainers had had to be thrown out after I'd left the hospital. They were already old, and they'd deteriorated during my impromptu marathon. I still hadn't replaced them.

"Good morning." She followed me as I went for the staircase. "That's a bold dress."

With her at my back, I let my eyes roll at her tone. Yes, it was a shorter dress than what she might deem modest, but it was also sweltering, and I loved the feeling of barely-there clothing when it was hot. "Thank you, Hanna. I think yours looks cute too."

Holding the banister, I made quick work of the staircase, aiming for the front door. Hanna was no doubt going to suggest I join her for singing in the common room or a high tea or whatever social event she'd organized for the several other guests. She'd been doing her best to catch me most mornings when I emerged for the free continental breakfast. I couldn't understand why she cared so much about her guests' involvement.

I wasn't interested in group activities, and if I'd known the hostess was going to hound me daily, I would've told Raine to take me somewhere else. That Sunday after brunch, she'd said she knew a great place. I wondered if she'd thought it would help to send me to such an overly friendly inn. Perhaps that was a weird form of support around here.

"We're doing a group reading this morning," Hanna said, keeping up behind me. "You mentioned you like to read, so I thought you might be interested in participating."

Group readings should be abolished. "I can't this morning, sorry. I have to be somewhere."

From my peripheral vision, I saw a blur of people sitting in the common room to the left, but I didn't pay them any mind and instead opened the door and slipped out before Hanna could respond.

• • •

The sun beat on my back, now at its peak heat for the afternoon. I'd been walking for hours again. I couldn't be sure how many. My phone was back at the inn, and I was far from town. Far from the old brick buildings and the boutiques and the eateries. I'd ended up on a scenic route, narrow dirt paths shrouded with trees and thick bush. I liked the smell of the earth, the sounds of birds fluttering in the trees and cattle lowing in the distance.

The sound of running water became closer, and the shrubs on the left started to thin, revealing a shallow creek. Water rippled over rocks, the width barely more than six feet. The bubbling sound of its flow was soothing, and I slipped between the tree trunks and stepped carefully over the rocks and tree debris of the thicket floor.

As I came to the water's edge, I had the sensation I was being watched and whipped my head to the side to see a beautiful young horse sitting with her front legs tucked beneath her. Her nose was wet, like it'd been in the water, and she watched me with dark, almost black eyes. Her coat was a chestnut brown, and her mane was black. I stood still for a moment, thinking, waiting, admiring.

Carefully, I crept forward, hand outstretched. She was so beautiful. I'd only spent time with horses one other time, when I was in school and we went on a field trip to an equine sanctuary. It was still one of my favorite memories. I took slow, careful steps toward the horse, my feet a little unstable on the stones bordering the creek. She didn't spook; she just watched me as I got closer, my heart pounding with something other than anguish for the first time in more than two weeks. It was about as magical as seeing a unicorn as far as I was concerned.

"Hi." I spoke softly as I ran my hand along her soft neck. "You're so sweet."

When I felt like she wasn't going to bolt or panic, I sat down next to her, all of my movements slow, precise. The rocks were hard and uncomfortable under me, but I didn't care because I was sitting next to a magnificent creature, hand running slow strokes down her mane and onto her back.

With my legs up to my chest, I rested my cheek on my knee. This moment felt too good to be real, too fleeting. My smile faltered as I thought about it being over. Because it would be over, this burst of elation that had spread through my chest. It couldn't last, and I hated the fact that I couldn't stay right here forever. I couldn't figure out if I was chasing the high or fleeing from the low. Either way, I was running.

Suddenly, the guttural growl of an engine grew out of the woods, closer and closer until I peered at the trail and saw a dirt bike tearing toward us, a cloud of dust behind it. The driver came close, skidding to a stop and kicking the stand down. The sounds of nature returned when he killed the engine.

Zac swung a leg over the bike and stood beside it. His dark-brown hair was wind-blown, messy, and tossed into waves around his ears and the back of his neck.

"Beverly?" He wore blatant confusion on his face, and I looked away, focusing on the horse.

"It's Addie," I mumbled.

"Right." He walked slowly toward me. "What are you doing out here?"

Zac crouched on the other side of the horse, his large hand coasting down her back, being careful to avoid mine.

"I don't know," I said, answering his question. "I started walking, and I kept going until I ended up on this trail, and then I found this sweet thing."

"You like to walk, huh?"

His tone lacked the judgment he'd regarded me with before. Instead, he was curious, and I couldn't blame him. "Yeah, I do," I said, not bothering to elaborate.

When I peered over at him, he was already watching me, his focus soft and his gaze on my mouth for a moment. He cleared his throat and fixed his attention on the horse. Birds chirped in the treetops above, their wings fluttering, and the creek babbled. Zac's T-shirt sleeves stretched tight around his arms as he continued to pet the horse. He was crouched, his strong thighs holding him in place with minimal effort.

"You're always up to no good," Zac murmured, and for a moment, I thought he was talking to me. It wasn't until I looked at him that I realized he was talking to the horse.

"You know her?"

Zac's lips kicked at the edges as he kept his focus on the horse. "Mm-hmm. Lavender lives on the farm. She's in training before she's going to be sold early next year. But she likes to get out."

"She's got a free spirit," I said, recognizing within the horse that need to stretch your legs and discover new pastures. Find out what else is out there. "Maybe you should let her be. Let her live her best life outside of the confines of a barn stall."

Zac chuckled. It was low-pitched, gravelly. "It's not my call to make. She doesn't belong to me. I just do the work. Keep their stalls clean, keep them fed. Sales and training aren't my area of expertise."

"I get that. I run an event planning business at home and—well, I co-own it—or I did, with my sis, Margo—and she was the one who made the final calls, even if I did want to do something different. Something that might have been outside the box. I guess I didn't mind so much, though. She kept the business successful."

I sucked in a sharp breath, not sure where the sudden urge to share had come from. Tears welled as I thought about the life I'd left behind. I thought about Margo, the fact that she wasn't at home waiting for me. Taking a few deep breaths, I pushed it all back, pushed back the truth, the anguish, the despair. I refused to think about the reason I was here in the first place. Watching the creek, I let it all go.

"Raine told me," he said quietly. I didn't respond; I was doing my best not to break. "So, the business must belong to you now?" he asked.

"I guess. I don't know what to do with it, though. I don't know . . . how to do it without her."

"You have to decide if you want to do it for yourself. It's hard to work if you're doing it for the wrong reasons."

I couldn't talk about how I felt about the business. I didn't know how I felt. "Yeah."

"You plan on heading home sometime? Raine seemed to think you'd be moving on from here."

Zac was still crouching, watching me.

"I kind of feel like—well, when I'm here, it doesn't feel like there's this entire part of my life that's fallen apart. It's easier to pretend that this is my reality, rather than facing the one back at home. I'm alone here, but it's better than being alone at home, where I have to be reminded of what I lost wherever I look."

"So, you and your sister—Margo, was it? You were close?"

The question broke the dam. Close didn't begin to cover what Margo was to me. My best friend, my mom, my person. Tears streamed down my face as I saw a montage of our life. The nights we'd laughed until the sun came up, the tears she'd dried from my face, the hours we'd spent on road trips together. The chance to ever do those things again was gone, and it felt like a hand was crushing my rib cage.

"You don't have to talk about it," Zac quickly added. "Wanna come back to the house for a cold drink? I can give you a ride home afterward."

"Home." My laugh was humorless, but it broke through the tears as I wiped my face. "I'm staying at some little bed-and-breakfast on the edge of town. The Lemon Inn. Have you heard of it?"

Zac gave a slow nod, watching the creek with amusement. "Yeah, I sure have. I'm guessing that was Raine's suggestion."

"Yeah," I sniffed, my nose running due to the tears.

"That doesn't surprise me. Raine loves Hanna, and Raine also thinks people heal better if they're surrounded by the sort of nonsense that goes on in that inn."

"I've managed to avoid it so far." I stood up, brushing dirt and dust off my butt. Gesturing to the dirt bike on the narrow path, I said, "Are we going on that?"

"I'd let you ride the horse, but she's not quite there. I don't have a helmet, either. So, no pressure to get on."

"No, it's fine," I said, wandering over to the bike, aware of my flip-flops. I needed to get a better pair of shoes if I was going to keep going on long walks.

Zac grabbed a rope off the bike handlebars, slipped it over Lavender's neck, and clicked his tongue, getting her to follow him. He swung a leg over the bike and sat, giving the stand a kick before he threw his boot down on the starter pedal and the engine roared to life.

"Is she going to be able to keep up?" I asked, looking at the rope around the horse's neck, worried she might end up with rope burn.

Zac tried not to laugh, but I caught the grin on his face before he could palm his jaw and hide it. "She could probably run faster than this bike if she wanted to. She's a quick little thing."

"Oh, right." Still, I looked at the bike, hand going to my head, fingers caressing the skin on my temple. "I don't have a helmet."

"We'll crawl it back." Zac rested his hands on his thighs. "You'll be safe with me."

Hesitating, my mind tumbled over all of the potential dangers. One of those dangers included how close we would be when I got on the back of that thing.

"Hop on. I swear, I won't go fast," Zac said, and then he lifted his pinkie finger and swiped the side of his nose, remembering the promise I'd made up on the spot last weekend. Something warm tugged at the cold void in my chest, willing me to feel something better than the ache I'd become so familiar with.

Finally, I stepped up to the bike and held on to Zac's shoulders, keeping myself stable as I swung a leg over the seat and slipped in behind him. I leaned back, holding on to the back of the seat.

Zac turned his head, giving me a view of his side profile, his brow raised. "You're going to need to hold on to me."

My eyes coasted down the length of his broad back and the obvious definition under his shirt. It wasn't like I'd never touched a man before, but the thought of wrapping my arms around him made me stupidly nervous. I saw him crack a grin before he faced forward. Faster than I was prepared for, he revved the engine, and the bike made one strong jolt forward. The sudden stop caused me to fall forward into his back, and out of instinct and self-preservation, my arms wrapped tight around his torso.

"That's better," he called over his shoulder. I didn't respond, but I hoped he couldn't feel my heart racing against his back.

He started driving, and I noted how good he smelled, like earth and musk and citrus.

Zac kept his promise. He didn't go fast, and it made our ride back to the farm long, but it was a beautiful afternoon: the sun was warm, and the wind felt like a gentle caress against my skin. The entire ride was more relaxing than I'd expected it to be.

Zac put Lavender into her stall when we got back to the barn. It had a unique smell, but I didn't mind it. It reminded me of the barns I'd seen in movies. Peaked ceilings, horseshoes on the wall, saddles slung over beams of wood, strands of hay on the concrete floor. It was sort of surreal, being immersed in such a different world than I was used to.

Zac introduced me to Hallie, the horse trainer, as she passed through with a coil of rope over her shoulder and a bucket in her hand. She was in her sixties and seemed too busy to stop and chat. After we'd locked up the stall and Zac had double-checked the latch, we wandered out into the sun, a view of sprawling paddocks, horses, and blue horizons. I wasn't sure which direction we'd come from now, there was so much wide-open space before the land turned into tree and shrubs.

"Is this your . . . passion?" I asked, watching an older man in a ring; the horse with him was prancing in a slow circle. "Would that be the right word? Horses and that sort of thing?"

"I wouldn't call it a passion." He leaned a shoulder on the barn wall, looking down at me. "I enjoy it, I love the animals, and it's outdoor work. Can't ever complain about fresh air. But I think there are other things I'm more passionate about."

"Such as?"

He tilted his head and then straightened up off the wall. "I'll show you."

• • •

Zac took me on a short walk down the drive. It split off in several directions, and we arrived at a large shed. He pushed back the rumbling roller doors, the veins in his arms becoming prominent with the effort. I did my best not to stare, but he had the prettiest skin. Inside the shed, there was a maze of tools, car parts, and vintage cars that were in various states of repair.

"You restore old cars?"

"I do," he said, standing among the mess. "It's not much more than a hobby at the moment, but I've sold a few."

"Do you . . . do you live here?" I wondered if that was normal, for staff to live on the farm. Perhaps it was.

"Yeah, I do. I'm pretty hands-on around here." Zac sat on the hood of one of his cars, elbows resting on his knees.

"It's a beautiful house."

"Thanks. I helped renovate the entire thing about three years ago. Around the time Raine and Milo started dating. He helped out a lot too."

There was so much to look at. My gaze wandered over the bumpers, hoods, pieces of glass, mounds of metal and steel. "You're all so . . . hospitable."

"What goes around, comes around."

"True." I nodded.

"Want that cold drink?"

• • •

Zac and I sat on the back deck where we'd had brunch last weekend. Instead of using the table, we were settled in two outdoor armchairs that were part of a lounge suite. They were woven wicker, black with charcoal-colored cushions. The sun was beginning to set, and he'd just sat down after bringing my drink. He'd first offered me a beer. I'd always found that stuff gross, so I'd declined, and he'd brought me a cold glass of fresh-squeezed orange juice instead.

"That's . . . the best orange juice I've had, ever."

He lazily waved an arm toward the garden. "The oranges are from the orchard here."

"Really?"

He gave a quick nod.

I loved the thought of picking oranges from my very own garden and drinking their juice. It was so self-sufficient and organic. "It's so good. Thank you."

He lifted his bottle in salute. "Not a problem."

I settled into the chair. The leaves rustled around us. On the cloudless horizon, the sky was illuminated with soft oranges and purples, while the sun set on the other side of the house.

Two black-and-white border collies snoozed in their kennels. Farm dogs, I would have thought, except there were no sheep or cattle, and I didn't think horses needed to be rounded up. Perhaps they were just good old-fashioned furry companions. Before I could ask, the soft sound of approaching footsteps had me turning to the French doors, where an older man appeared in a robe and slippers. His brown skin was aged with wrinkles, and his pepper-colored hair was thinning. He walked with a slight limp, but his tall frame still looked strong.

"Zac." He grinned, and it was full and deepened the lines in his aged face. "And who's this?"

"This is Addie," Zac introduced me and sat up a little straighter. His thin white shirt stretched tight across his broad chest. "She was here last weekend—"

"Oh, Raine's friend," the man said, interrupting Zac, and sat down on the edge of the coffee table. "I'm Keith. Yeah, apologies for not being able to attend brunch. I wasn't feeling right. I hope the kids here were good company."

I could feel Zac watching me, perhaps waiting for me to tell this kind old man that Zac had been a bit of a dick when we'd first met. Instead, I smiled. "It was a great morning. I met Noah, and then this afternoon, I met Lavender."

"She got out again," Zac said, resting his beer on top of his knee. "Found her down on the river trail with Addie here. I think she sprung the little foal, to be honest."

"Is that right." Keith stared at me with playful suspicion. "That reminds me of this ol' mare we had when I was a teenager. She'd get out all the damn time, quite a jumper she was. So anyway, we were heading off down the river for a swim one afternoon, the fellas and I, and we thought we better do our extra best to keep her in while we were gone."

Zac wore a subtle hint of amusement in his grin. He winked and made a dramatic show of settling into his seat and stretching his legs out in front of him, as if to tell me these stories weren't the short and sweet sort.

Even though it did go on for quite some time, it was entertaining. Keith had such an animated way of telling a story. His voice was old and hoarse but strong and captivating. It was impossible not to hang on his every word with anticipation.

"So then we find the mare down at the swimming hole we'd been at earlier that morning, and there she is, in the water having the time of her life, meanwhile we spent the whole darn day searching high and low for her. Rascal, she was."

I couldn't help but feel that it was somewhat similar to how Zac and I had stumbled upon each other this afternoon, and I wondered if he thought the same thing, because when I glanced at him, he was already watching me. He was quick to dip his gaze to the label of his bottle, his fingers picking at the sticky paper.

"Well," Keith said, scratching his thin, wiry gray hair. His eyes moved quickly between Zac and me, and then he stood, slow and cautious. "I'll leave y'all to it. Don't forget to eat dinner, Zac. It's in the oven."

Zac gave a quick nod. "Yes sir."

"He's great," I said once we were alone again.

Zac tilted his head. "You think? Couldn't tell."

"What?"

"The first time I heard that story, I was in fits. You barely cracked a smile."

I'd been laughing, hadn't I?

"It sucks, huh," Zac said, facing the darkening depths of the rolling land, and I waited for him to elaborate. "Life goes on, sometimes it's even great, but loss fucking lingers over you like a cloud. It's this constant damper on your spirit."

He looked at me, but not with that familiar grim, tight-lipped pity that I'd seen countless times since Margo had died. It was a look of understanding, and for that I felt grateful.

The intensity behind his stare was beginning to turn my stomach over in knots. I swallowed. Over the back garden, the sun had set, and stars littered the midnight-blue sky. It was beautiful, endless and enchanting, as if the clues to the vast expanse of our world were in arm's reach. It felt like we were in the thick of the universe out here. It felt like Margo was right there, watching over me.

"So," I said, changing the subject. "How did you meet Keith?"

Zac leaned back in his seat and put his arms behind his head; his biceps flexed, and he narrowed his thoughtful gaze. "Must have been . . . at birth. Yeah, he was there from what I've heard. Holding Mom's hand until I made an appearance, and then he cut the cord."

"Wait—you're his son?"

He nodded.

"So, Raine is your sister?"

He nodded again.

"Oh! I didn't even realize."

"You seem surprised."

"No! I just—well, it's—"

"Because they have brown skin and I don't?" Zac laughed, and it was deep, invasive, and enticing. "Yeah, Dad is mixed, and Mom was white. I can tan in the summer, but Raine got Dad's complexion."

"I'm sorry about your mom," I said. "I lost mine too. And Dad. I was thirteen."

"Doesn't seem fair." His tone was softer, and the warm night breeze ruffled his hair. "You've been through a hell of a lot."

"This conversation keeps getting dark." I stood up and walked to the edge of the deck. My light laugh was meant to be dismissive, but I knew it was strained. "I should get going, I suppose. You don't have to drive. I'll call a cab."

The wicker of his seat creaked as he stood up to wander toward me. "We have a ton of rooms if you want to crash in one for the night."

"I don't want to impose."

"You wouldn't be. But it's no sweat. I can drive you into town."

"We probably should have considered the fact that you've been drinking."

"We can wait an hour. It'll be safe. I've only had one."

"Yeah, we should wait the hour."

"Or," he said, and I looked up and over my shoulder to find him close, staring down, "you can crash in one of the spare bedrooms. There's a lock on the door if that helps."

"Well . . ." I fixed the strap on my dress. "I wasn't worried before, but now that you mention it."

He winked and pushed off the wooden railing. I smiled and watched as he collected his bottle and dropped it into a bin at the bottom of the deck steps. He was so tall and defined.

The urge to call Margo and tell her about him was sudden and unexpected, especially because there was nothing to tell. It was just something that we would have giggled about. Well, she would have giggled and told me to snatch him up. I would have grumbled and told her there was no point. Men are disappointing, even if they do seem perfect.

"So, is Raine the big sister?"

"Yep. She's thirty-five. I'm thirty."

"She's thirty-five? Wow, she looks younger than me."

"Hmm, that's sweet, but I'd disagree." He chuckled and folded his arms. "She's a good person. She loves that little girl, Willa. I'm glad she found Milo." His brows pulled, and he looked at me. "You plan stuff, right? Events. What about weddings?"

"Yeah. I plan weddings."

"Should talk to Raine. I'm sure she said something about needing to contact a planner soon but not knowing where to start."

I twisted my hair around my fist and worried on my lip. "I don't think that's the best idea. I have no idea how long I'll be in the area, and I don't want to leave her stranded if I head off before her wedding. Plus, I just don't think I could do it without . . . Margo. She made all the final calls. And we have a whole team that helps. It wouldn't work."

He stood on the other side of the steps and rested his arm above his head on the wooden beam. "You don't have to explain, Addie. It was just an idea."

"Do you have to be so understanding?" I snapped. "You were kind of rude when we met, and now you're . . . I don't know . . . so damn polite. It's pity, right?"

He pursed his lips. "Can I be honest about something?"

"Sure." I felt a little embarrassed about my outburst.

"I was quick to pass judgment." He met my eyes with his, and even in the dark, I could see his sincerity as clear as day. "I saw this stunning woman in a beautiful dress and heard she was from Beverly Hills, and I made assumptions about the sort of woman you are."

Now I felt bad for snapping. "Well, even if I was some Beverly Hills princess, that wouldn't give you the right to assume I can't handle a little dirt or wouldn't enjoy meeting a donkey."

He ducked his head with a small smile. "That's true. You know, we had a houseguest a while ago. She was from . . . I don't know, L.A. or something." He stared out at the night with a humorless laugh. "She complained about everything. The smell. The animals. The early-morning starts and the accents."

"The accents?"

"If she could find something to complain about, she would."

"Why was she here?"

"She's Milo's niece or something. He didn't have room to put her up, so we offered. A damn long week, that was."

"You just assumed I would be the same?" I raised a challenging brow.

He grinned. "That'll teach me not to make assumptions."

"It better. I didn't immediately assume that you've slept with a cousin."

He let out another loud laugh. "Definitely haven't done that."

"I guess I'll take up that offer if it's still on the table?" He seemed confused. "For the room. Tonight. I'm tired, so I might get some sleep. It's been a weird week. I feel like such a floater."

"I bet." He pointed at the French doors. "I'll show you where it is."

We went inside, where most of the lights were off, apart from the kitchen. The beams came through into the dining area, where there was a long twelve-seater table. This one was a gorgeous red-brown wood with a glossy finish. The high-backed chairs were covered in a beautiful cream-patterned vintage fabric. It was quiet as we crept through into the main hallway, where a staircase curved upstairs. I followed Zac, admiring his broad back and shoulders. There wasn't much else to look at while it was so dark.

When we hit the top floor, we walked for another small stretch until he stopped, causing me to almost collide with his back, and he opened a white door with a satin-black handle. He reached around the wall and switched the light on. As far as spare bedrooms went, this one was simple but beautiful. There was a double bed covered in throw pillows, two side tables, a dresser, and a round mirror on the wall. There were more decorative details—a vase of flowers, a rug—and I almost missed the window seat, which had a small stack of books on it.

"Your spare bedrooms come with a complimentary pile of books?" I looked up at Zac; we were both squeezed in between the doorframe, and we were close. "That's not a complaint. Good luck getting me to leave this room."

He chuckled and rested his hand on the door handle. "Nah, those are Willa's. She got them out at the library after you were here on Sunday and spent about four hours up here reading yesterday."

I swallowed, touched at the fact that she'd actually decided to take my suggestions on board. "Is this the room she sleeps in when she stays over?"

"Yeah, but we have a few spare bedrooms. I just happen to think this one has the best view of the landscape."

I nodded and sucked in my bottom lip, gnawing at it. He was so close I could smell his fresh fragrance along with a note of sweat. It wasn't bad, though. Not at all.

"Can I offer you something to wear to bed?" His tone was low and quiet. "A T-shirt?

"That would be great, actually," I said, steadying my uneven breath. "Thanks."

His eyes dropped to my shoulder, where the strap of my dress had fallen again. His fingertips brushed my skin as he lifted it and slid it back into place. "No problem," he murmured, his lips barely parting to let the words out.

The air felt so tight that I could have sworn it had nothing left to give. Something was going to snap. Something was going to happen. It had to, because we could not continue to stare at each other like this without it resulting in a shift in balance.

And then I heard Margo. I heard her as if she was standing right beside me. *What about me?*

"I'm wiped." I stepped into the room and kept my back to him. "Don't worry about the shirt. I'll sleep in this."

There was no response for a while. I wondered if he'd left. But then his feet moved on the carpet. "I'll be right back with a shirt."

I turned to object, but he was gone. It wasn't long before he returned and tossed the shirt onto the bed, bidding me a simple good night before he closed the door. After I'd slipped into the shirt and climbed into bed, I lay in the dark, covers up even though it was sweltering, and I trembled. Margo would never have said something like that. *What about me?* That wasn't her. Not at all. That was me, and I knew it, but that didn't stop the sobs that racked through me until I fell asleep, not waking until I felt the weight of a person on top of me, the end of my screams bringing me out of another nightmare.

"Addie."

I couldn't see, it was so dark, and I was shaking so hard, just aware of gentle hands that were rubbing circles on my back.

"Addie." The deep voice was coaxing me out of the terror, gentle reassurances grounding me. "You're all right. Come on, Addie. You're safe. It's Zac. I'm here. You're safe."

# CHAPTER SIX

Zac walked into the bedroom with a cup of hot tea and a cold flannel. I was still curled up against the headboard, ashamed and embarrassed of the scene I must have made.

The bedside alarm clock read three in the morning, and I'd felt terrible for screaming the house down until Zac told me his dad would sleep through a tractor driving through his bedroom and Zac himself woke at about four most mornings so it was no big deal.

That didn't stop me from feeling humiliated.

He sat on the edge of the bed and handed me the cup. He was wearing a pair of black sweatpants and no shirt. If I hadn't been in such a state, I might have been able to appreciate the situation a little more.

"Here." He handed me the cold flannel. "Might help cool you down a bit."

My face and neck were drenched with sweat; tendrils of hair were clinging to my forehead, and the white T-shirt I was wearing was damp. I wiped my face with the cloth, but I knew I would need a shower to feel clean.

Zac ran his hand across his jaw, looking perplexed. "Is this about Margo?"

Lately, my throat squeezed whenever I tried to say her name. And not in a metaphorical sense. It hurt. Real pain. When Zac said it, he was so casual. It slipped right off his tongue, and his southern drawl licked at the roll of the R.

But I sort of loved that he called her Margo, rather than referring to her as my sister and nothing more. It was acknowledgment, and she deserved to be acknowledged.

I nodded and tried to expel the remnants of the nightmare that had become a regular occurrence.

"You were . . . there for her death?" he asked.

"I can't, Zac," I whispered and shook my head. "I can't."

"All right." He took the flannel from me and threw it onto the dresser. "You want to get back to sleep? Or come for a wander with me? Figure I'll get a head start on the chores."

"Chores on a Saturday morning?"

"Every morning." He flicked his head toward the door. "I'll get something better to wear?"

"For me?"

He nodded and stood, his skin pulling against taut muscles. "You don't have to come, though."

"No, no." I pushed the thin sheet back and got up as well. His gaze was fast and fleeting, but it raked me over from my bare legs to the white shirt pulling tight against my thighs. "I won't be getting back to sleep. I'll come. I'll even help."

"Back in a minute."

He gave me a pair of his mom's old farm pants after he made me swear that I didn't find it weird, a pair of her boots that looked as though they had never been worn, and one of his hoodies. The hoodie was entirely too long for me, and the sleeves had to be rolled up, but it was warm. We trekked through the back garden and down toward the paddock.

The sun wasn't up, but it couldn't have been far because there was a bright glow on the horizon, and it lightened the night sky to a cobalt blue. Birds were beginning to sing, and I couldn't decide if I preferred dusk or dawn out here. It was an even tie.

"I'm sorry, again," I said as he opened a steel gate and waited for me to follow through before he closed it. "For screaming and all that. Not the best houseguest."

"Would you quit apologizing?" He shook his head with amusement. "If I was bothered, I'd have left you alone as soon as I'd woken you up and told you to shut it."

I watched the ground, laughing lightly as my boots stepped over grass and dirt.

"I'm gonna get a real laugh out of you sometime," Zac said as he sauntered beside me with his hands in his pockets.

"That was a real laugh."

"Nope. A real, big, side-aching laugh."

"Why, what's the big deal?"

He nudged me with his elbow. "Because that would mean you're really happy."

My hair fell around my face when I ducked my head to hide the blush crawling across my face. We walked a while longer until we came to the enormous stable. It was red and white with a classic peaked roof.

There were thirty stalls in total, a grooming cubicle, a row of cupboards and shelving for equipment, and even a break room. Zac said that it wasn't used too often as it wasn't the most inviting place to eat, what with the stench of horse manure wafting through the place.

"Rise and shine, kids," Zac shouted as he pushed the doors wide open with one effortless shove. I knew first-hand how heavy they were; I'd tried to open one of them when we'd brought Lavender back yesterday. It had been embarrassing. Zac whistled and clapped his hands. "Who wants a bite, huh?"

There were a few responses in the form of neighs and whinnies. But Zac must have felt the enthusiasm was lackluster because he stood there with his hands on his hips and sighed.

"Not used to getting up for another hour." He laughed and wandered over to the left, where there were sinks, buckets, bowls, and bags of food. Lots of bags of food. Zac talked me through the process and explained the nutritional value of their food as we filled buckets with high-protein feed. It was a lot of information, but I listened and learned.

We split the stalls in half, and I took the front half while he wandered down toward the back of the barn. The instructions were straightforward: tip the food into the trough that wasn't full of water, give them a pet, and then double-check the door was latched properly.

It didn't take long before we met in the middle and emerged from two stalls side by side. Zac had a light sheen of sweat on his forehead, and he'd ditched his hoodie, now down to a black tank top. We double-checked our stall locks and then turned to each other, still holding our now-empty buckets.

He gave me a slow nod and tilted his head to peer past me. "You work fast. Which is great for me—I can get out of here quicker now." His wink was playful.

"It was sort of . . . fun," I confessed, feeling strange at how true that was. It was hot, it didn't smell great, and I had sore arms from tugging a full bucket of food to and from the stalls fifteen times. Still, the brief chitchat with the horses was more fulfilling than I'd imagined a one-sided conversation to be. "You do this alone on the weekend?"

He nodded and started back toward the front of the barn where the buckets lived. "Yeah, but there's less work during the weekend. It's just food and letting them out into the paddock. Perhaps a brush. During the week is the big stuff. Friday is the busiest. We do a full clean-out of each stall and a decent groom. It's not hard to keep on top of it if we do a bit each morning and afternoon."

"When do we let them out?"

He switched the basin faucet on and raised his brows with a small smile. "Uh, well, we can let them out whenever. Most mornings, I let them out at six."

"How do you intend on keeping Lavender in from now on?"

Zac laughed. "Ray, the neighbor, fixed the gate lock while we were having that drink last night. I sent him a text and had him pop over. He's up for doing odd jobs for us. Dad saved his farm from being repossessed a long while back. Not that a gate lock will keep her in. I'm pretty sure she's jumping the fences."

"Aw, that's sweet." I handed him my bucket when he was done rinsing his. "I didn't realize there were neighbors around here."

"Not neighbors in the sense that you might be used to. You could walk over to his place, but it'd take a while. I get there in ten minutes on the dirt bike."

"Right. So, what else does a weekend around here consist of?"

"Well . . ." He used the detachable faucet head and sprayed the basin to wash down the food scraps that had splashed up the edges. "Once I'm done here, I go and have breakfast—I have to work up an appetite before I can eat—and then I shower, do some work out in the shed, go into town. Just whatever needs to be done, I suppose. Changes week to week."

"What do you have for breakfast?"

He switched off the faucet and turned to me. "You ask enough questions?"

I winced. "Sorry."

He wiped his hands dry with a rag and grinned. "You're fine, ma'am."

I ignored the way I felt when he called me ma'am. "Can I try to explain something?"

"Of course." He put his back to the wall and leaned with his ankles crossed and arms folded, his expression intent and focused on me and me alone.

"Well . . . up until a couple weeks ago . . . I had . . . a life. I had a routine and a home—I mean, I still have a home—but I was at that home. I had . . . M-Mar—"

"I'm following, Addie. Go on."

I took a deep breath and gave him a grateful smile. "So, I had all of that. Work that kept me occupied, books that filled in the spare time. A sister with her own . . . stuff happening. There was always something to think about. And now, whenever I think about those things, it feels like I'm going to be sick. It hurts so much. So, I think I'm trying to think about . . . anything else. Whatever can distract me and help me feel like this is real and all of that other stuff . . . isn't."

He didn't respond, but he continued to watch me thoughtfully.

"That doesn't make sense, does it?" I asked quietly.

"I think it makes perfect sense."

For some reason, that was a huge relief.

"Can I be honest about something?" he said with a cautious tone. I nodded. "Is that . . . entirely healthy? Isn't there some benefit to dealing with . . . the truth?"

It was hard to answer. Mainly because he was right. I knew denial wasn't going to help me heal. But that didn't mean that I was capable of dealing with the truth yet, either.

"But I suppose I was a bit the same when Mom died." His tone was distant, his gaze unfocused. "I couldn't face it for a long time. It's only been a couple weeks since you lost Margo. You can ask me all the questions it takes to distract your thoughts."

There it was again, the one brief moment where Margo's memory didn't equate to a vise grip throttling my heart. Instead, it was sweet and honoring, even if it lasted no more than the second it took for her name to leave his lips.

"All right." I exhaled, releasing the tension on my clenched jaw. My newly formed habit of grinding my teeth was giving me headaches like nothing else. "I have another question."

"Please." He gestured to go ahead.

"How did your mother die? Though you don't have to answer if you don't want to."

"She was thrown off a horse and snapped her neck."

"Shit," I breathed.

"Ironic, right?" His eyes shifted over the stable. "I couldn't stand the horses after that. Hated them. And then I remembered Mom loved these creatures with her entire soul. She dedicated her life to training horses. Even aggressive wild ones that didn't have a damn hope. She didn't give up on a single one, and I know that she'd never have blamed them for what happened to her. She'd have said it was poetic, to be honest. If I had continued to hate these animals, she'd have been devastated. That might have been the biggest moment for me, remembering that. It was . . . therapeutic."

I admired that—more than he knew. "When did it happen?"

"When I was fifteen. Dad was never the same. He's still a great man. Loves to talk about Mom. Smiles a lot and all of that. But he doesn't go down to the paddock unless he has to. He just keeps it running from a distance. He keeps it running for her. So, I help, for him."

"You've dedicated your life to it even though it's not what you'd choose to do?" I asked, thinking about my own future and the business I'd left back home. Whenever I thought about going back to it, it was accompanied with a sense of obligation that I detested. I was sure it had something to do with why I couldn't stand the thought of returning.

"I do my best to keep a balance," he said. "Making time for my own interests while I keep Mom's legacy going. I'll admit, though, I don't put the same amount of love into it that she did. It makes me wonder if I should be doing it at all. I'm waiting for Dad to tell me he wants to sell up."

"Do you think he ever will?"

Zac shrugged. "He's made comments about it here and there, but I don't want to push it."

I chewed the inside of my cheek. "You should talk to him about it. You don't want to spend your life doing something you don't love, right?"

He swung his gaze to meet mine. "Do you?"

I dropped my stare to the ground. He was right. It was more

complicated than just letting go of things our loved ones had left behind. But the fact that he'd been doing the same thing for the last fifteen years made me fear I'd end up in the same guilt-induced obligatory line of work, and while I wasn't ready to think about the future, I knew I didn't want *that*.

"I feel sort of bad about leaving the business in Beverly Hills now."

"Did Margo love her job?" Zac asked.

"Probably as much as your mother loved hers," I admitted. "She took it over from our parents when she was twenty-nine. I was thirteen, so I was sort of . . . shoved into it. She had me help during the weekends, and then I left school and joined full-time. It just . . . happened. It was decided for me."

"Trust me, I get that." He gave me a tight-lipped smile, and I realized he did understand, probably better than most. "You two have a pretty big age gap, huh?"

"Yeah. Different moms," I explained and focused on breathing.

Zac straightened off the wall and stood closer. "What would you do, if you could do anything?"

"Horticulture." I met his stare. "I want to open a nursery and sell plants, seedlings, perhaps flowers too."

"Take it from me, Addie," he murmured softly, "don't let that dream go. Learn to love yourself enough to live for yourself."

My chest swelled on a deep breath. "You first."

The side of his mouth kicked up in a small grin. "Deal."

"Zac? Addie?"

We both turned around to the sound of Raine approaching with her brows pulled tight and her lips parted with surprise. She noticed I was wearing pants that used to belong to her mother, and for a moment, I worried she was going to flip out. But instead, she smiled and folded her arms.

"I didn't realize you two hit it off at brunch."

I looked at Zac and found him watching me. He quickly turned his attention to Raine and put a small step between us. "I actually hadn't seen Addie again until last night."

"And that was a coincidence," I added, not sure why we were so jittery about explaining ourselves. "I was out for a walk, and the foal got out, and then Zac was there, and he invited me here, and it got late. So, I slept"—I pointed up—"in the spare room, and we got up, like, really early, to do the chores."

"Yeah, that's more or less how it went." Zac chuckled.

Raine nodded with a brow raised so high it was beginning to blend in with her hairline. "Yeah. Sure."

I knew how this must have looked. As though Zac and I had been in contact since brunch and I'd slept with him last night and now I was wearing his mom's clothes while occupying each other's space first thing in the morning.

Yeah, I wouldn't have believed what I'd said either.

But even if she had been right about her assumptions, would that be an issue? Raine and I didn't know each other that well. It wouldn't be violating girl code. Or perhaps Zac had a girlfriend? Ugh. It didn't matter what it looked like. We knew the truth. There was nothing going on.

"We're just about to grab some breakfast," Zac said and picked his hoodie up off the ground. "You joining us?"

"No, I was just dropping something off for Dad," she said. "I need to get home and get some sleep."

"Just hang out and have something to eat," Zac insisted, and we all walked over to the gate. "I'll come back and let the horses out after."

That last sentence must have been for me since I was peering back at the barn over my shoulder. I gave him a small smile, and Raine agreed to have something quick to eat. That something turned out to be scrambled eggs and orange juice.

The scrambled eggs were the best I'd ever had. Just as good as they had been at brunch last weekend. Raine said it was because their chickens were able to roam free in big open spaces as opposed to caged eggs where the chickens were in distress their entire lives.

I hadn't even realized there were chickens on the farm. I wondered how far their land went before it became someone else's.

The farm kitchen was beautiful. It was all distressed white paint and wood with polished surfaces and brass handles. The oven, while brand new, was a large retro design. It reminded me of the sort of oven that could be found in old Western films, just more modern. Copper pots and pans hung above the kitchen island, and antique teapots and teacups lined a stack of shelves above the sink. It was very much French country vibes, and I loved it.

While we washed up, Zac turned to Raine, who was mid tonsil-baring yawn. "Could you could give Addie a ride back to the Lemon Inn?"

Oh no. I'd asked too many questions, and now he was sick of me.

"That's if she wants to go," he added. "You're welcome to hang around for as long as you want."

What was I doing? I was stressing out over whether this tall, gorgeous, well-built man wanted me around or not. How selfish was I? Margo hadn't even been gone for three weeks and I was thinking about men? Or, well, one man. I felt sick.

"I should go back to the inn." I dropped the dish towel. Zac leaned on the edge of the counter. "Thanks for having me last night, and I—" He'd told me to quit apologizing, so I didn't mention the 3:00 a.m. wakeup call. "Anyway, thanks again. I'll return the clothes later if that's all right? I promise I will. Or I can take the pants off now?"

"Don't stress." He chuckled. "I trust you'll bring them back. And no need to thank me. You paid the favor back this morning."

Raine made a choked noise in her throat, and I felt red-hot when I thought about how that sounded.

"All right. I'll—goodb—see you later, all right?"

"Yeah. Goodbye, Addie."

# CHAPTER SEVEN

I held my dress and shoes close in the front seat of Raine's cruiser and stared straight out the windshield, listening to that conversation back over and over again.

It wasn't just what had been said that had me in knots, it was what hadn't been said. The feeling of wanting to be near him, to let him make me smile, to savor those chivalrous moments—that was all so selfish, wasn't it?

When was the right time to start living again? Because right now, choosing to live when Margo couldn't would make me nauseous.

"I wouldn't have called that," Raine said after a tense few minutes of silence, subtle teasing in her tone. "Not at all. I'm blindsided. I honestly got the feeling, at brunch, that you thought my brother was an asshole. I'm shocked."

"I did think that," I mumbled, feeling a bit mean for admitting it. And to his sister of all people. "I meant it when I said I hadn't seen him again until yesterday."

She still looked disbelieving, so I told her the entire story, starting with the aimless walk and moving on to Lavender, to Zac, to the cold drink and the spare bedroom. The part I did leave out was the nightmare. I didn't want to relive it right now; it would be back again soon enough.

"Oh." She smiled even though she sounded disappointed. "Well, it's like fate then. You were meant to see each other again."

I wasn't sure how to respond to that, so I said nothing and watched the rolling land whirring past. The sun hadn't been up long, and it was already harsh. Harsher than I'd ever felt it at seven in the morning.

"Zac mentioned that he asked about the wedding planning," she said. "That he asked if you'd do it."

"Oh. Yeah. I'm sorry I said no. It's nothing personal. I just . . . I don't know what I'm doing right now."

"I understand." She signaled a right turn and slowed down at a light as we came into town. "I actually found this woman online, and we have an appointment next week on the fifteenth. I don't suppose you'd come with me? Just to get a sense of whether or not she's a decent planner and knows what she's talking about."

I laughed lightly. "You don't even know if I'm a decent planner."

"Yeah, I do. I googled you, and a bunch of reviews came up underneath the website." She looked at me and then back to the road. "There were a lot of good things said about your sister too."

My chest felt tight, and I struggled to swallow the lump in my throat. There were always good reviews and feedback about Margo.

"So . . . would that be all right?" Raine said after a few minutes of dead quiet. "If you came to the appointment?"

"Yeah, of course," I said. "If I'm still in town. We should swap numbers, just to keep in touch about it."

"That's perfect."

Raine stopped outside the Lemon Inn, and we said our farewells after we exchanged numbers. Inside, I went straight for the staircase and cringed when I heard the curious call of Hanna.

"Oh." She turned the corner and found me paused on the staircase, hand on the rail, one foot a step up so she couldn't mistake the fact that I was in a rush. "I thought that was you, but you're wearing pants! I wasn't sure."

"Yep." I nodded and drummed my nails on the staircase railing. That was when I noticed that one of the powder-pink gels had snapped off. Damn it. "I could use a shower, so—"

"You missed breakfast this morning," she interrupted and pulled her blue-and-yellow shawl tight around her shoulders. "Were you out all night?"

"Yeah, I was at a friend's place, and I helped him on his farm this morning. So, I really need that shower."

"Of course." Her smile was forced as she took in yesterday's outfit hanging from my hand, deepening the lines around her mouth and eyes. "You should join us for lunch this afternoon. We're going to have Melanie's niece doing a piece on her cello in the common room."

"Oh, that sounds nice." I knew I was doing an awful job of pretending to be interested. "I have plans, though. Next time?"

I didn't wait for her to keep up her interrogation. I waved and ran upstairs.

In the suite I was renting, I stripped straight out of the borrowed clothes and switched on the shower. The room was nice. Spacious enough with a vintage dresser and side tables. The bed had a steel frame with intricate patterns, and the wallpaper was the same mint green as the rest of the house.

It might have been a bit much if I didn't have grief filling all four corners of my mind and leaving no room for much else. Margo would have hated it. I liked the fact that there were three hanging plants in the corner.

After I was showered and dressed in a short, pale-pink romper, I fell back onto the bed and checked the two text messages I'd received while I had been washing. Both were from Raine.

It's Raine!
Text me if you need anything at all. :)

She was the sort of nice and sweet that I appreciated. Part of me regretted telling her I couldn't help with her wedding. It seemed like the least I could do considering how welcoming she'd been to me.

Dropping the phone, I thought about the fact that I had to go out and find something to do so I didn't end up being dragged into the common room for the rest of the afternoon. Once again, I found myself heading out for a walk.

There was an incredible spot I'd discovered about ten minutes from the hotel called Blue Hole. It was a river in a vast open space with concrete footpaths, little bridges crossing the water, and picnic tables. There were hundreds of people swimming, bathing, and jumping from the cliff faces that ran along the other side of the river. There were small waterfalls, no more than a meter tall, that raised the river higher in two places, and teenagers were walking across the top of them.

I sat on the grass, under the sweltering mid-morning sun, and watched with amusement as a group of girls who must have been around sixteen floated by on round tubes while they threw a ball to one another. Whenever it landed in the water, they'd all shout with protest and laughter because someone had to get out of their tube and get the ball.

I let my eyes close and imagined Margo was with me, bathing in the sun, lathered in sunscreen, of course. I would have objected when she tried to get me into the water because I preferred being on land with a book. Even though I'd grown up on the coast, I'd never become a strong swimmer. I could wade in shallow waters, but that was where my confidence ended.

I watched the families playing and laughing, the pure elation carried through the atmosphere on a soft breeze, touching each person there, causing an undeniable environment of excitement.

It made me wonder how many moments I had missed with Margo because I had been too tied up believing that the only way to create happiness was reading the fictional lives of characters on pages. Perhaps if I had closed my book and taken up one of her hundred offers to do something with her, I'd have found my own happiness. I'd have made my own story.

My heart was pounding as I stood up and tugged the straps of my romper down. This was for Margo. Margo was the reason I shimmied out of the one-piece until I was down to the new black bra and underwear set I'd bought earlier in the week. They were plain and simple, not lacy or obviously underthings, so I didn't feel an ounce of shame when I saw a couple moms watching me walk toward the water.

I crossed the little stones and pebbles of the shore, dipped a toe into the cool water, and then kept going until I was submerged. Of course, I didn't go out too far or too deep. A sigh of relief passed my lips; a break from the heat was just what I needed. I ran my hands along the surface, watching the ripples.

"Addie?"

I spun until I saw who had called out for me.

"Willa?"

She was lounging on a floating mattress, and her cute little one-piece was retro chic: a fifties-inspired swimsuit that had dark blue and white stripes from top to bottom. She grinned and waved as I moved through the water, avoiding the other people who were swimming and splashing. When I noticed Milo not more than a few feet from her, he gave me a wave too.

"Hello," Willa said when I stopped beside her pool bed, holding the side so she wouldn't float off. "Dad said I should say hello because you're alone."

I looked at Milo, who lowered his head, pinching the bridge of his nose. I laughed. It didn't bother me that she hadn't called me over of her own accord. She was ten, after all.

"You look relaxed," I said. "Living the life, huh?"

"Yep. We come here a lot because it's close to home, and we like to get out and let Raine sleep."

"Ahh, that's thoughtful. It's a good idea to make the most of the summer break too. When does school go back?"

"Thursday." She pouted. "The fifteenth."

"Don't look so sad," I teased. "School is a breeze compared to adulthood. Believe me."

"Well," she said, tilting her head to the side, "I think that depends on how you adult. Life is what you make it, right?"

"How old are you again?"

She grinned, and I noticed she had two teeth missing. Her vamp teeth, as I liked to call them. "I heard that in a movie. But I think it makes sense. I hear a lot of good stuff in movies."

"Life lessons, huh? Whatever works, I suppose."

"How come you're swimming in your undies?" she said, and I ducked a little bit lower into the water, mortified that I was being called out. To be fair, I hadn't planned on bumping into anyone I knew.

"Willa," Milo scolded, still floating a few feet from us. He seemed more relaxed now that I was here, holding on to his daughter's pool bed.

"It's all right." I chuckled and turned back to Willa. "I forgot a swimsuit, but I was desperate for a dip. So . . ."

I shrugged, and so did she, and then she said, "Whatever works."

"That's right."

"You wanna hear a secret?"

I leaned closer and gave her an eager nod.

"I think my uncle Zac thinks you're pretty."

My brows shot up, and I stared at her, not sure how to respond.

"He was staring a lot. At you. When we had brunch. Raine said that he wasn't, but I think he was. He doesn't have a girlfriend, you know."

Milo sighed again. "Willa."

He didn't need to be concerned. In truth, I was beginning to love this little girl. She had such a mature air about her, and her observations were a lot clearer than I'd have expected from a child her age. Even if she was wrong, she delivered her secret with confidence.

"Do you have a boyfriend?" she asked, waiting for an answer with raised brows.

"No. No, I don't. I'm . . . I'm not old enough to date."

She giggled. "Not true."

"So true. You have to be at least twenty-five to date."

"Well, how old are you?"

"Twenty-four."

She bopped me on the nose. "Well, I'm sure he can wait."

Her optimism was charming. It would have been unfair to explain that I wasn't in the right headspace to begin a relationship, and I wasn't sure when I would be. Guilt crept through my veins like a virus whenever I thought about Zac. He would be the perfect distraction, but that wasn't fair. I knew I wouldn't do that to someone—use them to get past grief.

"You could go to my daddy's wedding together," she said. Even if she was a mature little girl, she was still just a child.

"Ooh, when is the wedding? Are you going to be a flower girl?"

"Yes." She blinked frantically when someone bombed into the water and splashed us. "I'm wearing a pretty pink dress. Like your nails. I told Raine I like that color after we had brunch, and she said that it would look nice with my skin tone. So we found one online."

"She's right," I said, feeling a sting in my nose. I blinked hard and smiled. "It'll look gorgeous. You never told me when the wedding is?"

"I don't know. Dad?"

"To be confirmed." Milo squinted, since the sun was reflecting from Willa's pool bed. "We're thinking next summer. Or perhaps next fall."

"Fall would be perfect. The weather isn't as hot, but it's still pleasant. Fall colors are beautiful, there are a lot of potential themes to run with. The photos would be exquisite."

"I'll have to let Raine know," he said, his crow's feet deepening with his appreciative smile.

"Question," I said. "Raine said that you're both cops. When do you work?"

"Days," he replied. "I took the last three weeks of summer break off to spend with Willa. But our normal routine is that I drop her off at school in the morning, Raine picks her up, and I get home just before Raine heads out."

"Oh. Doesn't sound like a lot of time together."

"We make it work," he said, his smile full and his gaze distant. "We have Sunday together, and sometimes if she wakes up early enough, she comes to the station to have lunch with me. The main thing is that we don't blame each other or take the frustration over not seeing each other out on each other. If that makes sense?"

"Yeah, it does."

It made perfect sense, and I wished that I'd remembered that more when I had the chance.

# CHAPTER EIGHT

*A year and a half ago*

"Addie!"

My head snapped up from my Christmas gift. A book to be exact. It was called *Plantopedia* and was full of information about houseplants and how to care for them, what to feed them, how to clone them. Irie had given it to me, knowing how much I loved horticulture. Margo hadn't objected, but I could tell from her tight smile when I opened it that she didn't want me to get any ideas about leaving our business and starting my own.

"Yeah?"

Margo stood in front of the armchair while she slipped her hoop earrings in. Her dress was fitted, stretched down to her calf, and, paired with a little leather jacket, was the perfect look for a date. I wasn't sure which number date this was, but she'd been seeing this Jacob dude for about two months.

"Get up," she said, hands on her hips. "You're coming with me. Jacob is bringing a friend, and I swear he's cute."

"How old is he?"

She shrugged. "No idea. Why?"

"Uh, because Jacob is in his forties. So how old is his friend?"

"Oh." She laughed and gave me a slap on the leg. "Not as old as

Jacob. They work together. But who cares? Older men are so much better. More mature. More experienced. You would suit an older man."

"If he's older than thirty-five, I'm not interested."

"Sebastian Stan is forty."

I bit down on a guilty grin.

She pointed at me. "You would go there. You've said so."

"Yeah, but that's different. He's gorgeous."

She rolled her eyes, and even I knew that was a ridiculous argument. She slid her platforms on one foot at a time, balancing. The heel was sharp and tall. The other end of the shoe was thick and gave her another three inches of height. As she walked into the kitchen, I watched the amount of grace she carried herself with. There wasn't a tremor in her balance or the slightest hint at a rolled ankle. She didn't look like a deer on ice but rather a swan on water.

I could wear heels no problem. I was just certain that I didn't look as elegant as she did when I walked.

"Addie, we're going on a double date," she called over her shoulder. "You either get dolled up now or I'm dragging you out of the house in that flannel shirt. Which looks super cute, but still. I'm pulling rank. Get up."

"It's just unfortunate that I'm in a long-term relationship. Otherwise, I'd love to go on a double date."

"The couch doesn't count as a long-term relationship."

I sighed and stood up, dragging my feet as I walked into the kitchen. Margo was strutting around the kitchen, watering the plants on the windowsills and side tables.

"I'm doing your job," she said, pointing at a fern in a white ceramic pot with geometric designs. "As a favor. Now you do one for me and come on this double date. You'll like Brad, I promise."

"His name is Brad? Nope. I'm already uninterested."

She inhaled a deep breath and pointed down the hall. "Get dressed."

"Take Irie! She's always up for this sort of shit."

"Get dressed."

"Margo, I know you think just because you raised me you can tell me what to do, but I'm an adult, and I don't want to go on a blind date." I put a little bite in my tone to convey that I wasn't just resisting, I was refusing.

Margo put down the watering can and propped a hand on her hip, mouth tight as she stared at me. "You wouldn't go to the gala with me last weekend. You wouldn't do the speed dating event at the bar the weekend before that. I just want to go out and do something fun together."

"Mmm, no," I scoffed, giving her a look. "You want to get me married off and out of the house."

She shook her head. "You and your future husband can live here for as long as you want. I am not trying to get rid of you, I'm trying to make sure you have fun."

"Well, it's a good thing I was having fun a minute ago; now we're arguing, and I do want to move out."

She waved her hand and started storming out of the kitchen. "You do not. Come on, let's go, get dressed."

I ground my teeth together and followed her, clenching my fists behind her back and silently screaming. Instead of bothering to continue the conversation, I went back to the sofa, plopped down, and dragged my blanket across my legs. Opening my book, I tried to read, but I was busy listening to Margo's heels clopping up and down the hall. Eventually, she came back, and I peered up from the pages to find her scowling at me.

"You're going to make me show up to a double date without you?"

"You should've asked me before you planned it."

I could see her jaw working as she stared, doing her best to intimidate compliance out of me. "You might have a good time."

"Eh." I tapped the open book; the glossy pages smelled sensational. "This is a good time. If I want to meet some dude named Brad and go on a date, I'll organize it myself."

She recoiled and threw her hands up. "You will not. You haven't been on a date in months."

"Yeah, I'm still recovering from the last douchebag I gave my precious time to."

Margo made a disgruntled shout and snatched her bag off the corner of the sofa. "Whatever, I give up. Be a spinster for the rest of your life."

I watched her stomp toward the front entrance. "Elizabeth Bennet was quite happy to be alone. I'm just waiting for a Mr. Darcy."

"Good luck finding him on the fucking couch," Margo shouted, the door slamming shut after her.

It wasn't like I was completely closed off to falling in love. But I'd imagined it happening organically, perhaps in a library or during a job. Besides, I wasn't in the mood to dress up and go out for dinner at the last minute. The thought of meeting a total stranger with the objective being a potential romantic connection made the whole thing awkward, and it felt unauthentic. I wanted to get to know someone for their true self and not endure a front that gets put on in order to create a successful date.

• • •

I was in bed when I heard Margo come home. I was so familiar with her patterns that I could visualize her actions as she walked through the house. Shoes off at the door. The next light thud was her purse hitting the side table. Then the rustle of her coat being thrown across the sofa, and a few moments later, she pushed my bedroom door open and leaned on the frame. I wasn't sure if we were going to keep arguing or not. If she hoped I'd apologize, she'd be disappointed. I did not regret staying in for the night.

"I ended things with Jacob."

"What?" I closed the book I was reading and sat up, patting

the bed beside me. Margo wandered in and sat down on the edge. "What happened?"

"Well, we had an awkward dinner with his friend, whom you would not have liked at all. Total dick."

I bit back the "I told you so" and gave her a light shrug.

"Anyway, Jacob and I went back to his place, where we talked for a bit, and I decided to just bring up the fact that I want to have a baby of my own. You know he's got children, so I asked if he'd have more, and he was very sure that he did not want to have another baby. No matter if he ever got married again or how in love he was, another child is definitely off the table."

My chest tightened, and I ran my hands through my hair with frustration. I thought about the nursery at the end of the hall, still vacant due to Margo's insistence that I give her one more chance to find a partner rather than a sperm donor.

"Don't be upset," she said.

"Well, I am," I said, voice breathless. "I hate it when this happens."

"I'm getting used to it." She pursed her lips and shrugged, but I could see the glisten in her gaze. "I think it's time to just do it alone, with a donor and a surrogate."

"Margo." I scooted forward in the bed, the comforter bunching on my lap. "Please let me help. Please. What do I have to do to convince you that I can do this? That it won't be triggering or upsetting for me?"

"How can you be sure that it won't?"

"Because it won't be like the first time."

# CHAPTER NINE

Thursday morning brought overcast weather. It was still sweleringly hot, but the clouds gave relief from the sun beaming straight down on top of me. I was sitting outside the inn, under a tree, with a book open on my bare legs and an acute awareness of Hanna watching me through the window, bothered that I'd told her I didn't want to join her book club despite being an avid reader.

Yes, I love reading. Yes, I will talk about books whenever I'm given the chance to do so. No, I don't want to sit in a circle with a dozen strangers and have the spotlight while I share what I thought. She couldn't seem to understand the logic. I wasn't sure that I understood it either, but I knew that I had no interest in joining, regardless.

The fact that she'd told me I was "asking for trouble" when she'd glanced over my cropped T-shirt and short shorts had soured my mood too. I wasn't asking for a damn thing from anyone.

Eh, whatever. Hanna and her comments were distracting and made me frustrated enough to steal some of my consistent pain and turn it into a mild rage. Whatever worked, to be honest.

I must have read for a few hours, time lost on me, because before I knew it, a horn honked, and I peered up to see Raine at the curb in her cruiser. It wasn't hard to waste hours around here. There was a lot of peace being outdoors in the clean air, with the warmth and relaxed demeanor of the locals. Beverly Hills was warm, but the vibe was different. Aside from the hustle and bustle of it, it was where Margo lived.

As far as I was concerned, she was still there, walking down the street in her elegant outfits and towering heels, looking right at home with effortless ease. She didn't have to try hard at all; she suited Beverly Hills. She reminded me of one of the real housewives on the television show. Just with less drama and no facial reconstruction aside from a nose job she'd had done when she was twenty-six.

If I went home, it shattered that illusion. I wouldn't find her in our home office, answering client calls, sorting our finances, booking venues, and hiring caterers. I wouldn't watch her walk through the door from a doozy of a date, and I wouldn't sit with her while we scarfed ice cream and bitched about it. None of that would happen ever again. I wasn't sure I could face that, and I didn't know when I'd ever be able to.

Standing up, I stretched and brushed at the back of my legs, which were creased from the grass. Raine wiggled her fingers in a cute wave as I rounded the front of the car and slid into the passenger seat.

"I really appreciate this." She slid her sunglasses from her head and onto her face.

"Oh. Yeah, it's no trouble. I don't mean this in a rude way, but don't you have other friends you'd rather do this with? Like, I don't mind going, I just figured this is the sort of thing you do with a maid of honor or something."

She held the steering wheel with two hands and shrugged. "Yeah, I have a few girlfriends who will be bridesmaids, but they all work on the force with me, and none of them are particularly interested in this stuff. They would have done it if I'd asked, but it'll be great having someone there who actually enjoys event planning and knows what she's talking about. Plus, Willa is going to be my maid of honor slash flower girl."

"Aw. That's so sweet."

"I think she would have loved to have done this with us, but it's her first day back at school."

"I'm sure she'll find other ways to help."

"Oh, of course." Rain nodded with a light laugh. "She's writing a speech, and she'll throw petals as she walks down the aisle. That sort of thing."

We slowed to a stop at a red light, and I peered out the window at the car beside us. It was amusing to watch how focused the woman was. Two hands on the wheel, steely stare on the road in front of her. I could almost feel the tension radiating from her shoulders. I wondered if she had a legitimate reason to not want the attention of the police or if it was just one of those natural reactions to the potential of getting into trouble. People were so prepared for the worst.

And perhaps that was for the best. The worst usually came when it felt like nothing could ever go wrong.

"So," Raine said once she'd turned off the car in front of a little brick building. It was narrow and tall and had a few different store signs hanging from a steel bar above the door. "Where to next? Do you have a plan for your next adventure?"

For a moment I thought she was asking where she and I were going next. But then I understood, and I exhaled a sigh, not sure how to answer the question I'd been asking myself for a few days now.

"There's nothing keeping me here," I said. "But there's nothing for me anywhere else, either. I did contemplate going to Sicily to find my Nonna. But after a social media hunt, I found out she died a while ago."

"You don't have other family you could go and see there?"

"Yeah, there's a lot of extended family over there. I just don't know them at all. There was a lot of drama around my dad and Margo's mom before Dad left, and no one kept in contact. I'm pretty sure someone would host me, that's what it's like over there. But I don't think I'd feel comfortable going. Not right now."

"Fair enough. You should hang around here. You know us now. You wouldn't have to go somewhere and start from scratch. Plus, Willa told me she bumped into you at the river, and I think that's fate telling you to spend more time with us. What are the odds you ended up at the same river, at the same time, on the same day? Hmmm?"

I smiled, appreciating her optimistic outlook.

"You know, also, ending up here when I was right in the process of hiring a wedding planner. Could the stars be any more aligned?"

Her brows wiggled up and down, suggestive and sort of adorable. It might've been impulsive and somewhat of a bad idea, but her contagious optimism made it hard to resist.

"Look, I'll do it," I said, realizing that this might be just what I needed. It was a distraction, one that would give me a piece of Margo, one that would keep me occupied and close to someone who was so sweet that I couldn't resist helping. "I'll plan the wedding."

Raine's lips parted. "You will?"

"Yeah. I would love to. Have you settled on a date?"

She twisted in her seat, facing me with a teeth-baring grin. "Next October."

"A beautiful fall wedding," I said, ideas already forming. "Ideas for a location?"

"I'm not sure, but I do know that I want to cut costs on the venue in order to spend more on a dress."

We both laughed, and I assured her I understood that logic. After she'd phoned in and cancelled her appointment with the planner waiting upstairs, she drove us back to the inn. During the ride, I brainstormed some ideas for the theme and suggested the farm as a good location. It was free, and those big barns would make a gorgeous spot for the reception.

Raine drummed her fingers on the wheel as I unbuckled my belt.

"How's it going here?" she asked. "Do you like it?"

"Hanna is . . . a bit much, if I'm being honest."

Raine winced, nodding. "Yeah, I was hoping she might be a friend of sorts, since I knew you were all alone, but she's not everyone's cup of tea."

"I appreciate the thought." I reached for the door handle.

"I have an idea," Raine said before I could leave. "Now that you're going to be hanging around, you should definitely find somewhere more permanent to live. Paying by the night is going to be so much more expensive than paying by the month. Plus, I'm sure you want to get out of Hanna's hair as soon as possible."

She wasn't wrong, but finding somewhere to live sounded so strange. I had a place to live. I just also happened to not want to go back there for the foreseeable future.

"What about the farm? Dad has a ton of room. It'll be no problem at all."

"Oh, no, I couldn't." I went straight to thoughts of living under the same roof as Zac, and for some reason, it made me blush. Not only that, but the potential of screaming down the house in the middle of the night because of nightmares was too embarrassing. It had happened at the inn several times, but no one had commented on it, likely because I didn't talk to anyone long enough to give them the chance.

Raine wouldn't hear my argument about being an imposition. "I'll talk to Zac and tell him to pick you up tomorrow afternoon. You two can discuss rent and whatever else."

I was in a daze as I walked back to my room. It all felt surreal, where I was, what I was doing with my life at the moment. Such an abrupt change in circumstance was hard to wrap my head around, but it felt like the only thing keeping me going.

• • •

The next afternoon, I sat in my suite and tried to ignore the heat while I read a book on my bed. The AC unit obviously wasn't up to the task of keeping one small room cool enough to function in. There was a sharp knock on the door, and I assumed it was Zac, showing up early to get me after Raine had texted to confirm I could move into the farm house. Pulling on a large T-shirt, because I'd been lounging in my bra and underwear, I went for the door as he tapped again.

"Good morning." Zac was leaning on the doorframe with two coffees from downstairs in his hand. "Mocha with almond milk?"

"Almond milk?"

He shrugged and slipped his hand into his pocket after I took the drink. "That's what all the girls in California are drinking, isn't it?"

"Again with the assumptions?"

He grinned, and it was full of guilt. "That was a joke. The kitchen had just run out of regular milk. It was all they had until tomorrow morning's milk drop."

He sipped from his to-go cup and smacked his lips. "It's not bad."

I smiled, my now-bare fingers wrapped around the hot cup. I'd spent an hour hacking at my gel polish the night before, peeling it off. I didn't want to lose them, but they were breaking, and there was no point in delaying the inevitable. "I thought you weren't meant to be here until the afternoon? And also, you do not have to agree to this. I hope Raine didn't make you feel like you had to say yes to me coming to the farm."

"I had to come into town and get a few things for dinner, so I thought I'd stop in and ask if you wanted to come with me now, or I can come back later. And no, Raine didn't pressure me into anything. It's no problem at all. Dad was the one who made the final call, anyway."

"Oh, right."

He smiled, still leaning against the frame, so tall and built that he almost filled the space. His gaze dropped and lingered for a moment on my legs, which were bare. My T-shirt just covered my underwear.

"I should come back, I suppose." His eyes met mine again. "Let you get sort—"

"Addie?" Hanna appeared from behind Zac, and he turned around, giving her a polite nod.

"Hello, Zachary," she said with that forced hospitable charm she'd mastered so well. "How's your father?"

"Great, thanks. How are you, ma'am?"

She shrugged and smiled as if to say she was so-so and then fixed me with that judgmental look that she tried and failed to hide.

"Are you in some sort of trouble, love?"

I frowned. "No. Why?"

"I saw you with the police yesterday afternoon."

"Oh," I chuckled. "That was Raine."

She parted her lips in a dramatic show of understanding and then looked at Zac again. "Yes, well, we're a family establishment, sweetheart. So we prefer that there's no promiscuous behavior going on. If you're going to have men in and out, it might be time to move on."

I stared at her with incredulity, speechless.

"Good thing I just asked her to move in with me, then." Zac winked at me and stood up straight, moving further into the bedroom. "We'll pack up as fast as we can, provided we don't get too *distracted*."

Hanna blushed a bright pink as Zac put his arm around me, fingertips gripping my waist. It tingled all over.

"Be out of here soon." He kicked the door shut, wearing a grin that had no right to be as gorgeous as it was. He dropped his hold and turned to me, sipping his coffee.

"That was cheeky," I scolded him.

He shrugged. "She's being like that because she still has a bee in her bonnet about Dad calling it quits on their brief fling."

I slowly shook my head. "No, I think she's just like that. She's been a pain since I got here."

He chuckled and looked around the room. "So, need a hand?"

Zac waited while I threw on some clothes and then helped me give the room a quick clean. I wasn't too worried about the state of the bed or the towels on the bathroom floor, but he put all of the washing into a pile by the door while I shoved my clothes into my backpack. I had a few more things now than I'd arrived with, so Zac held the bag, and I walked downstairs with an armful of clothes and a couple of books that I'd taken out at the library this week. It was hard to believe that I'd checked in almost two weeks ago. It felt like time had flown past and stood still all at the same time.

Hanna was stiff and didn't smile once while I checked out. She charged the total amount to the card that I'd given her when I arrived. I'd never been more grateful for Apple Pay considering I'd left my clutch at home, and my phone was all I had. Zac and I slid into a truck that was parked at the curb. It was a new one with big wheels and a lot of advanced technology on the dashboard. Zac suited it.

He started it up with the push of a button and relaxed into the seat.

"Raine said to discuss rent with you," I said, redoing my hair. "What's it going to be?"

He tilted his head, still watching the road with a contemplative stare, one hand on the wheel. "Two hundred a month?"

"That's it?"

He looked at me briefly, with a little smile pulling on the corner of his mouth. "You want me to charge more?"

"I'm just . . . that's low."

"You're doing this wedding thing for Raine, right?" I nodded. "How much are you charging her?"

"I hadn't thought about it."

"You run a business. You've thought about it."

He wasn't wrong. "I was going to charge her half of what the other planner quoted her."

He fixed me with a curious stare. "Why?"

I shrugged. "Because this isn't Beverly Hills."

He didn't seem to understand, but that was all right. I couldn't explain the fact that our usual fee felt superficial. It felt like it was too much to charge someone as sweet as Raine, who hadn't even hesitated to extend a helping hand toward me when I'd needed it. That being said, I did need to earn an income. Sure, I profited from the business, but now that I'd left Lo in charge, I was paying her a manager's salary.

"All right." He nodded and ran a hand through his dark hair. "You do Raine's wedding for free and you don't have to pay rent at all."

"You're negotiating in the wrong direction."

He laughed, and it was so full and masculine that it felt too big for this truck. It wrapped around me and pushed a chill up my spine. It was so unexpected that I inhaled a quick, quiet breath.

"We'll figure it out," he said. "No rush."

# CHAPTER TEN

Zac left me to freshen up in the room I'd slept in last time I was at the farm. I had a shower and went downstairs in one of the dresses I had on rotation. I followed the aroma of garlic and tomatoes and found Zac in the kitchen stirring a pot on the big retro stove top. Keith was sitting at the kitchen island, his hands clasped on the surface and his smile content.

"Hello, sir," I said. Zac turned at the sound of my voice. I sat on one of the stools, leaving one between Keith and me.

"Ah, good evening, darlin'." Keith grinned.

"Thank you for letting me stay here for a little while." I still felt like I was intruding, but Zac had spent the entire ride assuring me that I wasn't.

"Stay as long as you want, darlin'. We've got enough room. Can I give you a job to do each morning?"

"Oh. Yeah, please do."

He twisted in his stool, pointing out at the garden beds, visible through the large windows stretching across the kitchen. "Water and check for weeds? It's getting a bit tough on my back to bend down and give it a thorough check."

"You're the one who maintains the garden?"

"You seem surprised." He chuckled, and I felt heat creep up my neck at the thought of offending him.

"Not surprised, just—"

"My wife used to tell me that it was her favorite thing about me. A man's man that had a gentle, tender taste in flowers. Her words. Odd thing to love about a man, but it was an added bonus to have her approval."

I watched the spark in his gaze as he talked about his late wife; it made him look so much younger. As if his memories took him back in time.

"You have it," he said to me, his grin knowing.

"Have what?"

"Green fingers. You'll take great care of those flowers. Oh, the orchard too, darlin'."

Zac spooned sauce over a plate of pasta. I wondered if he'd made the sauce from scratch. He slid the plate to his father, who stood up and announced he was going to eat on the deck. Zac gave him a quick nod and went back to the stove to prepare another plate.

"Hope you don't mind being assigned a job within the first half hour of being here," he said once Keith was outside.

"Of course not. I'm glad I have something to do. I won't feel like a freeloader. Did you tell him I was interested in horticulture?"

"I didn't, actually." He brought our plates to the kitchen island and sat down beside me. "He's a wise old man, though. Suppose he saw something in you."

"I had a lot of houseplants back at home." I twisted spaghetti on my fork. "Outdoor gardens and greenery are a little more foreign to me, but it'll be a good learning experience."

Truthfully, I was excited about the chance to expand my knowledge.

• • •

In the morning, I woke up before my little bedside alarm could go off. The best time to water the gardens was before it got too hot. I dressed in a pair of jeans and a long-sleeved shirt before creeping through the quiet house. It was still a dark blue outside, the air cool but not cold. Midge and Toto, the border collies, came to see what I was doing as I dragged the hose across the lawn. Each of them got a good rub on the belly before I started watering the gorgeous range of flowers and vegetables.

Peace washed over me as I stood in the quiet morning. The birds were starting to twitter, and the air was so pure here, it felt like I could breathe easier than I ever had before. The stillness was like being in another world, where everything was slower, better, kinder. Looking out at the rolling land, the distant hills, the green pastures, it made it easy to forget about what cruel realities were still unfolding all over the earth.

When I was done with the garden, I wandered down to see Noah and gave him an apple from the trees in the orchard. Then I went down to the barns and sat on a weather-worn bench. It didn't feel like long before I heard footsteps crunching the gravel and then Zac appeared wearing a white T-shirt, jeans, and boots. His cap was on backward, and he paused his steps when he saw me.

"Mornin'." He smiled, his voice still holding the hint of a sleepy rasp. "You're up early."

"I couldn't sleep," I admitted, standing as he came toward me. "I finished up watering the gardens and orchard and thought I'd come down and wait."

He let his gaze sweep over me as he hooked his hand around the handle and rolled the barn door back with little to no effort.

"I, uh, I read about some really good garden food I'd like to get. If you don't mind taking me into town next time you go?" I asked.

"We can go whenever you want," he said, flicking on the light switch, casting a dim glow through the barn, bright enough but not too harsh. "You said you couldn't sleep. Something wrong with the bed?"

"No, just me."

He nodded, slipping his hands into his pockets. "You want to talk about it?"

"There's not a lot to talk about." I shrugged, staring at the boots on my feet, the ones Zac had lent me last time I was here. He'd left them on the porch for me last night. "I'm hurting. I'm doing my best to put one foot in front of the other and not let it consume me."

"Understandable."

"I keep on thinking about the fact that it wasn't even this painful when I lost my parents. I mean, that was hard, and I struggled, but this is—this—"

"Margo was all you had left," he observed, his eyes finding mine. "Losing your mom and dad wouldn't have been easy, but you had someone. You had Margo. I'm not surprised it's so much harder this time around."

My heart sped up, grateful for the words I hadn't been able to find. I felt myself smiling.

"You're sort of . . ." I looked for the right word. "Great. I—well, it means a lot to me when you refer to Margo by name. Rather than just calling her my sister."

Zac leaned against a small workbench and folded his arms, all of his attention on me. "I appreciate the same thing when it's about my mom."

"What was her name?"

"Annie."

I smiled. "Beautiful name."

"She was a beautiful woman."

"No surprises there after seeing you and Raine." My cheeks warmed at the compliment that had just sort of slipped out. I wouldn't take it back, though. He and Raine were beautiful.

He lowered his head, grinning. "Thanks."

Just like last weekend, Zac reminded me what we had to do, and we split up, feeding the horses, giving the stalls a sweep, and letting the horses out into the paddock. When I was done, I went out to find Lavender scratching her head on the wooden fence post. Zac told me where I could find a brush, and I went over, standing on the middle rung so I could reach her back. Lavender had no objections to a brush; she kept still and blinked slowly.

Zac appeared next to me a few minutes later. The sun was up now, and it was warm. "She likes you," he said. "None of us can ever get her to hang around for more than a few minutes. You got a secret?"

I huffed a light laugh and dropped from the wooden rung. "I don't know what her deal is, but she's a sweetheart."

He took the brush from my hand, his fingers grazing mine and his gaze lingering on me for a moment. Wind swept a strand of hair across my face. Zac reached out, pushing the hair back, his finger skimming over my forehead and down my temple until he'd tucked it behind my ear. "I might head down to the car shed for a while." He shattered the moment and waved the brush as he turned around. "I'll put this back."

"Can I come?"

He looked over his shoulder. "Of course."

When we got to the barn, Zac dragged a seat through the mess on the ground, one he must've pulled out of a car, and used a rag to dust it off. He gestured for me to take a seat once it was clean. He slung his hands low on his hips and looked around.

"This is a 1970 Buick Skylark." He tilted his head at the old car in front of us. It was a beautiful candy apple red with a shimmer in the paint. "Needs a new exhaust pipe and radiator, but she's almost done."

"Where does the painting get done?"

"A garage in town. I buy the paint, they do the work. I've come to know the guy well, so he's happy to do it. Plus I fixed his starter a while back."

"So, what does this go for when it's time to be sold?"

He leaned on the hood of the car, his biceps swelling and the veins in his forearm prominent as he thought about his answer. "Well, it's in good condition. New paint and interior. Total engine restoration. The colors aren't original, and the wheels won't be standard either, so be looking between eighteen and twenty thousand."

My lips parted in surprise. "What? That's insane."

"There's a big market for classic cars in good condition. Even in poor condition. People want them."

"So what condition do you buy them in?"

He lowered his head, biting down on a smile. I wasn't sure what he found so amusing. "I get them pretty beat up. Usually not running. Rust buckets. That sort of thing. I restore them, save most of the profit, and invest in the next project."

"Is the profit good? Like, once you've bought a new car and purchased everything that it needs, is there a lot left over?"

"Enough."

It occurred to me then, perhaps a little too late, that those were not the sort of answers I had a right to. "Those are invasive questions. I'm sorry. Your finances are private."

He chuckled and stood up straight. "You wanna go for a drive with me? In that?"

I twisted in the seat, following his line of sight where an adorable old car was tucked in the back corner, its own shed door behind it.

"The convertible?"

He nodded. "It's an Austin-Healey 3000."

"I would love to."

# CHAPTER ELEVEN

The Austin-Healey was gorgeous. It was from the fifties with that retro rounded look and original wire wheels, so Zac explained. He drove out of the barn and up a gravel path until we came to a long stretch of narrow road. The top was down, and the sun was bright.

"It was my grandfather's car first," Zac said, shifting through the gears. The muscles in his arm flexed, and I tried not to stare because it would make listening to him impossible. "He passed it on to Dad, and Dad never had much interest in cars, so he gave it to me."

"It's beautiful," I said.

Zac, who was wearing a pair of shades, looked in my direction and smiled before he picked up speed. We flew past tall trees that flanked either side of the road; the wind was loud, which made it harder to talk, but that was fine because I sort of wanted to embrace the peace that came with the feeling of floating.

I pulled my hair out of its bun and let it loose. It was wild and curled because it had been damp when I did it up, but I didn't care. It felt amazing to have the wind whipping at it.

Without asking, I wiggled up out of the seat and sat on the top of it, holding the windshield so that I could experience the full effect of driving with the top down. It was surreal. With my eyes closed, I could smell the river behind the trees, hear the birds, feel the sun, and absorb the exhilarating sensation of being weightless. Nothing had ever felt closer to flight, and I hadn't felt this at peace in weeks.

When I opened my eyes again, Zac was moving his attention between the road and me. His grin was full, and he had the most beautiful smile. I'd met a lot of good-looking men in my time as an event planner in Beverly Hills. There was no shortage of gorgeous singles. But Zac was a rugged, effortless, stand-out sort of beautiful, and he made me a little bit breathless.

We drove for a while, slowing when we left the road and drove through a narrow passage that was so overgrown with trees that Zac had to put the top up so that our hair wasn't caught on branches. We came to a stop at an opening. It was a pool with a waterfall pouring from the top of a cliff. It was gorgeous, secluded, and quiet apart from the tree leaves rustling and the constant whoosh of the waterfall.

Zac switched the car off and settled back in his seat, hands resting on his spread thighs. "Not bad, huh?"

"It's beautiful."

"Well?"

I turned to him and raised an uncertain brow.

Zac's smile was teasing. "I was just expecting a few thousand questions."

I laughed and twiddled with the soft center console. "I would've gotten there eventually."

"All right, well, I have one for you."

I nodded, gesturing for him to go ahead.

"Are you single?"

I ducked my head, feeling heat creep up from my neck and into my face. "Yes. Surely that's obvious."

"For the most part. I just wanted to be sure."

I still couldn't look at him. "Why?"

"Just because."

Finally, I looked up, but I couldn't see his eyes through his sunglasses. That didn't mean I couldn't feel them. "How about you?"

"Single."

"How come?"

He laughed, slowly shaking his head with a shrug, and then his expression became a little deeper. "I had a serious girlfriend, about five years ago. I mean, I thought it was serious. We were in the middle of building a house together, out on the farm. It was going to be our own little slice of land. The plans were all drawn up when she told me she'd been seeing some dude in Houston for the last six months and the two of them had just gotten engaged. She went there for work, so I never thought much of the weeks she spent gone. She used to call me and tell me how bored she was without me."

"I don't get it," I said quietly, watching as Zac turned toward me, curious. "I just, I don't get the cheating thing. I can't make sense of it. Just break up and be honest."

Zac's nod of agreement was slow, and he searched my face. "You too?"

"No," I admitted. "I've never really let anyone close enough to do that, or if they did, I didn't know about it. I had a lot going on in my teens, and then I started working for Margo. I went on dates here and there, had a few flings that lasted a month or two, but nothing serious. Margo got married when I was young, and her partner was just kind of . . . ick. He loved her, but he had a lot of expectations of her, and he didn't like when she didn't meet them. It sort of put me off the idea of looking for a man."

"I get it," he said, folding his arms and sinking further into his seat as he looked around at the scenery. "Kind of ended up feeling the same. I'm not opposed to falling in love, but I don't get out enough. Apparently, you have to leave the house to meet people."

An abrupt huff of laughter left me. "You sound like Margo."

"How so?"

I inhaled deep and let it go slowly. The fact that emotional pain could translate into such real, physical pain was something people needed to talk about more. There was a very real ache in my chest and nausea in my stomach when it came to talking about Margo in the past tense. But Zac made it easier; he let me talk about her as if she were still here, still with me. He let me forget for a moment that she was gone.

"Margo kept telling me that I need to find someone. Meet someone and fall in love. She tried to get me out of the house for that purpose all the time. I didn't listen, but now I feel like maybe I should have tried harder." Perhaps if I had, I wouldn't have been left alone.

"You shouldn't have to try. It should be natural and unexpected. It should just happen."

"That's what I thought too. But now—I'm—I don't know. I'm more alone than I've ever been, and I feel like I'm wasting time."

"How old are you?"

"Actually, I'm twenty-five today."

Zac's mouth fell open. "Today? Today's your birthday?"

"Yeah."

He folded his arms. "And you didn't say anything because . . . ?"

"What's the point?"

He gave me a tight smile. "Well, happy birthday."

"Thanks."

The truth was, the thought of celebrating a birthday without Margo was nearly impossible to comprehend. She'd been involved in them all. Made it a big event. Bought presents and cake and forced me to have a good time even if all I wanted to do was have a quiet dinner and a movie. She wouldn't have it. She told me that I was worth celebrating. She said that each year I was still alive and healthy and happy was a reason to celebrate. She was like that. So optimistic. So appreciative of everything that she had. Including me.

"Can I buy you lunch? For your birthday?"

"I won't say no to that."

We had lunch in Georgetown central. The historic buildings were beautiful. Enchanting almost. The atmosphere was relaxed, and the people were nice.

Zac and I sat opposite one another in a small café in between a clothing boutique and a pet shelter. The windows at the front of the shop were floor-to-ceiling, and we sat at a two-person table, watching the world moving outside. Well, Zac might have been watching. I had been staring at the menu for fifteen minutes.

"Sorry," I mumbled, pinching my lip. "I hate this part of eating somewhere new. I can never decide what to get."

He leaned back in his seat, hands behind his head. His black T-shirt clung to his arms and chest. He shrugged. "No stress. Take your time."

It was almost hard to turn my attention back to the menu. I let out a breath and grumbled.

"Y'all ready to order?"

I peered up at the waitress, who wore a sweet smile on her full lips; her tight black ringlets were in a bun on top of her head, and it looked like a fountain. "I'm sorry." I winced. "I'm hopeless. Recommendations?"

She tilted her head and pursed her lips. "Hmmm," she hummed as she thought. "The salmon salad is good. And the carbonara is a crowd favorite."

"Ooh, I do like pasta."

She nodded with an encouraging smile. "It's good. I promise."

"Okay. I'll get that." I handed her the menu and looked at Zac, who was already watching me with a soft smile. He handed his menu over as well.

"I'll have the BLT, thanks."

"No problem."

"Oh," Zac added as he halted the waitress. "It's her birthday."

My lips parted. "Hey—"

"Happy birthday," she chimed. "Drink on the house? What'll it be?"

"Oh no." I shook my head. "You don't have to—"

"Or I can bring out a cupcake with a candle and have the chef sing."

"I'll have a lemonade."

She laughed and spun to head off. My glare fell on Zac, who was looking relaxed and rather proud of himself.

"You are so lucky that no one is singing happy birthday to me right now."

He bit the inside of his cheek, attempting to hide his grin; he was all sorts of gorgeous when his thick black lashes were framing his smiling eyes.

The carbonara was mouthwatering. We talked about light topics and interests, and I asked Zac a lot of questions about his cars and about the horses. The different ways he talked about the two topics made it obvious that classic cars were his passion, even if he refused to label it a passion. I wondered if that was a subconscious thing, if he didn't want to admit that he loved something so much more than the job he was doing day-to-day.

After that we stopped at an auto parts store so Zac could pick up a few parts he'd ordered for his various projects. It felt so normal, us spending the afternoon together, me following him around while he ran his errands. It felt as if we'd been doing it forever, but the blatant staring from people he knew made it clear that this was not a regular thing for him. It wasn't the norm to have a woman in tow while he shopped around town. For some reason I didn't want to evaluate, I liked that.

When we were on the road again, I checked my cell phone, something that was becoming a rarity for me. Even though I knew it wouldn't happen, a small part of me, the tiniest whisper of hope, longed to see Margo's name on the screen, asking me to come home because she missed me. And the fact that she never would was a brutal reality check, reminding me that everything that had happened was real, no matter how hard I tried to escape it.

I had a few text messages. One from Lo, wishing me a happy birthday and letting me know that things were fine at home and she was booked up with events right until Christmas. July through to January was our busiest time. There were a ton of events. Fourth of July parties, Halloween, weddings, Thanksgiving, Christmas, New Year's. I felt bad for leaving her short-staffed at a time like this, so I tapped out a quick response.

Thanks. Hire an extra temp or two if needed over the next few months.

There was one from Irie.

Happy birthday baby girl. Missing you! Come home soon, all right? You can come and stay with me if you need. I'm here for you.

I didn't respond to that one. If I did, she'd call me straight back, and she wouldn't stop until I answered.

The next message was from Ange, Margo's childhood friend. She'd moved to San Francisco a while ago, and we didn't see her a lot because she was busy being the ultimate wife and mother, but she called Margo all the time and had come home for her funeral.

Happy birthday, Addie. Miss you and Margo more than I can tell you. Love you.

"Everything okay?" Zac asked.

"Oh. Yeah. Just birthday messages from a few . . . friends."

Friends didn't sound right. I mean, I'd had friends in high school, and whoever Margo spent time with, I did too. Subtly. On the outskirts. It was like I did all of my socializing without putting in a lot of effort. It was secondhand socializing, and I hadn't even realized at the time how lonely I really was.

"That's nice of them," Zac commented. With one arm on the door and the other hand holding the steering wheel from the bottom, he made driving look like a far more seductive activity than it really was. "People must be missing you?"

"Well, the first message was from a staff member. The other messages were from Margo's friends. That sort of sums up how missed I am."

"Quality over quantity, Addie." He smiled.

I didn't know how to respond to that.

"They reached out," he added. "More than some people do."

"Are you trying to get rid of me? Get me to go home?"

I was teasing, but his mouth pulled down. "Not at all. I'd miss you."

I swallowed and stared out the windshield, wondering how he thought he could miss me after knowing me for only a couple weeks. In fact, he didn't know me at all. I didn't even know who I was anymore.

But I knew I would miss him too.

When we got back to the farm, we split up to shower and change. Zac told me he had a few things to do in the afternoon, but he wanted me to meet him in the kitchen at four. Which wasn't that far off. I had a feeling he had a plan up his sleeve, and I wasn't sure how to feel about it, but I didn't argue.

I wandered out into the garden with a book and sat down underneath a big oak tree. The branches stretched, and the thick leaves sheltered the two doghouses. Midge and Toto must have been inside the house somewhere, likely with Keith.

It had been hard to read lately. Whenever I sat down, leafed through the pages, and absorbed the words of a fictional world, I could hear Margo telling me that my own story wouldn't start until I was the one who was living out those moments.

She didn't want me to never read. She wanted me to find balance. I felt like I had been doing more of that in the last few weeks. Which made me feel guilty. I was living when she couldn't.

In hindsight, I should have made the most of every opportunity that she'd presented. We'd have more memories than we did now. Memories that didn't consist of me resisting her efforts to help me find love or friends or fun. I should have listened to her more.

# CHAPTER TWELVE

"Addie?"

I looked up from the page that I had been staring at and saw Zac standing over me.

"It's four."

"What?"

He pointed over his shoulder toward the kitchen. "It's four. Remember, we were supposed to mee—"

"No, I know. I just . . . lost track of time. I'm sorry."

"Don't be. You weren't hard to find."

I looked down at my book and realized I was on the same page I had been when I'd opened it. Which had to have been two hours ago, at least. I snapped it shut and stood up quickly, meeting Zac's eyes with a smile that wouldn't let him know how rattled I was. Not that he would mind. He was so patient and understanding, but I didn't want to dwell on the fact that I was struggling to breathe.

"You free for the rest of the afternoon?" He stood close and slipped his hands into the pockets of his jeans, which were a faded wash; his powder-blue T-shirt hugged his arms and chest.

"As you can see, I'm not the most in demand person on the planet. So I'm free. What's the plan?"

He kept his eyes on me but reached out and took the book from me, and then, to my surprise, he took my hand in his. It sent a warmth right up my arm, and a tingle spread fast.

I trailed along behind him, not protesting when he carefully tossed the book onto the deck and then headed for the paddock gate. He was quiet as we walked, but he didn't let go of my hand. I watched it the entire time, fascinated at how it encased mine and felt so warm. I was sure that having my hand held had never felt like this before. Consuming.

"Surprise!"

He stopped abruptly. I hadn't been focusing on our surroundings at all. I had been too occupied watching our intertwined hands and his chiseled back, which I tore my gaze from to see a large, beautiful horse. She chewed on grass as her tail swished at the pestering flies. She was saddled up, and the saddle extended over her backside into a tray-like device that had a picnic basket strapped to it.

"What's this?"

Zac shrugged and gestured his head at the horse with a grin. "A different sort of ride. If you're up for it."

My stare fell to the ground while I hid the blush crawling up my neck after I unintentionally heard a different meaning than the one intended. He must have caught on.

"Head out of the gutter, Ads." He laughed, and I looked up in time to see him wink at me. It was the nickname that snapped me out of the amusement. It sounded so familiar, yet I'd never heard him call me that before. It sounded right. It fit.

"Is this a birthday present?"

"Nope." He waved me over beside the horse. "Just something to do on a Saturday night. You know Nellie. She's our big girl. Better for tandem riding."

Beside him, I tilted my head so that I could look up at his gorgeous face. Angular and dark in the most alluring way. His lashes were so full. His eyes were such a dark brown that his pupils were almost indistinguishable, and his stubble was rugged, perfect.

"A date then?" I had no idea what had possessed me to say that, but I regretted it the moment it left my mouth. He chuckled and slipped around me so that he could put his large hands on my waist.

"Foot in the stirrup please, ma'am."

My stomach turned over itself, but I did what he told me to and suppressed a squeal when he hoisted me in the air, instructing that I throw my other leg over and straddle.

Before I knew it, he was behind me, and his arms came around on either side, gripping the reins. My body sank back, his firm chest behind me and his chin above my head.

"It could be a date," he murmured beside my ear. I felt his breath on my cheek, and it made me shiver. Not just shiver as in "it felt sensual and therefore I was affected." No, this was a full-body shiver that made him laugh.

"It's cold," I said, filled with humiliation that would last until further notice. He continued his low laughter as he gave the horse a gentle nudge in the side, and she started to walk. I paid attention to the commands and the actions of riding, in case I was ever given the chance to get on by myself. I hadn't asked because most of the horses were in training or being rehabilitated, but I wouldn't mind learning to ride if the chance presented itself.

"You wanna go back and change into something warmer?"

There was no chance I would do that. The weather was scalding, and he knew it, which was the reason I was wearing a pair of loose cotton shorts and a tank top. A thought occurred to me.

"How come you don't have a pool? It's so hot here, and the place is enormous."

"We do," he said from behind me. Nellie was moving slowly, but it was still a jostled ride, and I was taking subtle peeps at Zac's forearms on either side of me.

"Wait, what?"

"On the other side of the house. It's gated off with a tall fence."

Now that he mentioned it, I did recall seeing a gated area from the downstairs bathroom window, but I hadn't seen what was on the other side of it.

"Good to know," I said.

We rode for a while. The relaxing jostle could have put me to sleep if I'd let it. But my heart was sort of a mess the entire time due to how close Zac and I were. It was so intimate, and though neither of us said it out loudly, it was romantic. It was something I'd read before. I could have sworn that it was a scene plucked straight from a romance novel. But it was happening to me now. Margo would have been ecstatic. Just thinking of how loud she'd squeal when I called her to tell her what I was doing made my heart pang.

We remained on a narrow dirt trail the entire time. Sometimes it was bright and open and sometimes it went through the thick of trees and forest. But I noticed we were on an incline and getting higher. I could see more of the landscape: it stretched on forever.

"So, where are we going?" I said, wiping at my damp brow. It was sweet and romantic, but it was still hot, and I was sweating.

"We're not far," he said, and he meant it. A few moments later, we came around a corner of shrubs and were on the top of a large cliff face.

Zac asked, "Look familiar?"

"Should it?"

"It might soon."

He hopped off Nellie first, and I watched him secure her lead to a tree trunk. She was sheltered from the sun and had a lot of greenery to eat. He sauntered over to me and offered a hand down, which I accepted just to be sure that I didn't land on my face and ruin his sweet gesture. When my feet were on the ground, he took my hand for a second time, and I wondered if he was thinking about it just as much as I was. Or maybe I was overthinking it. That was possible too.

"Recognize it now?" he said when we got to the edge of the cliff. Just below and to the side was a running river that fell into a waterfall, and below that was the large waterhole that we'd been parked at that morning.

"I like the view from up here," I said, looking out over the treetops that surrounded the water below. There was another car there now, and I smiled, wondering but not entirely wanting to know what they were doing. The car was low and looked like something a teenage boy would drive.

"That's Tyler Adler," Zac said from beside me. "Raine's had to talk to him a few times because people call him in for his car. It's loud, and he drives like a bit of a dick. She doesn't bother him too much, though, just has a chat with him and lets him go with a warning."

I gave a conspiratorial nod of understanding.

"He's probably down there with his girlfriend. He's not a bad kid. Likes to drive. I've fixed his car a few times for no charge. And he's obsessed with his girl. Fiercely protective of her. Her dad's a dick, so I think they have plans to ditch Texas after graduation."

"You know a lot of people around here. Ya know, for someone who doesn't get out a lot."

He chuckled and turned on his heel, sauntering over to Nellie. "Yeah, well, I've lived here forever, and it's not so much that I get out a lot but more like Raine comes across a lot of people through her job, and she's the friendliest person ever. So she gets to know people, and then I get to know them through her, and so on and so on. Plus, I'm the go-to mechanic when people don't want to pay full price."

"Ahhh." I nodded. "I'm surprised Raine hasn't found a nice woman to set you up with, then."

"Oh, she's tried." Zac laughed and unstrapped the picnic basket from Nellie. The sun was still up, still warm, but the sky was beginning to change color,

"But nothing stuck?"

"Not so far." He set the basket down and lifted the woven wicker lid, getting a blanket out. "But perhaps it will soon."

He straightened after he'd laid the blanket flat, and his gaze swept over me. His jaw twitched, and his chest rose and fell with a deep breath. "I'm—" I stammered and swallowed. "I'm—I think you're really attractive and sweet."

Why had I told him that?

He slipped his hands into his jeans pockets; his eyes didn't stop moving, traveling my frame from top to bottom as his teeth sank into his bottom lip.

"What I know about you," he said, his voice deep and invasive in the best sense, "I like a lot. You're beautiful. Smart. Strong. Outspoken."

I winced at the outspoken part. I'd never been too afraid of telling people what was on my mind, and I had never cared how people received that side of me. But now I was nervous.

"No." His laugh was low as he shook his head. "I like that. I like that you tell me how it is. Takes out the guesswork. Not that you wouldn't be worth figuring out."

"I don't like to pretend," I said, my confidence returning. "I call it like it is."

His gaze swept over me again. "Good. Don't ever stop."

Somehow, without me noticing, he'd crossed the picnic blanket and now stood in front of me, his skin kissed by the dusky orange sunset. His gaze lowered to my mouth, head on a subtle tilt. Lifting his hand, he swept my hair back over my shoulder and ran his fingertips down the length of my arm until he reached my hand. Tingles swept through me, and I peered down at where his large hand held mine. Breathing felt impossible when I lifted my face and found him close. He looked at me with a softness in his stare, a soul-searching sort of appreciation.

Even though we were surrounded by vast space and air to breathe, I'd never felt so suffocated with tension. It was as if we were in a box and the air was running out, and perhaps if we kissed, we'd be able to share oxygen.

Zac was so close, all it would take to kiss him would be to lift onto my tiptoes, and I could feel it. I could feel how his soft lips would feel on mine. I could feel how his large hands would cradle me against his firm body. I could feel the world melting away if I were swept into his embrace and allowed to breathe in a different sort of mind-numbing emotion. I could trade emptiness for the fulfilment of desire.

Zac's jaw fluttered as I got closer, his nostrils flaring as he inhaled a deep breath. He was just as nervous as I was, and I realized I couldn't use him like that. I couldn't let this sweet man be my distraction.

"Should we eat?" I whispered, but my voice was abrupt and unwelcome.

Zac's eyes flickered as he stepped back a little. "Yeah. Sure. Let's eat."

My entire body felt like Jell-o as he fixed his backward cap and flicked the picnic basket lid open.

• • •

We ate while the sun set, though I passed on the wine he offered. Eventually, we ended up lying on our backs while we stared up at the starry night. We hadn't stopped talking since we'd begun eating, and I found myself laughing more and more.

"He did not," I giggled.

"I swear," Zac laughed and rolled onto his side, leaning on his elbow as he stared down at me. I had to work to focus on what he was saying. "I was seventeen, it was eleven at night, and my chem teacher was stuck in the school parking lot because his car wouldn't start. So I had to go and help him out."

"Why not call an actual mechanic?"

"He knew no one would be open at that time of the night. But it worked out well. My grades were perfect in that class from then on."

I laughed, so wholly, and Zac's attention lowered to my mouth. "There it is," he whispered. "As beautiful as I thought it would be."

My heart hiccuped and his lip twitched with amusement, as if he heard that too. The moment was broken at the sound of gravel crunching and footsteps approaching. Zac didn't move, but he peered over his shoulder, and then a flashlight shone on us, and he stood up, fast. I stood up as well, but he pushed me behind him.

"Who's that?" he said, shielding his face. The light lowered, and I peered around him to see Raine in her uniform, grinning.

"Your big sister," she sang. "And who is that? Who are you on a cute date with?"

So she hadn't seen me. This might be awkward. I stepped out from behind Zac and gave her a small wave. Her mouth fell open.

"I knew it."

Zac sighed. "Stop."

"Cuuuuuute," she drawled.

"Cut it out," Zac said.

She stuck out her tongue.

"What are you doing up here?" Zac asked, slipping his hands into his pockets.

"Got a tip about a car down at the waterhole. The tip was anonymous, but I know it was Mrs. Kroger. Grouch. Anyway. It was just Tyler and Amber. But then I heard you laughing. So I thought I would come and see what's going on. Because you know I have to arrest you for being up here."

"Wait, what?" I stared at her.

She walked over to a thick bunch of hanging vines and pulled them back to reveal a sign that warned this area was off-limits.

"It can't be that serious if there are no gates to keep people out," I said in a curious tone.

"Yes, but everyone knows you're not allowed up here. It's dangerous. People fall. People die—"

"People come up here and get drunk and act like idiots," Zac interrupted, sounding bored. "We were just having something to eat."

"Mm-hmm." Raine gave an exaggerated nod. "Sure. Eating."

"It's my birthday," I said to deflect the sibling banter from becoming about Zac and me and what we may or may not have been doing up here.

Raine put her hands on her hips. "What? For real?"

"Yeah. Zac was helping me have a little birthday dinner. Something small because it's not a big deal. I guess we should go, though."

"Happy birthday!" Raine ran forward and pulled me into a tight hug, and I returned it. "All right, well, I won't arrest you, but move on. I'm not the only cop out tonight."

"Yeah, all right. Thanks, Raine." I could tell Zac was trying to keep the sarcasm out of his tone.

"Yep." She backed up toward the path. "I'll see you both tomorrow morning for brunch. And I'll have presents."

Before I could object, she spun and walked off. We stood still, listening to the sound of her feet getting further and further away.

"I sort of feel like a teenager again." I laughed. Zac faced me, standing close.

Again, there was a searching look on his face, paired with apprehension, and as his gaze drifted to my mouth, I realized I wanted to kiss him. Not just for a distraction, but because I was feeling things that were unfamiliar but so demanding. I swallowed, and Zac's eyes quickly met mine again.

"Addie," he started, jaw tense. "You're— are you sure there's no one waiting for you at home?"

My brow furrowed. "What?"

"A man . . ."

"No." I was quick to dispel that thought.

His shoulders released some of the tension he was holding, and he nodded. He was worried I was going to leave and go home to another man. Just like his ex had. That was a reasonable fear considering I did have to go home again soon. I pushed that thought back, refusing to acknowledge what was waiting for me. I did my best to give him a reassuring smile, but I wouldn't close the distance between us tonight. The thought of hurting him when I left made me nauseous.

He ran his finger down my cheek, tracing the outline of my smile and making it near impossible to breathe. And then he leaned in and kissed the spot where his touch had just left a chill. "Happy birthday, Addie."

# CHAPTER THIRTEEN

A week after Zac had taken me on our spontaneous date, we were gathering for Sunday brunch again. I'd looked forward to this meal all week. Not only was the food incredible, but the people were fulfilling as well. Everyone together at the table, happy and sharing stories of their week. Something within me craved this sort of company. Needed it.

Zac and I had been swamped on the farm over the week. Well, him more so than me.

Several acquaintances had brought their cars in at the end of the day, which meant he'd had a lot of late nights. I'd occupied myself with horticultural studies in my spare time and was learning a lot.

I'd planted some Tahoka daisies with little soft, purple petals, which sat among Texas bluebells, a pinky purple flower with a black center.

"Mornin'." Keith stepped out onto the back deck, looking jovial as he pulled out a seat and lowered himself into it. His thin wisps of dark-gray hair were combed over, and as usual, he was wearing a plaid shirt and big navy-blue sweatpants. He sat opposite me on the same side of the table as Willa, Milo, and Raine. The seat beside me was still vacant. I wasn't sure where Zac was.

"Willa, honey," Keith said. "Look at your pretty hair. Who did that?"

Willa smiled and touched her long, black French braids. "Raine did it. We were practicing ideas for the wedding."

"Very clever, my Raine." Keith started dishing eggs onto his plate.

Another job I'd adopted was collecting the eggs from the coop each morning. The chickens were so cute—visiting them was the perfect start to the morning.

"Thanks for breakfast, Milo." I took the bowl of eggs from Keith as he handed them over the table.

Milo stretched his arms above his head and yawned before he slipped his shades onto his face. "You are most welcome. So, how's it all going out here? Missing home?"

I wasn't sure how much Milo knew about my situation. He knew I'd lost Margo and come here on a whim, but other than that, I wasn't sure. The only person I'd shared with, in depth, how much I didn't want to go home was Zac, and he didn't strike me as the sort to share our conversations with anyone else.

"I love it here," I told him truthfully.

Raine peered over at me while she buttered her toast. Her tight coils were up in a bun on top of her head. "What do you love about it?"

I lowered my head and hid a grin. She had been fishing for information since she'd caught me and Zac on the clifftop last weekend. She'd even threatened to withhold the gift she'd gotten me if I didn't tell her. Of course, she gave it to me, too excited to watch me open the little necklace in the shape of a horseshoe. It was gorgeous. It wasn't that I wanted to keep secrets from her or hide whatever this thing with Zac was—but that was just it: I had no idea what it was.

There were feelings when I was with him: it felt breathtaking, the sensation of being swept off my feet, butterflies and giggles. The whole deal. But when I was in bed, alone with my thoughts and the haunted dreams of a dead sister, I felt immense guilt and grief. Life couldn't stop when someone else's did. We had to keep moving, breathing, eating, being. But it felt wrong. I'd never been more conflicted. On one hand,

I wanted to live for her, and on the other hand, I wanted to lie down, sink into the dirt, and cease to be, just as she had.

"I love all of it." I answered Raine's question and forced myself not to look up at Zac when my peripheral vision caught him appearing from the French doors. "There's a lot to do. A lot to keep me occupied. It's nice."

"Yeah." Raine nodded with a teasing grin. "There is a lot to keep someone occupied around here, isn't there?"

I inhaled a deep breath and refused to react to her implied meaning. Zac pulled out the seat beside me and sat down. His freshly showered aroma hit me, and I felt my pulse quicken in response. He smelled sensational. When I finally peeped at him, I noticed his damp hair tousled in a mess, his fitted T-shirt and black cargo pants. He was watching me and winked, causing my entire stomach to turn over itself.

"It's hot." Willa fanned at her face, and Milo immediately sat up so he could pour her an ice water from the pitcher. "Can we go for a swim after brunch?"

Milo slid the glass toward her. "We can't hang around today, bub. Raine has to get her sleep, and I have to finish painting the windowsills at home. I thought you could help me."

Willa pouted, but she didn't argue.

"Zac and Addie can watch her," Keith piped up. "If they're not busy."

"Yeah." I nodded, smiling at Willa, who was beginning to perk up with hope. "I mean, I can't speak for Zac. But I'd be happy to watch her."

"Yeah, no worries," Zac added and slung his arm over the back of my chair. It was so natural and intimate, but I was aware of the attention it received. Four curious gazes felt like bullets pelting me from across the table, but I ignored all of them and instead let my heart flutter.

"Yeah, that's all right," Milo said. Willa jostled with excitement. "You can hang around for a swim. You have a swimsuit here?"

Willa nodded and pushed her seat back, sprinting into the house.

"Hold on, Will, finish brunch first!"

Willa either didn't hear her dad or didn't care because she didn't come back, and we could hear her footsteps thudding upstairs. There was low collective laughter around the table, and Keith pushed his chair back next.

"You all right, Dad?" Zac asked, and Raine joined him in observing their father get up, slow and careful.

"Yeah, of course," Keith said. "Just full. Food was excellent, thanks, Milo. I've got some paperwork to deal with in the office, so I'll head off."

"It's Sunday," Raine said. "Relax, Dad. It can be done tomorrow."

He waved her off and headed inside. Zac and Raine looked at each other.

"I'm worried about him." Raine ran her hands down her face. She seemed exhausted most Sunday mornings after she'd been working all night. She told me that Saturday nights were her busiest. A lot of juvenile arrests for drinking or street racing. And more than the usual bar fights and domestics. But this exhaustion was paired with worry over the well-being of someone she cared about, and that was an entirely different level of tired. "He seems so doddering and fragile at the moment."

Zac pushed his food around with a fork and shrugged, his arm still on the back of my seat. "He's all right. He's gettin' old. Stiff joints. The usual."

He said it like he meant it, but I knew he worried too. I'd seen it more than once over the past couple weeks. He'd watch his dad at the dinner table, or he'd watch him when Keith was sitting in the sunroom, sipping a coffee while admiring the views from the window. Zac always asked his dad if he was all right.

"I'm ready to swim." Willa appeared at the French doors and bounced on the spot. She was in another retro swimsuit. This one was a yellow gingham two-piece with high-waisted bottoms that were more of a boy short shape than a brief and a wide top with a bow on the left strap.

"Let Addie and Zac finish their food, sweetie," Raine said, exhaling as she pushed her empty plate into the middle of the table.

Willa rested her chin on the back of the seat and grinned at us. I giggled when she mouthed, "Hurry up."

"Will," Milo warned.

"Well, I'm done," I said. "How about I go and get into my suit and we'll get in the pool?"

"You're going to swim too?!"

"Yeah." I gave her an enthusiastic nod and stood up so that I could head inside. I was sure the pool would be shallow enough. Zac's fingers grazed my lower back as I stood, and the brief touch was igniting.

"Do you have a proper swimsuit this time?" Willa said, and I tore my attention from Zac to find her tilting her head with the question. "Last time you just had underwear."

"In fact, I do have a proper swimsuit," I laughed as we wandered through the dining area. "I went and got one when I found out there's a pool here. I haven't had a chance to use it, though."

"It's really cool. And big. I love swimming."

"I can tell. You have super cute swimsuits as well."

She followed me upstairs. "Thanks. There's this one that Allie wears in *The Notebook*, when she's at the swimming hole with her friends. I love it, but I couldn't find one the same. I found a few different ones, though. Well, Raine did. She said she really likes my style."

"She's a good stepmomma, huh?"

"The best." Willa grinned when we came to my bedroom. "I'll wait downstairs."

She skipped off again. She wasn't as shy as she had been when we met, and she seemed a lot more comfortable chatting to me now. I quickly changed into the new bikini I'd bought during the week, an olive-green one with a push-up bust and a cheeky pair of bottoms. I slapped on some sunscreen and then headed downstairs. Instead of going back toward the dining room, I slipped through the living area, through the sunroom, and out a different set of French doors that opened onto a narrow deck.

Willa was waiting by the fence at the bottom of the steps. She swung a towel around her wrist and let it unravel again.

"Sorted?" I asked.

She startled and then smiled when she saw me. "Yep."

I could tell where the gate was in the fence, but I had to peep around to figure out how to open it, and then I saw the latch at the top and sighed. Sometimes being short was such an inconvenience.

"Hmm." I rested my hands on my hips and stared up at it, squinting at the sun. "Maybe I'll have to give you a boost?"

"Let me," I heard a deep voice say behind me, and then I felt a firm, bare chest against my back as Zac reached over me and opened the latch with ease.

Willa rushed straight in.

"Don't run, Will," Zac shouted after her. He was wearing a pair of trunks low on his hips. His gaze moved slow and sweeping from my head to my toes. "Addie, we're supposed to be watching Willa."

"Yeah?" I laughed lightly.

"I'm not going to be able to keep my eyes off *you*."

My teeth sank into my bottom lip. He cupped my jaw and used his thumb to tug on my lip. I could feel the tension pulling like a rubber band and knew how easily it would snap and become uncontrolled if we pushed it further.

"After you." He gestured at the gate he was still holding open.

"Thank you." I smiled, wound up.

"No, thank you."

"For?"

"The view," he said from behind me and winked when I looked over my shoulder.

Willa was sitting on the edge of the pool when we came in. She slipped off and into the water as soon as she saw us. The pool was gorgeous. It reminded me of a watering hole. It was edged with stone; at one end of the pool, the stone extended upwards, and a slide was built into a rock feature. There was a waterfall with lights at the bottom. Willa hopped out of the pool again and started climbing steps that were hidden behind the slide.

"This is beautiful."

Zac hummed with agreement from close behind me. We could hear Willa in the slide. Before she emerged, Zac slowly pulled my hair behind my shoulder, his fingertips grazing my neck. The effect it had on me was surreal and something I'd never experienced before. I'd had butterflies. I'd had first moments. But I'd never felt so strongly moved from the mere touch of another person.

Willa whooshed out the bottom of the slide into the pool and then popped up out of the water, inhaling a breath and rubbing her face. My grin dropped when I felt a strong pair of arms hoist me up, and then Zac was jumping, both of us plummeting toward the deep end. In the split second it took me to realize what was happening, I squealed, "I can't swim!"

We plunged in. The water wasn't cold, but it was cool enough that my body got a shock. Zac kept hold of me the entire time, and when we resurfaced, I sucked in a big breath and wiped the water out of my face.

"You can't swim?" Zac shook his hair off his face and blinked, clearing the drops off his lashes. He held me under the knees and around my back. It was then that I realized I'd wrapped my arms around his neck, our wet skin pressed against one another.

"I can sort of swim. Ish. I'm not confident in the deep."

He stared down at me, the water rippling around our chests. "I got you," he murmured, his wet hair in a gorgeous mess. His fingers pressed against my ribs as he kept a tight hold.

"I can stand in the shallow end."

The water droplets on his hard chest glittered in the sun. He swallowed. "I kind of like holding you."

My heart hiccupped, and then a big stream of water hit Zac in the face and he spluttered, both of us looking over at the edge of the pool where Willa was aiming her water gun at us. "Kiss."

My cheeks erupted with heat, and I wiggled in his arms, not caring if we were in the deep. Drowning seemed like a good idea at this point.

"How am I supposed to kiss her when you're firing water at my face?"

Willa's laughter was a squeal as she ran back to the slide, giggling and blushing about her uncle admitting he wanted to kiss me.

Zac waded through the water until we were in the shallow end, and I slid out of his hold until my feet hit the ground. He didn't let me go, though; his hand rested on my hip, my back to his chest. My throat felt tight, my pulse was hitching, and I was so aware of where I could feel him.

Zac's hand slid up my wet torso, gliding across the front of my ribs, his thumb grazing the underside of my breast as he kissed the side of my head. "You want me to teach you how to swim?"

I shuddered at his hands and then Willa flew out of the slide and went under the water. I turned around, putting a step of distance between Zac and me before she surfaced.

"How much of it will be teaching and how much of it will be touching?"

He tilted his head, his eyes making slow work of drinking me in as he smirked. "Guess we'll have to find out."

Willa shot out of the water, and we looked at her, both of us remembering we were here to watch her and not let our simmering tension get the best of us.

We messed around in the pool for a couple of hours. Willa used the slide at least a thousand times. We found a ball and threw passes. Zac pushed Willa around on an inflatable pool bed, and I watched him interact with her, admiring how patient and gentle he was. Zac was true to his word, though, finding it somewhat difficult to stop staring at me. I couldn't begin to process how his attention made me feel, but it came with flutters and smiles, so I decided to enjoy it.

It was the middle of the afternoon when Willa hoisted herself onto the edge of the pool, claiming that she was starving. So we got out and made her something to eat, having lunch while we bathed on the deck. We went down to the orchard and picked some oranges to squeeze juice. We went and saw Noah the donkey and fed him a couple of apples.

Willa and I wandered along the dirt trail together after we'd seen Noah. Zac had run off to check on the horses' water and food, so we'd said that we'd meet him at the house. Willa's hair was still in French braids but was taking a long time to dry, and the tips had left damp patches on her pale-blue T-shirt. She didn't seem to mind. The little girl took me by surprise when she slipped her hand in mine. I said nothing, but the gesture warmed me. It warmed me so much that it was startling. It was an onslaught of sudden emotion, and I felt tears start to well. What in the hell?

"So." I cleared my throat and resisted the urge to hug her and tell her she was my new best friend. All that would do was scare her. "How has it been since school started?"

"Mmm." She shrugged. "Fine. I have a new teacher, though, and I don't know about her."

I giggled at her mature tone. "What's wrong with her?"

"Well, we do our trips to the library, but she only lets us borrow from the children's section. My last teacher let me get whatever I wanted. But my new teacher thinks I'll get something with sex and stuff in it. But I wouldn't because I know I'm not allowed until I'm older."

I wanted to protect this little girl with my whole heart. "Doesn't sound fair. Have you told your dad?"

She watched the ground as we walked. "Nah. I think he'd just tell me, *That's life, Will.*"

"You never know, he might talk to the new teacher and explain the situation. Wouldn't that be good?"

"Yeah. It would be."

"You'll never know unless you ask."

She nodded. "I used to use the adoption card when this sort of thing happened. I don't know why, but it worked when I wanted something and I wasn't getting it. But then Dad told me I wasn't allowed to do that. It was extortion, he said."

"Adoption card?"

"Yeah. I'm adopted."

I sucked in a sharp breath and had to remind myself to keep walking. "Wow. I didn't know."

She shrugged. "It's not a big deal. My dad is my dad. Grandpa Keith always tells me that choosing family is a much more powerful love and connection than acknowledging someone just because their blood is tied to mine."

I smiled, but I couldn't shake the tingle at the back of my neck. "That's true," I said with a thick throat. "It's about who shows up and puts in the effort. You were chosen. I think that's beautiful."

"Me too." She grinned.

"So, you've never met your birth parents?"

"No." Her voice sounded a hint more solemn.

I felt nauseous. We wandered through the garden gate, and I stopped at the garden beds for a moment, admiring the flowers and wondering how to casually ask when Willa's birthday was.

"These are so pretty." She knelt beside me, running the tip of her finger across a bright pink petal.

"Aren't they? Maybe we could plant a flower for you? Perhaps the color of your birthstone."

"Oh. I don't know what that color is."

"Well, when's your birthday?"

"May sixth."

My vision blurred, and my heart beat so hard that I couldn't breathe. "Emerald." I had to put my hands in the grass beneath me so that I didn't lose sense of my surroundings. "Your color is emerald."

# CHAPTER FOURTEEN

*One year ago*

Margo and I had a small slab of concrete for our "back garden." We were on the second floor, so it was a balcony with a steel railing surrounding it; there was enough space for a sun chair and a little table. There was also a decent-ish view of the street below. Not that it was all that interesting. Just cars and more condos across the road.

School was out for the summer, so not only were the local teenagers out and about, roaming the streets, but also tourists in strong waves. There was a constant hum of chatter below me and feet scuffing the sidewalk. It didn't bother me enough to flee from the sun, but it was mildly disturbing while I tried to lose myself in the world of Violet and Finch. I was invested in both of their happiness. I needed it more than my own.

A low, hoarse voice that I recognized as Margo's when she sang Miley Cyrus came from the living room, and I laughed at her rendition of "Wrecking Ball." She'd been at a sweet sixteen that she'd organized, and the theme had been Malibu.

She wailed the chorus as I peered over my shoulder to see her flailing her arms and legs around in some sort of possessed impressionist dance as she came toward the balcony. ". . . so hard in loooooove. All I wanted—"

A voice came from the street below. "Shut up. You suck."

Margo stood at the railing and peered down to the street below, where a group of girls laughed as they walked past.

"Kids have a lot of nerve these days." She frowned and sat on the end of my lounge chair.

"Forget them. You sounded beautiful."

"Don't lie to me."

I raised my book to hide the guilty grin that I wore. No, she couldn't sing well at all, but she had a good time doing it, so I dealt.

"*All the Bright Places* by Jennifer Niven," she said, reading the cover that I was still hiding behind. "Sounds cute and uplifting. But it also sounds like it can wait. We should go and get a picnic and head to the beach."

"Why?"

"Because it'll be fun."

She and I had different ideas of fun. The thought of sand getting all over me and our food was enough to make me frown with resistance. But I knew Margo would be itching to get out of the house on her first free Saturday this summer.

The sweet sixteen had run from ten this morning and was meant to end officially at three. But during one of our meetings with the client, I'd overheard the birthday girl on the phone, making plans for after dark while her mother was out of the room. I'd kept quiet about it.

"Yeah, all right." I tried not to sigh with boredom and stood up.

"Get a swimsuit!" Margo called over her shoulder as she ran inside ahead of me.

• • •

We laid our towels out in a semi-secluded spot. Not that there was a whole lot of that at the moment. Santa Monica beach was packed to the brim, which was to be expected at this time of the year. Margo wore a wide-brimmed hat and a one-piece that had cutouts on the sides. She looked like a swimsuit model with her slim figure and enormous sunglasses. She was just a bit too short to fit the role.

I was on my stomach, book open in front of me. The breeze kept catching the pages, so I had to rest both hands on either side of it. All of a sudden, I felt the string of my bikini being pulled, and I gasped, peering at Margo as she settled on her stomach beside me.

"Dude?" I questioned.

"You don't want tan lines."

"I don't want my boobies falling out either."

She giggled. "Relax. I'll do it up when it's time to swim. Not that you'll get in the water."

I sighed but didn't move. I couldn't move. Wretch.

"So, next week." Margo watched a group of fit men walking past. "Changed your mind yet?"

She was referring to our first appointment with the IVF clinic. It'd been about six months since she'd agreed to let me be the surrogate for her child. But it had taken us a few weeks to find a reputable doctor. Margo said if she was doing this, she was doing it with the best. And the best was booked out for months. So it'd been a long wait, but I was sure it would be worth it.

"Of course I haven't changed my mind," I said.

I couldn't see the top half of her face behind the glasses, but I could sense her relief. She might have insisted that I shouldn't be the one to carry her baby, but I knew she was excited now that she'd made the appointment and the plan was coming together.

"Carrie told me I was being selfish," Margo said, resting her head on her arms.

"Selfish? What for?"

"For surrogacy. For not adopting a baby instead. She told me that I could help an existing life instead of creating a new one. Especially since I obviously was not intended to have kids."

"She's a bitch," I snapped. Carrie was Margo's personal trainer and self-appointed advice guru.

"You know she's just honest."

Too honest in most cases. She never gave her speeches with vehemence or judgment but with a "compassionate" and "concerned" tone, yet she still managed to hit right where it hurt.

The sun whipped my hair in front of my face, and I got flustered, holding my bikini while I flicked it back. "Don't even listen to her."

"She said that women like me were specifically put on earth to save the babies that needed a loving home. It's all about balance and opportunities for all. She thinks the fact that surrogacy even exists is disgusting."

"That's ridiculous." I was almost shouting now, and I wanted to sit up. I felt like I needed to get in her face and slap those thoughts out of her head. "It's called personal choice, and we're all entitled to it. The fact that some women can't have babies is just an awful genetic curse. Is she a weird cult fanatic or something? I've never heard something so stupid."

Margo's mouth lifted into a soft smile. "I get where she's coming from, though. Don't you? I'd have thought you of all people would appreciate the option of adopting."

My throat went thick. "I appreciate adoption, surrogacy, IVF, foster care, whatever other options there are. Like I said, it's a personal preference. We shouldn't give people a hard time for choosing how to have a family."

She didn't say anything for a while. "Do you think about her a lot?"

"Margo."

"Do you?"

"Of course I do. I gave birth to a human being and then never saw her again. I have a child. *A child*, Margo. And I don't know a damn thing about her. Of course I think about her. Every single day."

"We could look for her."

I shook my head and felt restless. "Tie my bikini up."

"Nope," she refused, and I had the urge to hit her again. "I mean it, Addie. We could look for her."

"I can't. Legally, I can't, and you know that. But the agency said she went to a good family, and that's the main thing."

Margo rolled onto her back and pulled her hat further down, shielding her face from the sun. With some careful maneuvering and keeping my bikini top in place, so did I. The clouds were pushed by the soft breeze, white pillows floating across the blue blanket above us. Watching such weightlessness made me seethe with envy. What I'd give to feel that light.

"I saw you after you let her go, Addie," Margo said, so quietly that I could hardly hear her against the crashing waves and my pounding heart. "You—you weren't okay. And that's an understatement. I don't want to put you through that again."

"It's different. It won't be my baby. I'm going into it knowing that I'll be giving the baby to you at the end. It's your DNA. It's not the same at all."

"You think people don't struggle handing the baby over, even if it isn't theirs? Even if they're prepared? It still takes a huge emotional toll on some women."

My hand sifted through the sand between us until I found hers. "I want to do this. For you. You deserve this after everything you've done for me. I want nothing more than to see you hold your own baby in your arms. It'll make me happy. Not upset."

I heard her sniff quietly. "I should have pushed harder to keep Baby Bianchi."

"I think who I am now, I could have handled watching you raise my baby," I said thoughtfully. "But not back then. I needed a clean break. I couldn't have had one foot in, one foot out. It would have been too hard. But I always felt awful for taking that chance from you. Especially after you found out that you can't carry to term."

"Don't think like that," she said, squeezing my hand. "I understood why you didn't want me to adopt her."

We lay there for a while, hands intertwined while we let the last of the setting sun warm our skin. Evening was upon us, and I could smell the aroma of restaurants on the pier The Ferris wheel was turning, and the jingle of rides echoed on the water.

I meant what I'd said to Margo. It wouldn't hurt this time because Margo deserved to have the one thing that she wanted more than anything else.

Giving up my baby had left a hole in my chest that had never healed. Whenever I thought about her, it was like rubbing salt into the wound. It was a brand-new kick in the stomach that winded me. I'd always feel like a part of me was missing.

The only relief was knowing that she was with a family who chose her. Who wanted to give her the love she deserved. Love I didn't think I'd had when I was fifteen.

It didn't matter that I had it now. It was too late. And I would never replace her. I'd had my chance. I'd let it go, and I wouldn't try and fill that space with another baby. Not ever.

# CHAPTER FIFTEEN

"Addie?"

"Addie?"

"Ads?"

I blinked and peered up at Zac, who was standing beside the arm-chair I was curled up in. Willa and I had come into the sunroom to read for a little while. I looked over at the sofa, worried that I'd zoned out for too long and she'd wandered off somewhere, but she was asleep, her book open on the floor beside her.

"Oh." I closed my own book and whispered, "That's so sweet. She must be exhausted."

"She's had a long afternoon. You looked like you were asleep with your eyes open. You wanna head upstairs and have a nap?"

I did feel tired, but that wasn't the reason I was having trouble remaining in the present. "No, no. I'm fine. Just daydreaming."

He held out his hand, and I only hesitated for a moment before I took it and let him pull me up out of the seat. I hadn't even noticed that Keith was on the other side of the room with a tall glass of beer. As usual, he was staring out the window.

"You all right, pops?" Zac whisper shouted.

He waved over his shoulder. "I'll keep an eye on her."

Zac wore a soft smile even though his dad wasn't looking at us, and he kept his fingers laced with mine as we climbed the stairs. We passed my bedroom and carried on down the hall until we reached his. His room was simple: cream walls with framed photos of his parents and canvases with old cars printed on them. The sun was low enough outside that it wasn't sweltering through the window.

He climbed onto the bed in the middle of the room and pulled me down with him, shuffling us both until my head was on his chest and his arm was wound around my shoulder.

"What are we doing?" I asked.

"Just relaxin'. That all right?"

"Yes. I suppose."

"I can feel the tension in your shoulders."

What I'd learned this afternoon did have me wound up so much that my jaw hurt from clenching it so hard. There was a chance I was wrong. Perhaps Willa wasn't the baby girl I'd given up for adoption when I was fourteen. America was huge. There were probably a lot of little girls given up for adoption on May 6, 2013.

Still, I had a feeling. Call it a maternal feeling. It was her.

Not to mention the similarities. When I'd first arrived, I'd thought she reminded me of Margo. But perhaps it was a subconscious deflection, not wanting to admit that she had the same nose, skin tone, and hair as me. But there were smaller things too. Her passion for reading, which admittedly wasn't a rare trait to have, it just happened to work in this argument. She also did this thing when she was off in thought— her tongue would tap the top of her lip. Margo used to tell me if I kept doing that, I'd get chapped lips.

"You wanna talk about it?" Zac offered, his breath warm on the top of my head. His hand rubbed up and down my arm, and as wound up as I was, he provided a sense of comfort.

But I couldn't talk about it. How was I meant to bring something like that up? How was I meant to confess that there was a good chance I'd given birth to Willa and by pure coincidence I'd ended up back in her life?

I shook my head and snuggled in closer to him. "Just the usual."

"You think about her a lot, huh?" he murmured. "I notice you zone out quite a bit."

He wasn't wrong—even if it was different this time, I was thinking about Margo all the time. I nodded and let him think that was the current problem.

"You ever thought about keeping a journal?"

I blinked, surprised at what he said. "What?"

"A journal. Write down all the thoughts and the feelings. Write down the pain. A therapist I saw after Mom died told me it was a good way to let some of it go. An outlet. I think the reason they pushed the journal so hard was because I was a teenager and a lot of teenagers use—"

"Alcohol." I nodded, and he kissed the top of my head; it made my stomach tighten. "Yeah. I'm not a big drinker. There's no chance of that happening."

"I didn't think there was." I could hear the smile in his voice. "Could still help. I know it helped me."

A flicker of hope ignited in my chest. "Really?"

"How about I show you?"

I leaned up with a palm on his chest and saw the genuine need to help in his soft gaze. Soft but so strong.

"You want to show me your grief journal?"

His brows raised. "I never called it that. But it works. Yeah, it's not a secret. Well, I wouldn't give it to the general public, but I think I can trust you."

"You can." He got off the bed and headed over to his closet. I was thankful for the distraction, to be honest. Not that I would treat this as a simple distraction—he was sharing a huge part of his past with me. But it was nice to have a shift in thoughts.

He sat back down with a worn leather notebook. He leaned against the headboard, raised his knee, and rested an elbow on it while he held the book and flicked through the pages. I folded my legs beside him and waited.

"All right." He clicked his tongue, his eyes roaming over the words. "Uh, here we go." He cleared his throat, loudly and dramatically. He grinned when I laughed. "Shit, my handwriting was awful. I'll read it out."

Something about his confidence and ability to share made him so much more attractive than he already was.

"I didn't date these, but it doesn't matter, I suppose. And don't laugh, I titled all of them *Dear journal*."

I bit down on a grin, raised my pinkie, and swiped the side of my nose. "I would never laugh."

His lids became heavier as his gaze swept my face, lingering on my mouth. The moment was brief, and then he inhaled, looked down at the journal, and cleared his throat.

"Dear journal," he said. "This is stupid. Jennifer said that I should write all of my sad, angry, and happy feelings down, but I never feel happy and who really wants to talk about being angry and sad? I'm always angry and sad. It's just whatever at this point. I guess that's the good thing about this weird journal thing. I can say it like it is because no one is looking at me like they feel bad. People do that enough already, and it pisses me off. Thanks for reminding me that my mom is dead with one damn sad smile. Today Raine wanted me to go horse riding, but I hate them. I hate them. They killed my mom. She loved them, and they killed her. She's dumb for trusting them. She's dumb for loving them. She should have chosen us, and now she's dead."

Zac looked up at me, and I snapped my mouth shut.

"Yep. I was mad. Mad about all of it."

"I get that."

"That was an earlier entry. I'll read the last one that I wrote."

I rested my hand on his knee, and his gaze flickered toward it for a moment, a small smile lifting his lips before he returned his attention to the journal and flicked toward the back.

"Dear journal. I rode. I got on Maisy and I rode her until I arrived at Mom's burial plot. She'd have been proud of me. She'd have told me that forgiveness washes away the bitter taste of resentment. She'd have been right. I'm not upset with her. She lived her life for others, animals and humans alike. She impacted lives. She gave her entire heart to the rehabilitation and training of horses. She died, but she didn't leave. She lives on in this farm, in these animals, in her cause. I'll keep on loving them for her, and I'll give them an extra carrot from Mom to remind them that she's looking out. For all of us."

I wiped at the tears that had gathered in the corners of my eyes and tried to smile when he closed the journal.

"I want to get there so bad," I sobbed and felt humiliated at what a mess I'd become. Not that he was ever bothered. He gripped my wrist and pulled me to him so that I was straddling his lap.

He held my face. "You will. There were hundreds of pages between those two; it took time. You'll get there."

"But I'm not even angry with Margo. I'm just—I'm upset, and I'm angry at me or disappointed that she died before she got everything she wanted, and I—"

"Shh." Zac pulled me in and kissed my forehead, his lips lingering for a beat. He had no idea what I was talking about. He knew some of it, but he didn't know all of Margo's lifelong dreams or what stole them from her. He kissed me again and then looked at me. "Write it down. Write it all down. Just—let it out. I can't promise it'll solve it all. But it might help. It helped me."

I sniffed and nodded.

"I'm always here, though, if you nee—"

The door swung open, and Raine stood at the threshold in a T-shirt and a pair of denim shorts. She winced but didn't retreat. I slid off Zac's lap, even though I could feel his grip and knew he didn't want me to move.

"Neither of you better deny this budding romance again. Caught red-handed."

Zac sighed and palmed his jaw.

"Anyway, is this what y'all call babysitting? Leaving Willa alone while you canoodle?"

"Canoodle? You sound like Gran," Zac teased, and we both stood from the bed. "Willa was asleep, and Dad was watching her. We came up here for a nap."

"Mm-hmm. Whole lot of sleeping going on around here."

Zac gave her a gentle shove in the shoulder, and she punched him. Raine went downstairs, and we joined her in the kitchen a moment later. She started scrounging through the fridge.

"Is Willa still asleep?" Zac asked, leaning around his sister so he could get a beer out of the fridge. He gestured at me in question. "Want one?"

"I'm all right, thanks."

"Yep, Will is asleep. I'm going to snatch your girl for an hour so we can sit on the deck with wine and gossip."

Zac used an opener and flung the cap off the bottle as he sauntered toward me with total confidence. He rested his hand on my waist and gave me a kiss on the cheek. "Have a good afternoon."

"Watch Willa," Raine shouted after him. I was busy fighting the heat that was taking over my entire face when Raine spun around, grabbed a bottle of wine from the rack along with a couple of glasses, and ordered that I follow her outside.

We sat on the sofa, and she set down her goods on the glass coffee table in front of us. All that was left of the sun was a dusting of dark orange atop the green hills on the horizon. Beautiful. Like a painting. But now that I was out here, alone with Raine, my thoughts shot back to this afternoon's conversation with Willa, and it put a ball of nervous tension in the pit of my stomach. I couldn't have downed the wine that she slid in front of me even if I'd wanted to.

"Sleep well?" I asked Raine before she could ask me about her brother. I could tell she was gearing up to tease me.

"Oh, mm-hmm. Yeah, I slept fine. How was your afternoon with Willa? Did she behave?"

"Would she ever not behave?"

Raine grinned and pulled her legs up under her bum. "She's a good kid."

"She told me sh—"

I paused. I knew I could trust Raine. If I was going to tell anyone about this, she'd be the best person to tell. But Willa's words continued to echo loud and clear. *Choosing family is a much more powerful love and connection than acknowledging someone just because their blood is tied to mine.*

Her blood was tied to mine, but I hadn't chosen her. Not in the sense that might matter to a little girl. I'd given her up because I'd believed that was what was best for her. I wasn't able to raise a child at that stage of my life. But what if none of them saw it like that? There was a good chance that if the truth came out, that would be the end—I would be asked to leave.

But I had to know for sure.

"She told me she's adopted," I finished, throat thick. Raine recoiled with a wide stare.

"She did? Huh, she must trust you."

That made me feel ten times worse.

"She's not secretive about it, but she doesn't come right out and tell people. Well, not like she used to when she was using it to her advantage." Raine rolled her eyes as she sipped the wine. "But now she prefers not to mention it. Most people don't even look twice at us as a family. Between Milo and me, she looks like a mix of us. Lighter than me but darker than her dad. It's cute."

I could tell that Raine loved the family she'd made for herself. Would she feel threatened if she knew the truth?

"Do you know much about her adoption?"

Raine slowly sipped again, and I wondered if she was hoping to nurse that drink so it lasted all night. "Not even Milo and his wife knew a lot. They chose to adopt because she couldn't get pregnant. So they went through an agency that ended up finding someone in California. The details on the woman were scarce, but they knew she was young and couldn't raise her. I don't think Milo ever met her. It was all closed and done rather fast. Willa still had goo on her when they handed her over to Milo and Siena."

"Was she born in Santa Monica?"

Raine paused with the glass in front of her mouth. She stared. I stared back. She didn't need to verbally confirm it; her expression said it all. But she answered anyway.

"Yes."

I nodded and felt tears welling. I couldn't see. All this time I'd been spending with her, I'd been getting to know my . . . well I didn't want to use the term *daughter*. She wasn't mine to claim. But the girl I'd given birth to. A piece of me. I'd agreed to a closed adoption, which meant I wasn't allowed to look for them and vice versa. But here I was. It looked bad. It looked like I'd shown up here on purpose.

"I was in Santa Monica with Margo—she had to travel for work—when I went into labor."

Raine scrambled up out of her seat and fell into the one beside me. Her cheeks were quivering, and her brows were pinched. "She's yours?"

"Only biologically."

She stared at the ground, gaze wide. "How do you know? Are you sure?"

"It all adds up. I didn't know until a few hours ago, though, I swear."

"Hell, you must have been, what, fourteen?"

I nodded, wiping my face with my palm, not that it helped as a fresh stream of tears poured down my cheeks.

"This is unbelievable," Raine murmured. "It has to be fate. It has to be."

I whipped my head toward her and stared with disbelief. How did she seem excited about this? "I don't think Milo is going to see it as fate. I signed an agreement. A legal one. To surrender all rights and never make contact in regards to Willa. He's going to be pissed. And Willa? She might want nothing to do with me. And fair enough too."

"No, no." Raine shifted beside me and came even closer if that were possible. She swiped at her damp cheeks. "You don't understand. Willa wanted to find her birth parents a while ago. She insisted that she at least get a name or a photo. All we managed to find was a name. Addison Bianchi. But as far as our searches went, that person stopped existing around the time that Will was born. After that, there were no records of phone numbers, licences, rentals, nothing in that name."

"You're cops. Seriously?"

She laughed through a sob. "We didn't use all of our resources. It would've been a breach of confidence according to the signed agreement. As it was, sourcing a name was more than we should've done."

"Bianchi was my birth name. Legally. I changed my name later. After the adoption. It was Margo's idea that we change our last name to May. The month Willa was born. A subtle way of honoring her."

She nodded, and we fell into a quiet lull. The only sound was the swish of tree leaves in the soft breeze. The jangle of dog collars as the border collies ran around the garden together. The far-off whinnies of the horses in the paddocks. These sounds were becoming soothing and familiar the longer I was here. But perhaps moving on was closer than I thought.

"I should've put it together when I heard the name Addison. But your last name was May. So I didn't think twice. Still, I can see the resemblance. I don't know how none of us acknowledged it sooner."

I shrugged. There were similarities, but she might have taken more after her birth father. Not that I could remember what he looked like.

"What do you want to do?" Raine asked, breaking the quiet.

"What do I want to do?" I echoed.

She nodded.

"It doesn't matter what I want. It's up to Milo and Willa. And you. You're the mother figure in her life now."

"Okay, but forget about all of the complications. What do *you* want? If anything were possible. Would you want to get to know her? Be in her life?"

"It's not that simple."

She sighed. "Just answer the question."

Tears pricked at my eyes again. "Yeah. I'd want to be in her life. As a friend. I don't want anyone to think that I'm trying to swoop in and take her, though."

"I don't think that'll be what anyone thinks."

I looked at Raine and saw the face of kindness staring back at me. "You really don't think that I came here with ulterior motives?"

"Of course not." She put her arm around my shoulder and sniffed. "I know what happened with your sister is true. The story checked out. I just . . . I don't believe you'd be selfish enough to do something like that. I can't explain it. I just think this was meant to happen. You were meant to be here."

She had no idea what that meant to me. "What should I do now?" I whispered.

"If you'd prefer, I can talk to Milo. Explain it. Gauge his reaction before he sees you again."

"That might be best."

"You should tell Zac, though."

I winced.

"Whatever is happening between you two, that's something the other person should know about."

There might have been a lot that Zac should know about. That didn't make it easy to confess.

"He's pretty understanding. Most of the time."

Even if she told me that he'd handle it with total understanding and could assure me that he would be supportive and caring, I still wouldn't feel better about having to tell him this truth when I was still hiding and denying another truth.

• • •

Zac was watching a movie in the living room when I found him. He was with Willa, and I could tell his focus was elsewhere. She was watching something in black and white. I might have sat down and asked her to tell me what it was about if I hadn't been so distracted with nerves of telling Zac the truth.

Still, my gaze lingered on the sweet little girl. Beautiful. My heart seemed to hammer whenever I looked at her now. Disbelief that I'd ended up here. Sadness that I hadn't been strong enough to keep her. Grateful that she'd been placed in such a loving family. That was what trumped all else. I couldn't be more relieved to finally know for certain that she was safe. I'd been wondering ever since I'd let her go.

"You all right?"

Zac's voice startled me, and I looked at him, sitting relaxed and casual with his arm across the back of the sofa. I nodded.

"Can we talk for a minute?"

He must have heard the tremble in my voice because his brows pinched and he stood up fast. "Of course. Will, I'll be outside. Keep watching the movie."

"Yep."

I followed Zac outside. We passed Raine as she was heading in, and I saw a glimpse of her supportive smile. I thought Zac would stop on the deck. But he didn't. We kept walking until we came to his shed, and he pushed the door open before moving to the hood of a car and leaning on it. He pulled me between his spread legs and held me at the waist.

"What's going on?"

"I just—I need to tell you something. About me. It's part of—part of who I am. My past."

He nodded and gave me his full attention. My hands rested on his chest, and I could feel his heart beat underneath my palm. "I'm listening."

I took a deep breath, and then I started. Right from the beginning.

# CHAPTER SIXTEEN

## August 2012

Another text blipped on my phone, and I knew who it would be before I read the name across the top. Margo.

> Come home to celebrate the end of summer, Addie. We're having a good time. I'll even let you have a glass of champagne.

Margo thought I was at a sleepover with Kelsey. Which wasn't a total lie. We were together. But we were at her big brother's party with a bunch of seniors from the high school. A lot of them were looking at us with sideways glances and judgment. We'd dressed up, but it was obvious that we were too young to be there.

Even in my wedge heels and halter dress that sat at my thighs.

It wasn't that I was mad at Margo and didn't want to spend time with her while she tried to step into the role of being a parent; I just didn't want to be at home. I hated it at home right now. Reminders of Mom and Dad were all over the house. Their scent still lingered, and their footsteps still echoed in the halls. I couldn't stand it. I couldn't be there.

Margo had promised me that we'd move soon. In the meantime, I avoided those walls as often as possible.

Kelsey fell into the old sunken couch beside me. I could feel the springs, and it smelled like stale alcohol. She handed me a bottle of vodka and threw her platinum-blond hair behind her shoulder. Kelsey and I hadn't run in the same circles until recently. She hung out with older kids; she had big boobs and an overall womanly figure, and due to that fact alone, she appeared more mature than a lot of the other girls in our grade.

She'd always been known for rolling with an older crowd, drinking, smoking, and having sex. Things I'd had no interest in until she'd invited me to a movie one day. It was out of the blue, but I didn't decline because I was in need of a distraction. We sat in the back of her brother's car before the movie, and she lit up a joint.

I'd never done drugs before, and I'd been told never to touch them. But she and her brother watched me expectantly, and so I took it and ended up as high as a kite. It'd been a good time, though. Kelsey must have deemed me worth her time because she carried on inviting me to parties and sleepovers. Her methods of fun were everything I knew I wasn't supposed to do, but they worked so well. I forgot about real life when I was with her.

"You remember how I was telling you that my brother's ex-girlfriend is pregnant?" Kelsey said from beside me. I nodded. "She's here with her friends. She isn't drinking or anything, but imagine coming to something like this when you're pregnant. Trashy."

"Yeah. Like, go home. That's so weird. How old is she again?"

"Si—oh, hey!" She waved at a couple of girls from school that were passing. They gave her a smile of acknowledgment but didn't stop. Older girls. Probably didn't want to be seen with us. "Sixteen," she finished and guzzled her drink.

"It's not your brother's, though, right?"

Kelsey shook her head, her hoop earrings swinging with her unstable movement. "Nope. Kane isn't that stupid, and they split ages ago. But I'm pretty sure she's still into him. I saw them while I was getting our drinks. He literally mouthed 'help' at me."

"Ew, how desperate." I gagged, and we both giggled.

"Right. I would fucking die if I got pregnant at that age. Like, nope. Get that thing out of me. Fuck, I don't know if I ever want kids."

I agreed with her that it wouldn't be an ideal situation, but I had to admit that I'd never thought of myself as someone who would get an abortion. Not that it was worth thinking about unless I was enlisted to be the next Virgin Mary.

"I want a cigarette—come outside with me?" She opened her palm, and I laced our fingers. We wove through the crowded living area. It was dark and loud, but we made it to the back doorstep and pushed through people gathered on the concrete steps until we landed on the large deck that extended over a pool.

Lights at the bottom illuminated the water. People were swimming; girls were shrieking when they were pushed in. I held on tight to Kelsey and hoped that no one would find it entertaining to hurl us into the water. She placed herself on the edge of a circle that was gathered, cigarette smoke billowing into the air, and started asking around for a lighter. She had her own pack, one that Kane had gotten for her.

Although it was obvious that we weren't welcome, no one was outright rude to Kelsey or me because they knew her brother was the basketball captain, and that held rank at these parties. The popular kids were untouchable, and so, by association, we were untouchable too. Otherwise, we'd have been sent packing a long time ago.

Kelsey handed me a cigarette and the borrowed lighter, and we stood there, bopping along to "Womanizer" by Britney Spears. Kelsey was deep in conversation with some girl from the cheer squad who didn't want anything to do with us until Kelsey started asking her all about cheerleading. The girl was more than thrilled to talk about her passion without a breath in between. I was about halfway through my cigarette when someone bumped into me.

"Oh, my bad."

I turned and came face-to-face with a superhot guy. He was lean, sort of tall. He had a big T-shirt on and loose track pants. His hair was dark, but his skin was pale, and he had a lip piercing that he put between his teeth as he looked me over. He couldn't have been older than sixteen, but I was still surprised he was showing any interest in me.

"Can I have a drag?" He gestured at the half cigarette in my hand, and I looked down at it, brain going slow. I snapped out of it and nodded, handing it over. "Thanks."

He watched me as he wrapped his lips around the stick and inhaled. My stomach twisted into a knot of tension when he leaned in close, and then he came closer and closer until his lips were on mine, and he blew the cigarette smoke into my mouth. My eyes widened, and I coughed, cheeks emblazoned red at how stupid I must have looked.

He didn't seem to care, though. He chuckled and leaned back again, slipping his free hand into his pocket. I looked over at Kelsey, who was staring at me with her jaw clenched and her grin full of intent. She fanned at her face and gave me a thumbs-up.

"You want this back?" He held his hand out, and I shook my head. "You can finish it."

He winked, and it made my stomach go stupid. I'd almost forgotten that we were surrounded by an entire party full of people when his gaze singled out me and me alone.

"You go to St. James?" he asked.

I nodded and wondered if I should clarify that I was a freshman. "I'm a freshman there."

He nodded as if the news were uninteresting to him. Finally, someone who didn't care if I was younger than the rest of the students.

"How about you?" I tucked my hair behind my ear. It was smooth and straight tonight, different than its usual wave. Kelsey had said it made me look older.

"I'm in town visiting a friend." He finished the cigarette and flicked the butt into the pool. I winced—gross. But I looked up with a startle when he stepped forward and closed the space between us.

"You're hot as fuck."

I swallowed. He was so blunt, and we'd been standing here for five minutes at the most. I guessed I couldn't blame him. He was hot too, and he must have known it.

"You're really hot too," I said. His gaze moved down to my mouth. My face heated up. That was such a lame attempt at flirting. But it must have worked because he lowered his head and kissed me. I'd only kissed one other boy before. But it never involved tongue. So when his slipped inside my mouth, I wasn't sure what to do. I tried to mimic his movements, rolling my tongue against his. His hands went into my hair, and he held it tight.

How did people not overthink this sort of thing? It felt so weird. I mean, I liked it. But I was so worried that I was doing something wrong. Especially when he broke away and leaned back.

"Mmm. Your lips are so fucking big and soft."

"Thanks." I touched the tip of my fingers to my bottom lip and lowered my head. No one had ever told me that before.

We made out for a little longer. For a while, I think. I lost track of time. But eventually we found ourselves against the house, tucked away in our own world. We hadn't gone far from our original spot, but when I looked around, I couldn't see Kelsey anymore. I hoped she wasn't mad that I'd become distracted. I pulled out my phone while the tall, gorgeous stranger checked his own phone. I didn't even know his name. I'd have to ask him once I was done with this message.

Lost you. Sorry. I'll ditch this guy. We should get something to eat maybe?

She replied a moment later.

Don't even stress girl. Get it! He's sooo hot and he seems into you, don't blow it. I'm inside with Kane and his buddies. Kitchen if you need me.

"Hey, I need to charge my phone," the guy said, interrupting me before I could respond to Kelsey. "Want to come help me find a charger? It's an iPhone. There'll be one in the house somewhere."

"Oh. Sure." I nodded and let him lace our fingers together.

I followed him through the crowded house. The living room coffee table was broken now. There were shattered bottles in the hall and guys passed out on the floor. The later it got, the more the antics turned up. I worried about Kelsey for a moment until I remembered that she was with her brother.

We wandered upstairs and opened three bedroom doors, finding all the rooms occupied until we came to the fourth. This house was huge, likely gorgeous when it wasn't trashed by teenagers. I didn't even know who it belonged to, but that didn't stop this guy from closing the door behind us and heading straight over to the double bed under a large window.

He searched on either side for a charger and rummaged through the side table drawers while I stood at the foot of the bed and looked around. There were posters of half-naked girls on the wall, lacrosse gear on the floor, and study books on the desk. Whoever lived here was on the team.

"Found one."

It was dark in the room, but I could see his silhouette leaning on the bed as he plugged it in. When he was done, he stood up and sauntered toward me. My heart started hammering again as his arms stretched out and gripped my waist, pulling me into him.

"Your body is so hot," he mumbled and then smashed his lips against mine. There was something different about this kiss. It was more frantic. Faster. Stronger. He spun us around, lips not leaving mine, and pushed me down onto the bed.

We kissed like that for a while, clutching at each other, breathing heavily. It was nice, I suppose. It felt good.

His hand slipped up under my skirt, and I felt like I was going to pass out when he started shifting my underwear to the side. This was new. So new.

I wasn't sure I was ready for it. I was also . . . nervous. He didn't even seem awkward when he started playing with my genitals. His fingers pressed over it, rubbing. It felt good, but my face was so hot. It was awkward.

And then he slipped his fingers inside me and started going in and out, faster and faster. I swallowed and breathed through it.

It wasn't awful, but I couldn't shake the feeling of humiliation. Especially when I moaned. I didn't even know his name.

His lips left mine and he sat up, spreading my legs and kneeling between them. "Fuck, you're so wet."

Kelsey had used that phrase about guys before. Honestly, half of it was gibberish to me, but I knew enough to know that it meant I was in the mood. Except I was half frozen with nerves. I didn't want this. My heart was pounding so hard it hurt when he started pulling my underwear down.

I wanted to tell him to stop or ask what he was planning to do or anything that would start a conversation and we could slow down. But I couldn't find my voice.

What if he got mad? What if he called me a tease?

I'd heard Kane use that word a lot when he talked about girls. *Yeah, she sent me all of these pictures and told me she was going to suck me off and didn't even fucking show up. Fucking tease.*

What if he thought I wasn't attracted to him or thought he was the problem? I didn't want him to think that. I wasn't cruel. I wondered what to say that wouldn't make me the problem.

"I've never done this before," I stammered as I watched him pull himself out of his own pants. I'd never seen a penis in person before, and I couldn't even look at it. "I don't know what I'm doing."

Maybe he'd think I was a waste of time if I didn't know what I was doing.

"You don't kiss like you've never done this before." His voice was low and full of intent.

"Oh, uh, thanks. Yeah, but I haven't. This is—I haven't done anything before."

"Don't worry, baby." He fell over me again and started pulling my dress up over my hips. "I'll guide you through it. Fuck, you're hot. So hot. I want you so bad."

He started kissing me again, and I felt flesh against my vulva. I didn't think my heart could beat any harder. It was nice to be wanted, but I didn't want this. I wasn't ready. I didn't even know his name. This wasn't special.

But I didn't want to make him feel rejected or hurt. It wasn't his fault that I wasn't ready. I didn't want to upset him by telling him to stop. He might think I didn't like him.

He leaned up on his hands and started pushing further in. I opened my mouth. I had to tell him something. Make something up.

"I'm—I jus—" My words were halted when he thrust, hard. It was a painful, stinging, searing sensation. I cried out and felt tears welling.

"It's okay, it'll get more comfortable," he said, giving me a quick kiss before he inched back and hovered over me, sliding in and out. It felt like I was tearing from the inside out. He sped up.

"Oh fuck. You're so tight. Fuck it feels good. You're so good."

It was too late now. It was done. So I lay there and felt relieved when the pain started to ease a little bit. Just enough for it to be bearable.

• • •

"I couldn't remember a lot the next day," I told Zac, who had been breathing hard and fast throughout the story. He seemed wound up. "Which I thought was weird because I felt fine at the time, you know? Like, in that moment, I felt coherent. But the next morning, so much of it was a blur."

• • •

Now that I was older, I'd realized that would be the shock of trauma causing the memory to be a blur. I'd learned a lot about my reaction and my feelings with the help of a therapist Margo had encouraged me to see.

"Did you tell someone what he did?"

I shook my head. "At the time, I didn't see it as assault. I figured because I didn't fight him off or kick or scream, or outright tell him no, it wasn't rape. I didn't realize that rape can come in so many different forms. I was ashamed about what had happened; I didn't want to talk about it. But I didn't understand why. Not until I told Margo what happened sometime later and she was furious. At him. Not me."

"Well, yeah. You were just a kid," he mumbled, tugging me in a bit closer, as if he wanted to protect me from long-gone danger. "He took advantage of you. Hell, it won't even be that long before Willa is fourteen, and I can't even imagine someth—" He shook his head and clenched his jaw.

"Yeah, that's the other thing." My fingers curled around each other, gripping the front of his shirt as I shifted, feeling the weight of this confession putting so much pressure on my chest that I expected my rib cage to crack. This was harder than telling Raine. He watched me, waiting. "A couple of months after it happened, I found out that I was—pregnant."

He stilled, and his gaze widened.

"I tried looking for him after that. I guess I felt like he should know. But he was gone. No one that I spoke to knew who he was, and I didn't even have a name to search. So I forgot about him, and I guess I finally opened up to Margo. Leaned on her. Let her support me. It brought us closer together, although I ended up placing a little girl up for adoption—" I choked on sobs caught in my throat. I always did when I thought about it. "I gave her up for adoption on the sixth of May, 2013."

He was still, so still as he watched me and realization dawned on him. It was a subtle flicker in his awestruck gaze. "Willa?"

I nodded, swiping at tears on my face. "She's my—daughter."

# CHAPTER SEVENTEEN

A comforting voice pulled me out of the horror occurring behind closed lids, and I felt a hand pushing hair back from my face.

"You're all right. It was just a bad dream."

I opened my eyes to Zac kneeling on the bed beside me, his face full of concern. He was shirtless, and his hair was a mess. I took it all in, adjusting to the waking world and doing my best to shed the lingering nausea of the nightmare.

"Move over," Zac mumbled, pulling the comforter back. He slid in beside me, his arms wrapped around me; my frame molded into his, and I rested my cheek on his chest. We settled like that, my breathing starting to slow, and I blinked back the dampness gathered on my lashes.

Zac kissed the top of my head and murmured, in a voice so soft it could've been a whisper, "What's bothering you tonight, baby?"

My breathing hitched at the nickname, and I snuggled in closer. "We haven't heard from Milo and Raine."

It was understandable. The decision whether to allow me into their lives was huge, and I expected it would take time to process. But it had been radio silence for almost a week, and all I wanted was a hint at what they were thinking. Even just a message to tell me they were still thinking. Something. I wasn't sure if Zac had talked to either of them. If he had, he hadn't told me.

"We have to give them time," Zac whispered, his hand coasting up and down my back in slow, soothing movements.

"I know that. It's just—it's hard to wait. As much as I understand waiting, it's still turning my stomach into knots." I slipped my legs between his, totally encased and more comfortable than I'd been in a long time. "Did Raine tell you that she thinks me ending up here is fate?"

"What do you think it is?"

"I don't know," I confessed. Deep down, I wanted that to be true, and I wanted Zac to be part of that fate too, and that scared me. "It could be fate. But that would have meant that it was—for it to be fate, Margo's death would have had to have played a part. And I'd hate to think that she died just so that I could find Willa."

"Or," he said as he rested a hand on my waist, "Margo's death has nothing to do with it, and the events that happened next were just something the universe took advantage of."

"I like that theory better."

"I'm glad."

"Because life would have been fine the way it was. I mean, no, I didn't know Willa, but I didn't know anything different. As far as I was concerned, she was with her adopted parents living a good life. I could have continued living that life, with Margo, happily, even if it meant I didn't know her." I exhaled a deep breath. "Is that awful to admit? That's awful, isn't it."

"No, I don't think so," he said. "It makes sense."

"I just wouldn't have wanted the universe to take Margo in order for me to meet Willa."

"I get it, baby," Zac murmured, his thumb moving in slow circles on my waist. He kissed the top of my head again.

• • •

I must have drifted off, soothed and settled by Zac's presence. However, when I woke up, he was gone. I figured he must have left me to sleep in while he started his morning chores. As sweet as that was, I knew I wouldn't get back to sleep. The alarm read six, so it was later than I was used to. I rolled out of bed and dressed in a pair of jeans, a tank top, and a baseball cap. I went downstairs, being quiet so as not to wake Keith. The sun was up, the morning glow bright.

Midge and Toto wandered over while I was standing at the garden beds, holding the hose and showering the flowers with a light mist. It was later than I liked for watering, but it'd have to do. The dogs sat on either side of me while I let my mind wander, thinking about Willa, how desperate I was not to lose her now that I'd found her. I'd been content to live my entire life never meeting her. I'd come to accept that. But now I knew her, and I cared about her. Losing her all over again would kill me, but I was doing my best to understand that I might be asked to leave and that would be it. I couldn't argue; I couldn't fight it.

Margo flittered across my mind, her smiling face. I imagined the joy she'd feel over meeting Willa. My chest tightened at the visual. Holding her heart and covering her mouth. Her eyes would crinkle; she would flick her hair behind her shoulders and fan at the tears on her face. She would stretch out her arms and ask for a hug.

As much as it hurt, it made me smile because I knew exactly how Margo would react, and conjuring up the scene in my head was so beautiful, it was somewhat of a comfort.

• • •

"Morning."

I startled. Zac was approaching at a slow walk, hands in his pockets. My heart did its usual little hiccup when I saw him. His tall build and his sun-kissed arms, the veins prominent, one thick one running up his bicep.

"Hi," I said, looking back at the garden, small puddles starting to form on the soil.

"You good?"

"Yeah," I murmured, not sure if I was telling the truth.

Zac stood beside me. "I went and saw Raine at work."

I whipped my head up toward him. "How come?"

He inhaled deeply, raising his shoulders. "Wanted to find out what was going on with Milo. Where his head's at. He's processing. It shook him, but he's thinking things over and just needs a little time to figure out what to do next."

Relief made me sag, and I nodded, moving over to a new section of flowers. Zac followed. "Yeah, that's fair. I understand." It was better than him asking me to leave and not giving it a second thought.

"I'm sorry I wasn't there when you woke up."

"Doesn't matter. Look," I said, pointing at a fresh plot of flowers that had been removed from a plastic pot and planted in the soil. They were green roses.

From the corner of my eye, I could see Zac watching me, slow to tear his gaze away. But then he did look at what I'd planted. "Those are nice."

I laughed lightly. "Such a male response."

He laughed. "They're stunning. Spectacular. Outstanding. I give them a gold medal. Better?"

I looked up at him, peering out from under the brim of my baseball cap. "Yes. Much. But besides that, they're for Willa."

"Really?"

"Yep. I told her that I would plant some emerald flowers for her. Since her birthstone is emerald. It was hard to find the right color. But I thought this would do."

"You were wearing emerald the first time we met," Zac said, and I felt my lips part on a silent gasp. "That little silk dress."

"You remember what I was wearing the first time we met?"

"I don't think I could ever forget."

Lashes fluttering on rapid blinks, I stared. All other thoughts eddied from me, and all I could do was search the tender face of the man staring back at me.

"I remember a lot about that morning," he continued. "I remember how your face lit up when you ate. Like you appreciated the hell out of a hot meal but you kept the appreciation quiet. I remember how pissed off you looked when I insinuated that you wouldn't want to meet Noah. That fierce scowl. I thought you might have slapped me right then and there. I remember the way that you softened when I promised to take you and Willa to see Noah, and I couldn't decide what I liked more, the harsh scowl or the soft smile. Turns out, I love both."

I felt like I couldn't breathe. "I—you noticed all of that?"

"I was transfixed from the get-go, Ads. Couldn't help but notice." He lifted his pinkie finger and swiped the side of his nose.

Zac stepped in close, his gaze focused on my mouth, and the world around us faded out. My heart had never beat harder. My entire body was alight with anticipation, and my lips parted. There had never been a moment in life that I'd gravitated so hard toward a man, as if I was powerless against the pull. There were a dozen reasons I'd told myself we shouldn't kiss, but none of them came to mind as he kept his eyes locked on mine and took the hose from my hand, dropping it in the grass.

One hand slid onto my waist, and with the other one, he lifted the cap off my head and put it on backward. He never broke focus, not for a moment as he lowered his hand and palmed my nape, fingers curling around the back of my neck.

"You mind if I kiss you, Addie?"

My breathing was harsh as my tongue flicked out at my lip, and his attention zeroed in on it, his fingers tightening on me.

Zac lowered his face and tilted my head to the side so his lips could coast along my jaw. "Can I kiss you, Addie?" he whispered, sounding like a man undone.

"Ye—"

I didn't get to finish the word before his mouth crashed down on mine, and my knees weakened to the point I thought I might lose my balance. Zac's hands lowered, his arms wrapping right around me and tugging me hard into him. Our bodies were flush, not an inch of space between us as our tongues collided, and I got the first taste of what I'd been reading about all these years.

I pushed my hands into his hair and lifted onto my tiptoes, desperate to get closer, to have more, to sate this insane need that I'd never felt before now. Zac deepened the kiss, his hands sweeping from my back to my waist to my hips and back up to my ribs. It was like he couldn't decide where it felt best to settle. His hands were so large, consuming me. Holding the nape of my neck, he inched back, capturing my bottom lip between his and sucking it. Then he rested his forehead on mine, his breathing harsh. I still had a grip on his hair, and I kissed him again, just one rough kiss that made him groan, the sound reverberating in my core. He deepened the kiss again, holding my jaw and angling my face so he could swipe his tongue into my mouth and taste me completely, as if he wanted to be familiar with every ridge and corner. We stood under the sun, the hose pouring into the grass at my feet while we grabbed at each other, kissing so desperately I felt half insane. I couldn't get enough, my body arching into his as if I could disappear, folded in by him and his consuming hold.

I pulled back enough that I could see his face. My hands held his shoulders, his hands held my face, and both of us were breathing hard and fast. I'd never been kissed like that before, like I was someone's reckoning. Zac tugged me back in and kissed my forehead, his lips lingering as he took the hat off my head and put it on his.

"You made a mess of my hair, ma'am," he teased.

"You made a mess of me." I clutched his shirt and leaned in, hiding my smile. He laughed, the noise rumbling in his chest, and I rested my face on his chest, letting the sound surround me. He kissed the top of my head, and his fingers cradled the back of my neck.

I touched my lips with the tips of my fingers and felt like stars were dancing in front of my face. "So." I swallowed and took a small step back, relishing the way he couldn't take his hands off me. They fell to my hips and kept me close. "The flowers?"

His low laugh was raspy. "They're great, baby. I love them. I do."

It felt like we'd just charged up a current between us—every move, every word, every look, was electric.

"They represent hope and optimism," I said, doing my best to think about something other than the throbbing between my legs.

Zac dropped his arm over my shoulder and tugged me into his side. "Hang in there, Ads," he murmured, kissing me on the head. "You'll see her again soon."

I was so grateful for his understanding, for knowing how much I needed to hear that.

# CHAPTER EIGHTEEN

There was an enormous superstore in town that had a range of random stuff. Kitchen supplies. Food. Towels. Beach gear. Fix-it solutions. Light bulbs. Home decor. It was one of those stores that had almost everything under one roof.

And it was all discounted and super affordable. I wandered down the stationery aisle with a basket, slow and careful to scan each item so I didn't miss something.

It wasn't just stationery. It was stickers, stencils, paper, ribbons, little chalkboards in different shapes that could be set on a stand or stuck to the wall. I grabbed a dozen and dropped them into the basket. They would be perfect for table settings at Raine's wedding. The chalk was right next to it as well. The convenience. I looked over our list once more.

*Glass bowl things that a little candle can sit in? Something cute like that.*

I chuckled and snatched a reel of white-and-orange ribbon. That would be useful. It might have been a bit premature to be sorting out little bits and pieces like this, considering the wedding wasn't until next October. But Margo and I had learned that collecting decor and small details early on was a lifesaver later.

It meant there wasn't a big rush right around the corner from the wedding when bigger details needed attention, such as rehearsals and bachelorette parties, that sort of thing. Plus, it was fun.

Margo and I used to do this together.

My fingers ran over the soft edges of a 3D velvet sticker. It was a rose.

*No, we don't need this, Addie. Put it back.*

*We might need it. It's not expensive. And even if we don't use it this time, we can keep it, and I'm sure we'll use it later.*

*We need to keep on budget, Addie.*

*It's four dollars.*

*You want it because it's cute.*

*Yeah. Of cour—*

"Ma'am, can I help you find something this afternoon?"

I looked at the store clerk. He was wearing a pin-striped apron, and his name tag said Brenn.

"Oh, no thanks." I smiled and shook off the lingering sensation that I was over-shopping. Margo used to think that she knew best, just because she knew my heart wasn't as invested in event planning as hers was. But I had ideas too, things to contribute. I put the sticker in the basket and kept walking.

Half an hour later, I put a full basket on the counter and smiled at the girl behind the cash register. She was tall, blond with pale-blue eyes and a little nose that looked too small atop her swollen lips. She smiled. "Hi, how are you today?"

"Good, thanks." I read her name tag. Amber. "You?"

She shrugged as she scanned items and dropped them into a paper bag. "The usual. Here till ten tonight. School at seven tomorrow. Good stuff."

I winced and noticed her manager glaring.

"Well . . ." I looked at the clock on the register. "Just four hours to go. You can do it."

She looked as though she really wanted to smile back at me. Poor girl. I couldn't imagine that she was here for the hell of it. She must have needed the job.

She peered up and did a double take at something behind me, and her entire expression morphed into elation. It was like staring at a different girl. I turned and saw a tall, I mean tall, teenager walking toward us with a bag of food. He had dark-brown skin and dimples on each cheek.

"Brought you dinner. I'll wait over here." He passed the register and headed for a bench beside the store windows.

"That's so nice," I said, glad that the girl was happier now. She nodded and bit down on her lip as she stared at the screen and tapped in the total.

"He's the best. Uh, that's one hundred and eighteen dollars and nineteen cents. Cash or card?"

"Apple Pay."

I brought up the company card on my phone and touched it to the machine. After all, this was all for a job. Raine had told me to give her the receipts for these purchases so she could compensate me for them. I made sure I kept them all. That was all the financial contribution she was making in regards to my planning her wedding. She'd insisted that I ask her for some sort of fee. But I'd refused.

When I got back to the farm, I had an overwhelming urge to send her a text message so that I could let her know what I'd bought. She'd want to come over and look through it all. She was the excited, impatient sort of bride-to-be.

I had a feeling she'd have been getting hitched far sooner if it weren't for finances and planning that required them to go slow. But I still hadn't heard from her since I'd told her I gave birth to Willa, and I knew it was probably out of respect for Milo. He obviously wasn't ready to talk, and I doubted she'd have been able to resist telling me what he was thinking.

She'd been keeping her distance. Well, that was what I'd told myself. I was worried I'd upset her somehow, even if she'd seemed excited about it all last weekend.

With the wedding supplies stored in the closet, I wandered downstairs to look for Zac.

The back deck was warm when I stepped out and hit the evening sun. Midge and Toto were darting around the garden, panting, tongues out. Someone had set up a little inflatable pool for them to cool down in. Zac was nowhere to be found, so I wandered off toward the back gate.

I found him in the paddock near the barn, in a tank top and jeans, sweat gleaming on his golden skin and hair a damp mess. He was hauling big bales of hay from the back of a truck and into one of the many small tin sheds. Gloves protected his hands.

Sometimes I just watched him for a little while and imagined a song, as if we were in a movie. Sometimes I heard it loud and clear. I didn't often decide the song, but it always suited the situation. That was probably information I shouldn't share because it made me feel a little bit unstable, but it made me smile too, and right now, that was what counted.

"Hey." I walked forward, and Zac made a subtle sweep of my outfit. A fitted pair of short overalls and a tank top. He smiled and wiped his arm across his brow.

"Had a good afternoon?"

"Yep. Just did a little shopping for Raine's wedding." His expression softened into a sad smile. "I'm fine. How's your afternoon been? Hot?"

"Not as hot as it is now." He winked, hauling another bale of hay, his biceps flexed as he threw it into the shed. I blushed. Of course I did.

"Can I help?"

He stopped between the shed and the truck, and his firm chest rose and fell with ragged breaths as he looked me over. "Those are heavy, and the hay itches."

They didn't look light. I mean, he was throwing them around with ease, but he was feeling it, that was for sure. However, now that he'd told me they would be too heavy for me, I was determined to do it. I walked over, grabbed the thin rope around the square bale, and dragged it off the truck. It fell straight onto the ground.

"Don't laugh." I pointed at Zac, who held his hands up innocently. I could see it, though. He wanted to laugh. "Well, if I can't lift those, what can I do?"

"Sweep the loose strands of hay out of the truck for Tom? There's a broom in th—"

"Got it." I spotted the broom leaning against the inside of the truck bed.

The truck was a little high for me to climb into, so I braced my palms flat on the lip, but before I could jump, a pair of hands wrapped around my waist and spun me around. Zac lifted me in one swift hoist and sat me on the edge of the tailgate. He moved between my legs, held the front of my overalls, and pulled me into a bruising kiss. My legs tightened around his waist, and I could feel his smile on my mouth. Our tongues brushed for a brief moment, and then he let me go and stood back.

"I'm just going to grab a towel and some water," he said, taking a slow stride backward. "Want anything?"

"You."

He bit his bottom lip and started sliding the gloves off his hands. "To be continued." I stood up, watching him with butterflies as he turned around and walked away.

He disappeared, and I thought about how selfish it was to want him so much. Selfish. Margo didn't get her true love. She didn't get her child. Those were things she'd wanted and tried to get. Here I was, running, refusing to face the truth, and it was all falling into my lap. It didn't seem fair. I didn't deserve it.

"I swear to God, Margo," I mumbled, snatching the broom and aggressively sweeping at the strands of hay, "if you went and died just to orchestrate my happy ending, I will—"

"Miss?"

My head snapped up to see a man standing at the back of the truck. He was wearing a plaid shirt and had a missing tooth, which I noticed when he grinned at me. He wasn't wrinkled and his hair wasn't thinning, but he sounded and seemed old. It was confusing.

"Oh." I pointed behind me at nothing in particular. "Is this—are you Tom?"

"Yeah, this is my ol' truck here. You are?"

"I'm Addie," I explained, twisting the broom handle. "I live here. I was just helping Zac. He'll be back in a second. Like, super soon."

His brows pulled at the over-explanation of Zac's whereabouts. I couldn't help it, though. Margo and I had been on our own for such a long time that we'd been vigilant about keeping ourselves safe. I was sure that he was just a regular farmer, but habits were hard to break.

Instead of letting him know that I was being cautious, I smiled.

"So, whe—"

"Tom." Zac appeared; he was wearing a backward cap now and had a towel around the back of his neck, draping down his front. He looked at me and back at Tom. "Dad sorted the check?"

"Yeah, mate." Tom slapped Zac on the shoulder. "Good ol' Keith is slower, ain't he? Hmm? Better start thinkin' bout sending him off. A home. Ooh, he'd love that."

Zac smiled, but it was forced. "He's fine. You want a drink while Addie finishes sweeping out the back?"

"Nah." Tom waved a dismissive hand. "Need to keep movin'. I'm due home to the missus. She'll have my head if I'm late tonight. You didn't mention you had a gal."

Zac looked at me, and this time, his smile was genuine, one that turned his eyes into half-moons and exaggerated his thick black lashes. I'd never believed that a smile could be one of those features that made your heart soar.

I'd thought that was a thing in novels. Something authors wrote about to add to the character's appeal. But when Zac smiled, it sent me into a tizz. Butterflies. Genuine appreciation for something so beautiful that you can't believe you've made it this far in life and never known a smile can do that to a person. I smiled back, a big one that I didn't have to force. Zac's eyes flared with emotion, and I realized that my smile meant something to him too.

• • •

The stars were out tonight. It was becoming one of my favorite parts about Texas. Among other, obvious things. Zac and I were in his car shed. I had a coffee, which I clutched while I sat curled up on the back seat of a convertible Mercedes that Zac was working on.

He'd found it after it had been in a wreck. The owner had been drinking during the accident, so it wasn't covered by insurance, and he couldn't afford to fork out for the repairs. Zac had bought it for four hundred dollars, determined to sell it for the fifteen thousand that it was worth. It was going to require a lot of work. But that was what he was best at.

I watched him leaning over the front of the car, which had been crushed. He was still wearing his backward cap and tank top, looking like an absolute heartthrob. He inhaled a deep breath. "I'm going to have to cut the entire front off and rebuild it."

It sounded more like a comment being made to himself, but I nodded in agreement, as if I knew what he was talking about. He straightened, holding something that he'd tugged out of the engine, and his tank top clung to his defined torso. He studied the piece in his hand. "That's fucked." He tossed it off to the side. "I don't think any of this is salvageable."

Again, I nodded and sipped on the hot coffee.

"Oh." He looked through the windshield at me. "I got you something."

I jolted with excitement and watched him head over to his truck. This was so exciting. My heart was fluttering away at the fact that I was on his mind enough that he'd gotten me a gift. I hadn't even seen it, and it was the best present I'd ever received.

He shut his truck door and wove through the mess of car parts, tools, and wheels on the floor. He held the car door as he leaned down beside the back seat and handed me a pale-pink leather-bound journal. My fingers skimmed through the blank pages.

"You don't have to use it," he said, still holding the door. "I just thought, it helped me. It might help you. You like that color, right? You had it on your nails when we first met. There were no emerald-colored journals."

I bit down on a grin and caressed the soft front cover. "I love it. You didn't have to do that, though."

"I wanted to."

I stood up and gave him a careful hug. Both hands were full, and I didn't want to spill coffee down his back. He hugged me, his hard chest against my head, his lips on my hair when he bent to kiss me. It made me shudder, and I heard him laugh. Damn tingles exposing me in full force. I couldn't help it, though.

He stepped back, and his hooded gaze swept over me as he took the coffee and the journal from me, placing them on top of the car. He put his arm up, encasing me against it as he leaned in, so close that I could feel his breath on my neck.

"I love making you tremble," he whispered, his lips grazing my nape. It made me weak and breathless. "I think I can do better, though."

I swallowed, nodded, unable to form a response. His gaze settled on my lips, and then he leaned in and kissed me with that slow, sensual pace that he had down to a fine art. He didn't need to rush or become frantic. I was a trembling mess at the slow lap of his tongue on my lips, nipping, tasting. His free hand gripped the hem of my overalls, and his fingertips grazed my thigh as they caressed the fabric.

"Ooh, Uncle Zac and Addie, sitting in a tree."

Zac and I parted so fast that I banged into the car and the coffee mug slid off the roof, shattering on the concrete floor. Willa didn't seem to notice. She continued singing.

"K-I-S-S-I-N-G! First comes love, then comes—"

"Will," Zac sighed, standing behind the car door in a particularly discreet position. "What the hell is going on?"

Milo wandered in next, his hands in his track pants pockets. My heart quickened. This was it. He was going to tell me that he didn't want me around Willa. We'd made an agreement. Well, he and I hadn't. I'd never met Milo or his late wife. But we'd still made an agreement, and I had no right to think he might want me around just because I'd shown up by accident.

This was the sort of thing parents were protective over. Their role. I realized that I hadn't moved a muscle since he'd stepped into the shed, but Zac was now bent down, cleaning up the shattered mug. He looked up, his face hidden from Milo and Willa by the car door, and mouthed, "Are you okay?"

I nodded.

He stood up, hands full of broken ceramic, and gestured at Willa. "Come and help me get a couple of cold drinks, kid. You want a soda?"

"Yes!"

The two of them left, Willa skipping beside Zac, who gave me one last reassuring look before he disappeared and left me alone with Milo. I felt like I needed to apologize to him for showing up and turning his world upside down.

"I'm sorry," he said, beating me to it.

"What for?"

"Oh, just going off the grid. I got a shock, I guess. Needed to process. Can we talk now?"

I nodded, dumbfounded. "Of course. But don't apologize. There's no need."

He ran both hands down his thick beard and leaned on the hood of Zac's truck, several feet from where I was still leaning on the wrecked Mercedes.

"I guess the first thing I need to know is, what's your plan? What are you doing or where are you going? Because I need to think about Willa here. I'd hate for her to find out about her birth mother and then have you take off again. Abandonment does terrible things to a child."

The word *abandonment* felt like a sucker punch in the stomach. He was such a good dad. I knew I'd have to go home again eventually. It was out of my control.

"Whether I go home or not, I wouldn't abandon her ever again. That's all I can really offer right now, Milo. I wish I knew what I was doing. I just . . . don't. That's as honest as I can be."

He nodded, gaze downcast. "I appreciate that. So, what, you'd keep in touch?"

"If I ended up leaving, of course. Yeah. I couldn't imagine not keeping in touch."

"And what if this thing with Zac ends sour?" he said. "Still plan on keeping in touch?"

"Willa has nothing to do with Zac and me. I wouldn't involve her in something like that. She's just a child."

He nodded again. It was so slow and thoughtful. I wondered if I was passing his test. "How much involvement are you hoping for?"

"I don't want to take your place, or Raine's. Or her mother's. I'd just like to be her friend. That would mean a lot to me."

He folded his arms, and I suddenly felt what it would be like to be interrogated by Milo as a police officer. It made me squirm and fidget. Milo had been relaxed and lighthearted whenever I'd seen him before. Smiling, laughing, sighing at his gorgeous daughter. This was an officer getting his answers. Protecting. I wanted him to trust me so much.

"She's always been curious about her birth mother," he finally said, brows tight like that fact bothered him a little bit. Perhaps I was just reading him wrong. He looked at me. "So, I'm going to allow it. A friendship and the truth. But I think it'd be best that you spend some time with her first. Let her get to know you before we tell her."

As much as I wanted to agree with whatever he said, I couldn't. "At the end of the day, this is your decision. You make the final call. But I have to say that I think it'd be a bad idea to let her spend all of that time with me just to tell her the truth later. I think she might feel . . . betrayed. Like we all knew this secret and she didn't. Personally, I'd rather tell her and let her come to me on her own terms."

He was almost blank as he stared, the only sign of life his rapid blinking. He did another slow nod. "I guess that's a good point."

"I also don't think I should be there when she finds out," I added, on a roll. "She might feel pressured to react a certain way if I'm watching."

"That, I most definitely agree with."

It felt so positive to be on the same page, to have an understanding of how this entire thing should proceed. Talking to Milo had lifted a weight off my chest and allowed hope to move in. Hope that I would get to have a relationship with the little girl I'd never stopped missing.

• • •

When Zac came back to the shed, I was alone, sitting on the back seat of the Mercedes, knees facing out, head spinning, heart pounding, throat closing over. Zac knelt in front of me and encased my hand in his. Such large, strong hands. Ones that weren't too soft or smooth, but rugged and rough. Hands that worked hard.

"You all right?" he asked.

"Milo and Raine are going to tell Willa tomorrow and then bring her to brunch on Sunday if it all goes well."

Zac's brows raised. "That's good. That's great. You're not worried, right?"

"I mean, a little. She might not want anything to do with me. She might hate me."

He clicked his tongue with disapproval and stood up, pulling me with him, his hands sliding down to my hips. "She knows you. She doesn't hate you. You're friends."

"That could change when she knows the truth."

Zac towered over me, as usual, but he held the nape of my neck and stared down, his expression full of patience and understanding. Part of me wanted to believe that he'd really come to know me so well in such a short amount of time. But that was impossible. This wasn't me. This was a version of me. The one that ran away and started building an entire new life in another state while she hid from her grief.

My words rang in my ears. *That could change when she knows the truth.* Would it change if *he* knew the whole truth?

He gave me a soft kiss on the forehead. "She isn't going to hate you."

Suddenly, we heard the pop and crunch of gravel and headlights illuminating the entrance to the shed. Zac peered over with his brow furrowed, and as the car got closer, noisier, he relaxed with recognition and mumbled, "What is it this time?"

A silver car stopped just outside, and a familiar tall kid hopped out of the driver's seat. Zac walked over to him with his arms spread in question.

"Hear that?" the kid asked. It was the kid from the superstore this afternoon. The one who brought his girlfriend dinner.

"Yeah, I hear it," Zac answered, shouting over the loud engine. "Sounds like you've blown the intercooler pipe again?"

"I know it's Friday night, but please can you help me fi—"

"Yeah, of course." Zac twisted so that he could look at the shed, possibly searching for a clear space, which there wasn't a lot of. As his gaze swept past me, he smiled and winked, and I felt my heart rate increase.

"Let me move some shit around," Zac said. "Then we'll bring it in, all right?"

. . .

It didn't take too long to clear a parking space for the kid, who I found out was Tyler. Zac moved his truck out, and then we all worked together to move car parts and rubbish off the ground—Amber included, who was the girlfriend who worked at the superstore. Georgetown wasn't small, but it seemed that in this little corner, on the outskirts, they were all familiar with one another. It was endearing.

Tyler assisted Zac with the car while Amber and I sat on a set of bench seats that had been pulled out of . . . something. It was impossible to keep up with it all. She was still wearing her pin-striped apron and name tag.

"Made it through the shift, then," I said.

She looked confused for a moment. "Oh, right. You were in there this afternoon. I thought you looked familiar. We get a lot of customers."

"Yeah, I bet."

"But yep. I made it through. A miracle."

She sounded exhausted: fatigue laced and slurred her words; purple shadows contrasted on her pale skin. But somehow, she was still strikingly beautiful. She almost suited the purple. It accentuated her pale-blue eyes.

"So, how long have you and Tyler been together?"

Her expression lifted in an instant. "About eleven months."

Well, that explained it. Honeymoon phase. I smiled.

"But we've been friends since we were seven."

"Aw." Friends to lovers was a special sort of relationship, I gave them that.

"Yeah. We're getting out of here after high school. I'm going to do medicine in college. He's going to open a workshop—he builds," she said with an excited little shuffle where she sat. "Once I've graduated college, we're going to get hitched, he's going to build our dream home, and we'll have babies before we're thirty."

All I could do was stare. I'd never heard someone sum up their life plan in such a short breath and announce it with that much confidence. She did not hesitate. Not even Margo had spoken with that much conviction. I couldn't help but dwell on it for some time before I finally said something.

"Can I ask you something?"

Amber nodded. "Yeah."

"How are you so sure? Like, with Tyler. Doesn't it scare you? You're both so young, and it's sort of impossible to know what the future holds. Especially when you hear about how many young couples don't make it."

Amber stared into the distance for a moment, thinking about it. "Can you guarantee, without a doubt, that it won't rain next week?"

I smiled. "No."

"Does that stop you from enjoying the sun while it's out?"

"No, but I wouldn't make plans to go to the beach if I didn't know what the weather was going to be like."

"But if you don't make the plans, and it is a good day for the beach, then you've missed out on what could have been because you were more focused on the potential negative outcome."

I nodded. "Plan for the best, be prepared for the worst."

She shook her head. "Plan for the best and deal with the worst when and *if* it happens."

I couldn't say that I shared her outlook, but I admired it. From the way those two looked at each other, it was obvious they were in love.

"My sister would have liked you," I said.

She gave me a knowing grin. "Was she optimistic too?"

I laughed and gave her a nudge in the side, noticing Zac look up from the engine and smile at me. He seemed to love it when I laughed.

"I'm not a pessimist, if that's what you're hinting at."

"Okay, sure. We'll call it a realist, then," Amber teased.

I'd liked to think I was a realist until she said it like that. And then

I thought perhaps I was on the pessimistic side. It almost confused me. I had no idea where I stood on all of this, and it was so sudden that I felt winded. I'd always been sure.

True love was rare, apart from the exception.

You should make plans for a future that secured yourself. Whimsical sweep-her-off-her-feet romance was for books and books alone.

But now, as I watched Zac leaning over a car, grease on his hands and arms, sweat causing his shirt to cling to him, well, I wasn't so sure.

• • •

It was close to midnight when Tyler and Amber left, the car repaired. I leaned against the open shed door, looking up at the stars. It was so beautiful, never ceasing to amaze me. Zac finished cleaning up, switched off the lights, and rolled the doors closed. His truck was parked in the grass, and he took my hand, not speaking until we reached the back of it and I saw the bed had been packed with pillows and blankets.

He leaned his elbows on the edge and looked down at me, winking.

"When did you do this?"

"While you were talking to Milo."

I grinned, tapping my hands on the edge with excitement.

"We can go inside if you want, but I know you like looking at the stars."

"I do," I said, my chest filling up with overwhelming appreciation. Zac stepped back and pulled the handle, lowering the tailgate so I could climb up. I made sure I left my shoes on the ground and then I got comfortable, smacking the pillows. Zac climbed in next to me and did the same thing.

When we were side by side, I turned my head to look at him. "Did you do this so we can have sex without Keith hearing?"

He burst into laughter—deep, rumbling laughter.

"You did, huh?"

He was still chuckling as he rolled onto his side and propped himself up on his elbow. "Do I think about having sex with you? Hell, all the damn time. Would I lure you into looking at the stars with ulterior motives? No, baby. I wouldn't. Keith wouldn't hear us inside; his room is far enough from either of ours."

I believed him, of course, but it was fun to tease him. I mirrored him, rolling onto my side and resting my head in my hand.

"Oh, I get it," he said, his grin playful. "You're thinking about having sex with me, right?"

I laughed and shrugged. "I might be."

He slid his hand over my waist, teeth sinking into his lower lip. "You are the most beautiful woman I've ever met, Addie," he said.

Scooting closer, I kissed him, hands resting on his neck. My tongue lapped out at his, and he sucked it in between his teeth. "Addie," he murmured, lips still grazing mine, lifting on a teasing smile. "You haven't even looked at the stars."

"Well," I whispered, hand on his stubble-coated jaw, "how about you put me on my back and I can look at them while you're inside me."

He groaned, his grip on my waist tightening. "You want that?"

He kissed me again, and I nodded, becoming restless.

"You want me inside of you?"

"I do."

He pushed me back and hovered over my frame, keeping his weight up on his strong arms.

"Oh." I pretended to pout. "You're kind of blocking the view."

He smirked, shaking his head. "I can put my face between your legs if that helps?"

My stomach flip-flopped so hard it winded me. "You promise?"

He dropped his head. His laugh was so sensual it made me throb. "I promise I'll do whatever you want me to. How does that sound?"

My gaze searched his face, so beautiful, so unreasonably gorgeous he didn't seem real. I imagined men like him belonged with five-foot-nine girls with washboard abs and long legs.

"What's going on?" he asked, his gaze searching.

"I don't know how this happened," I whispered, hooking my legs around his waist. He kept his weight up with one arm; the other hand gripped the back of my knee, and then his palm coasted up my thigh, toward the crease of my hip. "I don't know how I got . . . you."

His brows flinched as he stared down at me. "Baby, I've been asking myself the same damn thing. The moment I saw you crouching in that garden, I couldn't believe how fucking beautiful you were. The more I get to know you, the more gorgeous you are."

My throat felt thick.

"Believe me," he whispered, his hand on my thigh moving up and down, "I do not deserve you."

Using my legs, I tugged him down, his hard length pressing into me and our lips colliding. The kiss was desperate, our mouths moving fast, tongues tasting, teasing. Hands clawed at each other. An ache gathered between my legs, so insatiable, so mind-altering I barely even recognized myself. The more aroused I became, the wilder and more uninhibited I became. The things I wanted this man to do to me.

His hand slid under my shirt and curled around my ribs, his thumb brushing over my nipple. My hips shifted as I tried to gain more friction between my legs, his length hard and hitting that sweet spot. Zac groaned, dragging his mouth down onto my throat, sucking the skin beneath my ear. It ignited my entire body with a burning chill, and I tipped my head back, lips falling open on a moan.

This was what I'd been missing out on, this feeling, this consuming desire that was so feverish I felt insane. In all the sex I'd ever had, nothing had ever made me feel like this. Zac's tongue lashed out on my throat, swirling, dragging his teeth down until his kisses peppered my collarbone. I was shuddering with need, our hands still searching. Zac leaned up, his breathing hard and his mouth glistening.

"I'm going to take your pants off now." He reached between us, his fingers popping the button on my jeans without even looking. "You want me to stop?"

"No, don't stop, at all."

His sensual laugh raked down my spine, and I sucked in a sharp breath. "Listen to me," he said, eyes locking on mine. "Don't be quiet. Don't pretend to like something if you don't. Don't keep going if you change your mind. Don't. Be. Quiet. You got it?"

That might've been the sexiest thing ever said to me. I nodded, and he kissed me, hard, before he sat back and tucked his fingers into the waist of my jeans, dragging them down my legs. I lifted my hips and watched this beautiful man, the dark night behind him, the smattering of stars as his backdrop. This was another world, somewhere beautiful that was just ours, and I never wanted to leave. He slid his fingers under the band of my underwear next and raised a brow, checking in to be sure I still wanted this.

Instead of answering, I lifted my hips and pushed them down, leaving myself bare and exposed but not embarrassed. Never with him. His gaze turned dark as he finished helping me rip them off, and then he wrapped his arms around my legs and settled in. His face was so close that I could feel the breath on my wet entrance. His tongue lapped out, licking up until he reached my clit and sucked it between his lips. My chest rose and fell on deep, erratic breathing, and I did, in fact, look at the stars while his face was between my legs. My hands slid into his hair, and I pulled it as he ate. I couldn't tell if I wanted him to stop or keep going. It was so overwhelming in the best sense, the sensation unlike anything I'd ever felt. His stubble scraped the inside of my thighs, a little bit of pain and a lot of pleasure. I moaned, practically whimpering as I watched a star shoot across the expanse above me.

My legs tightened around his head as pleasure exploded in white-hot heat, searing from the inside out. My entire back arched off the blankets, and I was seeing stars behind my closed lids. Suddenly his mouth was gone, and he knelt between my legs, unzipping his jeans as he watched me, mouth wet with my climax.

"You taste like an angel." He pulled his cock out. I was restless, waiting for him, and then he reached into his back pocket and pulled out a condom.

"Zac." I leaned up on my elbows, watching him as he tore the foil with his teeth. "I thought this wasn't planned."

"It wasn't, but I've had it in my pocket for a while." He shrugged, watching me with hooded lids as he pinched the tip and slid the condom on. "Thought it'd be better to be prepared if we got caught up in the moment."

I nodded, still up on my elbows. I wasn't upset. "You should take your shirt off," I said, grinning when he laughed. Of course, he obliged, gripping the back of it and sliding it over his head. He took my breath away, his firm chest, that smattering of hair on his pecs, the defined V lines trailing down to his cock, which was hard and exposed by his jeans unzipped and hanging open.

"You comfortable?" He fell over me; his hand settled on my jaw, and his mouth feathered tantalizing kisses along my cheek. I practically panted as his tip teased me, pressing, pushing. "Talk to me, baby. You sound like you want it."

"Because I do," I breathed, words hitching as his hand moved down from my jaw and onto my nape, thumb caressing the ridges of my throat. "You're all I want, Zac, I promise, there's no doubt, there's—"

My words turned into a gasp as he thrust and slid inside, all the way to the hilt. He grew still, hissing through a clenched jaw. His face fell into the crook of my neck, and his light laugh made me shudder.

"Shit," he grunted, lazily kissing my ear. "You feel like a dream, Addie May."

My heart thundered: something about my name in such a guttural voice made me feel like this was special to him. It wasn't just sex. It was him and me.

I shifted my hips up, and he groaned beside my ear. "Hang on."

He took a deep breath, and then he slid out, nice and slow, right to the tip, and then he slammed back in. My nails dug into his back as he carried on, thrusting hard, getting faster until my head was banging into the back of the truck bed. Zac didn't even pause as he slid his hand onto the top of my head, cushioning the impact. My moans drifted through the quiet night, the clash of our skin, the deep grunts from Zac as he slammed into me.

Pressure built in my core, and my nails sank into his bare back. He was so big, encasing me underneath him, his hand easily cradling my head and his cock creating a delicious stretch as he slammed in hard and fast. He kissed me, tongue dipping in and our teeth clashing as we jolted on his thrusts. I moaned into his mouth, and he sped up, vigorous and undone.

"Requests?" he breathed against my mouth.

"What?"

"What do you like, baby? Tell me how you like it."

He made me feel so safe. "Turn me over," I panted, and he didn't hesitate. He slipped out and flipped me onto my stomach in one quick movement. He brought his hand down on my ass, and I gasped as he palmed it.

"You are unreal," he groaned, and then he grabbed a pillow, shoving it underneath my hips. I loved how strong and in control he was, while being totally at ease doing whatever I asked him to. He nudged my legs apart with his knee, and then I felt him at my entrance, sliding inside.

I buried my face in the pillows, clutching the blankets with tight fists as he moved, the new angle making me delirious, my climax building. Zac gripped a fistful of hair and wrapped it around his hand, going so hard while I did my best to push back. The pleasure was so intense I started to slide forward, my body inching away, but my building orgasm craved more. Zac slipped his other hand onto my hip and held me in place.

"You okay?" he asked, sounding breathless.

"Yeah," I moaned, head tipping further up as he pulled my hair. I whimpered. "It feels so good."

My words must've spurred him on because he started going so hard I couldn't even breathe, and then I felt it, the blinding release—the unbelievable sensation made me convulse, and I couldn't even scream, I was too busy trying to inhale a decent breath. Zac collapsed over me, kissing the spot between my shoulder blades.

We were both spent, and I shifted my hips, causing Zac to hiss.

"Keep still, baby." He laughed lightly, still inside me. I did it again, rolling my hips. He groaned, dropping his forehead onto my back.

I rested my arms under my face and couldn't stop smiling.

Zac eventually stood up, his feet hitting the ground with a thud, and I rolled over, watching him, shirtless with his jeans hanging loose around his hips as he slid the condom off and tied the end. He looked over at me and winked while I admired his capped shoulders and rounded biceps.

"You got more of those?" I asked.

He tipped his head back, grinning up at the stars. When he looked at me again, he slowly nodded. "I do, up at the house. Give me a minute to recover, though. Yeah?"

"Mm-hmm." I settled down in the blankets and covered up, releasing a quiet, satisfied sigh.

We ended up wrapped up under the blankets, his arms around me, legs entwined. I loved how I absolutely sank into him, like he could completely surround me and I'd disappear. We watched the stars from the bed of the truck, Zac kissing me on the head, his arms tightening in a squeeze once in a while. His bicep cushioned my head, and his fingers traced circles on my skin. I melted into him, content to remain there forever.

# CHAPTER NINETEEN

Clouds rolled across the dawn. It was the first day of bad weather that I'd seen since I'd arrived here a month ago. I hoped there was nothing symbolic about the patters of rain that hit the stable roof, echoing, thundering in time with the pounding of my heart.

Today Willa was coming for brunch, and I had no idea how it was going to go down. I stood in the stables, leaning against the wall while I watched the rain becoming heavier outside, curtaining the landscape, dimming its perfection. Not that it wasn't still beautiful in its own way.

There was a distinct whinny from behind me, and I turned to see Lavender staring over her stall door. Her black mane needed a brush, and it almost looked as if that was what she was suggesting as she shook her head and neighed a little louder. I smiled and collected the brush. Getting into her stall was a bit of a challenge. She'd bolted on Zac more than once when he'd gone in to clean out her trough.

If I'd been tall enough, I'd have just slung myself across the door, but that wouldn't be happening. Especially in the skintight jeans I was wearing.

"Please don't bolt on me," I whispered, and her quiet neigh sounded like a scoff.

The door creaked, and I pulled it open just enough so that I could slip in without a gap. The entire time, Lavender remained statue still, watching me. Sometimes she seemed far too aware and mischievous for a horse.

"Good girl," I said when I pulled the door closed behind me and stepped up to start brushing her mane. She did a slow blink as the bristles combed through her smooth coat and hair. Her relaxation was a sense of accomplishment I'd never known before. It was odd how one horse's gratification could be so pleasing.

"You ever miss your momma?" I asked, standing in front of her now and brushing her forehead. Her slow blink continued. Zac had told me that the mare who had given birth to Lavender had been sold after she had weaned. I knew it was natural, and I knew that animals didn't often remain with their moms. But I felt sort of sad for both of them.

"I can't be Willa's momma, but we could be friends. If she lets me." I inhaled a quiet breath. "I hope she likes me, Lavender. I know it sounds like we've never met, but it's different now. I don't want her to think I abandoned her. Or didn't love her. I gave her up because I do love her."

Lavender had a relaxed jaw, and I chuckled when she dribbled and breathed out through her nose. "Zac told me what that means, and I've totally forgotten."

"It means she's happy."

I stifled a squeal and spun to see Zac leaning over the stall door, elbows resting on the top.

"How long have you been standing there?"

"Long enough to tell you that you shouldn't worry so much." He tilted his head. "Will is a smart kid. She'll understand, and I bet she'll be damn excited that she gets to meet you."

I exhaled a soft breath as I ran a hand down the front of Lavender's face with gentle strokes.

"She likes you a lot," Zac said. "The dribble, her soft round nostrils, her relaxed jaw. You've got the magic touch, huh?"

I smiled. "Guess so."

"We're in the thick of a storm," he said, gesturing toward the barn doors. The rain was pelting on the top of the barn shed, getting louder. "We'll leave them in the barn until it's passed. Shouldn't be long. You wanna head in with me?"

"Yeah." I gave Lavender a kiss on the side of the face and walked through the stall door when Zac held it open for me. As usual, when we left our little escape artist, he double-checked that her door was secure, and by the time we reached the barn threshold, the rain was so thick that we couldn't see six feet in front of us.

I was preparing to make a run for it when I noticed Zac beside me, hands in his pockets as if he was out for a casual stroll when he walked into the downpour.

"What are you doing?" I shouted from under the shelter. He spun around, walking backward as he watched me through the haze of rain.

"I'm making the most of the rain. It's fresh. Smells good. Keeps me cool. You coming?"

My smile was involuntary, and I slowly shook my head, biting down a grin when he turned and kept going. As infectious as his attitude was, I didn't love the feeling of consistent pelts hitting my skin, so I began a quick sprint toward the gate, passing him as I ran. It was useless for the most part. I'd been in the rain for eight seconds, and I was drenched.

Eventually I made it to the gate, flung it open, and started up the mild incline of the gravel road. However, I hadn't anticipated that wet gravel could be so slippery, and before I had time to brace myself, my feet came out from under me and I landed front-first on the ground.

A rumble of thunder echoed in time with my laughter, but my breath caught and I inhaled raindrops when I was gripped under the arms and lifted to my feet.

"You all right?"

Zac watched me from under the brim of his cap. I couldn't stop laughing, which was somewhat of a struggle when the thick rain was making it hard enough to breathe and see. Still, I nodded through my drowned giggles and felt my heart accelerate when he smiled back.

I was a little bit worried that I'd reached an unhealthy level of hysteria due to nerves over seeing Willa. But if it was coming out like this, I wouldn't complain. We stood there in the downpour, the haze of rain distorting the rolling land around us. As usual, he treasured my laugh and drew closer to me as if to hear it better. I think I'd been waiting all my life for someone I could weather any storm with, and right now, the rain had never been more beautiful. I leapt up, threw my arms around Zac's neck, and kissed him. His hat fell off when my forehead hit it, but he didn't hesitate to clasp his hands behind my back and kiss me back.

We stood like that for a while, tongues moving together, breaking apart for air over and over again because the rain made it hard to breathe. But that didn't matter. For some reason, right now, nothing did. He thawed out all of the pent-up anxiety, and he gave me the air that I needed to keep going.

Upstairs, in the bathroom, both of us drenched from head to toe, we stripped out of our clothes while the shower warmed up. Zac took his shirt off and watched me with hunger as I used the wall for balance and peeled my jeans off.

"They'll be here soon," I said, referring to Milo, Raine, and Willa. "We don't have time for a long shower."

I crossed my arms, gripping the bottom of my top before I lifted the hem and pulled it over my head. Zac came closer, his clothes gone. I unclasped my bra and let it slide down my arms.

"I guess we better be quick then," he mumbled, leaning down and hoisting me up, hooking my legs around his waist before he stepped into the warm shower.

. . .

Zac and I emerged from our bedrooms, clothed, twenty minutes later. He'd kept true to his word, and we hadn't been in the shower for long. The aroma of bacon and fresh bread hit us both as soon as we reached the staircase. That meant Milo was here, cooking. I paused, holding the rail as I heard Willa talking to Keith.

"It's okay." Zac took my hand and made me look at him. "It's going to be okay. They're here. That's good."

I nodded, but I was lost for words. My heart pounded as we stepped into the kitchen and found everyone gathered around the island. Milo was at the oven, and he glanced over, giving me a small smile. Raine was looking at my hand enveloped in Zac's, but my attention went straight to Willa, who was watching me with curious kindness. She didn't look upset. She didn't look angry. My heart pounded as she walked straight toward me and offered me an envelope.

"Dad said that writing down what I wanted to say might be easier than trying to say it."

I didn't realize that I was trembling until my fingers clutched the envelope, and I gave her a slight nod. "Can I read it now?"

Willa nodded, and then, as if she was done with the moment, she went back to the stool she was sitting on at the island. Zac watched me, giving my hand a squeeze.

"I'll be back in a minute," I whispered.

"Of course." He kissed me. "I'll make you a plate."

I headed for the reading room when Raine intercepted me and pulled me into a fierce hug. It startled me for a moment. Shit, did she know the letter wasn't good and she was offering me her condolences? I panicked.

"Don't look so terrified," she whispered while she still held on to me. "You'll like the letter. I promise."

My shoulders, stomach, and the band of tension around my skull relaxed, and I felt a huge weight lift off.

"Thanks, Raine," I said when we parted. I squeezed her hand and slipped around her, more eager than ever to read what Willa had written. The large armchair swallowed me up in its pastel floral pattern, allowing me to feel hidden as I tore the envelope open and tried to stop trembling.

I couldn't believe how much life had changed in the month I'd been here. I was living in a gorgeous farmhouse, sort of seeing one of the most amazing men I'd ever laid eyes on, and now I was reading a letter written to me by the daughter I'd given birth to all those years ago. It was unfathomable. It hardly seemed real.

Her handwriting wasn't bad for a ten-year-old.

*Dear Addie,*

*My dad just told me that my birth mom had made contact and wanted to meet me. He didn't tell me it was you at first. But I was really excited anyway. I love my dad. Raine is the best too, and I'm happy all the time. But I really wanted to meet my birth mom for a long time because I wanted puzzle pieces. Hopefully that makes sense. Raine describes it like that. Puzzle pieces. You can have some of the pieces already. But if some are missing, it makes your picture incomplete. So that was why I really wanted to meet my birth mom.*

*So I said to my dad that I was excited and, yes please, could I meet her. And then he said, well, you have, it's Addie. I was so SHOCKED. But when I knew about it for a bit longer, I thought, well, that does kind of make sense. We actually look kind of the same. He said that you hadn't come here looking for me, but you realized that it was me when I said my birthday and talked to Raine and stuff. He asked if I wanted to be friends with you, and I said yes but only if it didn't hurt my daddy's feelings. He said it wouldn't because he knows that he's my dad.*

 *Raine and Dad said that I should write all of my feelings down. Stuff I might have felt weird saying out loud. So I guess I just want you to know that I'm not angry that you gave me up for adoption. Dad explained lots while I was growing up that it was because you wanted me to have a good life and that's why you had to let me go. He said it would have been hard for you but you put me first. So I'm not mad. I understand. And I would really love to be friends with you. I think we have a lot in common and you seem really nice. So we should hang out. I hope you'll stay in Texas for a while. I'm really excited to get to know each other.*

*Love, Willa xoxo*

I could hardly see as I stood up and practically ran back to the kitchen. Tears were streaming down my face as I stopped beside the island. Everyone was watching me, but I could only look at Willa, who smiled.

"Can I have a hug?"

She nodded and slipped off her stool, so I leaned down, opened my arms, and hugged her so tight that I was worried I was crushing her. She didn't complain. She was hugging me just as tight.

After such a long time, after feeling the ache of her absence from the moment I let her go, the emotion of holding her for the first time was so overwhelming that all I could do was sob into her hair. She was the missing piece of my puzzle, and she was finally found.

• • •

Milo was kind enough to allow me to take Willa out for the afternoon after brunch. He didn't have to do that. What if I had been some nutcase that decided to steal her and jet off? That would have been a concern to me, but he confidently let me know that he didn't believe I would do something like that, and even if I did, he'd find me.

He was so relaxed and sure of himself when he said that that I knew he meant it. Willa probably had a tracking device in her shoes or something. He and Raine were police officers, after all. Their daughter's safety wouldn't have been left to chance. Obviously, I wasn't going to kidnap Willa, so the conversation ended in good humor, and Zac gave me the keys to his truck.

The rain had stopped, and the earth smelled fresh, like damp soil and bark. Whenever the breeze lifted, the tree leaves shook water droplets onto the ground, and it sounded like a symphony of nature's finest tunes. Everything felt sharper this afternoon. Clearer. I knew it was because of the little girl walking along the sidewalk beside me.

We'd come into town and decided to head into the library. It was her idea, and I didn't argue. There was a common ground here.

The public library was like a lot of the other local buildings, large and red brick. Inside, there were dozens of sculptures of various items including a brass Western woman, an eagle, and a little girl reading. We headed for the classic romance section. Willa was in charge. She led the way, and I felt light and excited watching her long black hair bounce as she walked.

I was at the library with my daughter.

Surreal. The words kept rolling over in my mind, but I kept them to myself. I didn't want to sound weird or possessive. It was enough just to know this information myself and embrace it, allow it to soothe some of the ache that had been keeping me hollow for so long.

"I tried." Willa slipped a copy of *Pride and Prejudice* off the shelf and waved it at me with a defeated smile. "I just couldn't get through it. The sentences confused me, and I didn't know what most of the words meant."

I gave her an understanding nod. "I get it. The vocabulary in these books isn't really taught in school anymore, so I'm not surprised. Even I didn't know what a lot of the words meant. I spent so much time pausing and googling."

That made her laugh as she slid it back into place with her palm flat against the spine. "Did your sister like to read?"

My chest tightened. "Uh, no. Not a lot. She did once in a while if something sounded really interesting to her. But no, she was more of a doer. You know? She loved the beach, and she loved shopping. Also, she never let age stop her from going to the clubs and dancing. She was obsessed with dancing and dating and singing. She didn't sing well, but she loved it."

"She sounds fun."

Telling Willa about Margo should've hurt like hell. It did hurt, but getting to share memories about her aunt was a unique sort of special. Something I'd never thought I would do. I got to keep Margo's memory alive with a little girl Margo loved, regardless of whether the two had met.

"She was fun. She made lots of little moments fun too, you know? Like, she was so good at making pasta from scratch, and after it had been cooking in the water, she'd fish a piece out and fling it at the kitchen wall. If it stuck, it was cooked. Which a lot of people do, but she made it a game. We had little spots of light that came in from the kitchen window at dusk, and those were our targets. We had to hit them with the pasta. That was what Margo was like. She tried to make ordinary moments a little bit special."

She would have been an inspiring mother.

Willa was smiling, her attention all on me. We walked around the aisles while I told her about Margo. Aunt Margo to Willa. That was sweet. I told her about more of our special memories. The ones that we made out of seemingly normal circumstances. Well, I couldn't say we. It was always Margo who created the good times.

We stopped in front of a rack of newly released picture books. The illustrations were beautiful, little fairies that glittered and shimmered on the glossy cover.

"Margo would have loved to have known you," I said, picking up one of the fairy books, thinking about Margo and Willa in the same existence. "It was hard on her as well when I let you go. Hey, can I read this to you?"

Willa didn't dwell on the topic of Margo, sensing that I wanted to move on. It was beautiful to share those memories with her, but it was gut-wrenching to recall how much Margo had wanted to keep Willa.

"Yes, you can read that to me." She smiled and took my hand so that we could sit on the beanbags in the corner beside the window. There were about a dozen of them spread out.

Reading to my daughter was one of those things I felt I'd missed out on in the years after I let Willa go. It was one of those simple moments that I felt would have been a beautiful parenting experience. I couldn't explain it, but I wanted to create that moment now. Needed to, almost. It worried me—I didn't want to start stepping into the shoes of a parent, but there were things that I wanted us to do together so much.

I sat in one of the beanbags, and Willa sat on the floor in front of me with an eager smile and her arms and legs crossed.

"My dad used to read to me," Willa said as I opened the book to the first page.

"Yeah?"

"Yeah. But then I started reading books with kissing scenes, and he said, 'Will, I can't do this no more, kid.'"

We both laughed.

"That was okay, though, because he read kind of slow. I'm a much faster reader than he is."

"Well, now I'm feeling a lot of pressure to read this book fast!"

She laughed. "No way. It's different. This is a picture book. You can go slow."

"You're probably too old for this, huh?"

She shook her head. "No. I like older books, but I can still enjoy a cute picture book about fairies."

I smiled. She was so mature for her ten years of age. I'd heard from a few people that an oldest or only child can often seem older. I sort of loved it. I wasn't sure I'd have known how to interact with a little kid. Someone who wanted to play with building blocks and eat boogers. But that thought alone made me feel selfish. What, I gave her up and now I got to enjoy her at a more convenient age? That wasn't right.

"Addie?"

I startled, and life came back into focus. I had the worst habit of zoning out. I smiled and started reading. As I read, a little brother and sister hovered a few feet from Willa and me. They listened with cute interest, and in a heart-melting moment, Willa gestured for them to come and sit down with her.

Was this what maternal pride felt like?

A few more children came over, abandoning their own stories. Parents watched from a distance, and I tried to focus on the book and not the growing pressure that I felt to deliver this story with enough enthusiasm to hold their attention. It was sort of cute, though. I felt like a teacher, sitting at the front of her class. On cue, children would giggle, gasp, clap.

At the end of the book, I closed it, and a dozen little sets of hands began clapping, making me feel oddly proud. Especially when Willa stood up beside me and made it known that she was with me. Was she proud of me too? I internally scoffed and told myself to get a grip. I'd read to a group of children. I hadn't saved them from a burning building.

The group began to clear, and a librarian emerged from among the children who were returning to their parents. He was tall and lean with a thick southern twang and weather-worn skin.

"Willa," he said, grinning, his laugh lines deepening. "How are you, darlin'? Who's this friend? Surely a sister?"

I stood up, flustered for a moment. I totally blanked on how to answer. How did Willa want to answer? I swallowed and looked at her, but she was smiling at Hank, as his name tag said.

"This is my birth mom. Addie."

He gasped with an enormous smile. "Oh, my darlin', isn't that just beautiful. Your birth mother. Well, imagine that. Hello, Addie." He gave his attention to me now and gripped my hand in a firm shake. "It's such a pleasure to meet you. I've known Willa here for many moons. She's my favorite little reader."

He must have known that she was adopted. He seemed so genuinely excited for her.

"It's nice to meet you."

"You as well. You gathered a good crowd with that readin'."

"Oh. Yeah. I guess I did."

He folded his arms. "Don't suppose you'd be interested in doin' it again? I could keep the library open an extra hour on Sundays if y'all would come back to read to the kids."

"Oh, um . . ." I looked down at Willa to find her nodding with enthusiasm. "I could do that. Sure. Why not?"

"Oh, that's fantastic news, darlin'. I can't pay. Our readers do it as volunteer work. But our last reader, Kirsten, well, she slipped and hit her head while she was running in the rain a few months ago. Concussion, you know? She's not doing too well. So this is just wonderful."

My stomach turned over at the thought of this poor Kirsten woman. Images of her head bleeding swarmed, stirring me into a nauseated mess.

"You tell your daddy I said hello," Hank told Willa and gave us both another handshake, bringing me back from a mild panic attack. "I'll see you next weekend."

There was something seriously wrong with me. I needed to stop making commitments around here. And if I was going to be doing that, there were a few things that I needed to come clean about.

The rain had started again while we were in the library. It wasn't as heavy as it had been earlier, but it was enough that I didn't want to walk around town with Willa like I had planned to earlier. Instead, we sat in the car while I googled where the nearest cinema was.

"Addie?"

"Mmm?"

"Can I ask you about my birth father?"

I looked up from my phone and met Willa's curious little stare. Honestly, I could barely remember his face anymore. It was a distorted image of grunge hair, a hoodie, and a lean physique. Willa probably looked like him a little bit; I was sure I'd be able to see the similarities if I could remember his face.

"What about him?"

"Do you still know him? Did he ever want to meet me? That sort of thing, I guess."

The reality of what she was asking made me panic. How could I explain the situation to her without explaining sex? How much was she aware of? I put my phone down and turned toward her.

"How much do you know about how a baby is made?"

She almost scoffed. "Everything."

I felt doubtful. She was so young. "Really?"

"Yes," she stated with boredom. "The boy's private parts go into the girl's priv—"

"All right." I clapped and nervously laughed. "So you know what—"

"Sex is? Yes. I've had the talk."

Well, that made things a little bit easier. I clearly had no idea about a child's comprehensive range at this age. Or perhaps Milo was comfortable sharing these things with her because she was so mature. Each to their own.

"Well, the thing is, your birth father and I, we only knew each other for one night, and he wasn't—" I paused, exhaling because I didn't want to tell her the entire truth. I didn't want her to think her conception came from this traumatic event. "He wasn't interested in keeping in touch. I never saw him after that night. I don't know his name. I couldn't find him to tell him about you. I'm sorry I can't tell you more."

She slowly let her gaze move so that she was staring out the windshield. Rain pelted and drizzled down the glass, blurring the outside world.

"I'm really sorry."

"It's not your fault." She smiled, still staring out ahead of her. "I was just curious."

"If you really want to look for him, we could try?"

"No." She finally looked at me. "That's okay. I have a dad. If he just had sex with you and left, he's probably not really nice."

I chuckled. She had no idea. Granted, he could be different now that he was older. Who knows. He literally had no idea that she existed. But the choice lay with her, and she seemed sincere in not needing to know who he was.

• • •

Raine and Milo had a nice home in Berry Creek, Georgetown. It was two stories high, made of brick, with a beautiful front lawn, trees, and a double garage at the front of the house. The path that we walked to the front door was made of cobblestone, and the grass was perfectly trimmed.

My hand almost stretched out to ring the bell, but Willa went straight inside and called out for her dad. Inside, it was bright with white tile floors, cream walls, and lots of photos. The living room suite was brown leather, and the curtains were a similar shade.

There was a shelf beside the window, and it was covered in lustrous green houseplants. I wandered straight toward it while Willa flopped down onto the sofa and gave one more bellow for her dad. He must have been upstairs somewhere. Raine was sleeping, no doubt. I wondered how she didn't wake up with all of Willa's hollering. We heard Milo padding toward the room while I ran my fingertips along the leaves of a plant that was looking a bit lifeless.

"Afternoon." Milo sat beside Willa.

"This is a Calathea Ornata," I told him and touched the soil. It was dry. "This light is too harsh. It needs indirect light. Also, it helps to mist them. Is this a self-watering pot?" I lifted up the white pot and noticed there were no holes at the bottom. "I'd suggest getting a self-watering pot and putting it in a water tray. Keep it topped up. They need to be kept fairly moist at all times. You can put some pebbles in the tray or something to keep it looking nice. Try not to re-pot it more than once, though. They don't like it."

I set the pot down on a side table beside the living room threshold and looked at Milo, who was watching me curiously. Willa wore a soft smile.

"All right." Milo gave me a quick nod. "I'll let Raine know. Those are her plants. She's just got a few around the house. Said they add character."

"They do. Houseplants also purify the air."

His gaze widened. "I did not know that."

I smiled.

"So, how was the afternoon?" he asked.

"Good," Willa answered and sat up straighter with excitement. "We went to the movies, but first we went to the library and Addie read to me and then all of these other kids listened and Hank asked Addie to read on Sundays."

Milo chuckled and wrapped his arm around her shoulder. "Well, that sounds like a perfect afternoon, don't it?"

She nodded and scooted forward off the sofa. "I'm going to my room to get changed."

"All right, honey. You need something to eat?"

Milo looked over his shoulder and listened for Willa's answer, which she shouted from halfway up the staircase. "No. We ate. I'll have a lemonade, though!"

He chuckled and stood up. "Want one?"

"Oh, sure."

He circled the sofa, and I followed him toward the kitchen. It was crisp white and modern with a red feature wall and a breakfast bar cutting in between the dining area and the kitchen. I slipped onto a stool and peered out at the back garden.

"That's a cute little playhouse." I pointed at the back corner of the garden, where a wooden playhouse was tucked underneath large, sprawling tree branches.

Milo smiled, his focus moving between the lemonade he was pouring and the back garden. It was dead quiet apart from the liquid hitting the cup.

Finally, as he slid the glass across the breakfast bar, he said, "Zac and Willa built that last summer. I mean, Zac did most of it, but she was out there every day, hammer in hand. You should get her to show you it. It's her library."

"Really?"

He nodded. "There's an armchair out there, shelves of books, and a blanket. She loves it."

I could hardly wait to go out and have a look. Milo moved about the kitchen, putting the jug back in the fridge, wiping down the counter. I sipped the lemonade, and my legs jiggled as I tried to think of a new conversation. It was odd to think about the fact that this man had raised the little girl I'd given birth to. He'd been down the hall, he and his wife, waiting. While I'd been experiencing the worst pain I'd ever felt, he had been one room over, experiencing the greatest joy in his entire life. Now we were here, in the same kitchen, experiencing conflicting emotions. It was hard to process.

Milo leaned a hip on the counter and folded his arms. "So, how was it for you?"

My brow furrowed until I realized what he was asking me. "Oh. It was so much fun. She's a great girl. She didn't have bundles of questions like I thought she would. She's quite happy to just roll with the punches, isn't she?"

"Yep." Milo tapped the countertop with amusement. "She's an easygoing kid."

I thought I should tell him that she'd asked about her birth father. That seemed like the kind of information that I should pass on. "She did ask about her birth father."

Milo snapped his attention toward me.

"She just asked if he was in the picture. You know. Or what his role was. Raine probably explained that to you already?"

"She did. What did you tell Will? I mean, I'm not sure she needs to be hearing about rape at her age."

I was taken aback at the bluntness of his words. Perhaps being a police officer and dealing with that sort of thing on such a regular basis meant that it was just factual to him. Perhaps the impact wasn't as big for him. It still made me flinch, though. I'd have thought he'd be a little more sensitive given his position.

"Oh, well, she told me she knows what sex is?"

"Yeah." He dragged the word out. "There's a difference between consensual sex between two adults and rape and assault."

"There is." I nodded, feeling the need to make a point. I could hear Margo telling me to drop it. "But I think the two go hand in hand when you're having these conversations. If someone knows what sex is, they also need to know their boundaries, and they need to know they're allowed to say no and they don't owe it to anyone. And to listen when they hear no. They should understand what consent is and how to keep themselves safe. I'm talking in general now. For boys and girls."

Milo stared at me. I could have sworn he was pissed off. But I couldn't understand why. These conversations should have been first nature to him, having seen so much horror in his line of work.

"I didn't have a full understanding of boundaries and what level of respect I was entitled to when my virginity was stolen." I held the glass with a tight grip. "That's why I think these conversations are important."

He continued to stare, tapping his knuckles. I really had no idea what he was thinking. It wasn't obvious at all.

"I didn't tell her that I was assaulted or explain what rape was, because that's not my place," I said after I couldn't handle the quiet a minute longer. "But I still think it's a good idea to have those discussions with someone who has as developed comprehension as she does."

"Like you said, it's not your place. I'm her father."

"I know."

He nodded and started to relax a little bit.

"I actually didn't want to make her think she was the result of a really traumatic event. So I just explained that we only knew each other for one night and that I couldn't find him and he wasn't aware of her existence. I said if she really wanted to find him, I could do some search—"

"You told her what?"

I stammered at his angry tone. It was much harsher than it had been before.

"You don't get to tell her shit like that," he almost shouted, and I froze. "How dare you? You can't tell her that she can go and search for her birth father. You don't have the right. What the hell's wrong with you?"

Okay, he might have been right about that. "I'm sorry," I mumbled. "I wasn't thinking. I just felt bad that I couldn't give her any more answers, and I made an offer that I probably shouldn't have, but honestly it doesn't even matter because it'd be impossible to find him and—"

"You need to leave," Milo snapped, his breathing coming out harsh and fast. "If you can't respect the fact that you're not her parent, this isn't gonna work. You gotta go. You won't be seeing Will again."

Panic had me seeing dots in my vision. "Milo, please—"

"Go."

My shoulders fell, but I could see that he was in no position to be persuaded otherwise. Not right now, anyway. So I quickly made a dash for the front door. As I passed the living room, I saw Willa sitting on the bottom stair with a solemn look on her face. I froze for a moment, wanting to talk to her but not wanting to make things worse.

"Please don't give up on me again," she whispered, and my heart shattered into a million pieces.

I felt tears welling as I stared at her sweet face. A face that resembled mine. No, I wasn't her parent, but she meant the world to me, and I wasn't going to lose her again.

"Of course I won't," I whispered, forcing a smile. "I won't ever give up on you. I promise."

# CHAPTER TWENTY

The sun was beginning to set when Zac found me sitting in front of the garden beds, my knees drawn up, arms wrapped around my legs. Tears slipped down my cheeks, the ache returning, worse than ever before. This was what I'd been scared of. Losing her all over again. I wasn't sure I'd survive this one.

Zac crouched in front of me, tipping my face up with his finger on the bottom of my chin. "What happened?"

"I fucked up." I inhaled a shaky breath.

"How?"

I blinked, tears rolling down my face. Zac watched me, concern pulling his brows together as he searched my face. My chin quivered, and I wiped my face with both palms. It was like I could physically feel the fibres in my chest splitting, the healing stitches coming undone while I bled out.

"Willa asked me about her birth father. I told her a censored version of the truth and said that we could look if she wanted to find him, and then I told Milo about the conversation, and he lost it and told me I couldn't see Will again."

Zac's eyes flickered and darkened with anger, but he was quick to smooth the surprised outrage and offered me his hand, standing up.

"Come on. You want me to run a bath? You want a coffee or something to eat?"

"I think I'll just get into bed," I said, following him to the house, too exhausted to do much else.

Zac was waiting for me when I came out of my en suite in a fresh pair of clothes, teeth brushed, ready to turn in for the night at six in the evening. He watched me walk toward the bed, watched me stop beside it and fall victim to the defeat, watched me contemplate if there was any point. How long could a person keep going when their entire being was eclipsed in agony and loss?

"Addie," Zac mumbled, stepping closer when I looked up at him, the man who was patiently restoring pieces of my heart whenever I let him.

"I just—" I felt like I was going to keel over; the weight of the situation was too much. Zac quickly wrapped his hand around the back of my head, pulling me into his chest, where I fell apart all over again. "I just felt like this—this fucking ache was healing. Just for one second, I felt like—I don't know—whole again."

Zac held me tight, hands in my hair, lips on my head. He didn't push me to talk or offer me words of comfort. He just held me, and then we got into bed, and he kept me close while I cried. Eventually, I drifted off, Willa's words clamoring in my head. *Please don't give up on me again. Please don't give up on me again. Please don't give up on me again.*

• • •

The morning brought on another bout of despair, but I was rested now, enough that I could function. Zac wasn't in bed when I woke up, which wasn't unusual. As I got dressed, I thought up a game plan. I needed to give Milo some space—he needed some time to calm down—and then perhaps I could go to him with a heartfelt apology and the promise that I would never overstep again.

It was all I had, the hope that he would be reasonable if given enough time. Plus, Raine would find out what had happened, and I was sure she'd advocate for me. I went outside and started on the gardens. There wasn't a lot to do after all the rain. The soil was damp enough that I pulled a few small weeds, and then I went down to the barn to look for Zac.

Dawn was breaking on the horizon. Blue hues collided with the dark smear above us, and the sound of the world waking up was the soundtrack to a fresh start in the form of a sunrise.

The grass was moist for the horses. The fence smelled like damp wood, and beads of moisture hung from the shed awning, soon to be dried under the sun. I loved it when it rained, and I loved the morning after even more. The entire earth was rejuvenated, revitalized.

Zac wasn't at the barn, and the horses were still in their stalls, which was odd for this time of the morning. The trainers would be here soon to start working, but in the meantime, I knew what had to be done, and I was grateful for the distraction. Hallie and her husband arrived when I was halfway through cleaning out the stalls; we said a brief hello, but Hallie wasn't much for chitchat. Truth be told, I wasn't much in the mood for it this morning either.

When I was done, Zac still wasn't there. Weird.

The sun was up in full force when I emerged from the barn. Horses were being trained in the rings, and the others were grazing in the paddock. I shielded my face from the sun and searched for Lavender, who was nowhere in sight. Great. So much for the understanding we had. She'd obviously bolted after I let her out. I didn't know how to ride Zac's dirt bike, and I didn't want to panic the trainers by telling them Lavender was gone. There was a good chance she was down at the creek where I'd found her before. She liked to run, but she was always found.

It was a good thing I liked walking. Hopping the gate, I started off across the paddock toward the south boundary. The long grass and dandelion stems slapped my boots as I walked, and I listened to the slosh of damp earth. The crickets chirping, the birds whistling, the horses sighing and causing their lips to blubber. At one point, the grass was short enough that I could see some horse prints in the soil. I followed them until the grass was too long to see them again.

It wasn't as long a walk as I'd done before, and eventually I came to the tree line, walking the narrow path between shrubs and tree branches. The babbling river was within earshot, and I left the path, deciding to walk closer to the water so I could find her. From here, the river was about twelve feet below a cliff face, though I knew it became a shallow creek the further I walked toward town. The water was more aggressive here too, the current rushing, whitecaps bubbling with the speed.

I was watching the water when I heard a neigh and froze, spotting Lavender eating berries off a bush in the middle of the thicket. Letting out a breath of laughter, I shook my head at her. I wasn't sure how she cleared the fences around the farm, but I assumed she had a good jump.

"You aren't supposed to do this to me." I walked over to her. "We're supposed to be friends. You do the runners on Zac. Not me."

Running a hand down her neck, coarse hair beneath my fingers, I couldn't help but smile. "I get it, though. I get it."

She nudged me with her nose, and I giggled, giving her a good rub down her long face. My gaze coasted down her bare back and her mane. She seemed to trust me, more than she trusted the others. I wasn't sure why, but I appreciated it.

"Would you let me ride you?" I murmured, petting her back. It didn't look that hard, from what I'd watched on videos and read in books. I'd watched Zac when we went for the ride on Nellie, and that had looked effortless as far as I was concerned.

Searching the thicket floor, I looked to see if there was something I could stand on for a bit of height. There wasn't. No rocks or boulders. I stood back and assessed what kind of height I would need. She wasn't as big as some of the other horses on the farm. There was also no one around to laugh at me if I tried to get on and failed.

"Be cool," I said to Lavender, putting my hands on her back. "You be cool and I'll be cool, and if this doesn't work, we don't have to talk about it."

She kept still, almost as if she knew what I was doing. Bending at the knees, I sprung up and slid straight back down to the ground. Lavender continued to keep still, so I took that as a positive sign. If she didn't want me jumping on her, she'd bolt. I tried several more times and finally got a leg up, quickly throwing it right over her back. Huffing, I sat up and held on to her mane, laughing with disbelief.

"Oh my goodness, Lavender," I was quietly squealing. "You're being so cool right now."

Giving her mane a light tug to the left, I felt my smile grow as she moved, her hooves hitting the sticks and leaves on the ground. My heart was galloping, and my lips were getting dry from breathing so hard. "This is amazing."

I knew if I kicked her too hard, she'd run. Well, I thought that was what would happen. I wasn't going to test it. She didn't walk, she just stepped to the side as I guided her with her mane. Too afraid to kick her in the side, I just sat there on her back, pleased that she wasn't objecting.

"I know I'm supposed to make the calls here," I said. "But if you just want to head on home, that would be great."

Nothing.

"Please don't go nuts," I whispered and gave her a gentle tap in the side with my boots. It worked; she started a slow walk through the thicket.

"See." I grinned. "You and I are on the same page. This is good."

I knew we needed to get back on the path, but I liked the sound of twigs snapping under her hooves and the tree leaves brushing the top of my hair. All of a sudden, a ferret scurried out from behind a bush. I'd barely processed the little animal before Lavender was rearing, standing straight up so fast I didn't have time to react.

The lights went out.

• • •

My head was pounding, making it difficult to open my eyes. The ground beneath me was sharp, and confusion clouded my understanding of what was happening as I peered through narrow slits. Tree trunks, shrubs, spots of sun above me. Something warm tickled my skin, and I put a hand to my temple, pulling it back to see blood. Nausea rolled over me, my vision blurred, and my entire face tingled as I fought the urge to be sick.

"Addie," someone shouted, a desperate, deep shout. It sounded like I had cotton in my ears, muffling the volume. "Addie, don't move."

I started to shake, bile causing my jaw to tingle, and then I rolled over to vomit, but instead of finding the ground next to me, my body fell, too fast, too sudden. Water sucked me under, and I inhaled with shock, lungs flooding. It was black, nothing but the violent rush dragging me through the cold water. I flailed, not sure which way was up, which was down. I scrambled, hoping my body would find something solid.

Hope pushed through fear when my foot hit something hard and I pushed off, kicking and kicking until I broke the surface and sucked in a breath. It felt like my lungs were being speared by fire. Just before I went down again, I caught a glimpse of Zac swimming toward me. He was shouting, but I couldn't hear him over the rush of water in my ears.

I'd barely filled my lungs with air when I went back under, the crushing weight of suffocation pressing down on me. Not for one second did I stop kicking back toward the surface, occasionally popping up for another too brief breath of air. I thought about what I had to fight for. I thought about Margo and what she'd left behind. I thought about Willa, the unresolved tension with Milo. I thought about Zac, how I felt about him, how it scared me but how good it felt. I reached for him through the water, still being thrown around in the rushing current.

A pair of arms wrapped around me, and then the surface broke and I coughed up water, feeling as though I was still drowning. There was too much happening; the rough waters were still hitting me in the face as I kicked and fought to keep from going back down.

"I've got you," Zac said behind me, my head on his shoulder, his arms under mine. "Breathe, Addie. Breathe. I'm not going to let you go."

It felt like seconds later Zac was walking out of the water with me in his arms. I couldn't understand it. One moment we were in the water and the next he was looking down at me as he crossed the rocks and pebbles on the edge of the creek near town.

"Thank fuck," he mumbled. "Try not to go back to sleep, Ads."

"Sleep?"

He looked forward and shouted. "Here, she's here!"

"What?"

My head ached so much it was an effort to even turn it toward the noise, but I did, and I saw an ambulance parked on the side of the road.

"Zac." I felt a bout of panic surge through me. "What's going on?"

He didn't answer as he set me down on a stretcher, a couple of unfamiliar faces coming into view. Zac went to step back, but I held on to his shirt, meeting his eyes and communicating just how much I didn't want him to disappear. He was wet from head to toe, but that didn't stop him from giving me a reassuring look and climbing into the back of the ambulance with me. The paramedics were firing questions at both of us, but I was too far behind, too unsure of how to answer.

". . . told me she'd last seen her walking across the paddock." Zac was talking to the man sticking a piece of gauze on the side of my head. "I hopped on my bike because I had a fair idea of where I would find her, and I came across one of our horses, who—it'll sound weird, but the horse kind of showed me where to go."

"The horse did?" The second paramedic sounded amused, but I didn't look at her. I watched Zac tell us all what had happened while his hand held mine. His wet shirt clung to his chest and arms.

"Yeah." Zac peered down at me and brought my knuckles to his mouth, water dripping from his hair and rolling down his face. "I'm not sure what happened, but she was unconscious beside the cliff edge when I pulled up, and she was just starting to stir. I was on the phone with Raine at the time, asking if she'd seen Addie, so I told her to call an ambulance, and then I tried to get her to keep still, but she must've been dazed because she went to roll onto her side and went straight over."

"From the looks of you," the male paramedic said, pulling back the now blood-red gauze from my head, "you jumped in after her."

Zac kept his focus on me. "Yeah. She lost consciousness in the water after I caught up with her; she was in and out for about ten minutes. Threw up a little."

"I did?" I grumbled, embarrassed.

Zac gave me a half-hearted grin. "Don't worry, it washed off in the water." Under that grin was a hint of grave concern.

"This will need stitches, and she'll probably need a CT." The paramedic kept pressing the cut on my head, a pile of bloody gauze growing beside him. Fatigue swept over me again, my lids closing of their own accord as the voices around me drifted off on a wave of pain.

I was vaguely aware of the paramedics asking me more questions, but I was too tired to answer.

• • •

The wait at the hospital was long, even though I was asleep for the most part, only being woken on occasion by a question. *Can we take some blood? Can we clean up this cut? Allergies? Confirm your name and date of birth for me.* That one tripped me up a few times. Zac never left my side; he held my hand, checked in a few thousand times. Eventually, while I was staring at the ceiling in an ER cubicle, a doctor came to see me. I had no idea how long I'd been there, but I was ready to leave.

"Addison May." The young doctor gave me a warm smile. She had shoulder-length blond hair curled in at the ends. "I'm Dr. Marie, a resident here. You can call me Ashley. You feeling okay?"

"The painkillers have helped." I sat up and smoothed down my hair. I'd been given a gown so I didn't have to sit in my wet clothes, but my hair was still a mess, the front strands caked in dried blood. Zac stood at the end of the bed, giving me some space but remaining as a support.

Ashley perched on the edge of the bed and leaned in, assessing the stitches on the side of my head. "Those look good. The stitches are dissolvable, so they'll disappear in about six weeks. We'll make sure you have a prescription for some pain relief to take at home. I'd like to admit you for overnight observation, just to be safe. I think it's likely you've got a concussion."

"Can't I just go home?" I asked. "I'll have supervision the entire time."

"She will," Zac said, giving the doctor a reassuring nod when she peered back at him. He was standing at the end of the bed with his arms folded.

"Well, I can't force you to stay. I'd prefer it, but I can give you a list of things to look out for at home, if you *choose* to leave."

"Thanks," I said, relieved. I wasn't interested in spending the night in a hospital bed. I'd feel safer tucked up with Zac, knowing he'd fuss over me and be sure to check my vitals once an hour. When I peered at him, he was smiling at me, as if he was already thinking the same thing.

"I think we'd better do a CT scan before we discharge," Ashley said, lifting her iPad and swiping at the screen. "Is there any chance you could be pregnant?"

My lips parted to answer, but no words came out. My mouth went dry.

Ashley watched me, waiting for an answer I couldn't provide. I'd been avoiding this truth for so long. Deep down, I'd known it was bound to catch up with me, but for some reason, I couldn't bring myself to deal with it.

"Answer her," Zac said, his voice so sudden I startled and looked up, the pleading in his expression unmistakeable.

Ashley tapped the screen of her iPad again, reading with a knit in her brow. "Sir." She stood up and fixed Zac with a tight smile. "Can I ask you to step out into the waiting room for a few moments?"

His jaw fluttered, his gaze not leaving mine. I knew he wanted me to deny the potential of a pregnancy, but now that the truth had been unveiled, I couldn't put it back.

"He can stay." My voice sounded distant. "He's—he should stay."

I knew why she was asking him to step out. She was worried about me; she was worried there was a reason I was keeping my pregnancy from him. Perhaps he was violent and so I didn't want him to know. I understood her concern, but Zac needed to hear the truth. It was time to come clean, and as cowardly as it was, I was glad the choice to tell was being taken out of my hands.

Ashley hesitated, but then she gave a quick nod. "I just checked on the blood test that was done when you arrived. It does present a positive pregnancy. I think we should get you down to the radiation lab and perform an ultrasound. Check in on how the pregnancy is progressing and be sure it wasn't affected by the fall."

A positive pregnancy.

The words weighed down on my chest, and my breathing quickened. "I'll order the ultrasound and have someone come to collect you as soon as possible. Just ring the bell if you need anything in the meantime."

Her gaze darted to Zac for that last part, and then she slipped out through the curtain around my cubicle. Zac started pacing at the end of the bed, palming his jaw.

"Zac—"

"Are you running from an abusive relationship?" Again, he stared at me, his nose flaring on harsh breaths as he pleaded with his eyes, hoping I would tell him what he wanted to hear.

"No, I'm not."

He blew out a humorless laugh and shook his head. "So, what, what is this? You're pregnant with another man's child and sleeping with me?"

"It's not—"

"Did you know?"

I hadn't heard his tone so harsh before, not even when I'd first arrived and he'd assumed I was just a girl from California, too afraid of dirt and animals to participate in the activities on the farm. It would be easier to tell him the truth than listen to him hurl accusations at me.

"I suspected," I admitted.

His head dropped, and he held on to the railing at the end of the bed, knuckles white.

"What was the plan here?" he asked, not raising his voice, but the anger in it was loud enough. "Trick me into raising the child? You not know who the father is, so you figure you'll pick one? Or are you planning on giving this one up as well?"

I felt as if I'd been slapped. He knew how much giving up Willa had hurt me, and he threw it in my face. As desperate as I was for him to know the truth, perhaps it was better that he hated me. I had to go home. I had to face the truth, prepare for a future I couldn't understand. Dragging him into that mess wasn't fair, and leaving him would be painful for both of us. It was better he hated me enough to let me go. After all, he'd never asked for any of this.

"Get out."

He flinched. "What?"

"Get out. I'll get back to the farm myself, and then I will leave."

He swallowed, a range of emotions passing his face all at once. The most prominent might have been regret, but then again, I didn't know him all that well. He didn't say anything else. He walked out, throwing the curtain aside.

• • •

The ultrasound confirmed I was almost two months along. As I knew I would be. It was healthy, unharmed by the accident. Despite the doctor insisting I remain in the hospital for a night of observation, I asked to be discharged and caught a cab back to the farm. My head was a little sore, and I felt fatigued, but otherwise, the emotional torment was far more painful than the gash on my temple. In order to do what I needed to do, I had to tamp it down, forget what the last few hours had unveiled, and power forward.

The house was quiet when I went inside, no sign of Keith or Zac, which I was grateful for. Upstairs, I went into my room, closed the door, and started packing up the few possessions I had.

Half an hour later, after I had packed my bag and then paced the room while I wondered what to do with the rest of the clothes I'd accumulated, there was a soft tap on the bedroom door. I froze, standing at the foot of the bed. He must have come back to apologize. Perhaps he felt bad about how he'd handled it. I mean, no, we weren't ready to raise a child together, but we could make this work. Somehow.

I deflated with a harsh exhale. No, we couldn't make this work.

My hopes were shattered when the door opened and Raine peered through the gap.

"Oh, hi." She came in and closed the door. "I wasn't sure if you would be here. I've tried calling Zac, but his phone is going straight to voicemail. I wanted to see if you're okay after—"

Her sentence dropped off, spotting the packed bag and the remaining clothes folded in a neat pile on top of the drawers. My books were stacked. Toiletries in a plastic bag.

"What's going on?"

The fact that I had to tell her I was going back to Beverly Hills, when she'd been so supportive about my friendship with Willa, made it hard to look her in the face.

"You're leaving."

I nodded.

"Why?"

"I'm pregnant."

Her mouth fell open. So I explained. I explained from the beginning, and then by the time I was done, I was sitting on the bed with tears streaming down my cheeks.

"I can't believe he said all that," Raine murmured, sitting beside me. I looked at her through blurred vision. "No, I don't mean that I don't believe you. I'm just . . . disappointed in him."

I wiped my face with the back of my hand. "I don't blame him, I guess. I'd be upset if I were in his shoes. He thinks I'm pregnant with some dude's kid and I hadn't told him. It looks bad."

"I don't care how it looks. He should have let you explain."

I bit down on the inside of my cheek, not wanting fresh tears to fall.

"You don't have to leave, though," she said. "There's more here than Zac. Willa is here. You can come and stay with us if it's too weird being in the same house as my idiot brother."

I had major doubts that Milo would let me live under the same roof as him and his daughter, whom I was still not allowed to be near as far as I knew. "Is Milo willing to forgive me and let me see Willa?"

Raine hesitated, her face falling. "He will. I'll talk to him, get him to see reason."

"I appreciate that." I looked at her and felt an immense amount of love for this woman. She'd been nothing but supportive from the moment I'd stumbled into her life. "But I do have to go home. I can't just hang around and get more pregnant and not develop some sort of concrete structure for my life. That's not going to work with a newborn."

Her shoulders fell. "I guess."

"I just—I have things that I need to face at home. I just left. I left and went into total denial about the baby because—because I didn't know how to face it. I didn't want a child of my own. I was doing this for Margo. I got pregnant with Margo's child, fully intending to hand it over after it was born, and then Margo died. She's dead, and I'm carrying a baby that I didn't want, but—but it's the last piece of my sister I have left. How can I not keep it? It'd be like losing her all over again."

Raine exhaled and put her arm around my shoulder. "I can't claim to know what I'd do in that situation. It's unimaginable."

"And I can't go through the adoption thing again. I just couldn't. It would kill me. So I'm having my sister's baby, and I don't know how to navigate this entire fucking ordeal, but I have no choice. It's real. I have to go home and sort my life out."

She nodded. "Can I ask you something?"

"Yeah."

"How come you didn't tell anyone?"

"Margo died the morning after I was implanted. It was barely even a reality, and after she died, everything just sort of took a back seat to that. I think I also hoped that the implantation hadn't taken. But at the same time, I did want it to take. I was confused and compartmentalizing to forget, and I knew, I did know that I had to tell Zac. It just never seemed like the right time. It was wrong on my part. Super wrong. I know that. I just can't give any other explanation other than I haven't been okay in weeks."

"Like I said, I have no idea what I would do in your shoes. So I won't say what was wrong or right. Who could even say what the best thing to do in that position would be without having experienced it? Some things in life are in that gray space."

It meant a lot that she was so understanding, but I should have known she would be. That was her.

Our goodbye was emotional, tearful but also full of promises. I promised her that I would call when I got home, and she promised me that she would accommodate my friendship with Willa. I needed to hear that. I needed that hope, but I wouldn't bank on it.

# CHAPTER TWENTY-ONE

*Six weeks ago*

The salon was overpowering with the scent of lacquer, sanitizer, and harsh remover. The hum and spark of UV lights could be heard under the low hum of K-pop music in the overhead speakers, and the bubble of foot spas was a soothing, rhythmic pattern despite the assortment of other noises.

"What color?" Margo mumbled, staring at the wall of nail polishes, arranged in an intricate rainbow. There were hundreds of colors. Dozens of shades in each color. I'd been about to pluck a canary yellow down when she reached out for a pale pink. "This one."

"That's cute. I think I'll go for yellow."

"What?" She looked at me, palming the bottle in her hand. "We have to get the same shade. Toes, fingers, lips."

"I'm not putting nail polish on my lips."

"No." She laughed and linked her arm through mine, pulling us toward the tables that were arranged with manicure instruments. "I have a shade like this at home. It complements our olive skin. Trust me on this one."

It didn't bother me enough to argue. If she wanted us to wear matching pink nail polish, so be it. This entire afternoon was her idea anyway. A girls' date, followed by a night out to celebrate the fact that I had been implanted with her baby this morning. It wasn't a guarantee that it had taken—it never was with IVF. But Margo refused to believe that in two weeks' time, the test would be anything but positive.

So we were celebrating a new beginning. It was her treat.

Two technicians were smiling, waiting for us to put our hands on the rolled white towels in the middle of the tabletops.

"How are you today?" the technician with her hair in a tight ballet bun asked, dripping a few drops of oil onto my fingertips before massaging it into the cuticle area. I was feeling more relaxed already.

"Good, thanks," I answered. "You?"

She just nodded and kept her focus on the job at hand. It appeared there wouldn't be much chatting going on between us, and that was fine with me. I preferred less conversation from hairdressers, beauticians, and anyone else that was in my personal space.

There's something obligatory about salon etiquette and having to uphold a chat, a pressure that the stylist feels to keep the client feeling as though they are being paid attention to. I don't like my stylist to feel that way. There's no pressure from me. As long as my hair is done or my legs are waxed or my nails are painted, I'm happy.

Of course, Margo and the other nail technician with the fishtail were friends. They could have been. Margo got her nails done far more often than I did. It was a business expense. She had to keep up her appearance for events, whereas I sat behind a computer or did paperwork 90 percent of the job.

"Yep." Margo beamed, and I tuned in at the end of their conversation. "She's pregnant with my baby."

Her technician looked at me with total delight. Mine looked confused for a moment until she nodded between us.

"Congratulations, happy couple."

Margo's technician furrowed her brows at mine and gave a slight disapproving head shake for not understanding the context of the situation.

Margo grinned. "Thank you."

The conversation became quiet again for a moment, and only the filing of nails could be heard between our tables until Margo leaned toward me a little and said, "I think that we should move."

"Move?" My head whipped toward her.

Even though she'd suggested nothing more than the fact that she wanted to move, my imagination ran away, and I thought about all of the beautiful cities that we could explore in search of the right place to settle down. Somewhere with green rolling meadows and trees taller than the dull buildings that I saw day in and day out. There was so much potential.

"Yeah," she confirmed. "Into a bigger condo or apartment. I think we could use a bigger space to raise the baby in."

I swallowed down bitter disappointment and tried not to wince. "We?" I chuckled, hoping to hide the tightness in my voice. "What's this we? You're raising the baby. Not me."

Her brows pulled together, and she wore a small scowl that she was attempting to hide with confusion. "We live together. You're going to be the aunt. We are more or less doing this together."

"Less. This isn't my baby to raise. I'll be there, of course, every day, but it's not mine. You're the mother. You do the raising."

She exhaled, her shoulders fell, and she watched her hands instead of me. "Ever heard the saying 'it takes a village to raise a baby'? You don't have to be a parent to raise a child. Whoever is there and spends time contributing to their happiness aids in raising the baby. You're making this a way bigger thing than it has to be."

"I mean, I get what you're saying," I mumbled, feeling silly for flipping out. "I'm just . . . I'm not carrying this baby so that I can be a parent. Not at all. That's not why I offered. Just so we're clear. I'll be the fun aunt. I might even help with diapers once in a while. But it's yours."

It was quiet between us for such a long stretch that I looked over and saw Margo watching me with parental concern. It reminded me that she was right. She wasn't my mom, but she had raised me. She had stepped up when I had no one else.

"Is this about Baby Bianchi?" she asked.

"What?"

"You're so convinced that giving your baby up for adoption meant never being a mother again, which is stupid, but whatever. But if you're afraid to 'raise' a baby with me because you think it's too close to a second chance, that's ridiculous."

She knew me too well. I hadn't realized that was how I felt when I'd adamantly denied partaking in her baby's upbringing just now. But it was true. Whenever a small part of me craved the chance to be a mother again, I remembered the absolute desolating agony that tore through my entire body when my baby was taken, her cries fading and the sight of her pink fingertips disappearing as she was carried from the room.

· · ·

After our mani-pedis, Margo and I went home, changed into our cutest outfits, glammed up, and slipped into a cab. Margo was claiming tonight as her last night of wild life.

"You don't have to settle down," I said from beside her, tugging up my strapless dress. I so did not have the boobs for this outfit. But I loved how it hugged my hips. "You're allowed to go out and dance as a mom too."

She swiped gloss on and rolled her eyes. "I'm too old to hit the town. I mean, I love it. But I look ridiculous."

"You do not!" I argued. "You're a total babe at forty. Besides, there's no rule saying that you have to stop dancing at a certain age. Just have fun. Do you. I hate going out, so I'm never going to hesitate to babysit."

She laughed and slipped her gloss into her clutch. "Well, I'm glad you're out with me tonight."

"It's a special occasion."

"It's a miracle!"

I smiled, glad that she appreciated my company so much. Most of the time, she went out dancing with Irie or Lo. But tonight was sister night and an exception to my otherwise homebound life.

"Besides, the baby won't be here for quite a while. There's tons of time to get your dancing in."

She slipped her arm through mine and rested her head on my shoulder. "Nope. I'm committing to being part of this pregnancy as much as I can. You can't eat something, I won't eat it. No drinking. No wild late nights. We're in this together. Your suffering is my suffering."

"Wow. Suffering. And here I thought this was a beautiful time in our weird lives."

She leaned back and looked at me. "It is beautiful. I won't ever be able to stop saying thank you."

I gave her a pat on the head. Being pregnant was so different this time. Margo wasn't crying herself to sleep every night, worried about my future. She wasn't in a subtle but definitive state of sadness over the choice that I'd made to give my baby up for adoption. She wasn't moving around me carefully and concisely so as to not make me feel hated but definitely let me know that she was disappointed. She wasn't threatening to find the "no-good little shit" who'd done this to me and wring his neck.

The entire atmosphere was different, and it excited me. It excited me for her.

It seemed like as good a time as any to have a discussion with her. "I've been thinking that now might be a good time to start this horticulture course that I've been looking at online."

Margo looked at me, brows pinched, a burnt-orange glow illuminating her confusion each time a headlight passed us.

"The one that I talked about a while back?" I reminded her. "It seems like a good time. I'll still be doing the office work until the baby is born, but I can start this course. I could qualify and start selling houseplants. Which can be done from home too. And I'd learn so much—"

"Addie?"

"What?"

She leaned back in the seat and exhaled a quiet breath. "I need you committed to the business, now more than ever."

"Well, I am. But we could find a replacement?"

"A replacement? For May We? That's our name. Our brand."

"Well, sort of. I mean, we changed our name. But that's not the point. The point is, I want to do horticulture. I think I'm just past the event planning. It's great, and I'll still be involved, but I want to do something else."

"It's not a good time," she said, staring straight ahead at the dark road and bright city lights. "With the baby coming, I'm going to need a lot more help. Am I supposed to look after the business and the baby alone?"

I scowled. "That's not what I said. I said that I'd still help as often as I can. But I want to do horticulture."

"I need you right now, Addie. The business does. You can't just up and walk from it when we're about to bring a baby into the mix."

"Like I said, hire someone to take my place."

She bunched her hair in her hands and released a frustrated breath. "It's our business, Addie. Ours. I can't just hire someone to take the place of a May sister. I can't believe you'd pick now to do this."

"Seriously?" I leaned as close to the door as possible so that there was as much space between us as I could get. "Carrying your baby isn't good enough? I have to give up the only thing I'm interested in too?"

She whipped her head toward me, fast. "You pushed for that. Are you kidding me? You pushed so fucking hard for this surrogacy thing. I knew there was a reason we shouldn't have gone through with it. I knew something like this was bound to happen."

"Ugh. Whatever. No. I don't regret it. I'm glad you're getting the baby you've always wanted. And I'm one hundred percent happy to do it. It'd just be nice if I could do what I want to do. And that's learn more about the things I'm actually interested in. Plants and trees. That sort of thing."

"You know what," she snapped. "Do whatever you want. You were right, this is my baby, so I'm the one who has to worry about these things. I'll manage the baby and the business alone."

I felt hot all over as I leaned forward to the front seat. "Please turn the cab around and go back to where we started." I looked at Margo again. "You know what, you're the one who told me I was making a bigger deal out of raising the baby than I needed to. And now who's making a big fucking deal out of nothing. And being super dramatic."

"Dramatic?!"

"Yes! Dramatic. I just want to study horticulture, something that I'm interested in, and you're acting like I'm about to abandon you! I can still be at home, and I can still be hands-on and helping while I do what I want to do."

She waved her arms in frustration. "You told me to hire someone else to take over your part of the job. You want out. You have for a long time."

"So fucking what? Hire someone else. What's the big deal if the work is still getting done?"

"It won't be a May sister. I'll have to rebrand again."

"Ugh," I almost shouted as the cab pulled up outside of the condo. I handed the driver my card; my leg bounced, and my heart was beating while he swiped it. "We're going around in circles here. Your argument makes no fucking sense, and I'm sick of it."

Without waiting for her response, I got out of the car and walked through the dark toward the front door. She followed; I could hear the clack of our heels echoing through the quiet streets. Inside still held the lingering scent of our perfume and lipstick after we'd gotten ready not all that long ago. Margo threw her clutch past me, and it landed on the sofa.

I spun around and glared. "You missed."

"I wasn't aiming for you!"

We stared at each other, scowling and bitter while we took our shoes off, the heels hitting the hardwood floor. "Stop doing that," I seethed. Her knit brows drew even closer together.

"What?"

I spun around and headed toward the kitchen. "That stupid frown. You look at me like I'm a child. It's the same stupid look you used to give me when I was a teenager. The look I'd get for not only rebelling, but," I raised my voice, "not being like you."

She followed me. "Not being like me? What does that even mean?!"

"You have never been able to stand the fact that I don't have the same interests as you. Even when I was a kid. You were always carting me around and doing my hair and nails and forcing me to go to the park and the mall and then, as I got older, parties and social events. Even the career. I don't even remember getting a choice in the event planning. It was just decided for me."

"You're good at it!" she shouted, standing beside the fridge. I started filling up my watering can.

"That is not the point. It doesn't matter if I'm good at it. No, I don't hate it, but it's just—not for—I'm not passionate about it. Not like I could be. Besides, there's nothing wrong with changing careers. It's not a bad thing to do something new."

"You know, I didn't realize there was something wrong with trying to spend time with my sister and introducing you to my interests." She circled back to that argument, waving her hand with frustration. "But I didn't force you into anything! What teenager doesn't want to go to parties with their big sister?"

I barked with laughter. "Margo, you're sixteen years older than me! Your parties were wine and nibbles or lame open mic nights with all your desperate married friends who go out and pretend their pathetic husbands aren't sitting at home."

She recoiled with a harsh gasp. "That is so mean!"

"It's not even about the sort of party that it was! I wasn't a party person. I wanted to be at home. I liked being at home. Again, there's nothing wrong with that. But it bothered you that I might be an introvert because you weren't."

"You know what, I don't get you. At all. Never have."

"That's what I'm saying!"

"I just wanted you to get out there more. Make friends. Realize that life is fun when you're living it."

"Our ideas of living are not the same. We don't have to be the same. I'm not missing out on anything just because you're telling me that I am. Grow up and realize people have different personalities."

She was sobbing. It happened so fast. One minute I was screaming at her, and then she was wailing.

"Fine," she spluttered, not all that coherent. "I get it. We're not the same. Fine, leave the business. Fine, don't raise the baby with me. Just abandon me and live your boring, sheltered life."

"I don't want to abandon you, you idiot! I just want to be me without feeling pressured to choose and behave like someone else to please you."

Margo cried even harder, her makeup running, staining her cheeks. "We s-sound like an old married couple."

"Yeah, good thing there's a baby on the way to mend our broken marriage."

She laughed, sending a shower of saliva and tears out in front of her. So now she was sobbing through her laughter and looked like a real mess, which made me laugh, and we were both giggling ourselves stupid within a few moments.

Margo inhaled and then gasped sharply. She started coughing, her face becoming tight and red. She turned around and began pouring herself some water. I stepped closer, wondering if she needed me to pat her back. But as I stepped closer, she spun around and threw her glass of water at me.

The cold splash made me gasp, freeze, and quietly squeal.

"You deserved that."

"Me?!" I squeaked, wiping my face. "You're the one who's been a controlling bitch. And I'm carrying your baby! You deserve the face of water."

"Fine," she snapped and refilled the glass before throwing it at her own face. She gasped, and her gaze widened with the shock of cold water. "Better?"

"No, that wasn't even by my hand. I get no satisfaction from that."

She refilled the glass and handed it to me.

So I threw it. "Better." I turned around and left the kitchen.

"You have to clean this up," she shouted, getting louder with each syllable. Finally, she caught up to me, pushed past, and stole the bathroom before I could shower. Bitch. If she thought that I was going to occupy my time with mopping while she showered, she was wrong. I stripped off my cold, damp clothes, dabbed my neck and chest dry with the back of a T-shirt, and then put on a robe.

Half an hour later, I was in bed with the television on and the lights out, watching *Serendipity* for the thousandth time, when Margo slipped into the bedroom in her purple satin nightdress. She pouted and sat on the bed, watching me with cautious eyes, just as I was no doubt doing to her.

"Shower thoughts," she mused, not looking at me. "Seeking counsel from the showerhead. Not relief, those are two very different showerheads."

"Wow."

"Yeah, so anyway, I came to a sort of understanding. Or an understanding to not understand, but that's okay. If that makes sense? We are not the same, and I might not get the sort of person you are, but I can still support that person. And love that person and encourage that person. So, you should do the horticulture course. I'm sure you'll be incredible at it within the first two hours."

My chest expanded. This was what I had been waiting for. It was a quick moment, a brief chat about the change in attitude that she was having, but it felt monumental, like the weight had been lifted from me and I could stop dicking around and make some changes and choices. I had a fleeting thought that stopped me in my tracks. Had I, on some subconscious level, used carrying her baby as a bargaining tool?

I gasped, slapping a palm across my mouth.

"What?" Margo looked concerned, and I tried to hide a guilty grin before I dropped my hand.

"Nothing." I didn't want to tell her what I'd thought. The thought that perhaps we'd used a baby to save our relationship. No, that was ridiculous. Those were not the motivations behind the offer. But still, it fit so well with the situation. I had to laugh.

She climbed into the bed, lifted the comforter, and snuggled in beside me, resting her head on my shoulder. "I love this movie."

"Me too," I agreed.

"Sure. You don't even like romance. I don't know why you watch all these movies."

"For the same reason I read all the books."

She peered up at me. "And what's that?"

"Living vicariously through fictional characters who get a happy ending."

She was silent for so long that I would have thought she was asleep apart from the fact that she was tense, leg shaking.

"Say it," I sighed.

"You don't need to live vicariously through fictional people. You could have your own love life."

"Well, not now that I'm carrying your baby."

She gasped and gave me a slap in the arm, and we both laughed. "Don't start with me," she warned.

"Nah." I shrugged. "Happy endings don't happen in real life. Just stories. So, I'm safe there. I don't really see the appeal in going through a total heartbreak when I don't have to, and I can still get my fix of romance."

"This is going to turn into another argument," she said, her voice becoming monotone. "I do not understand, but I do accept that is how you feel."

"Okay." I laughed, not convinced at all, but that was as good as it was going to get, and it was better than ongoing arguments or just total submission to what she wanted. Balance.

She shrugged, and we fell quiet again, watching the movie. I got up just once for a glass of water and a bag of chips.

"That kitchen floor is still wet," I told Margo as I slipped back in beside her and opened the bag of salt and vinegar. I couldn't stand the smell of these things, but the taste was delicious.

"I'll clean it up after the movie."

"Will not. You'll fall asleep."

"Fine. I'll do it in the morning."

I grinned. "How about the first person to wake up cleans it up?"

"Sounds fair."

• • •

In the morning, I woke up in an empty bed. I'd been having a beautiful dream about who knows what. The memories were distorted, but whatever it was had left a good tingle up my spine and an overall warmth.

When I got to the kitchen, that warmth evaporated. The world evaporated, fell out of focus, and all I saw was Margo, face down, a pool of blood around her head, her visible eye open and unfocused.

"Margo?"

I stared at her back, waiting for it to rise on a breath so I could laugh at her elaborate prank. There was a niggling thought deep down, a truth banging on the door, a door I refused to open. It was still, silent. A tremor in my eyes meant it was impossible to tell whether Margo took a breath or not.

I crept across the kitchen, feet barely registering the liquid they stepped in. Sinking to the floor, I slid my arms under Margo and rolled her over, dragging her into my lap. The weight of her was limp, not an ounce of her assistance. With her in my lap, her face stared up at me, a gash in her temple now visible. It stretched from her hairline to her eye, swollen and bruised.

"That SFX makeup looks good," I said, the ringing in my ears drowning out my voice. "You're being weird, Margo."

Her blue lips were parted, a dark red smear on the inside of her mouth, trickling from the corner. It was all so convincing, so real. It couldn't be, though. This could not be real.

"Margo." I shook her, that vacant stare of hers aimed upward, not flinching, not seeing me and the desperation growing. "Margo."

*She's gone.*

"No." The door was inching open, the force of the truth too great to be contained.

*Look at her, she's dead.*

"No," I shouted, shaking her again, the desperation filling my lungs and expelling a scream—a scream so violent dots started to blind me. This couldn't be. Didn't Margo know I had no one else, didn't she know I would be left alone if she did this to me?

That lifeless gaze taunted me, refusing to blink with the promise of life. How would I get to school tomorrow? Who would look after me? I was just a child with no one left, no one to cook for me or drive me to my doctor appointments or watch my school productions. I couldn't be left alone.

"Mom?" I pressed my forehead to hers, whispering, pleading. "Mommy, come back. Please? I know I haven't been the easiest teenager, but please. Please. I'll be better."

She did not blink; she did not breathe. Her face was cold.

"Mom, please."

*She is gone.*

# CHAPTER TWENTY-TWO

That was it. That was all it took to lose the one person I needed in my life more than anything else. One moment we'd been having a girls' night, something we did all the time, so normal, and then the most unexpected circumstances pulled the rug out from under us.

The speed at which my entire life fell apart was so fast that it didn't feel real. It wasn't until Margo was being lowered into the ground that I felt the full impact of her departure. I would never see her again, never hear her voice, feel her hug. It was incomprehensible. My knees hit the freshly dug soil as her casket went down, down, down. I wanted to throw myself in after her, and when Irie held my shoulders, attempting to hold me through the mind-numbing despair, I pushed her back, stood up, and ran.

Margo's death was a simple accident, just a terrible tragedy, but the image of how gruesome it had all looked gave me nightmares and made me nauseous. When Mom and Dad died, I saw their bodies in their caskets. They had this eerie glamor about them. Beautiful clothes, hair and makeup done. But they were so expressionless, so pale, and I remembered thinking, as a teenager, that they looked like wax.

But Margo hadn't been to the mortician; she hadn't been cleaned of her wounds and blood. Her eyes hadn't been closed, and the smell of blood still made me curl into myself.

For a death that wasn't violent or malicious or even intended to happen, it had chilled me to the core and left me with serious terrors whenever it flooded my mind in sleep.

Irie said that seeing a body like that was bound to leave a mark, regardless of what caused the death. She kept on repeating how awful it was that I'd had to cradle Margo's body for a full hour and a half before I'd finally called the police.

Through the haze of trauma, I hadn't known who to call. An ambulance seemed pointless. In the end, a coroner and the police arrived. The events that followed were a blur of questions and visitors and friends of Margo who wanted to, but couldn't, help.

• • •

I'd decided to book a flight home, not feeling up to a long bus ride. Keeping up with the prescribed pain relief was helping, but there was still a dull throb in my temple as I stood on the doorstep of the condo. The awning kept the midafternoon sun off my face while I stood unmoving, my bag in hand. It'd been twenty-four hours since I'd left the farm. I'd slept in a chair at the airport while I waited for the first available flight, and while I'd had time to process what I was doing, it hadn't helped at all. I wasn't prepared for this.

This condo was the site of the worst thing that had ever happened to me, and I was not sure how I was going to put one foot in front of the other and go inside. The closer I got, the more real it became. As it was, I was having trouble breathing. What would happen when it all hit?

The first thing I noticed when I finally pushed the door open and dragged my bag in behind me was how familiar the apartment smelled. It smelled like Margo. Someone must have been here and aired it out because it didn't have the musty scent that I'd have expected after it had been closed up for over a month. The plants were all gone; Pete had obviously done what I'd asked and come to remove them all. It was emptier without them.

"Margo?" I didn't even recognize my own voice as I called out and waited for an answer that I knew wasn't going to come. My legs shook, but they carried me through the living room, and I veered off right before the kitchen. I couldn't look inside. I couldn't stop at her bedroom.

"Margo?!"

I flung the office door open, but it wasn't the office. It was the nursery. The one I'd set up in an attempt to convince Margo to let me have her child. And now here we were, or here I was, with that child and with the crib and the mobile and the change table and all of the things that she would never get to enjoy because she wouldn't fucking answer me.

"Margo?!" I sobbed, voice hitching as I looked around the room with blurred vision. "Margo?"

Somehow, I ended up back in the living room.

"Margo?"

She wasn't going to answer me. She wasn't going to walk out of her bedroom or the kitchen. She wasn't going to come through the front door.

The floodgates broke.

Everything that I had been holding in from the moment she'd died came to the surface, and it threw me down. My knees gave out. I hit the floor, and I gasped over and over again, trying and failing to breathe.

It didn't seem to matter how hard I tried, there was no air. No relief from the pressure forming around my skull. There was nothing for my hands to grab, nothing concrete, nothing that would stop me from feeling as if my mind was deteriorating. It all fell on top of me, and I couldn't seem to get up again.

"Margo," I cried. "Margo, please come back."

• • •

The sky outside the living room window was getting dark again when I woke to the sound of the front door being pounded on. How had he found me? I was pretty sure I hadn't given him an address.

"Go away, Zac." My voice was barely more than a hoarse whisper, but it must have been heard because the door opened and closed, and the sound of rushed footsteps forced me to turn my head toward the threshold, where Irie stood with panic in her enormous round eyes.

Margo's friend was a former runway model with no qualms about invading your personal space, telling you exactly what was on her mind, and being loud. So loud.

"Bloody hell," she screamed. Her accent was a unique mix of Jamaican, where she'd spent the first half of her life, and British, where she'd spent the second half. The six years that she'd been in America had made no impact whatsoever. "I thought I was about to find you dead on the floor. I've been knocking for too long! It's not funny."

I wasn't laughing.

"What the hell are you doing?" She stomped over to me and started nudging my arm with the toe of her platforms.

"How did you know I was home?"

"I asked the neighbor to call me as soon as she saw you," Irie said, switching the lights on and pulling the curtains closed. "She's a good sort. Don't mind her so much. She gave me a call yesterday when she saw you having a crisis on the doorstep. Too bad I was in New York doing an ad campaign. I don't walk the catwalk, but this bitch can for sure serve looks on camera. Thirty-eight years young, baby."

"Irie."

"Mmm?"

"Shut up."

"Attitude," she scoffed and collapsed onto the ground beside me. She lay on her stomach, just as I was, and we stared at each other. Irie had a beautiful complexion that truly did give her the right to call herself thirty-eight years young.

There was barely a line on her face. Her head was shaved, and she absolutely pulled it off with her sharp jaw. Her cheeks were supple. Lips full. Brows thick and lashes so long that she complained whenever she wore sunglasses.

"What are you doing here?" I asked.

"You smell."

"Thanks."

"What happened to your head?"

"I was thrown off a horse."

She stared at me for a while, nothing but silence and disturbed confusion between us. "I got the call about your arrival late afternoon *yesterday*," she finally said. "Please, please tell me you have not been in this same spot since then."

"I have not been in this same spot since then."

"That was a lie." She sat up and swatted me across the shoulder. "Get up. Get into the shower. You're probably dehydrated. I'll order some food because I doubt there's anything worth eating in here. Not that I'm all that keen on going into the kitchen, to be honest." She exhaled, a haunted look on her face. It only lasted a second. "Go on. Shower. Have you pissed yourself?"

"No." I was stiff, muscles aching in protest as I slowly stood up and stretched. "I haven't had anything to drink. So I haven't needed to pee."

Before I could walk to the bathroom, she stopped me. "Did it work? The embryo transfer. Are you pregnant?" I nodded, and she let out a sharp breath. "Wow. How are you doing?"

My gaze fell to the spot where I'd been lying just a moment before. "Not great, Irie. Not great."

"Got it. Go and shower. You need to drink some water too. You can't be getting dehydrated. It's not good for the baby."

She was right, but I couldn't exactly claim to have been the best thing for the baby lately. I'd been denying it even existed up until a few days ago. Although I'd passed on a lot of wine offers over the last month. On some level, I must have been considering it a possibility.

For a moment, I considered walking into the kitchen to get a glass of water. I hovered near the entrance; if I looked up from the floor, I would be able to see the exact spot that I found my sister.

But the thought of seeing that space made my heart do overtime, pounding so hard that it winded me. I rushed past and went straight into the bathroom, slamming the door closed and locking it. It wasn't going to be practical to live in a house if I couldn't even walk into the kitchen.

"Addie?" There was a knock on the door as I was about to switch the shower on. "I saw that. You know, avoiding the scene. Quite normal. Most people don't hang around in a house where their loved one died. So, what I'm thinking is, let's pack up a few things, and we can go to my place. At some point, we can discuss selling the condo. There's no rush, but I'm a bit worried about leaving you here and hearing you've starved to death because you won't go into the kitchen."

I slowly opened the door and looked up at the five-foot-nine goddess who was overwhelming at the best of times. However, she'd always been a good friend to Margo, and right now, she was being a good friend to me.

"Sell the condo?" I was stuck on that part. "This is her home. This is our home. We lived here together. I feel like . . . like I need to try to be okay here."

"This is just a space." She shrugged, an apologetic smile curving her lips. "This is just walls. You witnessed something traumatic here. Honestly, for the sake of your mental health, I think it would be smart to leave. How safe for the mind can it be to live somewhere that constantly reminds you of something like that? Personally, it would drive me mad. Like, mad. And the thing is, Margo is wherever you are now. She's in your heart. She's not immortalized in this one place. Wherever you go, she'll go. You don't have to torture yourself by staying here because you shared this home. You know she'd say the same. She moved you guys out of your parents' house after their death, remember? Because you never wanted to be at home, and she knew it was for the best."

Irie was right. Margo would tell me that. I smiled, or tried to. Right now, I needed someone to help me make a few decisions because my mind was not working, and if Irie wanted to extend her hand and be that help, I wasn't going to turn it down.

"I'll have a shower and then pack up some clothes."

"You shower." Irie shooed me further back into the bathroom and gripped the door handle. "I'll pack up the clothes. I know where the suitcases are. I've got it."

"Wait." I grabbed the door before she could close it. "What about her things? I can't just sell the condo without organizing her things. And I don't know if I can do that right now."

"Like I said, no rush. You're welcome to stay with me for as long as you like."

"I'm pregnant."

"I know." She grinned. "And I am so excited to meet the baby. Don't get all bothered, girl. I live alone, I have the space, I want you to come with me. Margo would have insisted that I take care of you."

"Yeah." I felt weak and let go of the door so that she could shut it and I could drink some water out of the faucet.

While I was letting hot water run over my body, thawing out the stiffness in my joints, I thought about the will reading that had been done two days after the funeral. The one where Margo had left me the deed to the condo, her car, her finances, and the company. She'd left it all to me and divided out a few little items to friends.

At the time, what she'd left me meant nothing—all I wanted was to have her back. Now, when I thought about it, I couldn't believe how much she'd left me.

I suppose there weren't a lot of options when it came to next of kin, though. When she was married, Pete was in her will; I was glad she'd sorted that out as soon as the divorce was final.

Irie was waiting in the living room with three suitcases full of my belongings when I emerged from the shower in a bathrobe. "How long was I in there?"

"Literally for bloody ever," she said, her long nails tapping at her iPhone. "Get on with it, yeah? I've ordered Uber Eats. We need to beat it back to my apartment."

"You didn't even ask what I wanted to eat."

"Pasta salad with a side of garlic bread and an orange juice." When I didn't respond, she stared up from her phone and raised a brow. "Am I wrong?"

"Guess not."

"I'm good with details, darling. You know I was a personal assistant before I modelled. Remembering useless information like what someone orders and how they like their coffee is ingrained in me now. Comes in handy once in a while."

"That's . . . great."

I dressed in a pair of jeans and a hoodie that she'd laid out on the bed for me. The closet and drawers were empty. Even my makeup was gone. She was quick, I gave her that much. But it did concern me to think about how carelessly she must have shoved it all in the bag. Eh. The concern was short-lived. In fact, I decided to check my attitude, because Irie was here when no one else was, and for that, I was grateful.

"Thanks, Irie."

She slung her arm around my shoulder. "You're most welcome, sweetheart."

. . .

Irie lived in a beautiful two-bedroom apartment on Wilshire Boulevard. It was all white walls, wooden floors, and modern appliances. It was an open plan with a kitchen and living area downstairs. The staircase that went to the second floor had glass in place of a hand rail, and at the top there was another small living area with a glass rail that overlooked the bottom floor. The bedrooms and bathrooms were upstairs as well. It was chic and sophisticated but a little sterile for me.

"We should get some houseplants," I said, still standing at the door after she'd closed it and started upstairs. She paused and looked around the apartment. "Houseplants add character and keep the air clean."

"All right." She cut me off with a light laugh. "We'll go shopping tomorrow."

"I'll go today."

There was a knock on the door behind me.

"Ooh, that's the food. I paid online, so just grab some cash from the side drawer and give him a tip for me, darl. We'll go plant shopping tomorrow. Let's just chill out for the night."

I watched her walk across the second floor and disappear into one of the bedrooms with two of the bags. There was no way I could stay in this house without some plants. It was weird that it was bugging me so much, but I couldn't cope unless I had them as soon as possible.

Grabbing a twenty from the side table, I tipped the delivery person and carried the paper bag inside. It smelled good, stirring my stomach awake. I hadn't realized how starved I was until now. Irie came skipping downstairs, clapping her hands with excitement as I settled into the sofa and put the food down beside me. She might have been right about relaxing for the evening, but I'd had so much sleep at this point that there was no chance I would drift off again for a while, and I would go insane if I just sat around and did nothing. Lose-lose.

"So." Irie fell into the sofa beside me and rubbed her shaved head. "This will be fun, right? Roomies. We'll have wine nights and watch movies, and I'm totally cool if you bring men here, as long as you're willing to replace anything that's stolen."

"I'm not going to be bringing any men here."

She shuffled through the food, her gaze darting between me and the containers. "Ads, where have you been, sweetie? You dropped off the face of the earth for over a month. Seriously, where were you?"

"I was in Texas."

"Texas?"

"On the outskirts of Georgetown, to be specific."

"How the bloody hell did you end up there? And for a whole month?"

I shoveled pasta salad into my mouth and chewed, thinking of an adequate answer. There wasn't really one. "I just got on a bus. Got off again. Did some walking. Met a girl who introduced me to her family. I ended up moving onto a farm, met a man who I started to fall in love with, and met the daughter that I gave up for adoption ten years ago."

Well, it was easier to sum up than I'd expected. Although I hadn't admitted out loud that I was falling in love with Zac until right now. That part startled me. I looked at Irie. Her jaw was on the floor, eyes wide. It was safe to assume that she was reeling with shock.

"M-man?" she stammered and blinked so much I thought she was having a fit. "Daughter? Farm? What the actual shit, Addie? You have a lot to catch me up on. I want details."

"I don't want to talk about Zac."

"Zac, huh?" She grinned. "Hot name. Is he cute?"

"I'm being serious, Irie. I don't want to talk about him."

"Fine. Tell me about the daughter. My mind is blown to heck right now. You need to fill me in."

So I did. Talking about Willa didn't hurt. It might have been the one topic I could have handled right now. I talked about her for hours.

• • •

I must've fallen asleep on the sofa, because I woke up in the dark with a blanket draped over me. My phone was ringing from the floor beside me. The glare of the screen was blinding, but the number wasn't familiar at all.

"Hello?"

"Addie, thank fuck," Zac breathed from the other end of the line, and I froze.

Zac.

His voice was like a shock wave, sending ripples of reminders throughout my body. It was hard to believe that Zac wasn't a dream. It was hard to believe that entire month had happened when now I was back here, drowning in guilt and grief. It felt so surreal to hear his voice.

"Addie." I heard him swallow. "I messed up real bad, Ads. I know that. I'm sorry. I accused you of something I should never have accused you of. Raine told me everything, and I jus—I'm so ashamed of how I behaved."

I didn't know how to respond.

"Addie?"

"I'm—" My voice was hoarse, so I cleared my throat. "I'm here."

"I'm so sorry, Addie. I wish I could put it into words how damn sorry I am."

"I forgive you."

And I had. I'd forgiven him before I'd left. His reaction had been justified, normal even. Sure, he could have given me a minute to let me explain, but it wasn't the first time he'd jumped to conclusions. This time, I saw it as a blessing in disguise. I couldn't have stayed there and kept on pretending as if my life was one iota of normal.

"You do?"

"Yeah." I sat up and folded my legs. "I understand why you were upset."

"No," he said firmly. "No, I shouldn't have responded like that. It wasn't fair. Addie, please come back. Please."

"Zac, I get that you're sorry, and I forgive you, and all of that is fine. But I'm still pregnant. I'm having a baby that I'm going to have to raise. That hasn't changed. You made it clear that you're not ready to play dad. There's no point in me coming hom—back."

"I didn't mean what I said, Ads."

"Really?" I asked, not believing him. "You're willing to be a stepfather? With a woman that you barely know?"

"I know you." His voice was low and desperate. "I do. Addie, I want to be with you. I'll come to California, I'll get on a flight tomorrow. I want to be there for you."

His words made me want to weep, but I didn't have tears left. Instead, I felt the immense pain welling up inside of my chest. "You don't know me. You can't. I haven't been me since I lost Margo. You've seen a version of me. A version that was trying to survive and plastering on a smile every morning and doing her best not to crumble. Zac, I ran away from home and spent over a month completely ignoring the fact that I was pregnant."

"I know." He exhaled. "I know, but it doesn't matter. I know how I feel about you. I know that I don't want this to be over. I'll be the stepfather. I'll be the best damn one. I want you, Addie."

I slowly lay back down on the sofa, not having the strength to remain upright. "Zac," I said, barely a whisper. "I'm doing you a favor, all right? I'm not coming back to Texas to be with you, and you can't come here—you have too much going on there. Go and find a woman who hasn't been pretending to be someone she's not the entire time you've known her. Start a proper family of your own. Fall in love with someone who isn't broken. You'll thank me for it later, trust me. I'm not the one."

"Addie," he pleaded. "You've never pretended. You've been honest about everything from the moment we met. My reaction, it was projection, fear I was being messed with. Again. I should never have compared you to what I went through in the past. Please, Ads. I know that I was an asshole and I don't deserve you, but please, give me a chance. I'll make it up to you."

It'd be so easy to give in and go back to him. My soul ached for the comfort that he provided. He truly had made it all so much more bearable when I was with him. But it wasn't fair. It wasn't right to change his life or expect him to cater to us, the baby and me.

Besides, chances were it wouldn't work, and I would end up right back here all over again. I hit End on the call and let the phone fall to the floor beside me. My chin started to quiver as the echo of Zac's voice started to dissipate from my memory. He was gone. Willa was gone. Margo was gone. Tears warmed my face as I shook with sobs.

And then Irie was there, crouching beside the sofa with a hand on my shoulder.

"Honey?" she whispered, but I had no response. I had nothing but the immense loneliness. My cries became so hard I couldn't breathe properly, gasping as I tried to fill my lungs. "Oh, sweetheart."

Irie climbed over me, the couch big enough to snuggle in and spoon me. "I'm here," she whispered, hand rubbing circles on my shoulder. Irie had been best friends with Margo; the two were like sisters, and Irie was the last person I had left. So I didn't reject her comfort; I embraced it, leaned into it. I let the last person I had left be the sister I needed.

• • •

Over the next two weeks, Irie and I developed a routine. She let me fill the apartment with plants and burst into shrill panic whenever I was at the top of a ladder, hanging a pot in a macrame hanger. I told her several times that the baby had already survived being thrown from a horse and falling off a twelve-foot cliff. She didn't appreciate that. Irie was in and out for work a lot, which worked well for me. I'd get a few days of peace before she came home and started forcing me out of the house.

I wouldn't admit it, but I kind of liked how much it reminded me of Margo. A little piece of her had followed me, just as Irie had said it would.

On Friday, Irie and I went to the hospital for a checkup. I had some more blood drawn, was told the wound on my head was healing well, and was reminded to take prenatal supplements for the remainder of the pregnancy. Irie went to the bathroom before we left the hospital, and I stood in the main foyer beside the vending machines.

Lately, I'd been thinking about selling the business. Irie had told me not to be hasty because having a successful business behind me would be secure. She wasn't wrong, but I couldn't imagine working without Margo. If I were to continue, it would be out of guilt and obligation. After seeing Zac do the same thing for his mom, I knew I wanted different. It wasn't that he was miserable, but it didn't bring him the same happiness his cars did.

My heart stung when I thought of him. The absence of him was so severe, which didn't make sense, not when we'd only known each other for such a short time.

"Addison?"

My head shot up, and I saw a familiar woman standing in front of the vending machines, her palm full of loose change. She was the same height as me, perhaps an inch taller; her chestnut-brown waves sat just below her shoulders, and she had the loveliest smattering of freckles across her cheeks and nose.

"Malia." She gestured at herself, but of course I knew who she was.

"Hi." I straightened up off the wall and accepted her hug. Malia and I had gone to high school together, both of us from wealthier families who wanted us in swank private schools. I'd left during the pregnancy and was able to keep it quiet until I returned and claimed I'd done an overseas exchange in Australia.

"It's so good to see you." Her smile was so genuine. I remembered that about her, her kindness and how she opened her heart to people.

Though she wasn't someone you got close to on a personal level. She had a lot of friends, and connecting with people on a superficial level was never her problem, but apart from her best friend, Paige, there wasn't a lot of depth to those relationships.

"How's Paige?" I asked.

"She's in at the moment." Malia tipped her head up, gesturing upstairs. "I've just started a new semester at college, so I'm swamped with coursework that I'm doing from her bed, but I'm used to it."

Paige had cystic fibrosis; she was in and out of hospital for months at a time while she waited for a lung transplant. I didn't know all of the details, but I did know that Malia had lived with Paige most of her life. Paige was one of the main reasons Malia still lived in L.A. For as long as I'd known her, she'd been desperate to spread her wings and travel, work in new places, vacation in new countries. But as long as Paige was waiting for a set of lungs, Malia wouldn't leave.

"How's the degree coming along?" I asked.

Malia scanned the vending machine. "It's a lot of work, but I love it. I have about three years to go, and then I'm looking at specializing in agriculture, perhaps a residency on a farm or a ranch."

"I just spent the last month on a farm," I said, and she oohed with interest. "In Georgetown, Texas. It was probably the best month of my entire life."

Not that I wanted to talk about what had made it so incredible. Just thinking about it hurt enough.

"I would love to experience that kind of life for a little while." She punched in a number, and we watched the metal coil unravel and drop a packet of chocolate-covered peanuts. "I better get upstairs and give these to Paige; she was craving a snack."

"Yeah." I let her give me another hug. "It was nice seeing you."

"You too," she said. "Tell Margo I said hi."

Malia spun around and walked toward the elevators, not at all aware that Margo had died. There had been posts made about Margo, but if Malia didn't follow the right people, she wouldn't have seen them. I certainly hadn't shared anything. Still, I stood and watched Malia disappear around the corner, sort of touched that in the mind of someone else, Margo was still alive and well. Tears pricked at the corner of my eyes as I smiled, grateful for that one moment more than I could understand.

# CHAPTER TWENTY-THREE

*Eight months later*

"Happy birthday, sweetie," I said to Willa over FaceTime on Tuesday morning. She wore a huge grin and rubbed her tired eyes. I'd wanted to make sure that I got a phone call in before she went to school.

"Thanks, Addie."

"What's for breakfast this morning?"

"Waffles with berries, syrup, and cream."

"That sounds like a sweet start to the morning."

She nodded, and Raine appeared in the background, leaning over Willa's shoulder. "Good morning." She waved. "Let me see the bump."

As usual, Raine wanted to ooh and aah over my stomach. I had been due seven days ago, so currently I was the size of a house. Their coos sounded over the phone when I lowered it and showed them my protruding belly under a tank top that left my midriff bare.

Nothing fit quite the same, but I couldn't complain too much. As far as pregnancies went, this one had been straightforward, mostly painless, and nausea-free. For that, I was thankful. It seemed like my string of bad luck was slowing. I raised the camera again and slouched further into Irie's sofa. Or *our* sofa, as she liked to call it. We'd been living together ever since she'd saved me from the condo.

Still, no matter how many plants she added to the decor, it still didn't feel like home.

"Willa," I said. "Can I talk to Raine for a minute?"

"Okay." She blew a kiss and handed the phone over.

"What's up?"

"I just wanted to make sure we were all set for the surprise?"

"We sure are." Raine grinned, the background moving behind her as she walked through her home. "We get on the flight straight after school. We should be in Beverly Hills around seven tonight. She's going to be so excited."

Since I'd left Texas, I'd been back twice to see Willa. And in between those visits, we spoke on the phone at least three times a week. Things were better than ever. We were close; we were best friends.

Willa made me feel whole at a time in my life when I'd never felt so depleted. Unfortunately, I was too pregnant to travel for her birthday, so Milo had graciously agreed to let Raine and Willa spend the weekend here in Beverly Hills. I couldn't wait to get my arms around her.

"Say hello." Raine turned the camera on Milo, who was in his uniform. He raised his cup of coffee in greeting, and I waved.

"How's it going, Milo?" I asked.

For the most part, Milo and I had resolved our differences and were getting along. Sometimes I got the feeling that he was still nervous about my part in his daughter's life. Worried that I might attempt to lure her in and have her choose me. He'd eased up over the last few months, though. I hoped he was starting to realize that all I wanted was to know her.

"Not bad." He nodded. "How's the little one growing?"

"She's growing," I said and felt my heart skip a beat, as it often did when I thought about the fact that Margo's daughter was growing inside of me. A piece of the sister I'd lost.

Milo excused himself and told me he was looking forward to hearing all about how our girls' weekend went.

"So . . ." Raine came back on the phone, and I knew where she was going with this conversation before she even opened her mouth. "Zac said to say hello."

I sighed. I'd managed to avoid Zac on both occasions I'd been in Texas visiting Willa. I knew I wouldn't be strong enough to see him, but I also knew it wasn't going to work even if I did. Not under these circumstances.

"He misses you."

"So you tell me," I said. "But he shouldn't. He should be well over it by now. We knew each other for a month. I've been gone for, like, eight. Surely, he's over it."

"Are you over it?" The lie I was about to tell got caught in my throat, and she gave me a smug stare. "So not over it."

"Raine, I'm not right for him. It's too complicated."

"You're being irrational. The fact that neither of you seems to be able to move on should attest to the fact that you had a huge impact on each other's lives."

"Zac has been single for how long? It's not unusual for him to be on his own," I pointed out. "Besides, I'm pregnant. I'm not on the market."

"Semantics," she scoffed. "You do realize you'll have to face him at the wedding." I'd promised to go to her wedding in October. Five-month-old infant and all. I'd agreed, but I was still wondering how I could get out of it. "Don't even think about it," she warned. "You're coming to my wedding. Willa would be crushed if you didn't watch her throw flower petals down the aisle."

"That is a low blow," I seethed. She was right, though. I wouldn't miss it. Hopefully by then, Zac would have moved on, and the thought of seeing him wouldn't send my stomach into a flutter of dancing baby limbs.

We said our goodbyes, and I assured her that a car service would be waiting at the airport tonight. Irie cleared her throat, and I rolled my head backward to see her leaning over the glass railing on the second floor.

"Am I invited to the wedding?"

"You hate weddings."

"I do not," she scoffed and started down the staircase. "Besides, I'll endure it if I get to meet this Zac fellow. He sounds gorgeous."

"You weren't invited."

"Well, excuse me, I'm about to let the bride stay in my apartment. I'm sure I could wrangle an invitation out of her."

She probably could; it was Raine, after all, just about the sweetest person I knew. Irie had work in New York over the next few days, so I was going to be in her room, Raine was going to be in mine, and Willa would be on the pullout sofa in the upstairs living space. However, Irie wasn't going to be leaving until after Willa arrived because she desperately wanted to meet my birth daughter.

"What time is Lo coming over?" Irie asked, flicking the kettle on. She leaned against the countertop and folded her arms.

"Ten."

"You need a hand to get upstairs and showered before she arrives?"

"I'm pregnant, Irie. Not an invalid. Thanks, though."

"Are you sure you want to do this?"

I stood up and sighed, certain in an uncertain sort of way. For the last few months, Lo and I had been in talks of her buying May We? The business had been everything to Margo, but I'd never loved it like she did.

With her gone, it was even harder to stay invested. It was time to let it go, and as hard as that was going to be, I knew it would be in good hands with Lo. She knew how much Margo cared about her work. She was the one who had kept it afloat since Margo died.

"I'm sure," I said and started waddling upstairs.

• • •

When I was showered and dressed in a floor-length summer dress, I hobbled back downstairs and found that Lo was already on the sofa with paperwork spread out on the coffee table. Irie was nowhere to be seen.

"Hey," I said, and Lo's pale cheeks lifted in a broad smile as her gaze swept over me.

"Wow," she said. "Not long to go, huh? You look radiant."

"Thanks, Lo." I lowered myself into the sofa next to her. "I don't feel radiant, but I appreciate that."

"At least you have an excuse." She pointed at her stomach. Lo was a bigger woman, but that didn't dim her beauty, not as far as I was concerned. Besides, when I wasn't pregnant, I wasn't exactly a model either. "Anyway," she added, waving a dismissive hand, "it's still so hard to believe her baby is in there." She stared at my stomach with awe. "She's gone, and yet part of her remains. Incredible."

"It is pretty incredible." I rubbed a hand across my stomach. "Sort of bittersweet."

"Mmm. Have you decided how you're going to raise her? As in, who you'll be to her?"

"I think I'm going to be Mom," I said. "She deserves that. You know? She deserves to have a mom. She'll know the truth about Margo, of course, but I don't want to make her feel . . . I don't know, isolated? It's hard to think of the right word. I wouldn't want her to grow up and not have the privilege of calling someone Mom. It would seem unfair to make her call me aunt or whatever. To never experience having a parent."

"That's very selfless of you," Lo said, and I nodded. It was quiet for a moment until she sniffed, straightened up, and looked at the papers. "So, should we talk business?"

"We should."

"Can I ask—" She paused before reaching for the paperwork. "What are you going to do now that you're not event planning?"

"I'm going to do what I've always wanted to do and study horticulture, perhaps open a small houseplant store or something like that. There's, um—there's a good chance I'll move out of Beverly Hills after the baby is born."

"Oh."

"It's just—it's not where I want to live. You know? At first, I thought it wouldn't be right to leave the place where I lived with Margo, but my therapist has been amazing at helping me sort through these emotions and allowing me to understand that Margo is gone and I can't let that stop me from living. She'd want me to be happy. Plus, her memory is alive with me. It doesn't matter where I am. Irie helped me understand that too. There are some things that I need to do for myself in order to heal. Confining myself to certain circumstances is actually going to do more harm than good in the long run."

Lo gave the top of my hand a gentle rub. "That's very true. I just hope I'll get to meet the baby before you leave."

"Oh, Lo, one hundred percent."

• • •

Lo left with a drawn-up agreement in hand. It would have to go through our lawyers and be notarized before it was official, but as far as I was concerned, she now owned May We?

And it was hers to do with as she wished. She'd mentioned that she would like to change the name but had asked for permission to incorporate Margo. That wasn't a problem with me. She meant a lot to so many people here in Beverly Hills. I hadn't been all that surprised to find out there were memorials and tributes going on for weeks after I left. Part of me wished I hadn't missed it all. Hindsight, I suppose.

That afternoon, I got a video message from Raine. She and Willa were at the airport, and the camera was on Willa while she looked around in confusion.

"It's your birthday surprise," Raine said, off camera.

I giggled at Willa's sweet face, alarmed and excited all at once. "Where are we going?"

"We are going to Beverly Hills," Raine said, and Willa's eyes widened. "To see Addie."

"No way?!" She bounced on the spot, and my heart felt as if it was going to beat right out of my chest. "Are we really?"

"Yep."

Willa clapped, bounced, and squealed. "Yesyesyesyesyes," she said in one short breath. The video ended.

• • •

The most I had achieved by seven that night was putting fresh sheets on all the beds—not an easy task with a giant stomach getting in the way—and setting the table for dinner. Irie was out getting Willa's favorite, enchiladas and egg salad. Well, her current favorite. Her tastes changed from month to month. The doorbell rang just before I planted myself back on the sofa, and I sighed with relief that I hadn't sat down. There was a butt mold forming from where I sat in the corner so often.

Baby started to kick, and I exhaled as I swung the door open and was met with two beautiful faces.

"Addie!" Willa squealed and launched herself at me. She was careful, though, and I pulled her in tight, squeezing her, holding back tears so she didn't think I was insane. I missed her so much when we were apart. It was hard to believe I'd lived without her for ten years. It was even harder to imagine I'd have lived a lifetime without her if I'd never ended up in Texas.

Raine slipped past us with two travel bags and closed the door. When Willa and I finally parted, I gave Raine a hug too.

"Pregnancy suits you," she said and winked, holding my belly. Her braids were wrapped in a bun on the top of her head, and she wore a hoodie and sweats.

"Sure. Hey, are you cold?"

"I'm not hot." She shrugged. "But I am used to the Texan heat, so don't mind me. This is a cute place."

"Yeah." I waved a flippant hand. "Irie's out getting dinner. Your favorite, birthday girl."

Willa gasped. "Egg rolls and fried rice?"

I winced. "Uh, no. But there is egg salad and enchiladas."

"Also my favorite." She grinned.

My heart sped up, and I pulled her in again. "I am so happy you're here. You have no idea. Should we go upstairs and put your things away? I'll show you where you're sleeping."

Raine and Willa followed me upstairs, and we stopped at the living area first. The couch was pulled out, and the curtains were still open. Willa immediately skipped over to the rectangular window that stretched along the wall, and I saw her jaw drop in the reflection. "Wow, this view is so cool. I can see the whole city!"

"Not bad, huh?"

"And you're thinking of trading this place for Texas?" Raine whispered so that Willa didn't hear her.

"Are you kidding me?" I whispered back. "I love it there. This is a great place, but it's just—"

"Not you," Raine finished and rolled her eyes with amusement. "This apartment is something you see on *Suits*. Or *Gossip Girl*. It's beautiful."

She was right. This place was beautiful. But beautiful didn't mean comfortable. It didn't mean home.

The sound of the door slamming shut startled me. Irie huffed and puffed into the kitchen with bags full of food. "Friday-night traffic is a fucking nightmare," she squawked, and I gave the girls an apologetic look. "I walk into the store, yeah? And the order isn't even bloody ready, even though I phoned it through, like, half an hour ahead of time. It's so damn packed in there that I'm about to kick off if one more asshole bumps into me. Barely room to breathe.

I think I inhaled someone's fucking fart. Turns out the daft bastards had given my order to someone else! So, I got the whole meal free and a couple of extra sides too."

Surely she was done. "Irie? Willa and Raine are here."

Her head snapped up, and she screamed, a loud, piercing scream that echoed through the apartment. She discarded the food onto the table and started sprinting up the staircase in her six-inch platforms.

"Where is she?" She appeared at the landing, and her sights fell on Willa.

"Stop." She clutched her chest. Irie had only seen photos of Willa; they were good photos, but it wasn't the same as seeing her in person. "Stop. No. She is so cute. She is beautiful! She looks just like you."

Willa wore a sheepish smile while she had the attention of the room, and then Irie stretched out her arms and wiggled her fingers. "Can we hug?"

Willa nodded.

"You don't have to hug her," I said, but Willa shrugged and let Irie scoop her up. Next to the former model, Willa looked so small.

"You must be Raine." Irie shook Raine's hand but still had Willa tucked in next to her. "It's nice to meet you."

"You as well. Thank you so much for having us."

"I absolutely love that accent," Irie said. "And not a problem. I wish I didn't have to leave. I want to get to know you both. But work is work. I am not willing to part with this lifestyle right now. So I do what must be done."

Raine nodded, and Willa stared up at Irie, no doubt in awe of her height. Or just her as a person.

"When do you have to leave?" I asked.

"In about an hour. So let's go and eat." She grabbed Willa by the hand and dragged her downstairs. "I want to hear all about school and gossip and whatever the heck you're into. What are you into?"

"Um, I really like books and movies. And swimming. Um, oh,

and my uncle has been teaching me about cars and stuff too. That's pretty cool."

I couldn't help but react to the mention of Zac. My instinct was to ask for more details. What kind of car was he working on right now? How were things with Keith at the home? I didn't know anything else apart from the one thing that Raine had shared. Keith had moved into a retirement village, but Zac was still at the house, where the wedding would be held. In terms of conversation surrounding Zac, it was off-limits. I didn't want to be updated on his life. It was too hard.

We ate together at the table—well, Irie inhaled her dinner—and then she left after a round of cuddles.

"All right," I said, coming back from upstairs with a big wrapped box topped with a ribbon.

Willa lit up from where she sat on the sofa. "Is that for me?"

"It sure is."

The three of us sat on the sofa, and I set the gift down in front of Willa, who immediately tore into the paper. Inside was a gift box of different assorted items. She gasped, gently taking them out one at a time and carefully inspecting them.

There were a few delicate ornaments wrapped in tissue paper: a ceramic book, a vintage fairy with transparent wings, a mushroom house, and a rocking chair. They were all so cute, and I'd bought them with the thought that she could put them in her outdoor library.

There were also a few sweets and treats, a notebook, and a set of vintage stationery with sunflowers and daisies on it. There were some books and gift cards in there too. It was hard not to go overboard while I was shopping for her. But I had to think about the fact that she had to fly home with all of it.

"I love everything," she said, shuffling through the tissue paper and coming to the last gift hidden right at the bottom. "No way!" She squealed and lifted a Polaroid camera out of the box. "These are so cool. They take the best photos that look old."

"Wow." Raine whistled. "You're a lucky girl, huh?"

Willa threw her arms around my neck and squeezed. "Thank you, Addie."

"You're welcome."

"Can we take a photo right now?"

"Yeah, absolutely."

We worked together to put the little stack of Polaroid sheets into the camera, and once we'd done that, I lifted the camera and the three of us put our heads together so I could snap the selfie. Willa could barely contain herself as the Polaroid printed.

"It looks so cool," she said when it was done, pleased with the vintage aesthetic of the photo.

"There's a few packets of film in there too," I said, knowing how fast she would go through them.

"You'll have to get lots of photos of you and your friends at home," Raine said, smiling with gratitude.

We took a few more photos, then we spent an hour or so chatting. Raine showered and called it a night after she'd tucked Willa in. Before I went to bed, I climbed onto the pullout sofa with Willa and aimed the remote at the television.

"Should we watch a movie?"

She grinned and nodded, then snuggled closer and rested her hand on my bulging belly, slowly moving it from side to side. Suddenly, the baby started to kick, and Willa gasped.

"Did you feel her?!" I asked, and she nodded. I put my hand on top of hers and held it tight. "She's kicking. Oh, that's so sweet."

"I've never felt a baby kick before."

"Cool, right?"

"Yeah. Do you know what her name will be?"

"I do," I said. "Maggie Pearl May."

"Pearl?"

"Mm-hmm. Margo means 'pearl.' Margo was big on using names to honor our loved ones. She would love Pearl."

"What if you and uncle Zac get married? Maggie Pearl Ryan?"

"Oh. My. Gosh. Willa?"

She giggled and shrugged as if she was totally innocent. "Just wondering."

I sighed and folded my arms, resting them on top of my stomach. "It would actually be Maggie Pearl May-Ryan. Because May is also sentimental. Not that it matters because I am not marrying Zac."

"You should. You guys are so stubborn."

"All right, miss." I playfully narrowed my stare. "Who have you been talking to? Hmmm?"

Willa didn't answer, so I started tickling her, and she squirmed and giggled and kicked around.

"Spill. Who's your source?!"

"Never!"

Eventually, we did watch the movie. But we must have fallen asleep halfway through because I woke up on the pullout sofa, right beside a curled-up Willa.

# CHAPTER TWENTY-FOUR

Willa, Raine, and I sat around the breakfast table on Saturday morning. I'd made waffles and bacon, which was not something I did often. It was a miracle if I could make an entire coffee without needing to sit down in the morning. But with the girls here, I wanted to make an effort.

"So," Raine said, leaning back in her seat with a coffee cup between her hands. "What's the plan for today?"

"I have a few ideas," I said. "I really want to take Willa to the Beverly Hills Public Library."

"Ooh," Willa enthused through a mouthful of waffle.

"Shopping, of course. We have to spend on Rodeo Drive. It's essential. But I wanted to ask for a favor while you guys are here."

"What is it?" Raine asked, interest piqued when she noticed that I was a little nervous.

"Uh, well, the thing is . . ." I chipped away at a mark on the tabletop. "I have to sell the condo that I shared with Margo soon, but before I can do that, I have to clear it out. I've done a lot of it already, but I haven't touched Margo's bedroom, and I was hoping that you guys would be able to come with me. I could really use the company, and—" I looked at Willa "—I'd love it if you chose anything you want to keep while we're there."

"Me?" Willa asked.

"Yeah. Clothes or jewelry. I want you to have first choice."

"Okay." She wore a small smile. "Won't the clothes be too big, though?"

"Probably not for long. Margo was a super small woman. Honestly, you probably aren't far off being the same size as her. She has a ton of designer items as well. Which might not be your style. But have a look anyway."

Raine sat up straighter. "Designer items?"

"You can try your luck." I laughed, eyes sweeping her five-foot-seven frame. "I'm not kidding about the height, though. Margo was an inch shorter than me."

Raine let out an exaggerated sigh. "Typical," she teased. "But of course we'll come with you."

"Thank you," I said. "I'm finally at a place where I'm ready to do it. With some assistance."

"We're always here for you." Raine put her hand on top of mine. "Whatever you need."

The condo looked so much bigger without all my things in it. Over the last couple of months, I had been coming through and boxing up bits and pieces. Most of the furniture was in storage and would be sent to Texas when I found a place to live, and the rest of it had been donated to women's refuge centers. Willa, Raine, and I moved through the vacant living room, our voices echoing.

"Great sunlight," Raine noted, staring at the living room window. She was right. It was great sunlight. It used to stream through onto the corner of the sofa where I would read and get a dose of vitamin D at the same time.

I stood at the threshold between the kitchen and the living area, sorrow seeping in. It would never not hurt. But eventually, I had found the strength to face the scene. Images of Margo flooded to the forefront of my thoughts, but they didn't cripple me the same way they once had.

"This is . . . this is where I found her," I said, pointing at the kitchen floor. "Irie cleaned the kitchen out for me."

Willa and Raine didn't say anything, but I felt a little hand slip into mine, and I looked down at Willa, courage surging through me. Courage and strength. She was a reminder of how much I had to live for. One of the reminders, anyway. My free hand cradled my baby bump.

"Margo's room is down here," I said, keeping hold of Willa's hand as we moved up the corridor. "She, um—she never made her bed. Or put her stuff in the closet. She has a chair. You know, the chair, where everything gets dumped."

Ripping the bandage off, I flicked the handle and let her door swing open. Everything was as she had left it the night that we were meant to go out and celebrate.

The armchair in the corner was covered in different dresses that she had tried on and discarded. Her closet door was still open, shoes spilling out; her comforter was crumpled; and her makeup was all over the vanity.

The only thing that had been touched when Irie came in here was the window so that the place could be aired out.

"What can we do to help?" Raine asked.

"We'll start with the clothes. Whatever you two want to keep we can throw into the hall, and everything else we'll make a couple of folded piles."

"Are you going to keep some clothes?" Willa asked.

"I've got a sweater and a necklace at Irie's apartment that she collected for me a while ago. That's all I need."

"Let's get started, then."

The three of us worked with a never-ending stream of chatter between us. It was a good distraction. Willa sat beside the chest of drawers and held out garments, assessing them so she could decide whether she wanted them or not. If she wanted them, she threw them to Raine, who put them in a box; if she didn't want them, she threw them to me, and I made a Goodwill pile.

Raine complained plenty of times whenever she loved a dress or a skirt but it was too short for her. I decided to cheer her up by telling her to go through the collection of jewelry. There was a ton of it.

"This is nice." Willa held up a knit sweater. It was white with a round collar and a fitted band around the bottom. "I'll keep this one."

"Good choice," I said.

"Will," Raine exclaimed, turning around with a silver chain in her hands. There was a little green pendant in the middle of it. "Look at this pretty emerald necklace. This is your birthstone. Want it?"

"Ooh." She sprung up from the floor and bounded toward Raine before turning around so that Raine could fasten the clasp behind her neck. "This is pretty."

I had no idea why Margo had an emerald necklace. I had never seen it before. But there was no denying how well it suited Willa and how thrilled she seemed to be wearing it.

"How about I go and get some lunch?" I suggested, feeling the emotion get to me.

"No, I'll go and get it," Raine said before I could start to get up from the end of the bed. "There's a burger joint just down the road, right? I saw it on the way here. I'll go and get a few burgers and fries. How does that sound?"

"Sounds yum," Willa said, and I nodded in agreement. We gave Raine our order, and she left.

Willa sat back down in front of the chest of drawers, the little emerald stone between her fingers. I stared at her for a while, absorbing how strange it felt to have my birth daughter in this condo. In this room. Margo's room.

Margo would have loved to have met her. It would have meant everything to her, and I could feel my chest tightening at the fact that she'd never had the chance.

"Are you sure you're okay giving all of this stuff to us?" Willa suddenly asked, and I quickly wiped a tear on my cheek. "Does it make you sad?"

"Oh, of course. It's really sad. I wish Margo was here and I didn't have to give any of this stuff away, but she's not," I said. "And you're important to me. You're family. So I'd rather you have some of this stuff and know that Margo's special items are going to someone who will look after them. You know? But I can't keep it all. I just can't, and she won't come back to get upset that I've given all of her stuff to Goodwill."

Willa and I shared a little giggle at that.

"She would have loved you, and she would have wanted you to have this stuff. She also valued charity, so she'd be pleased to know some of it's being donated."

"That's good." Willa nodded, holding a blouse in her lap without giving it much attention. "I wish I could have met her too. She sounds nice."

"She was. Come here." I slipped my cell phone out of my back pocket and went straight into the camera roll while Willa sat beside me. "I have a ton of videos of us together."

We sat there watching silly little videos that Margo and I had captured over the years. Some of them were of our time at the beach or videos of her awful but hilarious singing.

There were videos of her coming out of the bathroom while I hid and scared her. Messing around at the store. Working. Listening to her voice was always hard. All I wanted was to hear it again in person. But watching Willa's smile or hearing her giggle at Margo made some of the pain dissipate. I hadn't even realized that I was sobbing until Willa rested her head on my shoulder.

We sat in silence for a moment. The videos had stopped, and I embraced the comfort that her presence provided.

"Addie?"

"Yeah." I looked down and found her big brown eyes staring back at me.

"I was wondering something. You can say no, though." She seemed nervous, but at the same time, there was confidence radiating from her. "I wanted to ask if I could be allowed to call you mom."

Time stood still. I had no idea how to respond to that. Apart from the fact that I didn't know how to navigate a conversation like this, I wasn't even sure what I was thinking. Overwhelmed was the first thing. Honored. Happy. Nervous.

Every second that ticked by, I felt worse and worse because this sweet little girl was waiting for my answer, and I didn't have one.

"Never mind." She ducked her head.

"No, no," I said, panicking. "No. I'm seriously so flattered that you asked me that. You want to call me mom?"

She nodded but kept her gaze on her lap. "I know that we haven't known each other long, but you are my mom, and I wouldn't ask if my other mom was still alive. But she died. So I feel like it's okay. Because I really want to be able to have a mom that I can actually call mom."

"Well, what about Raine? She's going to be your stepmom."

"Yeah, I know. My stepmom. You're my actual mom, and you're making time for me and stuff. If you'd never shown up, I might have asked Raine if I could call her mom. But you're here now and I love you and I want to call you mom."

"Aw." I felt flustered. "I love you too, honey. And I love that you want to call me mom, but have you talked to your dad about this?"

The guilt washed over her face. "No."

"I think perhaps we should talk to him about it first. He got pretty upset last time we discussed certain subjects without including him."

"Yeah. I guess."

She didn't seem enthusiastic about the concept of talking to Milo about this topic, and that made me think he wouldn't be on board. If I was being honest, I really wanted Willa to call me mom. But I had to go about this with as much respect as possible.

Not to mention, I didn't want to upset Raine. How would she feel that the little girl she was raising on a daily basis wanted to call me mom instead of her? It was going to be a sensitive topic to broach, that was for sure. But I couldn't shut it down.

"I'm baaaaack," Raine sang from the other side of the condo, "and these burgers smell sensational."

That was the end of the conversation. Neither Willa nor I talked about it again while we took a short lunch break and then finished boxing clothes and belongings up. We were finished by two in the afternoon. Margo's bedroom was bare. The bed was stripped, the drawers and closet empty. We stood at the doorway, and I looked around at a space that now seemed so unfamiliar.

"You okay?" Raine asked.

"It was a big help to have you guys here," I said, nodding. "A good distraction. Honestly, it helps to remember that Margo is with me. She's not confined to this condo or bedroom. I'm not losing her if I leave or clear out her belongings."

"That's right." Raine nodded, pride in her smile. "She'll be with you wherever you go. I mean, her flesh and blood is literally in your uterus right now. She's actually with you."

"Ew." Willa screwed her nose up. "That's a gross way of saying it."

Raine and I laughed.

"Sorry," Raine said. "Her DNA is in your womb. Better?"

"Just say baby," Willa said, her tone suggesting Raine was being ridiculous.

I caressed the bump and knew it was true. Even if things were so far from how we had planned for them to be, I was grateful that part of my sister would remain with me. Most people weren't that blessed, and that was exactly how I chose to see it. A blessing.

We spent the rest of the afternoon on various activities. We went to the Beverly Hills Public Library, which blew Willa's mind due to the fact that it was so stark and modern and reminded her more of a hospital than a library. She preferred libraries that felt classic and authentic, which I understood. Next we went shopping on Rodeo Drive, and Raine almost had a heart attack when I spent seven hundred dollars on two outfits for Willa. But it was her birthday week, and I could afford it, so I told her not to concern herself, and we went in search of a place to have dinner.

Osteria Mozza was a place Margo and I had frequented due to its Italian menu, so I figured I would take the girls somewhere that had sentimental value.

I hadn't been there since Margo died. It seemed I was using the company as a crutch to get through a few things, but the girls seemed more than happy to oblige. Especially when they saw the menu and how delicious it all sounded.

"Can we start with a basket of bread?" I asked the waiter. He nodded and told us he'd bring a bottle of water too.

"I'm starving, and the bread here is so good," I said, watching Willa, who was studying the menu with a calculating glare. "See anything that sounds good?"

"The county lamb chops meal sounds kind of good," she said, still staring at the menu.

"It is! I always get that meal."

She looked up. "Really?"

"Yeah, it's my favorite. You'll love it. Whe—" My sentence halted when I felt a liquid rush between my legs. I wasn't even sure if rush was the right word. It was a damn flood. This was going to be so embarrassing. "I don't want to alarm anyone, but my waters have just broken."

Raine gasped and stared at my lap. "Shit," she said, panicking. "Shit. What do we do?! How are we—We need to leave, right now. I'll drive."

"Raine." I held her hand to stop her from shooting out of her chair.

"Relax. Yeah, it's a sign of labor, but I haven't had cramping yet. So it could still be a while. And the baby isn't going to fall out just because my waters broke."

"Really?"

"Yeah, really," I said and looked at Willa, who was watching us with alarm. "Labor takes a while. We should probably go, though, just because I'm soaked and the liquid is still coming. Ooh, that was a cramp. Or a mild contraction. We'll go and get it checked out."

"How are you so calm?!"

"I've done this before." I looked at Willa, and I was reminded of a time when it was her about to make an entrance. It had been so different then. A sorrowful experience from beginning to end. This time, I was allowed to be excited. "It's all right. I was in labor for a while with Will. Sometimes if you go in too early, they'll send you home until the labor progresses. Raine, can you go and let a staff member know that I've shed membrane all over their seat."

"Oh." Her mouth twisted for a moment. "Yeah. Sure."

Willa was still staring, her skin pale. "You're having a baby."

"I sure am. And you'll be here to meet her!"

# CHAPTER TWENTY-FIVE

Willa and Raine had meant to be on a flight home at two this afternoon; instead, they were out in the waiting area, running on little to no sleep because I'd been in labor all night.

It was three on Sunday afternoon. Irie, in scrubs and a surgical cap, was holding my hand and shouting instructions at me like she was a seasoned midwife.

My actual midwife, Laura, found her accent amusing.

"You should lie down," Irie said as I stood beside the bed with my palms on the mattress, sweat dripping off my forehead. "Lie down. What if the baby falls out and lands on its head?"

"Irie," Laura exhaled. "She's fine. The baby isn't going to fall out and land on its head."

"How fucking loose do you think I am?" I said.

Laura tilted her head. "Hmmm, that's not—"

"Oh, I know! I was just making a j—" Another contraction made me breathless, and I clutched the bedsheet in my fists. There was no way to describe contractions. It was like period cramps on crack.

Or if the Hulk squeezed a basketball in his fist—*squeeze, squeeze, squeeze*—and then, when it wouldn't pop, he loosened his grip a fraction, grumbled with frustration, and started squeezing again seven minutes later. And then five minutes later and then two minutes later. That was what my abdomen felt like right now.

"Deep breaths, Addie. Slow and deep," Laura instructed while she rubbed my back.

"Ha. That's what she said," Irie hollered.

Laura leaned down and whispered in my ear. "Do you want me to ask her to leave?"

"No," I panted. "No, I need the comic relief. It's fine."

The contractions were closer and stronger than ever at this point. I was barely getting a chance to breathe between them. Laura said that I was transitioning, and any moment now, I would be able to push.

"All right, we need to measure the dilation again. We should be at ten centimeters."

"We better be." I swayed. Remaining on my feet was getting harder and harder. "I can't do this much longer."

"See." Irie patted the bed. "Lie down so she can measure you."

"No, she's fine." Laura knelt down beside me. "I can do it here. Standing is going to be a lot easier when it comes time to push. Gravity really does help."

Because of how many internals I'd needed throughout the labor and how hot I was, I was in nothing but a sports bra. Dignity wasn't even a thing at this point. Nothing mattered except having this child. Laura knelt to the side of me and inserted two fingers.

Irie whistled. "Straight up cannot get over how pornographic childbirth is."

"Hey," Laura said to Irie, "how about you go and let Raine and Willa know that the pushing is about to begin. Give them an update."

"Is it?" Irie exclaimed.

"Yes." Laura stood up again and whipped off her latex gloves so she could replace them. "You're fully dilated, Addie. It's time to start pushing. Can you feel the need to push?"

Irie ran out of the room while I answered her. "Yeah. It sort of feels like I need to poop."

"Totally normal. Still comfortable there?"

"Comfortable?"

"Yeah, well." She hit the buzzer on the wall to alert the doctor and nurse that we'd be needing their assistance from here out.

Irie came back at the same time that they arrived. The three of them piled in and circled where I leaned on the bed. Laura had resumed her position, kneeling beside me. The nurse stood right back, waiting until she was needed, and the doctor knelt behind me. I might have been horrified at the thought of my ass being in his face, but right now, it wasn't a concern.

"How about we get her on the bed," he suggested. I couldn't remember his name or what he looked like, but I immediately shut him down.

"I want to stand."

A contraction started, taking away my voice and the ability to do literally anything except breathe. I vaguely listened to their debate while I focused on getting through the pain.

"I think as a safety caution, it'd be wise to get her on the bed," he repeated, more firmly. He must have been talking to Laura because she answered.

"She doesn't want to lie down. She wants to stand. That's how she feels comfortable giving birth, that's how we'll leave her."

"Mate," Irie snapped. "Are you the one about to push a little human out of your minge? No. Let her be, yeah?"

"Look," I groaned as the need to push became so much stronger, "I've done a lot of research. Hundreds of women said standing is a more comfortable position to give birth in. Not to mention faster. This is what I'm doing."

"She needs to start pushing," Laura said. "Get on board or get out, Doctor Beron."

He said nothing. Honestly, he could have left for all I knew. I didn't bother asking because another contraction came on fast and I started pushing, hard. At this point, the contractions didn't have a beginning or end. It was all pressure and unbelievable pain, all the time.

"Push, Addie," Laura instructed. "Push down, deep breath and big push."

I did what she said, pressure building in my head, face, and chest as I focused on forcing the big block out of the lower half of my body. I wasn't sure how long that had been going on before I was told to stop.

"The head is out," Laura said as I inhaled an enormous, ragged breath and panted. "I need to check the cord and the airway, and I know it's really hard, but don't push for a few seconds."

It felt totally unnatural not to push. My body was doing it on its own, but I tried to follow her instructions, focusing on my fists clenching the hospital-grade sheets while I took quick breaths in and out.

"Okay, good," Laura said. "Another big push. She's so close."

The time between pushing and finally feeling the pressure relieve could have been minutes or hours. It was impossible to tell. All I could focus on was the wailing of a newborn baby.

Margo's newborn baby. She should have been here; she should have been the one cutting the umbilical cord. She should have been the one who wrapped her daughter up into her arms and cried tears of total elation.

But she wasn't here. It was up to me to love that brand-new little girl. So with trembling arms and blurred vision, I let the nurse and Irie help me onto the bed so that I could lie down. Immediately, a fresh pink bundle with a surprisingly full head of hair was placed on my bare chest.

I couldn't hold her tight enough. The immediate need to protect her and let her know that I was going to keep her safe was overwhelming. Chills ran down my body, strong like vibrations, and Maggie settled. Her crying stopped—mine didn't—and she gurgled, and at that moment, I knew that Margo was with us. Hand on her daughter. Smiling at what she had created.

"She's beautiful," Laura whispered, using a soft towel to gently wipe at the excess goo on Maggie's body.

Irie stood on the other side of the bed. "She looks like she got dropped in a vat of discharge."

I sobbed out a laugh and was sure if I could see properly, Laura would be shaking her head in disappointment.

"But she is beautiful," Irie said, sincerity in her tone. "Margo would have been so proud. And she would have been the most incredible mother. And even though she can't be here, I know that you'll do just as well, love."

My tears started falling even harder, and Irie's arm slipped under my head, leaning down to give me a one-armed hug.

"We need to get her over to the scales to weigh her and do an overall health check," Laura told me quietly. Maggie was starting to stir again. "We'll do it as quickly as possible so that we can get her latched on for a drink."

"Okay." I nodded. "Can I get a proper look at her?"

She'd been put on my chest so fast that I had barely seen her face, but when Laura lifted her off my chest and angled her so that I could see that Bianchi nose and sharp chin, I knew that I would get to see a mini Margo every day for the rest of my life.

When Margo had chosen the donor, she'd chosen a profile that included a tall Italian man with dark hair and eyes. She'd wanted a donor who had similar features to her own so that she didn't have that barrier between her and her daughter.

So that people wouldn't ask things like, "Does she have her father's hair?" It might have been irrational, but she wanted as little reminder as possible that she'd failed at finding herself someone to share a life and child with.

When Maggie came back to me, she was wrapped in a pink swaddle with a beanie and booties on, and we were transferred from the delivery suite up to the maternity ward.

Laura spent an hour helping me with the breastfeeding process. It was trickier than other moms made it look. There was a technique to it, but eventually we made a comfortable latch, and Maggie guzzled while I watched her cheeks moving, her eyes closed, her skin perfect.

It was the most beautiful, rewarding, painful experience I had ever endured. I knew that I would never stop wishing for Margo to be here with me, to watch her daughter growing and reaching milestones. But I hoped that eventually, it would hurt just a little bit less than it did right now.

Maggie dozed off after she'd fed, and I held her while she slept. I didn't want to put her down. Irie went and got Raine and Willa from the waiting area and told me that she'd go home for a shower and change before she came back. As soon as they tiptoed into the room, I thanked them for waiting for such a long time.

"You must be exhausted," I whispered apologetically.

Raine pointed at Willa, who had beelined straight for the bedside and was busy watching her . . . her sister. "Willa slept on the seats," Raine said, looking jealous. "I'm a little wiped. But I'm not going to complain considering I didn't just give birth."

I smiled.

"She's so cute," Willa whispered, her eyes never leaving Maggie.

"Would you like to hold her?"

Willa's mouth dropped open. "Really?"

"Yeah. Babies will sleep on anyone at this age. If you sit in that chair over there, Raine can pass her to you."

Willa skipped over to the armchair by the window; her little legs couldn't reach the ground. Raine gently lifted Maggie from me, her lip pouting as she succumbed to the adorableness of my beautiful girl.

When Maggie was in Willa's arms, I felt a fresh set of tears forming and falling again. The daughter that I had let go of all those years ago, now back in my life, holding on to the daughter that had been left with me by the sister I'd lost. Life was a mystery. It was hard to make sense of. I'd lost so much, but I'd received so much too.

"I've been thinking," Raine whispered, standing beside me again, pretending not to notice when I wiped tears off my face, "what if Willa and I stayed for a couple of weeks? To help out while Maggie is so new?"

My mind went blank. "What? But—what about work and school?"

"Well, I have some vacation days that I have to use, and Willa goes on summer break in a couple of weeks. She could start early. I know that you've got Irie, but she works a lot, and the more hands the better."

The thought of having extra help made me want to beg her to stay. But I still felt bad accepting that kind of offer. "What about Milo? Do you think he'd be okay with Willa hanging out here for that long?"

"We talked earlier, and he was a little hesitant, but only because Willa wouldn't be at school. So I offered to send her home on a flight, but he thought it over and decided it wouldn't be so bad." Her brows rose a little as she stared at nothing in particular. "Actually, he said it might be nice for the two of you to get some decent time together."

That did surprise me. "Really?"

"Yeah. He's really . . . relaxed to the idea of you and Willa getting close. He can see how much she loves you, and he can also see that it hasn't changed his relationship with her at all. I told him he should apologize for that whole debacle back in Texas, bu—"

"No," I immediately said, watching Willa carefully cuddling Maggie, her focus totally on the baby. "No, he was right about that. I overstepped when I told Willa that I could look for her birth father. That was so stupid. He was right to be upset. I'm just glad that we overcame it. My life is better with her in it."

Raine peered behind her at Willa, her long braids tumbling over her shoulder. "Me too," she said. "And the more love, the better, right?"

I thought about the conversation that Willa and I had had — the one where she wanted to call me mom. It felt like so long ago now. I had no idea how I was going to bring it up, but it definitely wasn't going to be right now.

"So, what do you say?" Raine turned and looked at me again. "Should we stay?"

"Honestly, that sounds amazing."

• • •

The next few weeks felt easier than they should have, having a newborn. Between Raine, Irie, and me, there was always someone who had Maggie in their arms. I was the only one who could feed her, and I preferred to do the night routine alone because of how much help I was getting during the day, but I didn't know what I would have done without the girls. It was a blessing.

Willa and I also had so much time to spend watching movies while I was feeding and changing Maggie. Whenever Raine took Willa to the library, she'd bring back two of the same book so that we could read them together and talk about them.

We were all in a bubble of synchronized routine and existence, and I firmly believed that anyone who had a baby needed people around them in the beginning. Even if it was just for conversation or companionship.

Raine's vacation time was up the next day, and she had to get back to work. I wasn't too worried, though. I felt confident, I still had Irie, and it wouldn't be long before I made the move to Texas.

Willa was sitting on the floor, shaking a rattle for Maggie, who was on her back, staring at the ceiling, not really focusing on much. She was still too little to appreciate rattles.

"I wish I didn't have to leave," Willa said when I sat on the couch, taking the millionth photo of my girls together.

I had to be careful how I replied to comments like these ones, which I'd been hearing for about a week now. "I'm going to miss you too, Will." I desperately wanted to tell her that I was moving to Texas. But we'd agreed to hold off until I'd at least finalized a house.

"I'll miss too much of Maggie's growing."

"What if we FaceTime every day?"

She gave me a small shrug. "It's not the same. We can't cuddle on FaceTime."

"No, I suppose that's true. Well, I'll come and visit really soon, okay?"

"Promise?"

I raised my pinkie and offered it to her. "Pinkie promise."

Instead of winding her pinkie finger around mine, she raised it and swiped the side of her nose. It immediately reminded me of Zac, and my chest tightened. It was always hard not to bombard Willa and Raine with questions about him. Mostly, I wanted to know if he was dating. But I refused to cave and seem interested because Willa would tell him, and I would sound pathetic.

"Uncle Zac always promises like that," she said suddenly, smiling to herself.

"Does he?" I tried to keep my tone even, uninterested.

"Yep. He said it's the most official form of pinkie promising in the world. One time, he said he was going to take me down to the river on one of the horses, but he's really busy a lot, and the horses were getting sold and leaving the farm really quick, and I didn't think he'd actually take me, but then he swiped his nose and said he would never break that kind of promise, and then he really did take me for a ride. On Lavender!"

"Lavender?" I wanted to ask about the fact that he'd sold the horses. But I didn't.

"Yeah, she's a really good horse now and never runs away. She's the only horse left on the farm."

My heart was beating so furiously that it was deafening. He'd kept Lavender. He'd kept the horse that saved my life.

# CHAPTER TWENTY-SIX

*Five months later*

My heart was pounding, my throat thick as I drove through the farm gates and slowly made my way toward the area that had been designated for parking. There were cars and guests all over the place. Most of those people were looking up at the sudden influx of dark clouds that had started rolling across the sky, though the day had started as truly the most beautiful fall day that we could have been blessed with for Raine and Milo's wedding.

"Shoot," I murmured, getting Maggie out of her seat. The ceremony was outside, so I hoped it wouldn't rain until the reception at least. I tugged on the bottom of Maggie's dress, the same dark green as mine.

"Addie." I heard a squeal and turned around to see Willa running toward me in her beautiful dress, hair in two braids just like she'd wanted them done.

"Will," I gasped, looking at the light makeup on her face. A bit of blush and mascara. Nothing major. "You look beautiful, honey."

"Thanks." She grinned. "So do you. I like your hair."

All I'd done was some really loose curls that fell halfway down my back. It was more than I'd done in a long time; usually it was swept up in a bun. As it was, I'd have a hard time keeping it down when Maggie's fingers kept getting tangled in it.

"That dress looks perfect," I said to Willa as we walked toward the house. She was wearing a long pale-pink dress that almost touched the floor. She spun in a circle as we walked inside, and nostalgia hit.

Even with all of the people taking up space and the fact that I'd only spent a month here, this place was familiar in a sense that I couldn't understand. From the reaction I felt, you would have thought I'd grown up here.

"Aw, look at Midge and Toto," I said about the dogs who were sitting just outside the dining room French doors with little bow ties attached to their collars. "That's so cute."

"That was my idea," Willa said, full of pride.

"Such a good idea."

My eyes wandered the area, not recognizing most of the faces that passed. Keith came shuffling through in a sharp suit, and I gasped.

"Keith!"

He stopped, and his smile turned into total delight. "Darlin', how wonderful to see you, and look at this gorgeous little girl. Maggie, ain't it? Oh, she's sweet as sugar."

Maggie giggled. Her two front teeth had just broken through, and it gave her already beautiful smile a whole lot of character.

"We'll have to have a proper catch-up after the ceremony, darlin'." Keith was talking to me, but his attention was focused on Maggie. "I've been sent to gather everyone for the ceremony. Take seats. It's all about to start."

"Of course, we'll catch up afterwards." I wanted to hear all about how things were going for him in his retirement village.

"Willa," he said. "Raine wants you upstairs quick smart. Said you weren't supposed to be wandering off."

She covered her guilty smile with her hands and started running upstairs.

Rows of white chairs with dark-orange bows were arranged in the back garden. The flower beds sat behind a beautiful big awning that was wrapped in climbing vines and flowers. The pastor stood, waiting while guests took their seats.

The entire time I was slipping through the row of seats, I kept my head down and was careful not to look at the groomsmen lined up on the right-hand side, because I knew Zac was there, and I could feel him watching me. It was unnerving, knowing how aware of his presence I was.

And then, almost of their own accord, my eyes looked up and moved over his tall frame in a tailored suit that hugged him like a glove. His hair was tousled, and his stubble was short. He was so gorgeous that it winded me for a moment, and memories came flooding back in full force, threatening to drown me the longer our eyes remained locked on one another.

He let his gaze sweep over me; it was slow, intentional, and it was entirely too much; I had to avert my attention and focus on Maggie, who was sitting on my lap, gurgling.

She was such a relaxed baby; she didn't fuss a lot or cry unless she was super tired. It always felt like she was doing her best to make life easier for me.

For the rest of the ceremony, I didn't look at Zac. I watched Willa walking down the aisle, scattering orange rose petals on the ground, Raine appearing in her stunning dress. It was a strapless mermaid fit with a detailed lace back and a veil. I quietly and politely declined when a couple of old women beside me asked to hold Maggie. Willa gave a short but sweet speech about how much she loved having Raine in her life and how happy she was for her dad.

The ceremony was gorgeous, and when everyone wandered down to the barn, there was a lot of chatter about how beautiful it was. There was an antique wheelbarrow and wagon wheel and some hay bales stacked in the corner. It made the perfect place for photographs. Tables lined the outer edges and were decorated with glass centerpieces and dark-orange name cards.

Fairy lights started in the middle of the high ceiling and extended out to the corners. The table I was sitting at was occupied by Tyler, Amber, and a couple of other people I didn't know.

"So," I said to the teens, whom I hadn't seen in a while, prying a napkin out of Maggie's grip. "Did you guys end up moving out of town?"

Amber smiled. "I got accepted into Harvard. So we're living in Boston now."

"I can't even fathom being that smart," I said, inspired by her.

"She's incredible," Tyler said, watching Amber with nothing short of total admiration. "I just started working on a construction site. I did a summer internship and got offered a position,"

"Wow," I said. "That's great, you guys. You've done so well."

The room fell quiet for Raine and Milo's first dance, and the lighting dimmed, leaving a simple spotlight on the floor. They were so in love, they couldn't take their eyes off each other, and it was mesmerizing to watch. After the dance was over, Willa and Milo started to dance; she stood on his feet, and other couples joined the dance floor. Raine made her way toward me and melted at the sight of Maggie.

"Congratulations, beautiful," I said, standing to hug her with one arm. "You look gorgeous."

"I'm so glad you're here," she said. She was glowing, and her golden-brown cheeks had a shimmering layer of highlight on them. "Are you doing okay? I know you don't really know many people here, are you comfortable?"

"I'm fine," I assured her and handed Maggie over when she held out her hands. "I'm a grown-up, I can cope without someone holding my hand."

That might not have been true a while ago, but ever since Margo had died and Maggie came along, I'd had to step up and push myself outside of my comfort zones. A lot had subtly changed, and sometimes it was easy to forget that I'd spent a long time letting my big sister look after me.

"If you need to feed Maggie or change her or anything, just head into the main house."

I said nothing, not sure how to respond because the house belonged to Zac now—Keith wasn't even living here—and it felt awkward to accept that sort of offer without Zac being the one to suggest it.

"It's fine," Raine said, recognizing my hesitance. "Zac was the one who wanted you to know that you're welcome to put the baby down for a nap if you need to."

"He did?"

She rolled her eyes, amusement in her smile. "You two are hopeless. Yes. It's fine. Are you still good to have Willa tonight? We can drop her off in the morning if that's easier?"

"No, no. I'll take her with me tonight. Enjoy your wedding night alone."

Raine smiled. She and Milo had graciously agreed to let me babysit Willa while they spent two weeks in Fiji for their honeymoon. They didn't leave until tomorrow mid-morning, but it made sense to take Willa tonight.

Raine excused herself to mingle with some more guests, and I had a chat with Keith about life in retirement. He couldn't speak highly enough of the village he was in and the activities, the new friends, the comfort. He seemed more vibrant than he had when I was living here. I wondered if the constant reminder of life with his wife had weighed on him. After all, he'd remained in their home after her death. I imagined it was bittersweet to see the ghost of her every single day.

Maggie started to fuss around the time the meals were being served, but when it came down to her eating or me, she won. I could have fed her in the barn, but she'd need a nap afterwards. If Willa hadn't been coming home with me, I'd have just left, but she was having so much fun, I wasn't going to steal her away just yet.

"Addie?"

A chill ran straight up my spine at the sound of his voice. My damn body was still giving me away, reacting to him in a way that was obvious and embarrassing. I turned around and looked up at a face that had been visiting my dreams for months.

"Hi, Zac."

He slipped his hands into his pants pockets. His jacket was gone, and his shirtsleeves were rolled to the elbow.

His jaw clenched as his gaze roved my face with a heavy look, as if he couldn't help but remember a time when our bodies didn't hesitate to come together, when there was nothing holding us back. "It's nice to see you, Addie."

"Yeah, you too," I said, jostling Maggie, who was getting restless.

"She's beautiful." He smiled at my daughter. "Maggie, right?"

"Yeah."

Sadness seeped into his features, turning his dark-brown gaze into a whirlpool of emotion that wanted to suck me in and pull me under. He tried to hide it with a smile.

"You wanna dance?"

"Oh, um, everyone's eating." I looked around and shrugged. "And I have to go feed Maggie. Raine said it was okay to use a spare bedroom?"

"Of course," he said. "Yeah, please. Go ahead. Whatever you need."

"Thank you," I said, tasting regret on my tongue. How much I wished this wasn't the way things were between us. I'd never stopped wanting so much more.

But that was selfish because, at the end of the day, I was a mother. It wasn't just me anymore, and I couldn't ask him to take on me and a baby. He deserved a clean break and a fresh start with someone he could have a family with.

Outside, it looked so much later than it was. The clouds were low, dark; a rumble of thunder went across the sky, and I awkwardly ran the whole way back to the house with Maggie on my hip. Just as we reached the back deck, thick raindrops pelted the awning, and the downpour was furious within seconds.

"Seriously?"

The house was dim, not dark enough that I couldn't see, but I still switched on the light in the downstairs spare bedroom. Thunder boomed, startling me while I sat on the edge of the bed and fed Maggie. Lightning flashed outside the window. It must have been so loud on the barn roof. Although the music was probably offering good competition.

After I'd changed Maggie and pulled the mattress onto the floor, I settled a snoozing Maggie down with a blanket. She was rolling now, and I didn't want her to slip off the bed at full height.

Kissing her on the head, I pulled her headband off and left the room. There was no way I'd leave her in the house alone, so I wandered out into the kitchen and flicked the kettle on.

Watching the storm through the window was beautiful in a dark and haunting sense. There was something about heavy downpours on vast open spaces that was mesmerizing. Lightning cracked in the open sky, sharp prongs striking down on the fields and illuminating the entire horizon.

The kettle hadn't finished boiling when it switched off—along with the lights, the fridge, everything.

"Power outage," I mumbled, feeling a bit nervous at the sudden plunge into a thick wall of darkness. I pulled my phone out of my pocket and started texting Raine (not that she'd see it) when I heard the dining room doors open.

"Addie?" Zac called.

"In the kitchen."

His phone light was blaring when he appeared at the threshold with Willa behind him, wrapped like a cocoon in a blanket. "Why are all the lights off?"

"Uh, the power went out?"

"Oh, shit." He sighed and blew out a breath. He was drenched— his hair was wet, and his clothes were clinging to him.

"Did the power not go out in the barn?"

"No, it's run on a generator. We just came in to ask if you two wanted to crash here tonight? The storm is pretty bad, and it doesn't look like it'll let up anytime soon. That way you don't have to take Willa and Maggie out in this weather."

Admittedly, it wasn't a hard sell. The thought of being on the road in these conditions made me nervous, especially when I'd have two little ones with me that I considered more precious than life itself. "Actually, that'd be really great, Zac. Are you sure you don't mind? Will, you okay with that?"

Her blanket was covered in beads of water, but she gave her head a quick, enthusiastic nod. Zac quickly went over to the scullery and disappeared inside, coming back with a handful of candles that he made quick work of lighting, casting an ambient light throughout the room. Flickering shadows danced across his profile, making his chiseled features all the more alluring.

"Maggie is asleep in the bedroom down the hall if you want to share with her," I said. "We could put some candles in there too if you like?"

"On it." Zac put his phone light on again and turned on his heel. I watched his back, wet, white shirt stretching across his broad shoulders, and I wanted to put my arms around him more than anything.

Suddenly, Willa cleared her throat. It startled me, and I met her stare across the room. She stretched her mouth into a wide, knowing smile.

"What?" I said, suspiciously.

"Sleepover."

"Did you do this on purpose?"

She looked outside, confusion on her delicate face. "Yes, I am the goddess of weather."

"Very funny."

"I'm very tired." She dropped her blanket and skipped toward me. "I think I'll go and find some PJs and get into bed and go straight to sleep." She wrapped her arms around my waist; the front of her hair was a little damp, but she'd mostly managed to avoid the rain. "I love you."

My heart felt as if it could smile in moments like these. "I'll come and tuck you in. I love you too."

# CHAPTER TWENTY-SEVEN

Willa was tucked in on the mattress beside Maggie. She'd changed into a pair of PJs from the bag that she was bringing to my place. Plus one of Zac's hoodies because it was cold, but the heating wasn't on. It required willpower not to sniff the fabric because I knew it would smell like him.

"Maggie usually sleeps through the night, but I'll come back and check on you both before I come to bed."

"Will you sleep in here too?" she whispered.

"Yep, there's plenty of room. Will you be all right in here?"

"Yes." I could just see her wide grin thanks to the LED lantern that Zac had found in the hall closet. It was safer than candles. "This is fun."

"You're not scared of the storm?"

"No, it's just a storm," she said and snuggled further into the comforters.

Each little new piece of information that I learned about her was a gem in the treasure trove. There were years of missing pieces I needed to collect, and I couldn't get enough.

"Addie," she whispered. "Remember when I asked if I could call you mom?"

"Of course."

We never got to come back to that conversation. Maggie came

along, and by the time things settled again, I wasn't sure how or if I should bring it up. Willa didn't bring it up either, so I figured I would wait until she did.

"I still want to call you mom."

Luckily, because of all the time I'd had to think about it, I had an answer. "What if we talked to Raine and Milo, and maybe, if it's all right with everyone, you could call both me *and* Raine mom?"

Her expression brightened.

"How does that sound?" I asked. "I think Raine deserves to be called mom just as much as me, if not more. I mean, at the end of the day, it's your choice. It was just an idea."

"I love it." She kicked her feet with excitement under the comforter. "You're both my mom, so it's a good idea!"

"Yeah?"

She nodded, her eyes turning into little crescents and her cheeks dimpling.

"Okay." I leaned down and kissed her forehead. "We'll talk to your dad and Raine when they get back from their honeymoon. For now, you get some sleep. I love you, Will."

"I love you too."

· · ·

We said good night, and I told her I would be back soon. There wasn't much else to do apart from go to bed, but I needed to thank Zac for having us. As I wandered back down the dark corridor, I checked my phone and saw a text from Raine.

> Guests are heading home. Not many of us left. We'll be heading home soon too. How's Willa? You guys doing okay?

> Hey, we're all good in here. Willa is in bed, bunking with Maggie. Drive safe. This weather is nuts.

The front room was glowing with candles; their shadows flickered on the walls and ceiling. The windows along the front of the house revealed cars slowly leaving the property, their headlights illuminating the heavy downpour in front of them.

Zac was standing beside the window, his back to me with his hands in his sweatpants pockets. He'd obviously changed because he was now in a fitted white T-shirt that was just as alluring as the dress shirt he'd worn before.

"Willa's in bed," I said, avoiding his stare when he turned around. "I'll, um—I guess I'll just go to bed too. Thanks for having us."

"Addie," he said before I could turn around. "Can we talk for a minute?"

"Oh . . . umm, sure." I was so self-aware of every move I made and how Zac's attention was glued to me as I leaned on the wall. "Oh, I hear—well, Willa told me the horses are all gone."

"Yeah," he said. "It was time for something new, I guess."

"Cars?"

"Yeah. I'm selling muscle cars, and I'm a few months out from opening a showroom."

My interest piqued. It sounded like he was doing exactly what he wanted to. "I'm really happy for you," I said. "Where's the showroom going to be?"

"It'll be the barn that the wedding was in." He sat down on the arm of the sofa, legs spread and shoulders rolled forward. "It's still got some renovations to undergo, but it's getting there."

"I'll have to visit when it's done."

He met my gaze, and it was the first time we'd held eye contact since the afternoon. It took my breath away, meeting those familiar eyes, the depths of them containing memories of such a short but significant time.

"It's your turn," he said, and I remembered a conversation we'd had, a deal we'd made. "I'm pursuing my dream. Now, how's that plant nursery coming along?"

My heart hiccupped, and I felt the familiar warmth that accompanied the smiles he drew from me. "I'm working on it."

"Good." His voice was soft, and he scratched his brow with his thumb. "I did keep one horse. I kept Lavender. "

"Why did you keep her?"

"I promised her I would. She saved you that morning you went off the cliff. She found me at the edge of the woods and made sure I followed her. She deserves the best life I can give her."

My lips parted, and I inhaled a sharp, quiet breath. "Well, she's lucky to have you."

His expression fell a little bit. "How are you doing? Life with a baby and all of that. Raine said you're living here in Texas now."

"I am. Just around the corner from them. It made sense. I wanted to be close to Will." I'd moved into a beautiful little cottage with trees in the front yard and a garden in the back.

"You haven't come to see me," he murmured. It was quiet, as if I wasn't supposed to hear him.

"I didn't move back for you, Zac."

"I know." His smile was sincere, but there was sorrow in his stare. "I have missed you, though."

It was hard to remember all the reasons we shouldn't be together when he said things like that, when he watched me as if the space between us wasn't this giant chasm of complications that made it impossible to be together.

Still, I'd always been honest when it came to how I felt about him. "I've missed you too."

His brows lifted, hopefulness in his gaze. "Addie, I'm sorry," he said, sounding defeated. "I'm sorry for how I handled . . . everything. I'm sorry I wasn't there when you needed me the most—"

"Hang on. I didn't need you." I cut him off and straightened off the wall. "Yeah, I needed people around me, friends, guidance, and advice. But the help I needed went way further than a romantic connection."

"Yeah, of course—"

"You weren't the be-all and end-all for me, Zac," I continued, needing him to understand how much work I'd put into fixing the mess I'd become. "I needed things outside of what you gave me. You made me happy, and I felt a lot for you. But I needed to heal, and that wasn't something a summer fling could give me. I needed closure, and time, and therapy."

"It was more than a summer fling to me, Ads."

My breath caught. "It was for me too."

He tousled his hair, a sigh escaping his parted lips. "I'm still sorry for the way I reacted, Ads."

"I forgave you, Zac."

He stood up faster than I was prepared for and came close, towering over me. "I've never regretted anything more than pushing you away like that. But . . . I'd do anything for another chance. I still . . . I care about you a lot."

"I don't know how you could?" I had to tip my head back to see him. "You don't know me. Not really. You know the version of me that was hiding behind a lot of denial and trauma. Sometimes I'm not even sure if I know who I am, Zac."

"I know you," he said adamantly, pleading. "I know you. You might have been hurting and going through something when we met, but that just shows me that I'm right. You were going through all of that, and you were still caring, selfless, generous, ambitious." His hands came up and cupped my face, his forehead leaning on mine. "I know you."

He must have felt my hesitance because he stepped back and drew his bottom lip in. "Let me show you something. I'll be right back."

Before I could respond, he'd turned on his heel; the glow of his phone light could be seen for a few moments until his footsteps started running upstairs. Now alone, without his proximity drowning all of my senses, I could hear the thunder and rain again, the heavy pattering on the windows matching the speed of my pounding heart. I couldn't imagine what he wanted to show me, but I didn't have to wonder for long because he reappeared, clutching a leatherbound book in his hand.

"When I said that I kept a journal as a teen, I was omitting the full truth." His hand encased mine as he led me to the couch. "I've been keeping one since I was a teen. It became a habit. I don't write daily. Mostly when there's something worth writing about."

We sat close, and he leafed through the pages, a few labored breaths alerting me to how nervous he was as he stared down at the journal. He stopped on a page in the middle and swallowed, handing it to me. "Read from here."

"You don't have to show me this, Zac—"

"I want to." He held my stare, eyes traveling my features. "Please read it. I need you to know how I feel."

The candlelight on the side table was enough to see the neat words scrawled on the pages. His handwriting had improved a lot since he was a teenager.

*Dear journal,*

*Had this girl show up on the farm with Raine today. The whole thing seemed a bit weird. She seemed a bit weird. But I felt like an asshole after she left and I found out she'd just lost her sister. It made sense, I guess. She seemed pretty . . . sad.*

*Anyway, Raine has warned me about making assumptions before, and I'm always sticking my foot in it. I was rude as hell, but I can't help smiling when I think about this girl's zero tolerance for bullshit attitude. She didn't mind telling me what was up. And apart from all that, I don't think I've ever met a girl that beautiful before in my life. She stood up in the garden, hot little green dress hugging her hips, and I was literally fucking speechless. I stared at her for a bit, kept on thinking I needed to say something, even a hello would've been better than the mindless dickhead stare I gave her. But I didn't know what to say. I was worried if I opened my mouth, I'd admit she was the most gorgeous woman I'd ever seen. I've never liked to come across like a pervert, commenting on looks before I've even had a conversation with a girl. But shit, like I said, I was speechless.*

*Dear journal,*

*Addie showed up again. Found her sitting down at the creek with Lavender. I don't think I've ever seen Lavender so calm. Sitting there, allowing a stranger to pet her. Something about the serenity of that moment struck me. It reminded me that I didn't know anything about her and I'd been unfair to assume she was just some city slicker that cared only about superficial shit. I mean, just because she wore these gorgeous dresses that hugged her hips didn't mean there wasn't so much more to her. I was embarrassed at how close-minded I'd been, and suddenly, I wanted to know everything about her. I wanted to offer her a healing kindness that might cure some of that sorrow in her heart.*

The next few entries were about the nightmare I'd had that night. Working together to clean out the horse stables. He talked about the fact that I was a hard worker, and how much that impressed him. Reading his thoughts, his views on the encounters, made me breathless. To see evidence of the impact I'd made was overwhelming, and my hands trembled as I read the pages.

*Dear journal,*

*Addie moved in. Can't say I'm opposed to her presence. I can't explain it, but being around her is . . . it makes my stomach go stupid. We went for a drive in the Healey, and I could have sworn she was an angel.*

*She sat on the top of the seat while the top was down, and watching the wind in her hair and the carefree smile on her face was beautiful. I don't think I've ever wanted to make someone happy like I want to make her happy.*

*It means more to me than anything else, and it's new, sort of different, but damn I'm good to run with it. She might be the best thing that's ever stumbled into my life. We went on a date. It was my subtle way of giving her a birthday without giving her an actual birthday. I could tell she didn't want to acknowledge it without her sister there.*

*Couldn't blame her for that either.*

*At first, I thought about doing something that would involve her sister. I don't know, flying her to California wherever her sister was buried to have a picnic with her. But that would have been overstepping. Addie was still coming to terms with it. She needed to go at her own pace.*

*Instead, I took her for a picnic at the top of the lookout. Thought we'd be uninterrupted, but Raine of all people found us. Whatever, it was still one of the best dates that I've ever been on. I'm calling it a date. Addie can call it whatever she wants, as long as she was happy. I thought about kissing her, it kind of seemed like she was thinking about it too. Fucking nerves got the best of me. I started wondering if she had a man back at home, a life she would up and return to. It was irrational, but part of me couldn't help but thinking about how easy it would be for her to have someone waiting for her at home, and*

*I would never know. As soon as I'd asked her, I felt like an idiot. Of course she hadn't left a man behind. She was attempting to leave her pain behind, and all I really want to do is make it worth her while.*

*Dear journal,*

*Addie is Willa's birth mother. It makes total sense, they're basically twins. We're all idiots for not seeing it sooner. The only part I hate about this is the fact that I can't kill the son of a bitch who took advantage of Addie when she was just a child. It's getting seriously hard not to fall in love with this woman. She's gone through hell and back and she's still hopeful, sweet, optimistic.*

*Today I showed her my journal. She called it a grief journal. She cried for my pain, the pain that I'd moved on from a long time ago. She was so purely empathetic and honest. The fact that she still feels like that for other people when she's full to the brim of her own grief is just evidence of how beautiful her spirit is. Yeah, I knew what love felt like, and to be honest, what I felt for her was nothing I'd ever felt before.*

*Dear journal,*

*I kissed Addie today. I never thought I would put so much faith into one person's mouth on mine. But the things I felt when she pushed her fingers into my hair, when I held her against me, when her tongue lapped out and took what it wanted, it was impossible not to believe in a soul being matched to mine. How do I tell her I'm crazy about her? Is there a good time when she's still grieving her sister so heavily?*

*I understand her grieving, want her to go at her own pace, heal in her own time. Sometimes I catch her staring off into the distance, unmoving, unblinking, as if wherever her thoughts have taken her is so captivating that it's difficult for her to come back.*

*She's improving too, though. Fewer nightmares. Less tears. More smiles. And damn, does she have a beautiful smile. One that makes me stop and think, I've been right to wait for a woman to find me. I've been right not to rush it without feeling the connection I feel when I'm with her.*

*I'm grateful to Willa too, for giving Addie a chance. Selfishly, I'm hopeful that having Willa here will encourage Addie to hang around in Texas. If she wanted to go home, well, I couldn't stop her. I wouldn't have the right to. But if she's here for Willa, I won't be disappointed.*

*There's so much about Addie that I've come to admire. The fact that she uses whatever is within arm's reach as a bookmark. On Tuesday, I saw her slip a sock in between the pages of her novel because there was nothing else close.*

*She recites the alphabet when she's twisting an apple stem. Whichever letter it pops off at, she smiles and announces that her fate is in the apple's stem. I have no idea what she's talking about, but it's entertaining to watch.*

*Or whenever Addie is outside and she thinks no one is watching, she slips Midge and Toto pieces of bacon from breakfast, even if it means that she didn't get to eat hers. Or that she's nicknamed all of the chickens down at the coop and compliments them on their fine eggs whenever she goes to collect them.*

*Or that she's been making little three-flower bouquets from the garden, wrapping them in ribbon and leaving them on all of our pillows. Or that she treats the plants and the flowers with so much tender respect that it's captivating. As if they're intelligent and alive with a total comprehension of emotions. She cares for those plants better than I've seen humans care for each other.*

*She's made this her home, and I love it. The thought of going back to the house to find her either eating dinner or curled up with a book or chatting to Pops, it makes it easier to slide the shed door closed before the sun has set and head back up the hill, a damn sap of a smile on my face.*

*Dear journal,*

*Addie left the other day. My fault. She's pregnant, and I'm definitely not the father. But I hadn't given her time to explain before I blew up at her. It makes my stomach turn whenever I think about how I shouted at her, accused her, completely fucking ruined everything.*

*Raine ripped me a new one. Told me about how Addie is a surrogate for her dead sister. Her dead sister's baby is growing inside of her, and fuck, that has to be a lot of burden for one person.*

*She could have used some support, and instead I was a complete fuck. She won't call me back; she doesn't have to forgive me, I certainly don't forgive me. But I wish, more than anything, that I could take it all back. She could still be here if I hadn't done that. She could still be here, and I'd be holding her and telling her I would be there for her no matter what. But she's gone, and it's all my damn fault.*

*The more I think about it, the more I realize that stepping up and being the support Addie needs would be a privilege. To be her partner in parenthood, to raise a child with her, I couldn't imagine a better future. In such a short time, I realized Addie was the woman I wanted to stand beside in life. I want to experience milestones with her and witness her discover new passions and learn new skills. Her appreciation for such simple things is indescribable. It makes me crave a future full of living with her.*

*Dear journal,*

*Haven't written in a while. There's been nothing worth mentioning. Still isn't. I don't know. I was just having one of those days. Dad has been in the retirement village for a while. Last of the horses have been sold. Met with a bank rep about getting a loan today so I can open my own showroom. That's all good, I suppose. Life is moving along, but I miss her. I fucking miss her.*

*Nothing has felt the same since she left. She wasn't here for long, but she left her mark. She's embedded in every inch of this house. The pillow in her room still smells like her. Midge and Toto still sit at the back door waiting for their bacon in the morning.*

*I miss watching her when she'd sit at the window with her coffee, staring adoringly at the rolling land. I miss bumping into her in the hall in the evenings. I miss the way she came back from the hens and told me which ones gave her the most eggs.*

*I miss the smile she wore when she found new flowers blooming in the garden. I miss sitting on the back deck with her, under the stars, talking about anything and everything. I miss her laugh and the way that it sent surges of pleasure through me.*

*I miss watching her read and how lost she would get, completely immersed in another world, the expressions that she wore—the sadness, the happiness, the fear, the love. Watching her read was a journey of its own. I miss falling in love with her.*

Tears hit the page, dampening the paper. "Zac."

"Let me get to know you." He knelt in front of me and wiped my cheek with his thumb. "If you still don't believe that I know you, let me get to know you."

"It's more complicated than that," I sobbed, wiping my face. "I have a baby, Zac. You said so yourself, you're not ready for that—"

"What I said—" He lifted my chin. "It came from a place of jealousy. I didn't mean it. I was jealous at the thought of you having someone else's baby, and I was a complete dick about it, but I didn't mean it. You and Maggie are a package deal, I know that."

"What if she had been my baby?" I said, chin quivering. "What if I was pregnant by another man. Then what?"

He came closer, his jaw tense. "I can't convince you that I would've been okay with that. But I know how I felt for you back then, and I know I would've wanted to be with you regardless. I just have a shit reaction reflex, and I overreacted out of envy."

My lip shook and tears rolled over my cheeks, the taste of salt on my mouth. I could barely see him because of the blur. He was saying all the right things, and my heart wanted to believe it, but my head, my stubborn head, told me to think about how likely it was that one of us would get hurt.

"Let me take you out for dinner, movies, dates." He picked up my hand and kissed my palm, his eyes not leaving mine. "We can go slow, get to know each other again. We can go as slow as you want because you're it for me, Ads. I can't explain how I know, but I do, you're my future. So, we can go as slow as you want because we've got the rest of our lives together."

My loud sob was cut off when I threw myself forward into his hold and met his mouth with mine. He didn't hesitate: his arms encircled me, holding me impossibly close as he stood, drawing me to my feet. He was so familiar, it was like no time had passed since we'd last kissed. My fingers went into his hair as I stood on tiptoe, tasting tears between our passion.

My heart won, because sometimes hurt was inevitable, and it wasn't worth missing out on the sunshine because I'd held off on making plans just in case the rain fell. Rain would fall sometimes. Hell, storms would rage. But that didn't mean we'd drown. And the beautiful days in between were worth heading indoors once in a while.

Zac parted our kiss, breathing heavily, forehead on mine. "I'll do better, Addie," he whispered, his lips grazing mine as he spoke. "I'll be the man you deserve, and I'll never let you and Maggie down again." He leaned back an inch and swiped the tip of his nose with his pinkie finger. "I promise."

That was all I needed before I leapt back into his kiss. Our mouths collided, and Zac's grip tightened on me, desperation pulling me closer as he walked us back and pressed me against the wall. My hands traveled up his arms, feeling the swell of his delicious shoulders that I'd missed so much. Tears were still coating my lips as my fists closed on the strands of his hair, tugging it, both of us desperate to get as close as possible. Zac's hands circled my waist, squeezing before they traveled up to cup my jaw. His thumb pressed the bottom of my chin, angling my jaw up so he could drag his mouth down onto my throat, where he feathered kisses and sucked on my skin. I was trembling, the full-body chills that he'd been giving me from the moment he'd first put his hands on me. His low laughter tickled my damp throat.

"Glad to see you still tremble for me, ma'am."

I tipped my head back, and it hit the wall with a thud. The only light in the room was from the dim glow of a few candles, but it was enough that he could see how serious I was when I said, "You are the only man who has ever made me respond like that. I think you're the only man who ever will."

His eyes flooded with desire, and his attention fell to my mouth. The look was a man undone, and it overwhelmed me in the best sense of the word.

He crashed his mouth down on mine again, his hands resting on either side of my throat, cradling my face. I loved the way he held me when he kissed me: it was so consuming, so safe. Our bodies pressed together, and the friction of his hips on mine made me gasp, joining the sounds of the rain beating on the window and the thunder booming outside. It was a symphony that had never sounded sweeter. Especially when I pulled Zac's hair and his deep, unravelled groan joined in.

"Zac," I whispered as he ground against me, his fingers going into the strands of hair at the back of my head. His hands tilted my head so he could deepen our kiss, tongues gliding together.

"Yeah, baby. I know."

He sucked my tongue between his lips, and I almost collapsed. "This dress is fucking incredible," he said against my mouth, hands moving down over my rib cage to my waist, then to my hips. His hands were a form of appreciation all on their own, taking their time to feel every inch of my body.

"I swear," he murmured, still touching, still kissing me. "This afternoon I almost abandoned my fucking spot at the front of that wedding. You were all I could think about, all I could see. I wanted to hear your voice and see your smile. It was torture, ma'am. Pure fucking torture."

I couldn't stop shifting, trying to move closer. I could feel him hard against me, but his words, his confessions were driving me over the edge.

"I was smiling," I said, hands clasped at the back of his neck as he looked down at me, his focus mapping the planes of my face.

"I know, I was watching, soaking it all in. Fuck, I missed half of the wedding because I was watching you instead. Watching your happiness for Raine, your gorgeous tears, this fucking body."

His grip tightened on my waist, and he pulled me into him.

"I don't think Raine will be all that impressed to know you missed half of her wedding because you were being a horndog."

We both laughed, and he rested his forehead on mine. "She knew. I warned her I'd be a fucking mess as soon as I saw you."

I kissed him again, drinking him in, his feelings and his truth. "Zac," I mumbled, pecking his mouth. "I was so scared to see you today because I knew how I felt, and I didn't think I could have you. Just seeing you standing there almost ruined me."

He tilted his head, watching me with a softness and a longing that made me delirious. "You've had me from the beginning. You could've marched up to that podium and asked the pastor to officiate one more wedding and I would've been right there with you."

I giggled and felt another well of tears gathering in my eyes. Tugging on the back of his neck, I brought him down for another kiss, and it was so sensually soft; his tongue rolled against mine, and he sucked my bottom lip between his teeth, giving it a gentle nip. I was a quivering, panting mess again in no time. Zac slammed his hands against the wall on either side of me and looked down at me in the luminous candlelight. I loved how he encased me, but I missed his hands on my body.

"How do you want this to go, baby?"

"I want your hands back on me." I raised a brow and slipped my hands under his T-shirt, feeling the hard lines of his torso. He shuddered and closed his eyes, those beautiful thick lashes kissing the space beneath his eyes.

"If I put my hands back on you," he said, "I'm not going to want to take them off again."

"I'm failing to see the issue."

He clenched his jaw, a smile dancing on his lips. "Never afraid to tell me what you want, huh."

"Nope." I raked my fingernails down his stomach, and he sank his teeth into his bottom lip and groaned. "I want you, Zac."

"You have me," he promised, his voice deeper than I'd ever heard it. "But how do you want me tonight, baby?"

He took one hand off the wall and traced his finger down my cheek, cupping my face and dragging his thumb along my lips. "Do you want me to worship this body? You want me on my knees? You want my mouth all over you? Tell me how you want me tonight, Addison. Because I'm yours, and I'm yours however you want me."

"I want all of it, Zac," I whispered, tiptoeing and kissing him on the corner of his mouth. "Just touch me like you love me."

He hadn't said it, but I had a feeling that was just because he didn't want to scare me.

"That won't be a problem at all. I just want this to be perfect for you."

"It will be perfect, because it's with you, and you have always made me feel safe enough to communicate my wants."

Sure, he'd messed up when he found out I was pregnant, but I didn't want to hold that against him. Other than that, he'd always made me feel like I could be exactly who I was and tell him exactly how I felt. He listened and he heard and he respected me so much in a way that had never made me feel safer.

He stood up straight off the wall, looked down at me, and then hoisted me up at the back of the thighs, slamming me into the wall before his mouth was all over mine again. There was no restraint, no holding back as we kissed like our lives depended on it. Like we were making up for the months we'd lost. Suddenly, he dropped me and fell to his knees, shoving my dress up and over my hips.

"You don't mind if I take these off, right?" He slipped his fingers into the edge of my thong.

"Rip them off for all I care," I said, breathless.

"I wouldn't want to wreck this beautiful piece of fabric," he said, finger running down my center. My legs buckled, I was so sensitive and swollen, throbbing beneath the thong he'd started to roll down. I stepped out of it, and Zac threw it to the side before his hands were on the back of my thighs and he was lifting a leg over his shoulder.

Before I had time to brace myself, his mouth was on me, and I almost doubled over. "Zac," I moaned, legs threatening to give out at the sheer pleasure of his tongue making circles on my clit. "Zac, I can barely keep my weight up, I'm going to hurt your shoulder."

"That's cute, baby," he murmured against my wet heat. He slipped a finger in and flicked it. Paired with his tongue, I was on the brink, legs trembling as I practically collapsed on his face. I held fistfuls of his hair, whimpering, barely able to stand, and as soon as my climax hit, I started to slide down the wall. Zac splayed his hand out on my torso, keeping me up with almost no effort at all.

When he was done licking me clean, he stood up and kept his focus on me, rising to his feet as he tugged my dress down a little. I took note of the bulge in his sweatpants.

"So." He leaned on the wall, trapping me again, and blew out a breath. "I don't have a condom."

My eyes widened, and I stared at him. "You didn't think this was going to happen?"

He huffed an abrupt, disbelieving laugh. "No. I thought I'd be lucky to have a conversation with you tonight. I didn't think we'd get this far."

"That's kind of cute and sweet." I stared at his hard length.

"Baby, I was prepared to grovel for years if that was what it took."

I chewed the inside of my cheek. I was still breastfeeding, so my chances of getting pregnant again were a little lower. I hadn't had a period yet either, so we were safe-ish, if we decided to hope for the best.

"I know what you're thinking," Zac said.

"You do not."

"You're thinking we could chance it because you don't want me to be left with a rock-hard cock and no release, but you're not obligated to return the favor, baby."

Fine, he did know what I was thinking.

"I could . . ." I started lowering to my knees, but he gripped my wrist and tugged me back up.

"Let's go upstairs with a pint of ice cream and watch the storm outside?"

My heart tripped over itself. "You're so hard, though."

"That happens whenever I look at you," he said, leading me out of the living room and into the dark foyer.

Zac went to the kitchen, and I went to the bathroom to clean up a little before we met back at the staircase. In Zac's bedroom, we sat on the bed with the curtains open and watched the rain beating down on the window, occasionally illuminated by a flash of lightning. A candle sat on his side table and flickered. The ice cream was sensational too. I lay on my stomach at the end of the bed, legs kicking. Zac sat back against the headboard, legs spread, hand behind his head while he watched me slowly suck the spoon. I knew what I was doing. He knew that I knew what I was doing.

Zac was being a gentleman, not making a move even though I was doing my best to tease him into it. Eventually, I sighed and stabbed the spoon into the ice cream. "I've had enough of that."

Slowly dragging myself up, ass first into the air, I sat on my spread thighs and tousled out my hair. My dress was sitting so far up on my thighs, my bare center would've been visible to him, and I looked at where he was lying, his chest rising and falling with deep breaths. I had a plan, a little test that might've been a bit mean, but he'd be pleased in the end.

"Do you remember the first night I spent here?" I asked, and he sat up, watching me with the most arousing look I'd ever seen. "I was wearing a dress, and the strap kept falling off my shoulder."

He looked at my shoulder now, where I'd carefully pushed the strap of my dress down. He came closer, shifting onto his knees to mirror my position. Pushing the strap up, he nodded. "Of course, I remember. I fixed it."

"You don't have to fix it this time, Zac," I said, shuddering at his fingers on my skin. "I want you to be the one taking it off."

His jaw fluttered, and he swallowed hard as I reached into the middle of my cleavage and pulled a condom out, grinning as I held it between two fingers. His brows knit together.

"Where did that come from?"

"The bathroom drawer."

He tipped his head back and laughed. "I fucking forgot those were in there."

Throwing the condom at him, I pulled the hem of my dress up and gave him a gentle shove backward so I could straddle his lap. His hands slapped down on my outer thighs, and he thrust upward. I rocked my hips, creating a friction that made him hiss, his large hands coasting up and down my bare thighs and around onto my ass. He squeezed, and I splayed my fingers on his chest, holding myself up.

"I can't get naked right now," I confessed, not at all embarrassed. "My breasts are food right now, and I don't want to leak." That would kill the mood for sure.

"You're all good, baby." He gave me a shove backward, pushing me down far enough so that he could pull himself out of his sweatpants. Using his teeth, he ripped the condom open, and I watched with desperation as he rolled it down his length. As soon as he was done, he gripped my hips and brought me back over him with one strong pull. I reached down, holding him as I lined up and lowered myself. The stretch was delicious, and I sucked in a sharp breath at the same time he groaned, filling me until I was seated to the hilt.

He wrapped his hand around the back of my neck and tugged me down, pressing a bruising kiss on my mouth. We heard the side seam of my dress tear where it was bunched on my hips.

"Fuck," Zac murmured into my mouth. "I'm sorry."

"Don't be." I assured him that I didn't care because it was hot when he got a little rough.

"Fine." He grinned against my lips. "I'm not. I'd tear that whole fucking thing off you if I could."

He thrust his hips, and I gasped at the pressure in my core. "Tear it off," I panted, sitting up straight and spreading my hands on his chest to keep upright.

He didn't even hesitate—both of his hands gripped the fabric at my hips, and then he split it on one long tear from the bottom to the top. The fabric slid off my body, leaving me down to my bra. It was made for breastfeeding, but it was a cute lace design I'd spent more on than was reasonable. Zac looked at me like I was a dream, his teeth sinking into his lip as his hands coasted up my bare torso and onto my rib cage. My body was different now. I had stretch marks on my lower torso, and nothing was tight and toned, but the way he looked at me made me feel beautiful. It made me feel like I was a prize and he was so fucking grateful to be the winner.

"You are so fucking beautiful," Zac grunted, thrusting up, harder and harder. "I don't even know how to function when I'm looking at you."

He went for it then, holding my hips down and pounding into me so hard I couldn't even moan because I was so breathless. Then, in one quick movement, he threw me down into the mattress and climbed on top of me, pushing his sweatpants all the way off and shedding his T-shirt. Nudging my knees apart, he settled between my legs and slid back inside. There was no starting off slow: he slammed into me. When the headboard started hitting the wall, he gripped it with one hand and held it still, his strokes not slowing for even a heartbeat. Ugh, his effortless strength made me delirious.

"Fuck, you look so beautiful." He looked down at me, watching my lips parted on breathless moans. "Your hair spread out on my pillow is so much hotter than it should be, ma'am."

I managed a light giggle through the quiet gasps, and he lowered his gaze to my mouth, his eyes full of wonder.

"I love that noise. Fuck, I missed it so much."

"I missed everything about you," I countered, wrapping my legs around his waist and hooking my ankles at his back.

He peered down, watching where he sank into me; his beautiful arms bordered me, one still on the headboard, the other holding his weight up. I'd always loved his arms. The shape, the veins, the swell of his biceps. I coasted my hands along his shoulders and onto his back, nails grazing his skin and causing him to shudder. I followed his line of sight to where he was watching himself slowly sink into me, and the sight alone was enough to coax another orgasm to the surface.

I threw my head back, and Zac sped up again, harder and harder, faster and faster, and then white-hot pleasure exploded and all I could do was silently gasp, the breath being stolen from my lungs. Zac shuddered, his own release making him groan. He rested his forehead on mine, going still. I gave my hips a little roll, just because I liked to see him squirm. He hissed and lightly chuckled.

"Baby," he warned. "Be nice."

"I know you like that," I teased, doing it again.

He shook, and his breathing quickened. He kissed me on the forehead. "Please stay with me forever, Addie?"

I stroked the stubble on his jaw. "I'm home, Zac."

• • •

In the morning, I felt like the bliss in my chest would manifest in a bright light or a burst of stars. It felt so prominent that it should've been obvious I'd never been happier. Willa sat at the kitchen island, her feet swinging at the stool as she ate her scrambled eggs. Maggie had been up and fed in the early hours of the morning. She was still sleeping while Zac and I moved around the kitchen together, cleaning up the breakfast dishes and brewing coffee.

I stood in front of the window and looked out at the clear morning. The storm had passed, and the horizon was luminous with after-rain glow. The dew on the grass glittered, and there was a layer of thin cloud creating a fog on the hills.

Zac came to stand beside me and rinsed a spatula in the sink before moving behind me and slipping his hands onto my waist.

"You should sit down and eat," he murmured beside my ear, kissing me on the head. I sank back into him, a smile stretching from cheek to cheek. It wasn't just a safe feeling, it was a feeling of belonging here, with him, a man who'd patiently waited for me to come home.

I turned around and slid my arms around his neck, content just to stare at his face for as long as he'd let me. I'd missed his face. I'd missed how he looked at me with a thousand thoughts glittering in his dark-brown eyes and how the corner of his mouth would lift in a soft, appreciative smile. He made me feel seen, heard, valued.

"Can I be the flower girl again?"

Zac twisted, looking behind him, and I peered around him to see Willa watching us with a cheeky grin. She'd never been subtle about her hope for Zac and me to fall in love and live happily ever after.

"I would assume so," Zac said assuredly, as if there wasn't a doubt in his mind our wedding would be next. Butterflies erupted in my stomach.

Even though we'd been apart for a while, being together again felt like no time at all had passed. It felt as familiar as seeing a lifelong friend after months apart. As the sidewalks in Beverly Hills. As the Santa Monica sunset on a summer's evening. He was home, and nothing had ever felt more right.

From down the hall, there was a faint cry, the sweet sound of Maggie's little wails. The natural reaction my body had to her was still bewildering, something I'd never gotten to experience after Willa was born because she'd been gone. Those months after her birth, when I had to pump breast milk in order to relieve the swell, when I had to think about my empty arms not nursing a little girl, had been some of the darkest moments of my life.

Being able to nurse Maggie was something I didn't take for granted.

I stared at her little face, her cheeks and tiny lips. The wisps of dark hair on her head. Part of me never wanted it to end.

"I'll get her," Zac offered before I could leave the kitchen.

I paused, looking at him and the slight raise in his brow, waiting for permission.

"Sure." I gave a little shrug, pretending like it was no big deal and I wasn't all mush and butterflies at his immediate effort to be a partner. Because I knew that was what he was doing, showing me that he wanted to be involved.

He kissed me on the cheek and then stepped around me, leaving Willa and me alone. We stared at each other, both grinning, both listening. I half expected Maggie to start shrieking at the sudden appearance of a complete stranger, but her cries quieted and then Zac came around the corner with Maggie on his arm. She was pink-cheeked from sleep, lines from the sheets on her face and her gaze wide and unsure as she looked around the room.

"Hi, baby." I walked over to the two of them, admiring how gorgeous Zac looked with Maggie on his arm, her little frame even smaller next to him. I slipped my finger into her hand, and she smiled at me before looking back at Zac, inspecting his face. She did that for a while, her attention moving between the two of us.

"She's so damn cute," Zac mumbled, his large hand spanning the width of her back. "You know, she looks like you, Addie."

It was true; the older she got, the more she started to look like me. "Dad used to tell me I looked more like my aunt than my mom," I said. "I can see Margo too, though."

Maggie reached her little hands out and put her fingers on Zac's stubble, her fingers lingering at the strange texture, dribble rolling down her chin.

"The fact that she hasn't tried to jump out of your arms to come to me is impressive," I said.

Zac smiled at Maggie, looking at her with a thousand promises on his face. It was obvious that he meant what he'd said last night: she and I were a package deal. Part of me wondered how things would go when he was exposed to the harder parts. The late nights, the endless cries, the diapers.

"You sit down and eat." Zac gestured at the hot pan of eggs and bacon on the stove. "I've got her."

"Are you sure?"

He laughed lightly and settled a hand on my back, steering me toward the stove. "Yes. Have something to eat and then go and have a shower. Do whatever you need to. We'll manage, won't we?"

He bounced Maggie on his arm and then swiped up the pacifier on the countertop. As I scooped food onto my plate, I watched the two of them walk around the kitchen. Zac talked to Maggie about what to do with his morning, and then Willa hopped off the seat and followed them around, demanding a cuddle. My heart swelled to the point it made me breathless. I never thought I could feel like this again, like the chasm had repaired, refilled with so much to be thankful for that it was overflowing. It had taken a while, but this life was worth waiting for.

# EPILOGUE

*Two years later*

Hand in hand, Maggie and Willa walked between the greenhouses that lined the paddocks on the farm. They giggled and ran across the dewy grass, the fall chill causing swirls of cold breath to make little clouds in their wake.

I watched, smiling at Midge and Toto, who barked, chasing them with excitement. Maggie looked precious in her knee-high rubber boots, a snug coat on and a beanie atop her dark-brown curls. She was the spitting image of Margo, bringing me a piece of my sister each time she laughed or grinned.

"I love the new greenhouses, Mom," Willa shouted, running her hand along the thick plastic covering of the round domes. Recently, my thriving indoor and outdoor houseplant business had done well enough that I could expand production and even hire a couple staff members to help me.

Since I was loaded with experience running a business, it had been the perfect career move for me, combining what I knew and what I loved. I'd even done a couple of weddings as a horticulturist rather than a planner. There were some couples who preferred plants rather than flowers. Zac and I had made a deal, after all, and I was finally keeping my end of it.

Lavender whinnied from her paddock, and Willa looked over at her. "Can Maggie and I go for a ride?"

"Sure, you go and get the helmets," I said, starting a slow waddle across the grass so that I could collect my adventurous little daughter before she made a break for it. She was so like Margo in every way. Exploring, excited, undeterred by whatever obstacles might have been in her way.

Her cheeks were rose red, nose cold when she pushed her face against mine to give me a kiss after I'd lifted her up and perched her on the mound of my stomach. For being just thirty-three weeks along, I was carrying rather large.

Zac assured me that was because we were having a little boy, and he was going to be tall and built like his father. The thought made me smile—a little Zac, his golden skin and big brown eyes. Of course, there was every chance that our son could inherit my height, but Zac assured me that would be just fine too.

Lavender was part of the family at this point. She'd matured so well; she was gentle with the girls, obedient, careful and slow when Maggie and Willa were on her back. She was still the most self-aware horse that I'd ever met. Willa held Maggie's hand while I saddled Lavender up, and then we used the stepping stool so that Willa could climb on first. Next followed Maggie, in the front, little fingers wrapped around the reins.

"Ride Ladder," Maggie squealed with excitement; she couldn't quite get "Lavender" out at the moment. But Ladder was just as cute.

"Yep," I said, double-checking that her helmet was secure, Willa's too. "Ride Lavender. You say, 'Giddyup, Lavender.'"

"Gup, Ladder!"

Willa giggled and used the heel of her foot to give a gentle nudge in the side and Lavender walked. That was it. She knew she was only allowed to walk with the girls on her back. She didn't go far, either, wide circles close enough that I could talk to Willa and she would hear me.

Willa was growing into a beautiful young girl, so self-assured and sweet. After Raine and Milo's honeymoon, we'd spoken to them about Willa calling Raine and me both mom. While Milo had seemed hesitant at first, Raine was so thrilled at the idea, he couldn't say no. Raine was momma and I was mom; it made it easier to discern who she was talking to when we were all in the same room.

It never ceased to amaze me that not only was I in Willa's life but she loved me so much that she wanted to call me mom. I never felt deserving, but I cherished it.

Heavy footsteps pushed through the wet blades of grass behind me; the slight slosh of damp earth being pressed on and rising again made me turn to find Zac approaching in a thick parka, his hood up.

"You girls are up early." He stopped beside me and dropped an arm around my shoulder. "Happy Thanksgiving, baby."

"Happy Thanksgiving." I stood on tiptoe to give him a kiss and held the hand that he had dropped over my shoulder, toying with the wedding band on his finger. "The girls wanted to come outside and play. I forget the cold doesn't exist at that age."

"You should have woken me up. I'd have brought them out."

"No, that's all right. I wanted to check on the greenhouses anyway."

"Everything going well?" he asked, pressing a kiss against my head, his lips lingering.

"Yep. We have a few dozen orders to send out over the next week, so that'll keep us busy."

"How about I look after Mags then," he suggested. "I'll take her into the showroom, let her win all of the customers over. She loves hanging out with the cars."

"She does."

Zac's showroom was thriving too. He'd recently had a driveway laid that came from the road through the paddock to the showroom doors, with a little four-car parking lot that customers could use so they didn't have to come through the dusty, narrow track that used to be used for the dirt bikes and horses.

There was a constant stream of cars being imported and sold just as fast. Specialty cars, muscle cars, vintage classics. Whatever he could get his hands on. As well as the engine work that he continued to do in his new workshop. Between my plants and his cars, we had industrial-sized sheds all over the property so that we could keep stock and fill out orders.

"Dadda," Maggie squealed, pushing her ringlets off her face only to have them bounce back. She needed a bangs trim. "Dadda, ride Ladder! See."

"That's awesome, baby girl," Zac shouted back, giving her a thumbs-up. Maggie's little front teeth were on full display when she grinned and copied Zac's thumbs-up.

For someone who'd so adamantly claimed he wasn't ready to be a dad when he'd found out I was pregnant with Maggie, he'd taken to fatherhood as if he was made for it.

After we'd reconciled at Raine's wedding, we'd started dating again. It was slow in the beginning. He would pick me up with a house-plant—not flowers—and he would take me on a date and then he would drop me off at home, and we did that for about three weeks until we couldn't stand being apart any longer.

We were married within six months. I sold the home I'd bought when I moved to Texas, moved onto the farm with Maggie, and life had been beautiful ever since. We decorated a bedroom for her together, we had Willa every other weekend, and we saw her a lot in between. Zac and I continued to develop our careers while we raised our daughter.

There were still moments when I felt niggling bouts of guilt for living out the life Margo had so desperately wanted. But she'd wanted it for me too. She'd wanted me to be happy, and sometimes it was as if I could hear her thanking me for raising her daughter, for loving her, for finally allowing myself to love and be loved. I missed her, I missed the potential of our futures and the things we'd planned. I missed looking forward to watching her be a mother.

But the circumstances couldn't be altered or changed, and it would be senseless to sit down and let life pass by because I felt guilty that she wasn't here to live it with me. She'd have been furious if I'd done that. So, I was doing what she no longer could, and I knew she appreciated it. I knew I had her blessing.

Finally, after such a long time of hurt and loss and things going wrong time and time again, I felt optimistic and excited and full. It was as if I was being granted peace after surviving so much trauma. But I knew that no matter what happened, whatever obstacles life might have left for me, I had a lot of love around me to see me through.

I turned to Zac and pushed my fingers into his hair. "I'm in love with you."

His gaze was soft. "Well, that's a relief. After a year and a half of marriage, I wasn't sure." He kissed me, his hands cradling the underside of my bump. "I am so in love with you too," he whispered.

What did it all mean? Why did my sister die right before her life as a mother began? Why did I end up here, with the daughter I gave up, who happened to be family with a man whom I consider to be the other half of my soul? I don't know. I can't ever answer those questions. The way the world works is bigger than I am, and it might never make sense, but what I'm making of it now, that does make sense. I'll cherish it because one thing I've learned is everything happens for a reason.

# AUTHOR'S NOTE

To read the original draft of this book, including chapters from Zac's POV and bonus material, please feel free to check it out on my Wattpad profile, @tayxwriter.

# ACKNOWLEDGMENTS

I'm so grateful to have had the chance to publish this book. It was one of my favorite books to write, and getting to see it on shelves is a blessing. I want to thank Anna Todd and the team at Frayed Pages, as well as W by Wattpad Books for this incredible opportunity. Thank you to Margot Mallinson for her editing guidance. It was a pleasure working with you. Thank you to God for faith and guidance and providing me with such life-changing opportunities, not to mention blessing me with the gift of words. Special thanks to my mom, Barbara, and my sister, Sarah, for being my biggest fans. Thank you to Ashley Marie for being the best internet friend I could ever ask for, the endless promotional material, and aesthetic graphics she supplies me with. Thank you to Courtney, my soul sister who is so supportive and encouraging. Thank you to Jess, my longest friend, for the shared happiness. Thank you to my husband and children for believing in me and allowing me to work from home. Thank you to Andrea and the team at my favorite local café, Tonic, where I spent hours working on this book, supplied with incredible coffee and savories that fueled my days. Shoutout to Morgan Wallen for being in my earbuds during the entire editing process. Thank you to the readers on Wattpad for being the best people ever; the encouragement and love I'm shown is unreal, I can never thank you all enough. My career exists because of your support, and I'll always be more grateful than I can describe. I will keep writing and dedicating books to the readers for as long as you'll have me.

# ABOUT THE AUTHOR

Tay Marley is the author of the Wattpad YA hit *The QB Bad Boy and Me*, soon to become a movie. With a passion for romance, happy endings, and strong women, she loves to write stories that set the reader's standards for love oh so high. When she's not writing or reading, she's teaching her three children how to be their own leading characters. *Meant for Me* is her debut adult novel.

# MEANT FOR ME
## Discussion Questions

1. What is your favorite moment from the novel? Why does it stand out to you?

2. Addie's relationship with her sister, Margo, is the defining relationship in her life, so when she loses her, she doesn't know who she is any more. Do you think Addie is too hard on herself with her inability to move on? Do you think Addie's grief is reasonable?

3. Who is your favorite side character, and why?

4. Have you ever done anything as drastic as Addie fleeing her home and job and starting over from scratch? What was it?

5. Did your opinion on any of the characters change over the course of the novel? In what way?

6. What about Addie's choices or her past did you find the most interesting or surprising?

7. What do you think are some of the overarching themes of the novel?

8. How did Addie's journey make you feel? Did you empathize with her? How did she grow and change over the course of the story?

9. If you could have given Addie or Zac any advice during the story, what would it have been, and when?